MW00957654

DUNGEON DIVING 201

BRUCE SENTAR

Copyright © 2024 by Bruce Sentar

All rights reserved.

No portion of this book may be reproduced in any form without written permission
from the publisher or author, except as permitted by U.S. copyright law.

CONTENTS

CHAPTER 1

C rimson was still pouting as she pulled at her long, black hair, tightening it into a braid while flicking a spare hair band harder than a bullet. The band bounced through three low-level dungeon monsters and back to her.

"I mean, really, why did it have to destroy the potion's effect?!" She played with the hair band and put it on her braid after checking to make sure it had survived its passage through the monsters.

I gave her a sidelong glance as we walked through the dungeon on our way back to the Nagato Estate. "Limit break must not like the dye."

Crimson played with her hair while monsters died all around us. She was in a bit of a mood.

"I don't see what the big deal is—your hair is beautiful." Fayeth smiled at our teacher.

Crimson looked at Fayeth's hair, which looked like spun gold. Then she glanced over at Ami's, which was a pristine white, before looking back at her own black hair with a frown. "I finally got Ken to pick a really pretty rose petal red. It's a really rare hair color potion or I'd just drink one every day."

I didn't bother correcting her. She had placed a number of potions to change her hair color out for me and tried them as an excuse to kiss me.

It had been blatantly obvious that she wanted red when she showed up with twenty potions that were all different shades of red. Although, I would have said they were all pretty much the same. I honestly couldn't tell the difference between most of them.

I picked based on which one she seemed most excited about, only for it to fail the first time Limit Break activated.

"The potions do show up as a debuff," I added. Based on her expression, my comment was entirely unhelpful.

Crimson rolled her eyes. "I'm going to go find a master alchemist and hang them off a bridge until they fix it. Oh!" Her eyes shined.

"Or put them in front of the demon boss on the forty-fifth floor. He's a weird one."

"Wait, is that the one whose blood you gave to Desmonda to use on me?" I asked, suddenly interested. I hadn't heard from Demon Lord Snu Snu all summer.

"Oh. Yeah. The UG restricts access to his boss fight, but he's a really strong demon." Crimson grinned at me.

"Why is it restricted?" Fayeth asked.

"Lots of deaths there. He has a very powerful charm ability that kills whole raids by making the ladies kill the men," Crimson explained.

I nearly fell over. Of course that was how he killed adventurers. "You purposefully got me that demon's blood?" I stared at her.

"Yup," she shamelessly admitted.

"It's a fun ability," Fayeth added. "Whe—"

I covered her mouth. "Not around elves anymore, Fayeth. Besides, we are close enough that my grandfather could appear at any moment."

We had already seen several Nagato clan members. The ninja garbed adventurers had faded into the shadows after seeing who we were earlier in the dungeon.

My thoughts of them seemed to summon them.

"Young master." Several high-level assassins pulled themselves from the shadows and bowed. "Welcome home. Some of the new Silver Fang members have already headed back to school; however, Miss DuVell and Renard have remained," they reported.

"Perfect. I—"

"Come back here, you!" Grandpa's voice cut through what I was about to say.

A white rabbit bounded through the dark dungeon screaming. Tears were streaming down the bunny's face before he spotted our group and ran straight for us.

"You won't lose me you long-eared rat! You ate the cheesecake that I stole!"

Grandpa came around the corner of the ruins as Bun-bun successfully landed in Fayeth's arms and settled in like he'd been there for hours.

"There you are." Grandpa drew his sword before he realized who was holding him. "Fayeth! You're my best granddaughter." He picked her up, swinging her and knocking Bun-bun from her arms. "I'm so happy you are back."

I grabbed the rabbit before he got far. The troublemaker seemed like he'd grown as he looked up at me with a pitiful gaze, letting his eyes water.

"Don't think that's going to work on me. You caused this." I glanced up from the rabbit to Grandpa. "I'm back too, you know."

"Yes. Yes. But Fayeth is back, and Crimson is back!" He dropped Fayeth and tried to hug Crimson, who kept him at arm's length with a hand on his forehead.

"I don't like being touched," she replied.

"But you touch Ken all the time and even encourage him." Fayeth blinked.

Crimson gave her a light chop on the top of her head to silence her.

"Oww." Fayeth rubbed her head.

"Ami. How did everyone fare?" Grandpa became serious in an instant.

My butler straightened up and glanced at me for my approval before speaking. "Ken performed admirably, if slightly distracted while training in the Elven world."

Grandpa chuckled. "I bet he was distracted."

"Elysara, the next heir, joined my Adrel," I cut in. "Stop drooling, Grandpa."

He wiped at his mouth and turned furious. "You are a damned lucky man! Let those of us with less enjoy."

"Less you say?" Grandma Yui poured out of a cloud of mist, her eyes like two daggers pointed at Grandpa.

"Quantity, certainly not quality." He rubbed his hands and grabbed Yui's hand with a giant smile.

Crimson huffed. "Did he just call me ugly?"

Grandpa froze suddenly, realizing he was stuck between two very dangerous situations and his gaze shifted to me, his eyes full of pleading. I kept my mouth shut. The old man had made his own bed. I was going to let him sleep in it.

Crimson played with the length of her whip.

Grandpa swallowed and scowled at me for not saving him. "Now now. I wasn't saying that." He shifted gears. "You know what, Yui? I think we need to get Ken up to the estate. Sakura is beside herself, and I'm sure Hemi would love nothing more than to smother him until he has to go. Yes, let's get them up there."

"Wait one second." Crimson had a giant smile on her face and leaned on my shoulder. "I want to settle this."

Grandpa sighed while his eyes searched everywhere for inspiration and something clicked. "I didn't want to say it, but you are simply too young for me to find attractive." He pulled the statement off well. If I hadn't seen him reading the magazines that he does, I would have believed him.

"Alright, you are too slow. I'll take Ken." Grandpa's form shivered before I felt wind on my face and the world blur past me as he carried me.

"You damned brat, you almost got me killed!" he shouted in my ear.

"That'll teach you to tease Crimson," I warned him. "She's only mine to tease."

He laughed it off. "The danger is what makes it so fun. Fine, for you, I'll lay off your ladies. The rest of your class..."

"Is also off limits," I added.

"The Harem Queen?" he asked tentatively while racing through the dungeon.

"I want nothing to do with her. The angrier you make her, the better off I think the world will be," I answered.

Grandpa grinned like a loon. "Redheads are best angry. The hair goes so well with a fiery temper. I love a good redhead."

"But none of the grandmas are..." I stared at him.

He continued to move so quickly that the world was a blur. Soon he started whistling to himself, coming to a sudden stop as we exited the dungeon into the inner courtyard of the Nagato Estate.

I barely registered my surroundings before green hair fell over my face and I steadied myself. Charlotte wrapped me in a giant hug that pressed my face firmly between her two soft globes.

"Ken! One of the clan just notified us that you were on your way."

I had a feeling that Charlotte wasn't letting me go anytime soon. Yet I wanted to see her, and pulled her off of me enough to meet her gaze. "I love you too, Charlotte."

Her face turned pink with a light blush. It had only been two months, but I felt like she had matured slightly in that time. Her eyes held a little more depth to them.

She was the same beautiful, green-haired, green-eyed woman, and there was still a sweetness to her, but some of the innocence had been shaved off, revealing a genuine, caring person beneath.

"Stop staring at me so intensely." She blushed even deeper but kept on smiling.

A huskier voice spoke behind her. "Yeah, share some of the love with me." Desmonda Renard was even more attractive than before, if that was even possible. There was just a magnetism to everything about her as she walked forward.

She ran a hand through her purple hair, lifting it from the one eye that it always covered before letting it fall back down. The covered eye caught my attention. Rather than the red irises that she had since I met her, they now looked more pink, and to make things stranger, her pupil was now a heart.

I realized both Charlotte and Des had gone through drastic changes since I'd been gone.

I pulled myself free of Charlotte. "Love you too, Des. And I have good news. I think I can get you a princess to play with in the future. Maybe even an Empress."

Des purred as I stepped into her arms. It felt like the sound vibrated straight down my spine to my pants.

"I would *love* that." She kissed me and held the kiss, even as mist formed into Ami, Crimson, Yui and Fayeth.

It was Fayeth that broke us up. "Des!" She slammed into the other woman, breaking her away from me and taking just a quick kiss from the woman before shifting to Charlotte and hugging her. "We had the best time! But next time, you two are going to come with us."

"Wouldn't dream of missing it." Des winked at me. "However, we need to get going soon or we'll be late for the start of our classes."

Crimson waved her hand. "Don't worry about it. We'll get a lift there at the last minute. We can still have dinner here tonight."

I raised an eyebrow at her. "You are going to ask the head-mistress, aren't you?"

"Of course I am. Woman owes me a lot of favors, and let's be honest, portals are very convenient." She stared at me pointedly. "I did save her school from a Naga attack."

"Yes, you did, and portals are convenient. Now if only I could use my own," I huffed. "Grandmas."

I turned to see them walking across the lawn and hurried over to hug Hemi. I got a pat on the head from Akari before she decided to give me a big bear hug anyway, then I bowed to Sakura.

"Welcome home." Sakura smiled. "If we can have you for dinner, then that's what we'll do."

"I'm on it." Hemi rushed off to the kitchen to show her love through food.

Sakura watched her for a moment. "The Clan was quite lively this summer. The Silver Fangs made a grand re-entry into the world of adventuring." She walked slowly after Hemi, and the rest of the group sort of fell in line behind us.

"There have been a lot of changes," Des echoed her. "Not just here, but the adventuring world at large."

"Oh?" I was curious about what I'd missed. Crimson hadn't ex-actly been a fount of information on that front. She'd spent most of the summer slaughtering Naga and talking to herself, only to come back in a whirlwind.

"After the fight with the Naga, a lot of the top guilds started working together," Charlotte added. "My dad and Des's father are working on a few new projects with how they bring in new recruits. They're creating an intense training program."

"Isn't that what Haylon essentially is?" I asked.

"Yes and no." Des came up and walked on my other side. "Basically, humanity got its teeth kicked in. Yeah, we won, but really, it was Crimson who won." She glanced at said woman over her shoulder. "Without her... well, more than a few of the adventurers were humbled and realized that the situation would have turned fairly bleak if that matriarch hadn't been killed and the portal closed."

"Kaiming are being hunted down extensively. Any facade of decency has been stripped, and the UG crushed any business holdings they could tie to them through Gransmen Industries. They went to ground as a result, and we've even been sent after a few nests they've made." Grandma Sakura grinned viciously. "However, it always gets harder to clear out an organization the smaller and more fragmented they become."

"Frankly, it is kind of amazing." Des shook her head. "They became the instant enemy of all of Earth. There was no division among the nations, no sides. Just everyone against Kaiming after the Naga incident. If they are found, they are eliminated with prejudice."

"Wow." I hadn't expected the outcome to be so swift. "That's where the guilds working together began?"

"Some, but mostly, they feel like they need to step it up and humanity needs a few more on Crimson's level," Desmonda answered. "Oh, Crimson... I'm supposed to ask you where you got Limit Break."

"A secret boss on the twenty-eighth floor," she answered.

I glanced at her, and she smiled back at me. It felt like she was being honest, but my intuition said there was a little something she was excluding.

"See, that's the story you've always told. Yet, now years later, no one else has found it." Des raised an eyebrow.

"Yup." Crimson shrugged. "Don't know what to tell you. The whole situation was intense. The big, red lightning bird wiped out all of my party but me. Don't know what caused it or how to fight it again."

"That's way outside of the types of monsters on any of the different floor twenty-eights. Again, this is my father's question," Des pushed her.

"The UG has been asking me since my rise to prominence. Trust me, if I knew how to summon it again, I would. Then I'd stick Ken in front of it." She grinned. "It was not an easy boss and would be great training for you."

I rolled my eyes, not surprised that my training was where her mind immediately moved. Though, if she knew how to summon the boss, she was right that the whole adventurer community would be trying their best to farm it.

"Well, without some secret like Crimson's, the only answer for humanity is to push as hard as they can." Charlotte made it sound like asking Crimson more was out of the question.

Bun-bun looked both ways before bounding into her arms.

She easily caught him. "And where have you been?"

Squeak.

"Uh huh. That's not a likely story." She lightly rapped a knuckle on his head. "Don't go causing problems."

Bun-bun folded down his ears and gave her giant watering eyes as he let out a few pitiful squeaks.

Charlotte hugged him tightly. "No, I'm not getting rid of you."

The rabbit cuddled against her.

Des snickered, watching the whole thing with me. "He's trouble, but if he can evade your Grandpa's sword, he can dodge a monster."

"We've been working with him." Charlotte calmed the rabbit by petting his head. She glanced at Fayeth. "With you gone, we wanted a little tanking support, so we helped Bun-bun along in that direction. He has a few new skills, notably [Pester], [Aggravate], [Evasion] and [Fleet Feet]. We've turned him into a dodge tank, but he still has some trouble keeping aggression from the monsters."

"He actually does a good job." Des smirked as Bun-bun stuck his nose in the air. "Then he finally gets hit and runs back to Charlotte to heal his boo-boo."

The rabbit scowled at the beautiful warlock.

"Got a problem with that? Maybe don't go bringing your monsters back to us when you get your ear nicked next time." Des stuck her tongue out at him.

"You guys have grown." I smiled at them.

"Course." Des beamed up at me, and I once again felt like I was going to melt into a little love puddle under her gaze. "My parents brought me down deep into the dungeon and helped me unlock my unique heritage."

"Ah. That explains the eyes. I was wondering if it was rude to ask," Fayeth piped up.

Des pulled back her hair again. Both eyes were more pink than red now, but the one that was kept covered had that heart-shaped pupil. The more I stared into it, the more I felt both weak in the knees and like stealing her away to reconnect.

"Yeah, I got a class change with it too. I'm now a Demonic Mage rather than a Warlock. That means it's my power I'm using rather than calling on a demon's power." Des grinned.

"Secondary class?" I asked.

"Temptress." She licked her lips. "I've been aching with you away. Now that you are back, be careful, I might be more than you can handle."

I chuckled and kept my voice low so that my grandparents wouldn't hear, "I'm going to take that challenge."

"You'd better. That was the whole point," she whispered back and touched my cheek with a soft lingering kiss.

I cleared my throat and walked a little funny for a few steps. "How about you, Charlotte?"

"Oh. Still a druid. My mother pushed me hard, though." She showed me her CID.

My eyes opened wide. "That stamina." I glanced at her again to see if she was covered in scars. "Rough training?"

"A healer needs to survive. They are the beating heart of the party," she intoned. "At least, that's my mother's philosophy. As long as the healer can stay alive, then the rest of the party can be healed or brought back. I have a revive skill now, too."

Fayeth flexed her arm. "It's my goal to make sure you don't have to use it either."

"It is a nice thing to have." Charlotte nodded before she continued. "But not something we should ever plan for. It and my healing skill do no one any good if I die."

"Her mother was lovingly brutal," Des agreed. "Can't argue with the results though. Charlotte can take a beating when Bun-bun inevitably messes up."

The rabbit angrily squeaked at her, and Des pinched his cheeks, stretching them out as she taunted him right back.

"What about you?" Des asked as we stepped into the hall and got seated.

All of my grandparents were listening intently.

"Well... I leveled quite a bit, did some training, and figured out how to swap skills with Fayeth and Elysara."

Des leaned forward, causing the top of her shirt to part in an effortlessly seductive way. "Yes? And how is that accomplished?" She had a wicked grin on her face.

"Let me start from the beginning." I cleared my throat in an attempt to change the topic from how I was going to swap skills with Des.

It barely worked, but it worked enough that I was able to launch into a story of my summer adventures. Meanwhile, Grandma

Hemi started to come out of the kitchen with platters upon platters of food, like she was trying to make up for not having fed me all summer.

CHAPTER 2

After a long retelling of our adventure, I was ready to sneak away with Des, but Grandma Sakura pulled me aside.

She paused, making sure we were alone. "Ken, I need to warn you. Kaiming is trouble."

"Huh? I thought the UG was hunting them?" I was confused.

She slowly shook her head. "They are. The whole organization has collapsed and fragmented. We and the UG are picking off the group as much as we can, but the last several times we dug them out, we found evidence that they were tracking and waiting for your return."

I frowned. Why would they be after me?

"Some of the communications we uncovered show that some of their central figures that have risen in the fragmentation put much of their downfall on your shoulders. And the Naga have instructed them that they are to do all that they can to harm Crimson." She put her hands on my shoulders so that she was looking into my eyes. "Take caution as you dive. We will work on digging the rest of their organization out, but this is when they are the most dangerous. They have nothing left to lose."

"They are cornered and could choose to stick it to me as a final act," I sighed. "Understood, Grandma. I'll keep a watch out for any troubles."

She smiled. "I'm proud of you. Already, just your name has made the Nagato Clan re-blossom. You will do great things, so it is important to keep that head on your shoulders and let these ladies look out for you. Charlotte and Des put themselves through Hell to keep up with you this summer."

I felt a wave of warmth ripple through me. "Then I should get back to them to say thank you."

Grandma gave me a knowing smirk. "Yes, to say thank you. Don't be too loud about it."

"Huh?" I playfully cupped my ear as I stepped back. "Couldn't quite hear that last part. I'll catch you later, though." I slipped out before my grandmother started a conversation about the birds and the bees.

Luckily, she let me go, and I let out a deep breath, glad to avoid more of that conversation. I snuck back to the dining area, finding that it had been cleared, and Des had disappeared.

Rather than worry about where she'd gone, I figured that they were staying in the same rooms as last time, and went to the building they'd been in previously.

But as I walked in, the place was quiet. I quietly opened the door hoping to surprise them, but after only a few moments inside, I was sure it was empty.

Heading back out, I wondered where they could have gone. Turning back to where I'd be staying, I headed inside. Crimson was sitting at the counter pounding a beer while Fayeth took small sips from hers.

"You two having fun?" I crept in.

"Fayeth is too chicken to match me in a drinking contest." Crimson burped.

"Yeah, that's not without reason. Do you even get drunk?" I asked the high-level adventurer.

"Not really." Crimson crushed the can and threw it in the trash can where a pile had started. "But beer reminds me of easier times. Like times I wasn't hip-deep in Naga corpses. Fayeth, another."

The elf dutifully passed a beer from the fridge.

I rolled my eyes and kissed Crimson on the cheek as I passed.

She froze, beer halfway to the mouth. A small spark of red lightning spilled from her eyes, but it was gone after just a flicker. Crimson grabbed me by the lapel and kissed me more passionately, this time without the sparks. "Need to stop sparking when you surprise me."

"That's half the fun," I teased and pecked her on the cheek. Sadly, this time there was no spark before I came over and hugged the smallest of my ladies, planting a kiss on Fayeth's cheek. "I'm going to get some rest."

Fayeth giggled.

"Huh?"

"Nothing," Crimson said for her. "Go try and get some rest."

I rubbed the top of Fayeth's head, making her shrink down into her beer before picking it up and taking a long drink. Then she returned to her conversation with Crimson.

"So, then Miriam just let you?" Fayeth asked in disbelief.

I wandered off, having an inkling as to why they were being funny.

Moving silently up the steps and to my room at the end of the hall, I cracked the door open slowly, a theory playing in my mind. The dim lighting as if it was candle lit told me all I needed to know. I opened the door to Charlotte instead of Des.

A husky chuckle to the side told me she wasn't alone as Des closed the door behind me and slid her arms over my shoulders and pressed her chest to my back.

Something about the familiar touch made me want to melt into her, and I relaxed.

"Weren't expecting both of us?" Des asked, her breath brushing my ear.

Charlotte was blushing furiously and rubbing her thighs together. Her green braid was undone and brushed out. Her hair fell softly over her shoulders and down to her hips. It was long when it was out of the braid. She had on a sheer, white nightgown which her nipples showed through.

"Welcome home." She met my eyes and turned even brighter red.

"Welcome home," Des echoed. Her voice caressed my brain with pleasure. "We got into a slight argument over who got you on your first night. The only way to be fair was to share you." There was a slight edge of excitement in Des's voice.

She kissed the back of my neck softly, making little wet patches with her lips while her hands roamed down and started to work on my pants.

"You'll join us?" Charlotte prompted me.

I shook off my stupor. "Yes. Of course. It would be my absolute pleasure."

Both of them chuckled. "I think he's excited." Des had my pants down around my ankles a moment later, and her warm hand slipped inside my boxers to cup my quickly growing length. "Very excited."

She caressed me slowly, the pads of her fingers making warm shapes along the head and shaft while her palm pressed slow circles.

I sighed and leaned against her as I remembered just how much I enjoyed Des' company. Checking over my shoulder, her eyes drew me in, and I gave her a lingering kiss.

She broke the kiss, though, and pushed me towards Charlotte. "I think she should go first. You ran off with Fayeth so soon after she and you got started," Des whispered in my ear, no longer holding back her excitement. "Let's make her want to do this again."

***

Kai Ming was throwing everything he could into the CID on his wrist. He had just gotten to the latest safe house only for alarms to start going off. He grumbled, grabbing another item. This safe house was supposed to be secure.

He glanced up to watch the security monitors as they fizzled out one after the other, followed by an explosion rocking the bunker. Men were jumping up from their cots all around him, drawing swords and rushing towards the conflict.

"For the Kaiming!" one shouted, rushing towards the entrance and swelling grotesquely as his voice dropped an octave. His sword was stopped dead by a softly glowing hand that emerged from the hallway.

Kai's face fell as the high-level angel summon pushed back his man. The President of the UG was here himself.

Three spears shot around the first angel, impaling and tearing apart the swollen warrior.

"Fall back," Kai shouted at the rest of the men.

"But, Mr. Ming, this was our last safe house," one of his followers whined.

"I know. It's clear that either the UG has known where we are the whole time, or that we aren't able to hide on the surface. We'll push into a dungeon." Kai Ming swirled his hand in the air, creating a portal as some of his men chose to delay the angels.

Their efforts didn't do any of them much good. They were summarily torn apart by the high-level summons. Those with more brains than faith went for the portal.

Kai stayed at the edge of the portal until the large man came up from behind his summons.

"This ends," the President of the UG intoned. Adventurers in green vests poured out around the summons. Some healed the fallen men, no doubt to take back for interrogation.

"This ends when Ken Nagato dies." Kai grinned and threw himself through the portal, coming out around the corner from a dungeon entrance on the other side of the world.

His men had already gone to work on the UG staff at the dungeon entrance where he'd portaled them. There was no reason to be gentle, and in fact, they wanted nothing more than to inflict pain upon the UG who hunted him.

His men tore through the UG guards, the staff, and any adventurer that got in their way. Kai strode behind them, letting his shoes get a little bloody with each step. His men stalled as they faced off against a level thirty-five adventuring party.

With a flick of his wrist, snakes rained out of the ceiling and bit into the adventurers with deadly venom as the spell fell upon them. Another gesture and the venom blossomed in sickly green fire before racing through their system.

It was enough that his men made a hard push and cut down the party as Kai continued to debuff them.

"Go. We'll hide in the dungeon," Kai shouted to get them moving as they reached down to loot the dead. "Leave it."

He marched forward. Those surviving men of his rushed ahead as if afraid to be too close to him while he was angry.

Once, his organization had been well formed and powerful. Now, they were a shell of what they once were. And Ken Nagato would pay for what he had done.

***

Ken Nagato
Class: Emperor
Secondary Class: Demon Lord
Level: 25
Experience: 24%
Strength: 52 (+6)
Agility: 115 (+14)
Stamina: 82 (+4)
Magic: 78 (+4)
Mana: 75 (+6)
Skills:
Dark Strike, Earth Stomp, Charm, Metamorphosis, Sprint, Absorb, Discharge, Dark Blades, Shadow Arm, Camouflage, Shadow Ambush, Elemental Shield, Portal [Special] [Restricted], Mana Burn, Hydra [Elysara], Cleave [Fayeth], Spell Mirror, Dungeon's Blessing, Blades of Shadow, Mana Implosion, Shadow Wave [Desmonda], Heal [Charlotte]
Debuffs: Drained

I looked at the debuff on my CID as Des lounged in my bed with a smirk. Charlotte had already gotten up for the morning.

Des had enjoyed herself almost as much as I had last night. "So?"

I glanced at my CID again, focusing on the new part.

[Drained] - You survived a night with a temptress and have gained one stamina. It would be dangerous for you to attempt it again. [116 hours remaining]

"Well, you look positively glowing." I smiled at her. "The free stamina doesn't hurt, but the timer does. Five days?"

She pouted, and I wanted to push her back down. "I know. We need to work on your stamina so that the timer isn't so bad. That's what you'll get, though. Compared to the training required for stamina, it isn't half bad, is it?" She winked.

"Not at all. Charlotte got the same?" I asked.

"Yes, she did." Des grinned in satisfaction. "Think we changed her mind about joining us?"

"Probably. She's still going to be shy about it, though. You'll have to invite her, she won't invite herself," I answered. Des was anything but shy, stretching in my bed. "Okay, now out. And get dressed. If you don't, I'm going to have trouble not getting myself hurt according to this debuff."

My words seemed to satisfy Des. She hopped out of bed with a fluid grace and put on an outfit for school.

The outfit reminded me. We were heading back to Haylon today.

I slid out and got dressed myself, checking my CID to ensure that I had everything I needed. Elysara hadn't been shy about stuffing me full of camping equipment and supplies.

"You are taking a long time." Fayeth opened the door and peeked in. "Aww, Des has her clothes on."

"You'll have a chance in five days," Des said.

"Better than the week we thought it might be," Fayeth sighed. "I call next time. There is just something about you now that we've returned."

"It's the class upgrade," I said, finishing getting ready. "That, or you did something to me this summer."

"Got used to the frequency." Fayeth straightened up her green dress that I suspected she had been about to throw down on the ground. "Anyway, Crimson is ready to head to Haylon."

"Alright, let's get going then. Crimson doesn't have much patience," I said.

"She has none for anyone else. For you, she'll wait a few minutes," Fayeth teased and caught my arm as I made it to the door. "Charlotte and Des?"

I scratched my cheek. "An interesting dichotomy between cute and sexy," I admitted.

Des purred and took my other arm, making our group almost a little too wide for the narrow hallway. But we pressed together, making it work. "It was delightful. A nice break before we'll have to return to the dungeon." She narrowed her eyes and straightened up, losing some of that magnetic aura. "Ken, they are going to push us hard this year."

"How hard?" I teased.

She licked her lips. "My father said that the top guilds are going to steadily raise their requirements for entry. Meaning Haylon, the big four, and every other dungeon college is going to have to start putting out students at a higher level."

I blinked. The average Haylon student would probably graduate at level twenty five with a five level range on either side. "How much?"

"Five levels every year." She tensed her jaw.

I did the math. With four years total at Haylon, and three to go, that meant they'd expect us to be an average of level forty out of school. "Holy crap. That's almost enough to compare to someone like Penny's father. Actually, that is the average. The best of Haylon would be stronger than him."

"Yeah, and he's not the top grade of adventurers but he's a seasoned professional," Fayeth agreed. "This is all just to push humanity higher?"

"Yep." Des nodded. "I think we can go higher, though. If Ken can figure out his portal." She poked me, even though she had borrowed the ability from me and had it now too. "Then we can go hunt some events, but I expect this year to be a little different than most second years at Haylon. After all, most of us are capable enough to be in this year's graduating class."

"They are going to find a way to push us as hard as they can," I agreed and stepped out of the building with each of them on an arm.

Crimson saw us and put down her CID. "Just on time." She grinned, before smoothing down her outfit. It looked much the same, but I knew it was made from dinosaur leather rather than dragon hide now.

After my experience in the raid with her, I wasn't sure what was more terrifying, a dragon or a T-rex. Dragons flew around and breathed fire. A T-rex was all teeth. Lots of very big teeth.

I shuddered from the recent memories.

A portal opened up and Headmistress Marlow stepped through in a rush. "What's the emergency?" She narrowed her eyes, seeing us all standing around. "Crimson, you canno—"

Crimson stepped forward and patted the headmistress on the shoulder before turning and motioning to all of us. "Everyone through. Time for school."

Sakura caught me for a hug while my other grandmothers hugged the rest of my party. "Stay safe and watch your back."

"I have good ladies watching mine while I'm watching theirs." I smiled.

She patted my shoulders. "Alright. We've done the best we can to prepare them."

Grandpa slid in next to me, handing me a brown paper bag. "A present for your return. We'll send Ami down to you shortly; I suspect that we'll have some missions for you and your group in the near future."

I knew better than to think what was in the brown bag was anything about the missions. Stuffing it in my CID, I didn't want the Headmistress to see it.

"Hurry up." The Headmistress had her arms crossed as Crimson applied pressure. "If you call me for transportation enough, I'm not going to keep coming. We have an important entrance ceremony today."

"Yeah. Yeah," Crimson dismissed the comment with a wave. "Just taking five minutes out of your day to make sure your teacher and students are best prepared for success. We barely made it back from the Elven territory. Oh, did you know that Ken here married the next empress of the elves? You should treat him well. Maybe he'll even owe you a favor one of these days."

The gray-haired old woman narrowed her eyes on me before she forced a smile across her face. "Welcome back to Haylon." The statement was brittle enough that I thought she was going to crumble right there in front of me.

"Thanks." I stepped through the portal only to get shooed by Crimson to get clear as the Headmistress came storming through behind us.

"Unless there is anything else?" she asked Crimson with an arched eyebrow.

"Nope. Thanks for the lift. Though I'm going to have to drop you down a star on your rating. Poor personality for the duration of the ride," Crimson tsked.

A blood vessel threatened to burst in Marlow's forehead before she just stormed off, throwing out the last word, "I'll see you at the entrance ceremony."

I glanced at Crimson. "Must you antagonize her?"

"Yup." Crimson grinned. "Otherwise, she'll start to think that she's actually my boss. We can't have that."

I sighed. "Come on. You might be able to be late, but I can't be."

Chapter 3

I found our class's section of the large auditorium without trouble. Penny spotted me first and stood waving her hand to get my attention.

"Welcome back." The tall frost knight had a big smile plastered on her face as she welcomed me. "I knew you'd come back just fine."

"It was a near thing," I replied, sliding into four empty seats that had been left for our group.

Harley turned away from Bonnie, her eyes lighting up as she bounced over to give me a hug. "Oh my gosh. How was playing with the princess all summer?"

I cleared my throat.

Several of the other students in what was now Class 2-A turned around in their seats and stopped their other conversations to hear my answer. Suddenly, I was reminded of the smut story that was going around the school at the end of the previous school year.

"It was—"

"Quiet down." The Headmistress reappeared and scowled at me from the stage as if she had been talking directly to me. "We have all of the classes here today because there is news. First off, we are excited to welcome several new members of the staff."

She gestured to the side. Crimson, along with the other teachers I recognized, came out, but there were several new additions. One in particular caught my attention.

The Harem Queen walked out on stage wearing a dress that belonged at some wealthy donor function and not in a school nor a dungeon.

"Some of these you recognize, others are new," the Headmistress called them one by one to cross the stage and stand up front.

When the headmistress introduced the Harem Queen, the Harem Queen walked gracefully across the stage, making direct eye contact with me before coming down and standing near Crimson.

Crimson leaned over and whispered something that made the woman swallow a lump around her throat and stop making eye contact with me.

Des huffed. "Bitch can eat dirt. You are all mine."

I put a hand on hers. "That's a promise."

The Headmistress' voice pulled me away from Des. "As many of you heard, there was an attack on us and on Earth at the end of last school year. Several of the people here before me have volunteered to help us improve our teaching at Haylon. The expectation for all major guilds is that you are at least level thirty by the end of the year."

There was a gasp from the crowd of seniors and angry muttering. They had a longer way to go to reach that goal in time.

"No, I do not expect you to find this to be fair. But the fact remains that there is a hostile race that came through a portal to attack our world. We will adapt to this new challenge, and that means pushing our adventurers as hard as we can." The headmistress glared at the noisy group, waiting for them to quiet down.

Candice leaned over my chair. "My mother said the death rate in the colleges is less than three percent, but they are inflating the bottom two classes in size."

"Not the upper classes?" I asked.

Candice grimaced. "Pushing harder means more deaths. They estimate death rates at the big four will rise to ten to fifteen percent with the new training."

That fact hit me hard. Beyond the two students that Crimson had killed and that I had killed because they had gone after Fayeth, there was only one death in our grade.

I thought about losing those in our class.

"Don't be so glum," Candice snorted. "Like hell any of us would go and die. You'd better be more worried about the class C's and class D's. Honestly, you might see a class D get wiped out in the next few years."

"Brutal," Des said. "That's how the dungeon normally is. Most people don't have Crimson looking out for them."

"We will be fine," I answered with determination.

"This year is going to be a little different," the Headmistress continued, despite the noise only growing as all of the classes started to talk amongst themselves. "First years will have a mandatory requirement to break level twenty to return for their second year. In order to accomplish that, we will arrange transport to additional dungeon entrances to best help you level."

Even without her saying it, I knew the students would be brought from event to event.

"Last year, Crimson showed us the benefit of teaching from the dungeon to maximize the class's time in the dungeon, and we will be continuing that strategy for the newest class as well," Marlow continued. "For the second years, we have an inter-school competition. The raid on the thirty-second floor will become the grounds for your competition. That means you have to get there first." She stared up at our class and the two others. "Failure to reach the thirty-second floor before the end of the year will result in expulsion."

I blew out a breath, thankful that we'd trained all summer. Hitting that point would still be a hard push for all of us, but it was within the realm of possibility.

"Third and fourth years, the second year has caught up to you. Should you fail to stay ahead of them, you will be held back a year."

"WHAT!?" some students shrieked from the crowd.

The Headmistress grabbed the edge of the lectern. "Allow me to be clear. The level and quality of adventurers that we put out *will* improve. In order to do that, a heavy amount of pressure will be applied, as well as support from the college, to cut back wasted time."

I sighed. "It seems impossible to just demand it and have people suddenly rise to the occasion."

Candice leaned forward, still joining our conversation. "You apply pressure and suddenly the students are doing the math, cutting back on sleep and social time to grind more in the dungeon. The learnings from diving up and down from our first semester were important, but not absolutely vital. I'd be shocked if there aren't some lessons on how to fight other adventurers this year."

I frowned at the changes, but I stayed quiet. Honestly, with Crimson, I wasn't going to be able to slow down anytime soon anyway. My target had always been to get to the sixties to catch up with her.

"The UG, the guilds, and the colleges know that they would have been completely fucked without Crimson," Candice added. "They might not be able to solve it tomorrow, but they can be in a different place in four to five years if they invest in the right adventurers now."

I nodded in agreement; we'd be part of that solution. "So be it."

The Headmistress wasn't stopping for any of the chatter. "I expect Haylon to come out on top for all of the grades. Don't slack off and you'll get your name in the ear of every guild recruiter. They are all watching us closer than ever." She stepped back from the lectern.

Crimson moved up in front of our section. "Welcome back! Now get moving. Let's get to class so that I can explain to you how not to die."

***

Crimson closed the door behind us as the last student settled into their seat. "So, the Naga attacked, and humanity is scared because I might not always be there." She sighed dramatically. "Boo hoo. Anyway, they gave me free rein to push you as hard as I want! So, there is a silver lining in all of this."

Several of my classmates audibly swallowed.

"So, here's the deal. Raid on the thirty-second floor. You have to get there and clear the raid first. You are going to rotate in and out of the raid based on how many other classrooms there are. They want you to rest, recover, and level before going back for another attempt." Crimson patted the book in front of her but didn't open it. "Who can tell me about how raids work?"

Candice's hand shot up into the air, and nobody was surprised.

Crimson squinted at me as if asking me to raise my hand.

I sighed and raised it.

"Great. Go ahead, Ken, since you are so eager," Crimson pretended as if I had willingly volunteered.

"Raids are sections of the dungeon with larger, more powerful monsters. They are each more or less a boss monster. To make up for this, the dungeon allows for larger groups to enter. There are also raid bosses which are more complicated fights with even bigger monsters," I explained.

Crimson nodded along. "Bigger, more health, and more abilities. Only one group can be in each wing of the raid at a time. The level thirty-two raid has three wings." She turned around and sashayed to the chalkboard as she started drawing. "There are nine bosses total in the raid."

Her hand blurred, and there was a painful scraping of chalk before she stepped away and a detailed map of the raid was on the board. "This is the raid."

There was the sudden flutter of paper as we all worked to get our notebooks and pencils out.

"What's the environment of the raid?" she asked.

Candice's hand was in the air again as she sat stiff like she was urging her arm higher in the air.

Crimson sighed. "Candice."

"It's a mimicry of the Egyptian temples. Though, it is larger in scale to fit the Egyptian deities," she said quickly.

"Correct." Crimson made some notes on the board. "We could get into which came first, the myths of Egypt or the dungeon, but that's boring and mostly conjecture. Instead, let's talk about how to kill things and survive. Charlotte has a revive skill. Who else in here has one?"

Bonnie and Helen's hands went up. I raised an eyebrow at Helen.

"My mom." She shrugged.

"Okay, we need a few more to make sure that someone is alive at the end of everything to bring you guys back." Crimson pointed at Bonnie and Charlotte. "Make sure to keep those two alive or you are all dead."

Helen grunted.

"You're a tank. If other people are dead before you, it's best to just replace you anyway." Crimson rolled her eyes at Helen. "Besides, you are writing smut about Ken and didn't even include me," she grumbled under her breath.

"I'm no—" Helen groaned and sat back while Des snickered beside me.

"She's not really the one," Des whispered. "She told her mother that she's in love with you, and writes it to get back at her and to join Silver Fangs with the rest of her party."

Des's cheek pushed in as a piece of chalk hit her and knocked her out of her chair.

"Hush. I'm teaching," Crimson continued.

Charlotte raised her hand, making a sign with her fingers, and green healing light washed over Des as she pulled herself up, rubbing at her cheek. They were acting like this was normal, only making me wonder what they endured under my grandparents while I was gone.

"Alright, if there are no more interruptions about Ken's love life, let's continue with talking about surviving. The guides from the UG are pretty accurate. They oversell some of the danger of some abilities, but that's normal for their guidance. Fight the fights, figure out where you need to focus damage, healing, and damage mitigation. That's really what raid fights boil down to." Crimson continued making notes on the board. "Candice, why don't you run us through the easiest wing."

Candice cleared her throat and ran a hand through her straight, blonde hair. "It's called the scarab wing in the guide. I suggest it as the easiest because two of the three bosses are low damage, increasing likelihood to survive and making success reliant on our damage dealers' output."

"Fair," Crimson said. "Not a bad way to dip your toes into the raid. The raid will be the full twenty-five students in the class. Whichever team reaches the raid first will be the ones to reorganize the class for the raid."

Harley squeaked and turned to stare at me.

The class chuckled.

"Don't get too excited, Harley. Raids are no time to be goofing off," Helen scolded her. "They are also a deviation from the normal progression of leveling a ton. You tend to build raw stats more when fighting in a raid, and it is all about the gear. Doing this raid could easily set you up with gear you won't start replacing until the later forties."

"You can also speed up your leveling process in the thirties considerably with the better gear," Des added.

Harley laid on her desk and pouted, "No fair. My healer harem."

Crimson cleared her throat. "I stand by my word. Whoever can get there on their own power first gets to make the raid."

Harley leaned around Charlotte and whispered loudly at me, "Ken, can we ninja our way— Ouch." She rubbed her head where Bun-bun had smacked her. "Bun-bun, you aren't very cute and fluffy."

The rabbit huffed and curled back up on Charlotte's head. If he had fingers, I was pretty sure he would have flipped her off.

Penelope raised her hand. "Perhaps we should wait to learn much more about the raid until we are there? The Headmistress said that we could set up classrooms in the dungeon."

Crimson blurred. A moment later, she had a hardhat on her head and a toolbelt slung across her hips with a two-by-four over her shoulder and a nail between her teeth. "Don't worry. I'll make a big hall on the thirtieth floor."

The door to the classroom slid open, and the Harem Queen poked her mane of red hair through. "Ah, that's not necessary, Crimson. My harem has already started and finished construction on the thirtieth floor. It's a beautiful building with luxury for all." She winked at me.

The nail fell out of Crimson's teeth and clattered onto the floor. "Already?"

"Mmmhmm." The Harem Queen had a smug smile on her face. "Headmistress told me about the need a few weeks ago." She glanced behind her. "Alright, my students are on the move. I will see you all on the thirtieth floor."

"Wait, you have a second year class?" Helen stood up and slapped her hands on the desk. "Who was irresponsible enough to give you that?"

"Daughter, I am very responsible. And Teacher Sai suddenly dropped out at the last minute." She shrugged and pressed her lips flat.

I could imagine that she had something to do with Teacher Sai leaving.

"I must get going if my class is to hurry there." The Harem Queen closed the door softly.

The entire room was silent until Crimson's hard hat cracked between her hands. Then she crushed the entire thing in one swift motion like an empty soda can.

"Yeah, those things were never really very safe, were they?" Des commented as the yellow hat fell in little chips from Crimson's hands.

"Hard hats are really so that you just don't bump your head, not to save you from anything bigger than that," I said.

Crimson's whip crack silenced the class. "What are you all waiting for!? Get down to the thirtieth floor. I'll meet you there." She became a red blur, likely heading off to harass the Harem Queen.

"Well, that's our cue to go." I threw my notebook into my CID with the hastily copied map from the chalkboard. "Are you all ready?"

"Happy to follow you," Des said.

"Ready!" Charlotte snapped to attention.

"Let's go, my Adrel." Fayeth agreed.

Harley had fire in her eyes. "My healer harem depends on our success. By the way, what were you up to this summer?"

I gestured vaguely as we got going. "Things."

"That's code for banging a princess, right? Des, tell me that's code for banging a princess."

I sighed. "It's code for busy."

"Much less exciting," Harley sighed and patted my shoulder. "If you don't go banging princesses, how are you going to fill my spot when I leave you for my healer harem?"

"With literally any support," Des chuckled.

"Hey! I do solid work. Charlotte and you never run out of mana," Harley defended herself. "This is why my healer harem will love me. I'll inspire them with endless mana." She spun in circles as she dodged between the desks.

"He did actually bang the princess though." Des' words had the desired effect, and Harley ran into a desk before she spun to a sputtering stop.

"Why didn't you lead with that!"

"Because this way was more fun," I answered for Des with a big grin on my face.

It was nice being back with my party. I walked towards the door with a smile on my face, despite what we were about to be up against.

CHAPTER 4

F ayeth sprayed her [Agitating Spores] over the small encampment of trolls. They let out screams of rage that sounded more like animals than sentient creatures. They weren't exactly the smartest looking creatures, but they came in a variety.

Fayeth braced herself. Her spear butted against the ground as she held the last two feet of it steady at the charging monster. The biggest of the trolls was a hulking eight-foot-tall creature with a chest of green muscle that resembled a brick wall. She caught its face with her shield even as its hands slammed down on her shoulders that were both wrapped in the root-like armor.

"Got them," she grunted as she switched her grip and cleaved through the pack.

I moved in, throwing my hand in an arc shape and activating [Blades of Shadow], the ability that Elysara had given me from the Elven library. Eight shadowy magic blades fanned out and dove into each of the trolls, spreading dark lines from where each impacted.

I ducked a wide swing that was meant for Fayeth, but it came dangerously close to ringing my bell before coming in at a caster troll that was a few steps back from the rest.

"Earth Stomp." I used the ability to stop abruptly and the ripple effect to disrupt their cast.

The troll was a bent over humanoid with a giant nose and tusks protruding from its lips. If it had stood straight up, it would have been a foot taller than me, but right now, it was a hair shorter.

My blades flashed as [Dark Strike] activated and I tried to find its mana crystal in its chest. Unfortunately, I missed and just dealt some heavy damage.

The troll's eyes flicked towards me as I picked up aggro from Fayeth, but that was okay, I could handle a caster on my own.

A ball of mud formed in its hand as it curled its fingers and hurled it at me.

"Absorb." I caught the spell and threw it right back. "Spell Mirror."

The mud hit the troll in the face and covered its eyes. I'd already been hit twice, and it was fairly effective at blinding as well as disorientingly stinky.

The troll stumbled back and I pressed forward, entering my trained forms as my two jagged, black daggers tore into the monster. The troll didn't last long under a concentrated attack and puffed into black smoke as a mana crystal and loot fell to the floor. I didn't bother grabbing the loot, instead turning around and joining the party for the rest of the fight.

Harley was playing an upbeat tune with an occasional grating sound that sent a ripple to deal a weak AoE to the trolls.

Des stood back, making gestures with her hands. Pentagrams dotted the trolls as their veins turned purple and bled small wisps of black smoke from her curses. She flicked her hand to the side, and a wave of dark magic roiled over the trolls, dealing even more damage.

I threw another fan of [Blades of Shadow], reapplying my own damage over time and started working in from the edge.

Fayeth was a force to be reckoned with, partially rooted to the ground and swinging her spear back and forth in wide cleaves.

Charlotte was casting healing on Fayeth with mutters and hand gestures with one hand while the other flicked a wand sending white magical bursts into them at random. She wasn't aiming very well, but she also didn't need to be very precise when shooting into a mass of trolls.

With all of the area attacks and the damage over time spells on them, the trolls began to crumple one after another in short order.

I wiped at my brow and picked up one of the blue mana crystals, holding it up to have it catch the light. "We are moving up in the world. This is worth a hundred Ren."

Harley picked up a sword and inspected a piece of loot with her CID. "Junk."

"No, that's scrap metal." Des smiled. "Now that the Nagato Clan has a quest out for scrap metal, we are going to make some nice money."

"Doesn't Ken then sell it for more?" Harley asked.

"I'll pay you the bounty. No reason to cut you out," I said.

Harley bounced over and handed me the sword. "Money, please."

I rolled my eyes but put it in and tapped my CID to hers. "Done."

"Who knew being part of a guild would be so profitable?" Harley did a little dance and went back to checking on the loot.

"The profit is coming from trading with the elves," I explained. "Otherwise, we wouldn't have quests at such a low level."

Harley stuck her tongue out at me. "There were plenty of nice collection quests. And don't think I didn't see you cutting through a few extra boggarts on the first floor." Harley pulled out some of the moss that was highly regarded for low-level healing potions.

There was another quest from the Silverfangs for that material. If we weren't pushing ourselves to level so much, I might have tried to convince the girls to spend a little time on the trip down farming the boggarts before the first years swarmed the first five floors.

That wouldn't be out of the question for any Haylon student. This year was different, though.

As things were currently, we had made good progress.

"Call it for the night?" Des asked Fayeth.

The elf nodded with a one-word answer, "Tired."

"I can—" Harley was halfway to trying to perk her up with some buff before Charlotte put her hand on the flute to silence it.

"I'm tired too. If you have the energy, Harley, why don't you help set the traps?" Charlotte smiled softly at the bard.

Harley rolled her eyes. "On it. I see the dungeon wall there." She pointed ahead and started marching through the heavily wooded dungeon floor.

Fayeth cut ahead of her, putting her spear over her shoulder and keeping her eyes up ahead. As the tank, she was constantly vigilant for other monsters and seemed to be the first to hit her limit. She'd taken a lot of damage in the fights today.

We moved quickly through the trees to the dungeon wall. Charlotte threw down some camping gear while Fayeth checked both directions to make sure there wasn't anything lingering around the camp.

"All clear." Fayeth came back, planted her spear, and then hugged me. "I'm sleepy."

I picked her up off her feet. For someone who could successfully hold back giant trolls, she was pretty light.

"Hey, don't distract Ken. He's supposed to be working," Harley grumbled as she staked another warning line with a tin can full of bits and pieces.

Sometimes the simplest of solutions were the best.

I pulled out one of the tents that Elysara had given me. It was an Elven construction of a waxy leaf-like material, but I knew it was grown in this shape for this purpose. I hadn't explored much of it while I had been there, but the elves had very interesting plant-based technology.

The tent popped open on its own and expanded into a large room the size of a small apartment. The edges grew roots to stake themselves down; they'd have to be cut later.

Fayeth wiggled free and pulled out some water from her CID, pouring it on one of the sections where moss as soft as any foam mattress grew from the water.

"That's just not fair," Harley sighed.

"We can section off part at night. It's decently sound proof," I offered.

She nodded vigorously. "Yes please."

Fayeth fell down on the moss, and I pulled out some blankets from my CID to cover her.

"I'll help you with traps in a moment." I covered up Fayeth and tucked the edges of the blanket in around her to keep her warm. The current dungeon floor's climate was chilly once we stopped moving and fighting.

"Why don't you help me find wood?" Des asked, already picking up some branches from around our campsite.

Harley squinted at her.

"He's got more than four days on his timer with her," Charlotte sighed as she set up the cooking pot. "Not everything is about sex."

Harley pointed an accusing finger at Des. "It is with her. Not even my type and I'm a little jealous of Ken."

"As you should be." Des somehow made picking up sticks exciting with how she bent over.

I cleared my throat. "I'll work on picking up wood with Des. We should stock up on some from this floor so that we have enough for our whole dive."

Harley rolled her eyes. "We'll be on these five floors for a little while."

"I don't know, we might stretch up to the next set soon," I said. "I'm level twenty-five, and the rest of you are no lower than twenty-three."

Harley pouted as I pointed out that she was the lowest level, even Charlotte had edged above her. Des was the highest, and her stats had kept up too. Though, much of that might have been her transformation.

One day, I'd need to see if I couldn't shake more stats out of Demon Lord Snu Snu.

We stayed near the camp but wandered far enough to talk softly without being overheard. The current floor was mostly large trees with little to no underbrush; it was easy to see the troll packs, even if it was heavy woods.

"Go easy on Harley, okay?" I told Des.

Des huffed a little as she straightened up. "She's leaving us," she said, revealing she was truthfully a little upset by it.

"For her dream of a healer harem," I reminded her. "We sort of knew it was going to happen."

Des sighed. "I know, I know. That means we are going to end up with an open spot in our party."

"And there's your real concern. You want to keep the party balanced," I said.

She nodded. "That, and while Harley isn't joining us in bed, nor do I wish her to, she's been a very good and functional piece to our adventuring." She paused. "How does the princess look for joining us?"

"She promised to join us when she could. However, she's stuck in her role right now. With her father leading their elites to guard the dungeon where it connects to the Naga, Elysara is holding down the capital of the Elven world," I said. "Though, as far as a support, she'll do just fine. Her class is incredibly flexible."

"I'm sure she is." Des couldn't suppress the wry grin.

I rolled my eyes. "Down, girl."

"Can't help myself. You need to work on your stamina," Des sighed, putting another stick in her CID. "I knew I was going to get this ability with the change, and I picked it so that I could help give us all stats that would keep us alive." She poked my chest and then slid her arms around my neck to bring her face to mine and her lips brushing mine as she continued. "I need more."

Her words had a visceral reaction from me. "I know."

"Then work on your stamina, because I'm a little temptress, and once every five days is like fasting for me." She kissed me and melted into me.

All thoughts of picking up sticks vanished, and instead, I wanted to hide mine in her.

She broke the kiss after a moment, her eyes promising delight but her words pouring cold water over the mood. "You're going to get hurt if we keep going."

"The result?" I asked, debating if I wanted to continue.

"Stamina damage for you, stamina gain for me," she answered. "I actually gained three points last night. One in mana, two in stamina."

I raised an eyebrow. "Seems hard for me to keep up."

"That's kind of the point, I think." Des frowned and went back to finding firewood. "The demonic side of this would be to fuck my way to very high stamina and mana. Not that it is even an option. You are the only man for me."

I kissed her on the cheek. "Not worried about that. I'm worried about keeping up with you," I chuckled. "As for a new member of the party, let's let it happen more organically. To be frank, I'm not even sure who are the options?"

Des raised an eyebrow at me. "Really? Just pick one in the class and I'm sure they'll hop over. Candice might even be interested in pretending to be a support."

"Taylor?" I asked, doubting that one.

"She's pretty sick of being a tank with her DPS class. Even if she was running around with bandages and potions, she'd probably be happier," Des snickered. "Is that the one you're interested in?"

"No." I waved my hands. "I was just picking out someone who seemed unlikely."

Des clicked her tongue. "I got news for you, Ken. You are showing a large amount of potential, and the writer of 74 wives isn't wrong."

I shook my head. "You know who it is." It wasn't really a question; the way she said it was clear.

"Of course I do." Des grinned. "But I'll leave it to her to come out on her own. Now that she's stopped misrepresenting me in the fiction, we are cool."

"Uh huh." I watched her closely.

"There was a whole summer training arc, followed by you basically working your way through impregnating every elf in the Elven world. Actually, I think she depicted the Elven world like there were no males," Des explained.

I rolled my eyes. "Of course she did. What a harem thing to do."

Des shrugged. "Made for good reading. Not everything has to be realistic." She paused. "During your retelling of the summer, you sort of glossed over Ami, and also this Felin."

"Are you asking if there's anything there?" I asked.

"Pretty much." Des broke out into a wide smile.

"Ah. Well... Ami is a consummate professional. She's a butler first and foremost by a large margin. It is sort of hard to see the romantic angle through all of that," I admitted.

"At least you are honest. She's pretty, though." Des nudged me in the ribs.

"Yes, she is," I agreed. "When she takes her mask off. She likes to hide it."

"Well maybe she's the shy type," Des added. "Either way, I want to run my hands through that white hair when I see it. It looks so silky soft. I understand your view, though. Tell me about the curious Nekorian who bargained for your stolen clothing. Actually, tell me about Nekorians in general."

"Their tongues are like sandpaper." I started with the relevant details for a temptress.

Des made a face. "That's got to be a horrible blow job." She patted my shoulder reassuringly. "Sorry you miss out on that one. Holding them by their cat ears is probably a dream of yours."

I deadpanned. "Not even on the radar."

"Huh. Are you sure you have an incubus secondary class?" Des teased. "Are they more human or more cat-like?"

"More cat-like than I expected. They have a wicked set of teeth, and Felin is all about brushing against me. Oh, she tattooed me." I pulled up my shirt to show her.

Des poked the tattoo. "So you let the cat girl mark you?"

"Not like that, and stop calling her a cat girl."

"Seems like that's exactly what she did. Cool tattoo, though, kind of hard to imagine that it moves when she asks the dungeon to read your skills."

I pulled down my shirt. "It was an interesting experience. It was the second time I felt the dungeon focus on me. Hopefully the last." I shuddered at the memory.

"So, what about Felin? Is she cute?" Des smiled.

"She's got a lot of hair; a big mane of it." I held my hands out to show her.

"Still head hair?"

"Yeah, just frizzy enough that she seems to struggle to tame it. Then she's got blue stripes on her skin." I made motions along my abs.

"And her shirt shows off her abs," Des said, reading between the lines.

"Yeah, not much in the clothing department if I'm honest; those leather pants of hers were pretty much painted on. She's a shaman which is an important part of their culture and I think a class," I explained.

"Sounds like she could fill Harley's spot. I'd just have to buy you some extra shirts." Des was desperately holding back a laugh.

"Glad you are enjoying yourself." I rolled my eyes and picked up some more wood. "Let's head back before Harley hurts herself with her imagination."

Des let her laugh out at that. "She would. Though I feel bad for her when the cat girl tracks you down."

"What makes you so sure of that?" I asked.

Des gestured vaguely at me. "She's a cat and she steals your shirts. I'll bet you ten thousand Ren that she comes and finds you when she wants attention. Not sure how long she'll stick around, but she'll find you when she wants to. After all, she's marked you and has your scent."

"I'm not going to dignify that with a response." I rolled my eyes.

CHAPTER 5

I woke up to Charlotte rubbing my back. "My turn?"

"Figured we'd let Fayeth take the night off," Charlotte whispered. "You got the last watch."

I snapped a lazy salute at her and wiggled my way out of Fayeth's grasp as Charlotte slipped into the spot where I had been. Fayeth quickly snuggled up against Charlotte.

"Get some rest." I slipped out of the large tent and stretched my back as I pulled out a bottle of water and crushed it in a few seconds.

The morning in the dungeon was quiet as I pulled out two practice blades and started to move through my forms to warm up my mind and body. My blades cut through the air as I stepped through the familiar forms.

The first day back in the dungeon with the party had gone well. I had been a little worried that we'd have more to iron out, but after adapting to some new skills, we fit together like we were made for each other.

I blew out a breath as I picked up the speed, working on my agility. My stamina was going to need some extra attention, but that was a marathon, not a sprint.

The blades swished through the air in a rapid staccato as my movements sped up. I was at the peak of my speed, a level I didn't achieve during monster fights because they moved so much, and began to work on my footwork to help fix that.

That was when I felt a new presence.

The dungeon's attention was once again upon me, and despite my heart pounding a second ago from my exertion, it felt like my heart stopped. Everything felt like it froze for an eternity that lasted just a second.

The dungeon's attention lessened, and time returned, yet I could feel a distant prickle in the back of my neck, like something was still watching me.

I spun in place, replacing my practice swords with large, jagged daggers as I prepared for a fight. A set of eyes glowed in the darkness, and I didn't hesitate.

"Monster attack, wake up," I shouted at the tent, hearing rustling immediately.

My shout caused the glowing eyes to rush forward, a barely visible form of a prowling panther pulled away from the shadows of the trees. A faint spark of purple light raced through its fur as it leapt at me. The thing was huge, as big as an SUV.

I caught its front claws on my daggers and rolled with it, keeping myself from being crushed by its bulk.

The strange panther's eyes crackled as it spun around to meet me while I rolled to my feet and brought my daggers back up. Something was strange about this monster, but I couldn't quite put my finger on what was different.

"Shadow Bolt." Des appeared at the lip of the tent.

Her ability went right through the panther, like it was made of smoke, only for it to reform and charge me again with a rapid series of swipes.

"What was that?!" I shouted, blocking the paws and giving ground to the larger creature.

"I don't know!" Des shouted back, just as frustrated.

Fayeth came charging out next, her spear braced on her shield as she ran the panther through. Only, just like Des, she couldn't touch it. She still spun around and cleaved through its body, her spear passing harmlessly through.

I blocked again, driven back by the force in its paws. To me, it certainly didn't feel like I was fighting something made of smoke.

"Maybe only the paws are physical?" I offered.

Fayeth shoved herself between me and the monster only for her shield to pass through the claw as it reformed around her.

I hastily blocked the claw, feeling the jolt up my arm and a burning pain in my shoulder. "Just get back."

"Ken. What is going on?" Des asked.

"Focusing right now," I grunted as the panther sped up.

Its claws started coming faster and faster as it also started jerking to the sides in rapid motion to change its angle of attack. I cut its leg, my blades biting into its skin unlike Des or Fayeth's attack.

Whatever this thing was, it felt like it was made to fight me and me alone. But as it picked up speed, I was flagging in the attacks I could block.

"Heal!" Charlotte shouted, and I felt my exhaustion fade along with the pain in my arms.

That momentary respite was lost a second later when the panther's eyes flashed angrily. Apparently, Charlotte's heal had violated some unspoken agreement.

Those eyes felt like they consumed my vision before the panther disappeared and pain erupted all over my body. I saw my blood splash into the air and my vision rotated to see my decapitated body a moment before everything went dark.

***

"NO!" Des screamed activating [Metamorphosis]. Her skin turned a pretty pink while white horns jutted out of her forehead.

She started casting with both hands, throwing dark pink blasts of magic in rapid fire. Unfortunately, the spells did nothing to the panther who teleported behind Ken. It felt like the creature was gloating as it turned around.

Des' spells went through the monster, like she was trying to cut fog with a knife. Then after the gloating was done, it disappeared, melting away into the darkness.

Des panted, holding two spells in her hands as she spun around looking for the panther to come past again.

"What was that?" Harley was doing the same, looking for the monster.

"Don't know. Get him back up, Charlotte," Des demanded of their healer.

A small part of her was afraid that with all the abnormalities of that monster, Ken wouldn't come back with a revive. She wanted him back—that would be the only way she could feel reassured.

The panther was gone, and she let go of [Metamorphosis], rushing to Ken's side.

Charlotte was putting his head back in place. Every inch of him was covered in claw marks. That panther monster had destroyed him in that last instant.

Was it a reaction to him being healed? What even was that? She had too many questions circling her mind. For now, she needed to focus on Ken.

Charlotte had her eyes closed as green motes of light trickled out of her palms and settled into Ken's body, restoring his neck and some of the more major wounds.

Ken gasped a breath before wincing.

Des was there in an instant, cradling his head. "Don't move, let Charlotte finish healing you."

Ken coughed up blood. "Fuck."

"Not until you get rid of the blood," Des joked, holding back tears.

Seeing him injured and killed like that was crushing her new demonic heart. It physically hurt to see him in pain.

Her new class and secondary class came with some changes. For the most part, she found herself less caring about others, but in the same breath, she felt an attachment to Ken that she couldn't explain.

Having him back had been like the sweetest wine on her lips. Taking him back to bed had been heaven. And seeing him die, even knowing that Charlotte was nearby, was hell.

Charlotte continued to envelop Ken in green light until he was whole once again, though he'd need a new set of clothes.

The druid wiped her brow. "That was... something."

Des helped Ken up, unwilling to let him go just yet. "Going to explain that one?"

"I don't really know." Ken blinked a few times. "First I felt the dungeon focus on me again, like when I learned the Portal ability, then I felt the panther watching me. As soon as I shouted for help, it rushed me. I'm not sure if the dungeon warned me or summoned it." Ken shook his head, just as confused as the rest of the party.

"We clearly couldn't do anything." Fayeth was wringing her hands, and as much as Desmonda wanted to keep a hold of Ken, the elf clearly needed some reassurance.

"What did you do to piss the dungeon off?" Harley asked.

"Come here." Des pulled Fayeth close and then brought Charlotte into a large group hug. Harley put a hand on her shoulder in support.

"It's okay. The thing is gone and Ken is fine. He's just in slightly less clothing, though I'd argue it isn't a bad change." Des couldn't help the small smile as Ken let out a chuckle.

The group needed a few laughs right now.

"I... I think I killed Ken when I used my heal," Charlotte hesitated.

"The monster was speeding up on its own anyway. Honestly, I'm not sure how much damage I did, but I don't think I was going to kill that on my own. It felt like I was trying to block a runaway truck." Ken squeezed them all. "But it is gone and we are all okay," he repeated. "You guys can get back to sleep."

Des scoffed. "Not going to happen after that. Let's pack up and start the day a little early."

All the others nodded in agreement. After seeing Ken go down, there wasn't going to be any restful sleep until they processed the whole situation.

***

With the tent packed up, we pushed deeper into the dungeon. Soon we would reach level twenty-five and a boss that we'd have to work through.

"Do you think it'll come back?" Harley asked as Fayeth led us through the dungeon.

"Your guess, in this one instance, is as good as mine." I smirked at Harley.

She scoffed. "I wasn't hip-deep in Elven ladies all summer."

"It wasn't that bad, but he did get a lot of attention," Fayeth said from up front. "He brought yoga pants and sports bras to the Elven world. He really enjoyed workouts."

"Yup. All the Censors started wearing them and joined me and the princess for our workouts," I added on.

Harley slurped up a little drool that came out of the corner of her mouth. "And you came back?!"

"Yeah." I pointed to Des. "Could you walk away from that or Charlotte for long?"

Harley seemed torn with that question and decided to keep her mouth shut. "Still a very difficult decision."

"Thankfully, Elysara is going to come visit when she's free from the responsibilities," Fayeth added.

"I want to make a bet," Des blurted. "That Felin shows up before Elysara."

Fayeth hummed in thought. "Standard bet?"

"Yup."

"Can I get in?" Charlotte asked.

"Of course," Des answered. "I'm happy to take you both on. Felin shows up first."

"Deal. I think Elysara will," Fayeth agreed.

Charlotte thought for a moment. "I'll double up and say both show up at the same time."

"Deal," the other two said at the same time.

"Do I want to know what the 'standard bet' is?" I asked.

"Probably not." Charlotte blushed.

Harley grumbled, sounding jealous behind me.

"Trolls ahead." Fayeth stopped short and summoned her shield, the roots growing out of her forearm and forming the shield.

"Bun-bun, you'll get the second big one until we can take the first down," Charlotte said, the rabbit bounding out of her arms now that he had a job and stretched out.

"That's right, Lazy. Time to get to work." Des clicked her tongue at the rabbit who chittered back at her.

"He says you are the lazy one. You spend a lot of time sleeping," Charlotte translated.

"I do not and that's not what he said." Des squinted and pointed at her eyes then at him. "I'm onto you."

Bun-bun hopped forward like he was escaping and ran towards the trolls.

Fayeth followed right behind him, her spear swept to the side as she sprayed her spores onto the trolls and stopped short to swing through them with her spear.

"By the way, what abilities did you guys swap?" Fayeth asked as she fought.

Des chuckled. "I wanted his big Portal ability and his Absorb."

"You still passed out when you used it," I reminded her, rushing around Fayeth and throwing out my attack rotation for a group before focusing on the largest troll to get it down so that she could relieve Bun-bun.

"Ha! But mine made a spark in the air. I might not be far away from being able to use it." Des blasted off a wave of shadow magic into the trolls before working to put her curses and hexes on them.

Since I wasn't going for the caster first, I used the [Shadow Arm] and [Mana Burn] combo to burn away its mana.

"What about you, Charlotte?" Harley pushed.

"Absorb and Elemental Shield. I don't need to focus on doing damage, and Des has the larger mana pool. When Portal failed for her, I just focused on what would improve my survivability." Charlotte had a cute focused face as she healed Fayeth, keeping an eye out for Bun-bun and working to get in attacks with her wand.

"Now what did Ken take from both of you? Eh?" Harley teased.

"For someone who has no interest in joining me in the bedroom, you sure do want to know a lot of details about what happens inside," I teased and hurled Des' [Shadow Wave] ability as an answer.

"I'm just a curious girl. Not that kind of curious, but you have a very unique ability to swap out abilities," Harley spoke between playing her flute.

Fayeth absorbed a mud ball and flung it over at the troll that Bun-bun was tanking.

I activated [Cleave] with both of my daggers. Though it was better used with a larger weapon, I was still working on my rotation for larger monster groupings.

"I mean, this gives us a lot of cool options. If there's a spellbook that we all want, we just have to give it to Ken," Des said with a silly smile. "He can be like a big spell repository for us."

My [Mana Burn] brought the caster low enough that I tried out my new level twenty-five Trelican ability. "Mana Implosion." I put my palm against the troll's chest.

A small, blue bead with a black rim formed in its chest and sucked at its remaining mana. When it didn't find any more mana, it ripped at the flesh of the troll, sucking it in until it was satisfied.

I took a step back as the troll went off like a bomb, a blue ring erupting and injuring the nearby trolls and taking out the weakened large troll. The caster survived, but the troll had a hole in its chest that revealed the mana crystal. I quickly stabbed the mana crystal with a swift motion of my daggers.

The caster turned into black smoke.

"Okay, that's a cool one. Why didn't you take that, Des?"

"Well, I didn't know it would be that flashy," she admitted.

"It's a finisher. They are supposed to be big," I said, feeling buoyed by the cool new skill, even though I was feeling a little drained from using it. It had a high mana cost.

I moved through my forms on the remaining trolls as Bun-bun jumped over and hopped on Fayeth's head, screaming at the trolls before bounding off to the side.

Whatever the rabbit did caused the large one he'd been antagonizing earlier to focus now on Fayeth while Bun-bun fussed over his ears.

"Get back to work," Des scowled at him.

He squeaked back, pulling at his ears and pointing at something.

"It's so small I can't even see it," Charlotte sighed and cast [Heal] on him, causing the rabbit to glow green for a second.

He fluffed up his ears again for a second and then bound back into the combat.

"The little guy is getting pretty finicky," I commented.

Des rolled her eyes. "Tell me about it. You'd think he was preparing for a lady rabbit to stroll on up."

Bun-bun chattered back at her while his ears waved angrily side to side.

"He says that it's good to always look your best," Charlotte translated.

Des squinted at the druid before going back to throwing spells into the pack of trolls. "Sure he did."

We whittled down the rest of the trolls until there were no more. Then we began picking through the loot.

"Hey, this might be nice for you." Des tossed me a rusty short sword.

I caught it out of the air. "It is better, but so ugly." I checked over the weapon.

Ancient Blade: +9 Agility, +2 Strength, +1 Stamina

Ever since the event boss' epic quality weapons, I hadn't found an upgrade from the rank and file monsters until now. This one was just a magic weapon, but even the magic weapons at this level were bound to catch up.

"It has stamina too." Des pointedly poked at it.

"Good thing you like it. I'll wear it if you wear these ritual robes." I pulled up loot that was at my feet.

Des recoiled at the patchwork leather and fur outfit. "You want me to wear that instead of my dress?" she gasped.

"Wear it, wear it," Harley chanted. "You've said before that stats matter more than appearances."

"Have I?" Des put a hand on her chest. "I don't recall that, do you, Charlotte?"

"Don't think I do," Charlotte played along. "Wasn't there someone in our party who fought tooth and nail to wear a poofy dress even though she had out leveled it by the time she could afford it?"

Harley grumbled, "It was a spectacular dress. Bonnie liked it."

"Bonnie dresses like an old woman," I pointed out.

Harley gasped and threw a piece of troll liver at me. "Take that back."

I popped the liver in my CID. "What? She does. Someone back me up."

Fayeth pinched her fingers together. "She does dress like a prudish priest."

Harley huffed. "I think it's adorable."

"You just want to corrupt her," Des corrected.

Harley stuck out her tongue. "Maybe that too. Anyway, Ken, take the damn sword. Try it out and see if you'll keep it. We can't slow down because we have to get to the thirty-second floor first."

I sighed and shook my head. "We have to level on the way. We have two more floors and then a new boss that we will take seriously. That'll be the twenty-fifth floor and we'll have caught up to our levels."

"We should start to read up on the guide that the UG put out for the boss so that we are prepared when we come to it," Des offered. "I'd be happy to read it while Fayeth takes the lead."

"Please do. I'll keep an eye out for the next pack of trolls." Fayeth put her spear over her shoulder and started leading our group forward in the dungeon once again.

CHAPTER 6

I t took two more days before we made it to the boss on the 25th floor.

I sat down by the giant doors and waved to Candice's party who had beaten us to the entrance. The giant brass doors were a reminder of just how huge and powerful the dungeon was. Those doors couldn't be broken even by someone of Crimson's level.

Candice had her legs folded under her as she ate on a picnic blanket for lunch. Wendy's owl was flying lazily overhead while they enjoyed a small break.

"Took you long enough." Candice glanced up from her sandwich.

"This part isn't the sprint. We took our time killing as many of the trolls as we could." I plopped down next to her and pulled out a sandwich from Grandma Hemi. "At the end of the day, the race is how quickly we can get experience."

Candice finished her sandwich and dabbed at her lip. "Still, I wanted to propose something for this boss. It's a tricky one. I'd ask that you let us fight it while you watch and learn from our mistakes."

I glanced at Charlotte, already understanding what she wanted. "We'll be here to revive you if something happens?"

Candice nodded sharply. "Precisely. I knew you were smart enough to see where I was going."

I grinned at her. Candice was always a little rigid. "Fine, we'll hang out by the door. We'll only open it if you are in immediate danger; otherwise, I'll let you play it out. You can yell at us to open it too if you want."

"No need. As long as you are there to revive us, we'll do what we can to see the full breadth of the boss fight. Have you read up on it?" Candice asked.

"It's a group of trolls worshiping to start. The strategy is to kill as many as possible in the first burst. For each one that survives, the boss starts with 10% more health," Des spoke up, having read all the materials. "There's no tanking or healing during that part of the battle. Everyone is just doing as much damage as they can."

"We'll do better on that part, and it works well with Selene's class." Candice gestured at the healer with short, black hair. She drained the soul of her enemies and used it to heal her party. The fact that their healer naturally did damage was a big part of how Candice's party was able to progress quickly.

"I'm interested to see just how long that stage goes," Des agreed. "Will it be worth putting up my damage over time abilities, or are they close enough to use Area of Effects effectively?"

"Good questions and you'll get to see it." Candice nodded. "Then they summon the boss. It's a giant troll-shaped mud elemental. It takes damage fairly normally, blunt damage takes a small reduction."

"Of course these stinky trolls worship a big pile of mud," Harley grumbled.

"You are still just bitter that Fayeth dodged that mud ball and you got hit," Des chuckled to herself at the memory.

Harley shuddered. "That mud stank. I still swear that the stench was damaging my health."

"It was not. Though, it was foul," I admitted.

"There's going to be a lot more mud during this boss fight," Candice reminded Harley, who shuddered.

"I'll survive, and next time we are bringing more wet wipes," Harley sighed. "The things I do for my healer harem."

"You have to get there first," Candice reminded her.

"It's a marathon not a sprint. Besides, we have Ken. Though he isn't much on his own, he comes with an obsessed leather-wearing lady who could murder us all in a blink of an eye." Harley bobbed her eyebrows.

"Don't forget Helen's mom too," Selene added in. "We all saw that."

"Maybe you could get some mother-daughter action." Harley turned to me.

I took a deep breath and continued eating. "No."

"I bet she has some crazy skills you could take. At some point here, you are going to start selling access to that crazy Portal skill, aren't you?" Harley asked.

"My mother asked about it," Candice added in. "All of the high-level adventurers are interested in it. If you could really share..." She trailed off, not needing to list off all the favors I could get if I started sharing the skill.

We all knew that they'd go well out of their way to get access to it.

"It isn't that easy." Fayeth wrapped her arms around me. "You have to be Adrel, which means more than just having sex. You have to harmonize your soul to the Adrel."

Candice's eyes searched mine. "Understood. I'll relay that answer to my mother."

"Wait a second. I don't know if I want that going around." I held my hands up. "Last thing I need is your mom or her guild romancing me."

"What, you don't think Candice is cute?" Des teased. "Her mom looks just like her."

"Hush you. That's not what I said. Candice is plenty pretty." I poked Des. "You'll just try and fill my bed if it means you get to join some of them."

She stuck out her tongue. "Guilty."

Candice watched both of us with interest. "I see." She put away the remainder of her lunch. "Then we'll have to reach the thirty-second floor before your party."

I glared at Des in a 'look what you've done' expression. She just gave me a big smile back.

Candice's party packed up and headed into the boss room as we took up the back corner by the door.

"Remember, don't help," I told my party. "They are giving us a lot of trust."

At the higher level bosses, watching like this to revive wasn't uncommon. It was a big reason that guilds were able to grow faster than others with this kind of support. Yet, it gave the watching group a lot of power. It would be easy to intervene, enrage the boss, and wipe another party only to loot them after resetting the boss.

***

The boss doors closed. Candice watched Ken's party tuck into the corner while she and her party had moved to the center of the room.

The boss room was large enough that it was clear the boss fight wasn't going to be as small as the dozen trolls continuously chanting on one side of the room.

For the most part, the area was all stone, with interesting markings along the wall like a primordial language. Several carvings in the wall gave hints as to what they were going to summon.

Myrtle and Wendy were shifting their weight from one foot to another. Her party had fought bosses before, but that wasn't the reason they were impatient.

"Alright, don't be nervous just because Ken is watching." Candice ran her hand through her hair. She was talking to herself a little too.

"Right, just any other day in the dungeon." Wendy fidgeted and looked over her shoulder. Her two wolves whined, picking up on her nervous energy.

"Think of it as tryouts." Selene bit her lip while she played with her raven curls. "When we do the raid, he's going to get shuffled about. I mean, Fayeth will get put in a tanking group, and Harley is going to be put with a party of healers. Her mana regeneration is just too good to not utilize. That means he'll need someone to look after him."

Candice narrowed her eyes at Selene. "Then don't fuck this up. We went over the plan. All of you got it?" Candice looked around the group. Now was not the time for them to blush over Ken. "Got this, Meixie?"

The silent assassin nodded.

"Alright, Myrtle, give me a second and then start us off." Candice raised her attention from her party to the boss room. She pulled on a pair of leather gloves that made her hands feel suddenly lighter as she whipped a wand through the air, weaving arcane runes for a fan favorite spell, [Fireball].

She utilized another class ability to stall the activation of the rune and to set it on continuous fire while she worked on another rune.

"Going when you finish," Myrtle said, starting to walk forward and checking on Candice's progress.

"Go." Candice finished the second rune and slapped it, pouring more mana into it.

The first one went off a hair before the second, lobbing a purple fireball like a mortar shell. With that, Candice was focusing on the next rune and the next.

The first fizzled out while she was working on the fourth. Three fireballs lobbed together, crashing down on the chanting trolls. The blast was enough for two of them to be blown away into black smoke.

The radius of her attack caught half of the trolls, but it was dealing less damage the further they were from the impact. She finished the fourth rune and changed abilities to chain lightning; it seemed that would be better and less likely to hurt her party.

Meixie was running back and forth through a line of four trolls, hitting them with a dashing attack that built up the more she used it in sequence.

Candice finished her chain lightning rune to check on Selene.

The Soul Binder was pulling at invisible threads in the air and draining an ethereal blue current from one of the trolls. Selene didn't have any great attacks for how far the trolls were spread out, so instead she was just filling her reservoir of souls so that she could heal. Candice would have to assist in healing during the boss, but that was fine.

Wendy's wolves had pinned another set of trolls, and she had her crossbow out, firing at the one Selene was draining. Everything was going to plan, but the current stage was the easy part for Candice's party.

A moment later, the trolls all collapsed. While they dissolved, a giant muddy hand rose from the center and slapped down, knocking Myrtle away.

"Stop damage! Let Myrtle get a head start," Candice shouted. They shouldn't need the reminder, but it was always good to be clear. It kept the party on the same page.

Selene ignored her and continued, but Candice let that happen and instead switched, creating a rune that would pulse healing at Myrtle. The Earthen Guardian tore her spiked mace along the muddy hand several times while it pulled itself up.

This was the largest boss they had seen yet, and suddenly, the room didn't seem quite as overly large as it had when they had stepped into the boss fight. The figure was hunched over in the shape of a troll, with running mud instead of wrinkly skin.

Candice stood in a line with Selene and Wendy as the troll started with simply attacking Myrtle. The tank lifted her shield and grunted as the giant muddy hand crashed down on her, leaving her covered in mud as it lifted away.

"She's gonna need a bath," Selene snickered.

"We all will." Candice made another rune, this one to fire ice bolts that struck the giant mud troll and froze patches for the rest of her party to strike for additional damage.

Meixie jumped nimbly into the air, striking some of them before rounding on the troll's ankles and digging in with bursts of flashy knife work. Selene switched up her spells to start healing Myrtle.

The fight didn't remain simple for long.

The boss lifted its foot high.

"Back!" Candice shouted.

Meixie was fast and flipped backwards before dashing again to escape the wave of mud as the troll's foot slammed back down.

Wendy's wolves barely made it out with their raw speed; it was Myrtle who didn't stand a chance.

The mud washed out in a wave, catching Myrtle and then retreating back to a central point just in front of the boss before its hand slammed down hard on Myrtle.

A flash of a brown barrier surrounded Myrtle for a second before it shattered and she was encased in mud. There was a brief pause before the mud all pooled back into the boss and left Myrtle dirty from head to toe and staggering with pain.

"Top her up," Selene called out.

Candice was already on it, creating two healing runes for Myrtle in a row before returning to firing ice.

"I got a slow debuff," Myrtle said from the front of the boss as she continued to grunt while blocking the attacks. "Going to get even harder to dodge that."

"Clocked it at forty five seconds from the start of the fight." Candice checked her CID and the running timer in the corner.

The troll stomped at Myrtle and thrashed its arms, sending globs of mud at everyone in the fight, including Wendy's owl that was circling overhead.

Candice tried to side step, but the bolt of mud arced towards her and slapped into her side with a heavy thud that made her wince. She checked her CID; she was slowed by five percent. That level of debuff was not immediately lethal, but it was clear that the fight would get harder as it continued.

The troll raised its arms, clasping its fists together in a telegraphed move.

"Out of the way," Candice called and rushed to the side.

The hit was easier for Myrtle to avoid, who sidestepped twice to get clear. Candice checked the timer again and marked it with a tap.

The boss' fists came crashing down, and geysers of mud shot up in a wide arc in front of it.

Candice made it clear in time, barely. She waited for the mud to settle back down to see that Selene was clear as well, but they were both out of range of each other.

The boss thrashed and another bolt of mud came flying at her.

"Focus on damage. The slow debuffs are going to get to the point that we can't escape those big attacks." Candice also noticed that the mud from that attack hadn't retreated to the boss. The floor was now covered in a layer of slippery wet mud. She grimaced at that.

The boss lifted its foot again, and she saw what was going to happen before it occurred.

Wendy's wolves ran straight into the slick mud to get to Wendy and didn't make it. They were pulled in with Myrtle and packed into a ball before the boss crushed them.

Candice winced at their whimpers.

"I got them," Wendy shouted and took a break from firing her crossbow to heal her summons.

Candice took the moment to heal Myrtle and realized the current strategy wasn't going to be enough. Another wave of mud pillars came next, and Wendy got clipped, sent flying into the air only to take the fall rough enough to make Selene wince.

Candice did the math. She estimated that they could take two more rounds of the current attacks before they were too slow to dodge. Judging by the boss's health, she realized it was a loss.

"Alright, pack it up. We need to retreat," Candice said. "We are behind the ball and aren't going to recover."

"Backing it up. Get out and get clear," Myrtle confirmed.

The group backed up and Ken's party opened the door.

As soon as the door creaked open, the giant muddy troll took a step back and melted into the ground, pulling back all of the mud and even the debuff on Candice.

"That's nice." Selene brushed her arms. "Clean."

"No, you still stink." Harley plugged her nose. "The mud might be gone, but you are all still so terribly stinky."

Candice shrugged and made a rune above her that blew hot air out over her.

"You have a drying spell?!" Harley bounced from foot to foot. "How do you feel about being a healer?"

"That it is an unfortunate necessity that I can heal at all," Candice deadpanned and answered the other question that Harley was asking.

Harley pouted. "No fun."

Candice checked Ken's reaction, only to find that he wasn't even listening to the conversation with Harley. Candice tried to not be annoyed, but failed a bit. It was stupid and girlish, but she wanted him to hear her turn Harley down. "Ken, what did you think of the boss?"

"It's a giant damage check." He looked at the giant boss doors. "First the summoners, then the boss itself continues to slow the party until they get hit by everything. You can't heal or tank through it. You have to focus on damage or it won't work."

Candice nodded, thinking much the same. "I need to not get caught up spending all my time healing. If I hit Myrtle with haste before she has to run, or maybe with a protection ability, it'll save me the need to heal her after. And Selene can focus on her damage not healing if we avoid everything but the mud balls."

Ken nodded thoughtfully. "It sort of spirals out of hand. You get hit, you get slowed, you take more damage, and your focus is pulled away from the damage you need before you start getting hit with everything to the point that no healing is going to keep up. Alternatively, if you bring enough tanking and healing to just weather through it, you could probably just stand still and take it to the face."

"Eew," Harley groaned. "You would talk about a lady taking it on the face."

Ken rolled his eyes.

Candice found his insights to be the same as hers. The simpler path seemed to be minimizing healing and just crushing the boss, but he was right, a party could probably muscle through it if they had enough healing.

She didn't think that was an option for her party, but a setup like Helen and Penelope's party might make something like that work.

"I really need a movement ability," Myrtle blurted out. "That would make this much easier." Candice's tank glanced at Ken.

She sighed. That wasn't an option, at least not in the short term. "I agree. That's a priority. We should try the boss a few more times. If we can't get it, we'll skip it and go shopping in the safe zone."

CHAPTER 7

C andice's and my own definition of 'a few more' tries with the
boss were vastly different.

We ate dinner outside the boss doors with two more of our class's
parties.

"You should start running when it lifts its foot. It won't move
after that, I think," Penny said after Candice came back from her
last attempt. "You guys should take a break and level. At a certain
point, you are just ramming your head against a wall. Also, I think
another team should get a chance to go in."

Several heads swiveled my way.

"We'll take it up." I wiped my mouth with the back of my sleeve.
"We've gotten all the timers down from watching Candice's group
and have our own plan."

"Gonna let us watch?" Helen asked.

"That's your kink?" Des shot back. I had a feeling Des had been
saving that one up the entire time.

Helen scoffed and rolled her eyes. "I mean to have a revive on
hand."

"Wouldn't mind you poking your head in when the doors open,"
I admitted. "But I think we'll try it on our own first."

We'd have to pull out all the stops, and sometimes it was good
to keep a few fighting tricks to yourself.

"Suit yourself." Helen nodded. "I'll be at the door to step in
should it open without you guys."

I brushed off my pants and got up to stretch my back. Another
group moved our way, and I shielded my eyes and squinted in an
attempt to see them.

"That's a Class B party," Wendy stated, her eyes starry while she
looked through her owl's eyes. "The Harem Queen is with them."

"I thought Crimson would be chasing her around," Taylor said
over a mouthful of food. "Where is Crimson?" She asked me.

I shrugged. "If I could keep track of her I'd be a hell of a lot—" I
froze in my tracks as I felt the hairs on the back of my neck prickle.

Two daggers entered my hand, and like a team of seasoned adventurers, everyone reacted, weapons in hands and spells beginning to glow at the ready.

A pair of glowing eyes stared at me as the panther from before prowled out of the woods. Its body seemed to absorb the light as dark lightning crackled over the surface.

"You're fucking kidding me," Des spat. "Where did that even come from?"

"It's just a monster." Helen spun her mace and put it away along with her shield. "Why are you all worked up?"

"Stay back and don't heal Ken," Charlotte grumbled.

The other group frowned, suddenly far more curious.

I let them talk to my party as I spun my daggers to warm up my fingers. The panther closed the distance in a flash, and I parried its superior weight, striking back between its pace. I knew that if this battle was going to be like before, the panther was going to pick up speed.

A blast of ice came from Candice and went right through the panther like before.

"Why can only Ken fight it?" Kendra asked, sounding like they were getting the rundown.

"We have no clue," I growled and fought back, starting to trade blows with the panther.

This time, it wasn't going to get the better of me. I activated [Hydra], scales dotting my skin as I gained self-healing and some additional stats. The regeneration let me be a little more reckless and take some damage while dishing out more of my own.

Beyond the strangeness that others couldn't attack it, it was just a big cat monster. But its speed continued to increase like before with no signs of stopping, and my damage was barely wounding it.

Those claws lashed out and raked me repeatedly as I was forced to step back and cast Charlotte's [Heal] on myself to repair my bloodied chest.

"What are you all doing?!" The Harem Queen arrived instantly at my side, a giant sword in her hand burned with bright blue fire as she severed the panther's neck.

At least, she tried to.

Like everyone else, her blade cut through it like it was made of smoke only for it to reform after.

The Harem Queen stared at her blade for a moment before she really let loose. She stomped hard enough to shatter the packed earth around her, sending geysers of blue flame up from the cracks as her red hair fluttered behind her. She swung her large sword back over her shoulder and then down on the panther with such strength and speed that I almost missed it.

Five lines of blue flames exploded from the ground, completely obliterating the panther and everything else for a hundred meters in a ninety degree cone in front of her.

She had a satisfied smirk on her face as she ran her hand through her hair. "There that— what the fuck."

The panther reformed, this time turning to her.

"You want to fight?"

What happened happened in a flash. The panther stared at her, before the very fabric of the world frayed for the briefest of seconds and the panther was suddenly behind her.

Blood sprayed into the air from dozens of wounds on the Harem Queen, and she staggered back, mostly in shock.

"Ken, what is this?" She wiped blood from her painted lips and stared at the panther in shock.

"I have no idea. It attacked me once before and only stopped when it killed me. Charlotte was there to bring me back, though." I spun my daggers as the panther glared at the Harem Queen, as if debating something. "Step back. I think it's somehow just for me."

"If you insist," the Harem Queen said to save face.

The panther came back at me, but this time, its strength made my arm go numb even though I successfully parried the blow.

I took the next swipe from its paws while staggering back less successfully and my hand rolled on the ground, still gripping the dagger.

"Ken!" the ladies all shouted.

I ignored their yells. I knew I needed to fight through the pain. I let adrenaline flood my system, making my body block any reaction to the missing hand for the moment.

I rushed back in, using the panther as a whetstone and got inside its range slashing at its shoulders while using how close I was to lessen how much punch it could put in its swipes.

The panther snapped down on my shoulder and twisted.

That was enough pain for everything to go black and then wink out.

***

Helen watched as Ken rushed back into the panther fearlessly after losing a hand and the panther met that fearlessness with lethality. Those jaws tore half of Ken's torso off.

As soon as that happened, the panther puffed away in black smoke and the second half of Ken's torso fell to the ground.

Everything was quiet as the ladies watched on.

Helen acted first, rushing forward. "Divine Intervention!" she shouted and put her hands on Ken's body as a pillar of light slammed into him.

However, in the time it took her to do that, Crimson practically teleported beside Ken. The woman in red leather had wide eyes that took in the scene. Mainly, a dead Ken, torn to pieces, and the Harem Queen covered in blood with her sword out.

"Wait!" Helen shouted before there was a concussive shockwave that made Helen fall on top of Ken as her mother's voice faded off into the distance and booms exploded repeatedly in the distance.

"Oh shit," Harley spoke first.

Ken groaned under Helen as several flashes of healing magic hit him.

"You need to get him up and get him to Crimson before she tears your mother apart," Fayeth shouted over the noise.

***

I blinked back to life with someone pressed to my chest and hair over my eyes.

"I'm fine, Charlotte." I cupped the woman's hips on top of me.

The surprised noise that came out of her was not one that I was expecting. Helen pulled herself off me with fiery, angry eyes and fist raised in the air.

"Oh shit."

"Pervert." The fist landed to punctuate her words and knock me back to the dirt.

"Don't hit him!" Des shouted and pulled Helen off of me.

I realized that the sound of their words was distorted by distant explosions.

"Ken." Fayeth was there to pull me to my feet. "Crimson showed up right after the panther disappeared and she went wild on the Harem Queen."

I might have just died, but her words made the distant noises click in my mind to a horrifying degree. I could already imagine

Crimson losing control of Limit Break if she saw me like that, not to mention the blood that would have been on the Harem Queen.

The noise was easy for me to pick a direction and start running. "Sprint." I took off without explaining any more.

I ran for several minutes before wind buffeted me back from another explosive exchange from the two ladies, or at least I hoped it was an exchange and not some one-sided brutality.

My hopes were dashed a moment later as trees fell out of the way and Crimson had red lightning racing out of her eyes as she held a bloody and unconscious Harem Queen up by her hair.

"Crimson!" I shouted at the top of my lungs.

Her head snapped in my direction.

I didn't fear her, yet it was an intimidating sight to see one of humanity's most powerful adventurers laid out like this so quickly.

Crimson really was heads above the rest. I didn't blame the UG for trying to understand where she got Limit Break. It was a terrifying skill should the source ever really become known. I knew she was hiding the source, or at least a part of it.

The red lightning retreated from Crimson's form as I approached slowly and put a hand on the Harem Queen's neck to still feel a pulse.

"Heal." I knew the spell wouldn't do as much to a high-level adventurer like her, but she looked like she'd seen better days.

"Ken!" Crimson hugged me as I cast my second [Heal] on the Harem Queen. "I can't believe she did that to you!"

"It wasn't her, Crimson. You came at a very bad time." I patted the air for her to calm down. "Also, there were several people who could revive me nearby."

"Yeah. Yeah. So then what down here could cover her in blood? Huh? This makes no sense, Ken. We are on the twenty-fifth floor and she's in the fifties." Her eyes let out red sparks just talking about what she had seen.

I sat down, placing the Harem Queen's head in my lap to keep her airway open while I started to pump more heals into her. "You might not believe this, but there's a dungeon monster that's... hunting me."

Crimson froze, her brows pressed down. "Tell me everything."

I nodded. "Okay, so there's this panther. It has shown up twice and attacked me both times. No one else can touch it. The Harem Queen even let loose a pretty powerful attack on it but it did nothing."

"When someone else attacks it, does it just wipe out everyone present?" Crimson asked a strange question.

Now it was my turn to furrow my brows. "No, instead it just sort of teleports and shreds someone. When Charlotte healed me the first time, it just instantly killed me. When the Harem Queen interfered, it did the same to her, but she survived. That's why she was bloody. It was her own blood. Afterwards, it was too strong and quickly killed me. That's right when you showed up."

"Of course, I am tracking your CID." Crimson smiled. "I was at the safe zone when I saw that you died. Then I raced here."

"What about the other time?" I asked.

She poked at her CID angrily. "What other time?"

"The panther killed me the first time, but with its weird ability," I explained.

Crimson scowled. "We'll talk about this later. I might have some ideas. Until then, I think your healing is waking her up. She tried to save you?"

"Yup." I gave Crimson a look that made her roll her eyes.

"Ugh," the Harem Queen groaned.

"Good morning, Sunshine." Crimson smiled at her from a few inches away.

The woman in my lap jumped. "Crimson, I can explain."

"She knows." I pushed the Harem Queen back down on my lap, making Crimson pout. "Heal. I calmed her down and have been healing you."

The Harem Queen looked up at me through her lashes, and I got the feeling it wasn't even on purpose, she just automatically tried to manipulate using her looks. "My hero."

"Enjoy it while it lasts. Ken's lap is the best you are going to get," Crimson grumbled. "I might have jumped the gun, but you were covered in what I thought was his blood." She shrugged. "At least I didn't kill you. You keep fucking around with Ken and I might not be so lenient next time. Really, all of this misunderstanding is because of how aggressive you've been. So, sorry."

I gaped at Crimson as a realization hit me. "Was that supposed to be an apology?"

Crimson held her hands out helplessly. "I have to be bad at something."

The Harem Queen rolled her eyes before they shifted to me and she cuddled into my lap further. "I think I need quite a few more heals before I can get up."

"Listen you." Crimson went to grab her and I slapped her hand away.

"Let her rest for now." I didn't miss the sly smile from the Harem Queen. "This is the closest she's going to get."

Crimson chuckled. "Too bad for her, you can share your portal ability with people you have sex with."

The Harem Queen's eyes nearly popped out of her head.

I slapped my face and ran my hand down it. "Crimson."

"What? Someone was going to start to figure it out real soon. I think Des and Charlotte are probably less than ten levels away from having the mana pool to use it," Crimson explained.

I faced the Harem Queen. "It takes a lot more than just sex. Crimson is understating the situation." I glared at Crimson, narrowing my eyes. "And she knows it."

"What does it take?" the Harem Queen asked, snuggling into my lap further.

"Sorry, I don't think you are eligible." I smiled to try and soften the blow. Sadly, I had no interest in trying to join her harem, and she wouldn't exactly fit in my own.

"My daughter?" she asked.

"Not the topic of conversation," I cut her off. "It seems you are healthy enough to get up."

The Harem Queen groaned exaggeratedly. "I'm so injured from Crimson."

"She's clearly faking it." Crimson crossed her arms.

I wanted to kick her out of my lap. But Crimson had done a real number on her after she'd come to my rescue. I decided to provide comfort until she was ready to stand on her own.

It would also be a lesson to Crimson.

"Oh my gosh. You seduced the Harem Queen?" Taylor showed up first as the rest of the class ran over.

"Mom!" Helen shouted.

The Harem Queen cracked open an eye and spotted her daughter. "Daughter, I don't know if I'll make it. Ken has tried hi—"

Helen jerked her out of my lap. "Stop being a drama queen."

The Harem Queen fell onto her daughter, continuing to play up the situation. "Daughter, hold your dear mother in her last moments."

Helen pushed her off. "You are fine. I remember when you held a live grenade until it blew up as a party trick."

She stood up just fine on her own. "Really, daughter, you should treat your mother with more respect. What would have happened if Ken hadn't healed me?"

Helen scoffed. "You are fine, even better that I got you out of the clutches of that pervert. Now fix your clothes before you turn him into a wild beast."

The Harem Queen raised an eyebrow at me as if asking if I could please turn into a beast. When I did nothing, she turned back to her daughter with a slight smirk. "That's an interesting way to talk about the man you said you loved."

Helen froze, caught in the act.

Des bounded over with a giant smile on her face grabbing Helen's arm. "Don't judge how we all love each other."

"Of course." The Harem Queen held up her hands. "Now, I believe before I interrupted that you all were preparing for the boss?"

"Yeah." I scratched the back of my head. "My party was about to go in."

"Is that safe?" Candice asked. "You have some strange dungeon monster that's appeared twice."

"Yeah, but those were days apart," I argued.

"I'll come in with you and destroy the boss should it interfere." Crimson's tone wasn't an offer. She was stating a requirement. "We'll head down to the safe zone after that. All of you are expected for class down there tomorrow." She made eye contact with everyone in our class. "Alright, let's get going." Crimson waved us forward and started heading back like she hadn't just wrecked the dungeon.

"I'll see you tonight, Ken," the Harem Queen's voice warbled flirtatiously.

Crimson's jaw clenched. "Did I not teach her enough of a lesson? Maybe I'll have to teach that shameless woman another," she grumbled out the end of her sentence.

I put a hand on Crimson's back. "Everything is fine. I'm alive and well. No ill effects at all." I knew she needed a little more reassurance.

"Oh, I know," Crimson said. "Don't let her have you before I do."

"She won't 'have' me at all," I sighed. "There's no interest. She has a massive harem, and I don't really want to wait in line behind a hundred other men."

Des snorted. "You know, that's a smidge hypocritical."

I stuck my tongue out at her. "I have no interest in that large of a harem. A small Adrel is plenty for me, thank you. Don't let that smut author fill your head with lofty ideas."

CHAPTER 8

I pulled the boss doors closed and glanced at Crimson, who was standing with her arms crossed at the side of the room. "You won't cheat, will you?"

"No." Crimson's expression was hard. "You all need to learn how to fight bosses. That means learning to try new things in a safe manner."

"Like letting Candice's group go at it for a few hours to learn from their mistakes?" Harley asked.

"Won't always be an option, but considering you'll be working with the rest of Class A for the raid, I would encourage you all to continue working together." Crimson leaned against the wall. "Your thoughts on this boss?"

"Well, the big question is if I can Absorb the mud balls." I pointed at where the boss would come out of. "If I can, that means we can elongate the damage check, giving our party a substantial advantage."

Des nodded along. We'd already talked about our party's strategy for the fight.

"Not bad. You won't always have a cheat like that," Crimson cautioned.

"I know. We still want to measure our damage against the boss to make sure we are 'qualified', even if we are going to pad it for safety." I spun my daggers in my hand. "Unless you have more to say, I'm itching to fight after having to sit through and watch Candice fail."

"I'm ready," Charlotte said, holding out her wand.

"Everyone good? Need to run through it again?" Fayeth checked with everyone.

"Just go slap some trolls," Des laughed while we all nodded.

Fayeth didn't need any more encouragement. She rushed forward swinging her spear in wide arcs.

I slipped into the shadows and popped out behind one of the trolls with [Shadow Ambush]. My blades were already swinging as

I activated [Metamorphosis], and they transformed into claws as I tore into the troll.

Des transformed as well, and I was momentarily distracted as she grew a foot taller with pink skin and white horns. Her hair grew all the way down to the floor with the front swooping wider out to the side.

"Admire me later." She gave a throaty laugh as she threw her damage over time abilities on my troll and then started to go around the circle.

I had watched Candice's group do this part of the fight enough times to see the range between the casters. Even perfectly execut- ed, I'd only hit three trolls with my area attacks.

And I'd have to step back to get the range right. So instead, I'd decided to focus on each troll, hopefully leaving it weak enough for it to die from Des's abilities.

The caster ignored me and continued the chant to raise their god from the summoning circle. I bloodied the troll a good bit and jumped over on the next one. Des' curses would kill it.

Wind whipped past me as Charlotte threw around harsh winds that hammered into the trolls. Harley was on support, buffing Des, who was in her element. The monsters were too far apart for area attacks, making all of her damage over time abilities the best way to deal damage to multiple targets.

A younger me might have argued it was unfair, but the variation in parties made for very different difficulties on a wide range of bosses. Another boss fight that had monsters clustered might do very well for me. As it was, our party was balanced in a way that would serve us well.

Des kept up her role. Her metamorphosized form hurled spells as fast as she could form them. Fayeth swung her spear around, trying to do as much damage as she could.

We ended up taking down eight of the dozen trolls before a muddy hand slapped down on the ground and swallowed the rest.

"Great job." I jumped clear of the mud. "That's two more than Candice had managed."

"They didn't have me." Des flipped her hair as she reverted back to her normal self.

"Modest as usual," Charlotte added dryly.

Bun-bun chittered in agreement as he started bouncing angrily on top of one of the boss' muddy feet.

The boss did his first rotation, which meant I was about to find out if my [Absorb] would really work in the fight and give us a massive advantage.

I stepped back to see the mud ball coming and raised my hand. "Absorb." The ability sucked in the spell, and I pumped a fist. "Spell mirror." The mud ball shot back towards the boss, but the hit did nothing.

"Yeah, we thought it might not work that way," Fayeth grunted as she blocked again and swept her spear through the mud. "But absorbing was still the biggest part."

Harley trilled on her flute, and Fayeth was wrapped in faint light as the boss lifted its foot. I rushed out with [Sprint], and Fayeth kept up with me thanks to Harley's buff.

The wave of mud missed us both, but a muddy Bun-bun started hissing at the boss angrily while he waited for the ability to end so that he could go back in.

"I'll bathe you after," Charlotte tried to mollify the bunny.

Bun-bun hopped back and forth angrily.

"Amen, Bun-bun. It isn't fair for those of us not sleeping with Ken." Harley wiped some of the mud off her face. Unlike the rest of us, she was going to get hit every time. Yet as a support, she was a little more mobile, and we hoped could last longer.

The boss slammed its fist into an empty space as we rushed back in.

"Back to the mud pits with you," Des laughed. "Don't come back out until you kill the boss."

I rolled my eyes but settled back in on my forms that had shifted to add my abilities into the mix. My blades danced over the boss as I absorbed another mud ball and shuffled out of the second ability.

My focus was absolute. I was in the zone as my CID dinged in warning for each stomp and wave attack.

It was on the fifth round that the boss was looking worse for wear and Harley got caught in the wave, knocked high into the air. She screamed and had the wind knocked out of her on the rough landing.

Charlotte was healing her while shouting. "Back on your feet. You need to help Fayeth get out in time."

"Forget that. Push through." Des used [Metamorphosis] again and stopped using her damage over time spells as she started hurling streaming pink blasts at the boss.

I agreed with her, activating my own [Metamorphosis] and trying to pump out a last surge of damage. Charlotte started hurling storm bolts, and even Harley pulled out her crossbow to do a bit of damage.

"We got this. Just push a little harder!" I grunted with a deepened voice as the wave of mud hit me in the chest before dragging me back.

I charged forward, attacking as the boss raised its fist high, ready for another big smash. The hit never came. The boss shuddered and all of its mud collapsed down on top of Fayeth, Bun-bun and me.

We were pushed back away from the boss as the mud drained into the stone floor and oozed off of all of us.

"Eew." Des pinched her nose as she walked up to me and held her other hand out to help me up. "You are taking a bath after this."

"We all are," Charlotte agreed.

"I call dibs on the first," Harley called out distractedly as she moved to check on the loot.

"Anything good?" I asked.

"Good, but ugly." She held up a pair of muddy boots. "Really? Do they have to be permanently muddy?"

"The dungeon likes its themes. Plenty of people will wear a pair of muddy boots for those stats." Crimson swaggered up and patted me on the back. "Good job. The safe zone has bath houses, though they are a little pricey."

"Supply and demand at work," Des laughed. "I'm certainly willing to pay a little more for a bath right now."

The boss doors opened up and Helen stuck her head through. "You guys got it?"

"Without Crimson's help," I added. "Rough go of it, though." I picked at my clothes. "We managed to last until the fifth round of attacks by using some survival abilities, though we almost got hit by the sixth."

Helen nodded as the rest of the class started to look through to see the evidence that we'd won.

"How many of the casters at the beginning?" Candice asked.

"Eight." I pointed at Des who preened under the attention. "She blanketed everything effectively with damage over time abilities. Honestly, our area attacks just didn't cover enough of them."

The rest of the class nodded, most of them having similar assessments.

"Alright, let's keep this show rolling," Crimson shooed us away with our loot. "Next party, step up! Ken and company head down."

I picked up the remainder of the loot, finding a few items that might sell as resources, and a mace that had a mud ball at the end that slowly flowed, yet went nowhere.

"It's a caster item." I held it out to Des.

"For someone who uses Earth element. Honestly, Myrtle might like it," Des said. "I'm not interested in it for just the stats."

I shrugged and put it in my CID to sell or figure out something else to do with it. "Baths?"

"Yes please," Harley said.

"Bun-bun, stop." Charlotte fussed with the smelly rabbit as he tried to climb into her hair. "It will take me forever to get your stink out of my hair."

He continued to chitter at her.

"No. It isn't that bad right now, bad rabbit."

He seemed to collapse on himself and give her giant, watering eyes.

"You get to get in the bath with me if you don't try and nest in my hair right now," Charlotte bargained.

The rabbit looked to the side in thought before nodding and plopping back down on the floor.

"You need to stop causing so much trouble," I scolded him.

He rolled his eyes at me. The cheeky rabbit was constant work. I wondered if my Grandpa was right. Maybe he really was just a long-eared rat.

We headed down the stairs in the corner of the boss room to make way for the next group. It opened up into a huge, circular plain with a town built in the center. Rather than the entirely human ones of the past, for the first time, this one held different, alien structures.

Part of the settlement was covered in huge, solid-looking stone buildings carved with strange dwarvish runes, while another had buildings made of wood and hide with wide openings and Nekorians moving about.

The third section, the one that was closest to us was our destination.

"We probably should get those diplomacy lessons sooner rather than later," Des said as we saw the central area between it all create a mingling between the three races. The rest of the safe zone was a clear delineation between the three.

"This is the point where the dwarves and the Nekorian dungeons connect with ours," I observed, stating what we were all thinking out loud as we headed down into the human-built area.

There was a towering, white spire complete with Haylon's crest on the top.

"So... uh... do you think that's what the Harem Queen made?" Charlotte pointed at the structure.

"Or is that what Crimson made in response?" Fayeth offered.

We all looked at each other. As much as we enjoyed Crimson, she wasn't the kind to make such an opulent structure. Her idea of construction was a giant, overengineered square.

"Do we use it, or do we find Crimson's?" I asked.

"We find a bath!" Harley pushed me forward. "Hurry, hurry. I stink and I don't want Meredith or Bonnie to come out before I'm clean."

"They are going to stink too if they go through the boss," I pointed out.

"That doesn't matter." Harley rolled her eyes. "Men. You just don't get it."

"To be fair, you don't make it easy," I countered.

The human area of the safe zone was pretty standard. The UG had a very large presence with plenty of shops. As I looked around, I realized that the UG had a greater than normal presence on the current floor.

"It's probably the other two worlds," Des practically read my mind. "The UG shops probably also come with a number of people watching the dwarves and Nekorians while also ready to protect the path that leads back to Earth."

I nodded along with her. Her assessment made sense to me.

"Bath!" Harley grabbed my hand and jerked me to the side.

A stone building with a glass front filled my view before Harley pulled me through the open doors. Suddenly, the air changed around us, growing far more humid.

A handsome man with the kind of hair that would make most ladies jealous flashed Harley a grin. "Welcome, pretty lady." He leaned on the counter.

"Pass." Harley stepped over to the other person at the counter, a young woman with a warm smile. "We need a bath."

"Have you been here before?" she asked patiently.

"Nope."

"We offer private rooms or the public bath," the woman explained a few of the details, during which Harley hastily nodded to rush her along.

"We'll take a private bath," Des spoke up behind me. "Harley, just wear a towel."

"We will all wear a towel." I narrowed my eyes at Des.

"Of course." The lady at the counter ignored our conversation. "If you would like, there is also a UG terminal in the private room. Please feel free to complete all of your transactions there. Follow me and I'll show you to the changing room." The lady walked past the man with gorgeous hair, who seemed a touch deflated by Harley's rejection.

We all went back into a small room with just a handful of lockers and plenty of fluffy towels and robes.

"Please, get undressed and wash off briefly at the shower then you can enjoy the hot bath through that door." She pointed to the only other door in the room.

"Thank you, we've got it from here," I said, turning back to find Fayeth peeking out the door.

"It's so steamy, I can barely see," she said, steam leaking through the door and around her.

"That's kind of the point." Des was already naked and putting her clothes into her CID. "It's to preserve your modesty."

"What modesty?" I asked, staring pointedly at Des as she walked gracefully into the shower.

"For other people." She smirked, swaying her hips a little as she leaned forward and turned the water on.

The water was hot without needing to even heat up as she started to scrub down without closing the curtains.

Harley rolled her eyes. "Don't stare at me, Ken."

"Pretty sure his eyes are busy elsewhere," Charlotte shot back.

Bun-bun jumped forward and squeezed past Fayeth before a splash was heard through the door.

"You were supposed to shower first!" Fayeth scolded the rabbit who made a satisfied squeak from the other side.

"It's fine. He wasn't really dirty since all the mud was pulled away." Charlotte shrugged out of her own clothes and went into the shower with Des.

"Yes, join me," Des teased and soaped up her hands, waiting for Charlotte who only had a light blush on her face as she fell into the temptress' waiting hands to be lathered up with bubbles.

"No funny business. I want to shower and then go soak."

"Then can we do some funny business?" Des asked with a bat of her eyelashes.

"Maybe." I was fairly sure once we all got in the hot bath to soak, we'd relax. It had been a long day.

Des hurried up with Charlotte, and I stepped in to clean off, escaping Des' wandering hands and slipping out into the hot bath.

The bath was a large square with a few rocks in the middle, along with a facade of rocks on the walls to make it feel like a private hot spring in the mountains.

I slipped in and groaned as the warm water felt like it was soaking right into my muscles. "This feels so good."

Bun-bun squeaked in agreement as he floated past me with his eyes closed. The rabbit blew a few bubbles and kicked lazily to keep moving.

"This is nice." Charlotte came out next with a towel covering her as she slipped in. "You did good on the boss fight, by the way. I didn't have to heal you much at all."

I pulled her close to sit beside me, taking a rag from the side and wetting it with warm water. Then I folded it and placed it on top of her head. "You are doing an excellent job. Even without any supportive heals from the rest of us you are... well, I'd say killing it, but as a healer, you are doing quite the opposite. You are lifting us all up."

"Oh, that is nice." She melted slightly with the warm rag on her head and cuddled into my side before pecking me with a kiss on the cheek.

I wrapped my arm around her waist and held her close. "It is very nice." Though, we were talking about two different things. "Thanks for being our healer, Charlotte."

"Mmm," she hummed, just enjoying the water.

Des slipped in on my other side. "Charlotte's so cute." Des trapped my arm between her chest. With her hair wet, she pulled her bangs to the side, revealing her heart-shaped eye. "We all have done a great job. I just wanted to check with you, Ken. Sometimes, after dying people have a change of heart."

I blinked. I certainly hadn't considered anything in that realm, though I also hadn't fully processed the death. "No, I'm fine. Maybe it's the assassin training, but as long as I knew Charlotte was there for me, it wasn't really more than a large wound."

"You died," Charlotte murmured and squeezed me tighter.

Fayeth came in next, and the slim elf found her way onto my lap, laying against me and pressing me to the wall of the bath. "I couldn't even protect you. That's my job and I failed."

I rubbed the back of her neck with a hand to comfort her. "It's fine. Whatever that panther is, we'll find a way to deal with it."

Harley splashed into the bath, hidden somewhat by the fog. "Yeah, the panther will die. Ken will figure out its weakness. Got you, Bun-bun." There was a squeak in response.

"No playing in the bath." I closed my eyes, feeling very content surrounded by my harem.

"Yeah, no playing in the bath," Crimson's voice spooked me, and I had to look over my shoulder. I could barely make out her form as she moved through the fog and slid into the bath.

"Welcome." I somehow wasn't surprised that she'd found us.

"Thanks. The Snooty Queen is watching the rest of the parties go through the boss. I wanted to catch up to you in private. Because I think I know what that panther is." Crimson sighed as she slid into the bath.

"Oh?" I perked up.

"Please, don't wait on our account." Des turned and stopped teasing me with her hand under the water.

"Well, it's a bit of a story." Crimson crouched in the bath so that the water went over her shoulders. "I was about a year out of Haylon. At that point, we were on the twenty-eighth floor..."

CHAPTER 9

Malinda Crimson picked at her teeth as her party traipsed through the weird set of floors.

The white powder looked a bit like snow, but it was sticky. Given the monsters, Crimson was pretty sure it was supposed to be powdered sugar. She wasn't going to find out. It hadn't taken long to determine that eating the surroundings led to a nasty debuff.

"Like I said, one of these days soon, we are going to be one of the top guilds." Rick walked with his ax over his shoulder. "I mean, we all came from the big four. What's to stop us from stepping up and being something like The Verdant in a decade?"

"Survival," Heather reminded him. "We only have one party in the guild so far."

"Yeah, that'll be fixed as soon as we make a name for ourselves." Rick had his head in the clouds.

Crimson didn't blame him. He had a good hold on his berserker class; he was going to be a rising star if they could keep him alive.

Rather than go to one of the big named guilds, she'd decided to help this startup with the hopes of getting in on the ground level. That, and she really didn't want to go into a guild at the lowest rung and be someone's loot gopher for a few years or some other stupid shit.

"Up ahead," Crimson called out. She always had the sharpest eyes in their party. "Two candy cane men and a chocolate bunny."

"This is such a weird floor, isn't it, Malinda?" Rick turned to her.

She scoffed at him. "Call me anything but Crimson again and I'll show you your own intestines." She flashed her short sword from the sheath. Uncoiling her whip didn't have quite the same flare.

Rick held his hands up playfully as the ax stayed balanced on his shoulder. "Sorry, your Mistress." He did a little bow, only for the ax to hit him in the side of the head.

The party roared in laughter. Crimson quite liked the sound of that Mistress Crimson.

"I know you like to take a few hits, but don't smack yourself with your own weapon." Mike rolled his eyes and cast a healing over time ability on Rick.

It wasn't just for the bump from the ax; it was to spur Rick into starting the next fight too.

"Everyone got their shit ready?" Rick asked. "I don't think I'm going to have to dip into rage for a small group like this."

They all had taken extra precautions. Not only did they have survivability tools for the dungeons, but Rick had bought them all several abilities to escape a fight in case he ever lost control of his rage.

Berserkers had a reputation, after all. They might be strong, but it was safer to have tools like Crimson's [Retreat] and [Feign Death].

"I'm good." Crimson played with the handle of her short sword with one hand while uncoiling her whip with the other.

Rick swaggered forward, his oversized ax lifted off his shoulder like it was a toy. He was a big guy, even before he went berserk.

The two candy cane men shifted at his approach, and the giant chocolate bunny perked up with some of the powdered sugar on its face. At once, all three rushed Rick.

He spun with the ax right into them.

Crimson was a step behind, swinging into the chocolate bunny, and using her short sword to peel off chocolate strips from the comical monster. Her whip followed up a second later, with the snap of it blowing a chunk off its ear. With her whip out, she sheathed her sword.

This floor was a weirder floor, almost a little funny. It was like some twisted version of a children's game come to life.

[Pierce] activated, and she kicked with her heeled boot, blowing a large chunk out of the chocolate bunny. Then Crimson spun, activating [Sever] and cutting deep into the monster with her short sword.

Crimson could have dual wielded, but she liked mixing in abilities that used other parts of her body. It was just more visceral. And if she was honest with herself, the feeling of punching something never really got old.

She activated another ability as her fist became a fiery red and slammed into the chocolate bunny's side, melting a little more of the chocolate while her whip recovered from the last strike.

She glanced over, checking on the rest of her party.

Rick's eyes had the glazed look he got when fighting, and he was nearly frothing at the mouth as he'd put on another fifty pounds of muscle and tore apart the first of the candy cane men.

Sometimes, Crimson wished she had a different class. Berserkers were a cut above the rest.

Heather sat back, buffing Rick and turning the already strong fighter into a walking meat grinder, while Mike ensured his best friend stayed alive. Jane used her abilities to push and pull monsters around the fight while piling on damage.

The whole team was built around Rick. Technically, Crimson's job was to scout and bring in more monsters, but this floor didn't really work that well for that particular role.

Crimson jumped back, brought to the present again as Rick cleaved through the chocolate bunny and it exploded into black smoke. The pack was dead, and Rick stood nearby panting as he tried to recover.

Crimson knew better than to even speak at that moment. He needed to calm himself and that was best done without distractions.

She stood, coiling her whip, as a feeling of complete intensity rolled over her. Crimson struggled to even comprehend what was happening as a bird cry overhead shattered the moment.

"Above." Mike spotted the monster first, pointing at a glowing red bird.

Crimson frowned as she looked at it; the bird was made of red lightning.

Rick was staring up at it, his focus back on a monster.

The bird, however, swept down right for Crimson. She dodged back as lightning sprayed down among the powdered sugar, turning it to caramel.

Rick wasn't happy being ignored and jumped forward, swinging his ax. But when the ax made contact, red bolts jumped along the metal to his arms, making the berserker lock up and his teeth clack as he fell back down like a rock.

"Back up!" Heather shouted with fear on her face. "Get away from him, Crimson."

She didn't need another reminder and hurried away from the berserker who had just been shocked. His arms smoldered where the lightning had gotten his forearms.

The whole party winced. Getting shocked and burned did not make a berserker happy.

Rick spun as soon as he had control of his body again and his eyes went from the glazed battle fervor to red pin pricks as he searched for that bird in the sky.

Thankfully, the bird came back and was giving him an outlet for his anger.

"Jane, ground that elemental bird," Crimson spat. "If it flies away, we'll have to disappear for a minute while Rick calms down."

Jane wove a spell between her hands, and a purple cage of energy slammed down as the bird did another dive. This time, the bird was highly focused on Rick. Once again, Rick got shocked for his efforts as he tried to attack, and the bird broke apart into lightning to escape the cage.

"Just what the fuck is that thing?" Jane's jaw dropped as it escaped her spell.

Crimson could feel the bird's eyes on her as it circled around to come back.

"It's like a lightning phoenix or something," Mike named it.

The bird swept at the ground that had pulled back from Rick. Crimson struck out with her sword. This time, she hit something and drove the bird to a stop.

"That worked!" Heather shouted.

Rick recovered and was deep into his berserk. His eyes were nothing but red and he had tripled in size. All of that was nice if he were charging a monster, but he was coming for the four of them.

The berserker roared, spittle flying from his mouth as he cleaved into the bird and through it to Crimson. She barely managed to duck and roll out of the way, losing an inch of her hair in the process.

Jane wasn't so lucky. Rick's ax buried itself into her gut, and the lightning spread from the bird through his weapon to both of them.

"Holy shit, Rick! Calm down!" Mike shouted. "Jane! I got you, baby." He pumped heals into her. "We need to escape."

Crimson knew Mike wasn't talking about the monster; he was talking about Rick.

What was happening was essentially the worst-case scenario with a berserker. He couldn't seem to hit the monster that they were fighting, and it was only antagonizing him with shocks and burns.

The fact that he couldn't think clearly enough and had swung through the monster to hit Jane showed Crimson that even if she could hit it, she didn't want to be standing next to the monster.

Rick spun, sending powerful air blades out in every direction.

Crimson bailed, grabbing the limp Jane and throwing a potion in her mouth before chugging two agility potions and booking it. Heather screamed over her shoulder, and Crimson knew it wasn't the monster, or at least not the bird.

"I got you, Jane, but you need to wake up." Crimson slapped her stunned party member. "We need to use our abilities to get out of this."

Jane shook off her stun from the lightning. "Watch out!" She raised her hands and took the dive from the lightning bird, losing a good portion of her arm in the process.

Rick slammed down right behind Crimson, making her stumble as he still tried to cleave through the bird that he couldn't seem to hit.

Crimson had no idea what was going on, just that she needed to get out.

Mike was still trailing Rick, like the good little friend that he was, healing Rick as the man fucked up Mike's girlfriend. But Crimson knew that they could heal Jane's arm later.

"Let me go. I can stop him." Jane grit her teeth and was dedicated even while missing half an arm.

"You are all fucking crazy," Crimson hissed and dropped Jane on her feet only to dodge to the side as the lightning phoenix kept doggedly pursuing her.

She blocked two of its dives, trying to stay with her party, but the monster made it difficult.

A moment later, Mike's head rolled to her feet.

"Fuck this. I'm out." Crimson glanced over at Rick, who had a dead Jane at his feet. The rest of Mike's corpse was nowhere to be found.

Crimson activated [Feign Death], her body falling limp to the ground. The lightning phoenix did another pass only to leave her alone.

Rick wasn't done with it yet and charged again, only for the bird to turn and surge through his chest, burning a giant hole through him as if the monster was pissed off. Apparently, it could have ended Rick at any given time.

After the hit, it dispersed the lightning, bleeding into the ground.

"Holy fuck." Crimson turned off the ability and got to her feet. She stood in shock for a moment, seeing her party wiped out and the weird boss monster gone. "Mi…" His name died on her lips.

Their healer was dead. All four of her party members were dead, and Crimson didn't have anything to bring them back in time. She clenched her jaws and walked over to Rick's corpse, ripping off his CID. Her training had her recognizing the feeling of shock, at least logically.

Yet her mind was numb and she was having trouble thinking of what came next.

She moved around, collecting their CIDs. She and Jane had gotten along well enough that she knew she had a sister and Crimson would return her belongings there, along with letting her sister know what had happened.

***

"Wait wait wait," Harley interrupted the story. "Are you telling me that the next several floors have candy cane men and toxic powdered sugar terrain?"

Bun-bun squeaked along beside her.

Charlotte sighed. "No. The chocolate bunnies are clearly worse than you."

"That's what you got out of that story?" I asked. "Crimson, I thought the secret boss on the twenty-eight floor was where you got Limit Break?"

Crimson crossed her arms in the bath. "I was getting there before I was so rudely interrupted."

We all stared at Harley.

She held up her hands. "I'm processing, okay? Sugar Land holds a special place in my life."

I remembered her confiding in me that the little candy women in the board game was the first hint she'd gotten that she was interested in other girls. "Fine, so, your party wiped from this lightning phoenix and you returned the CIDs?"

Crimson nodded. "Yep. Well, most of them. Turns out that Rick was kind of a big fat liar and his father was very rich. Given that he had just killed my closest friends, I kept his CID."

"Of course you did." I rolled my eyes. "So what happened next?"

Crimson leaned back with a sigh in the hot water. "Well, the lightning phoenix showed up twice more after that. And I was getting frazzled because I couldn't dive the dungeon without this stupid powerful monster showing up."

Crimson locked eyes with me. "Ken, remember how I talked about taking the taxis deeper in the dungeon?"

I blinked. "Yeah, you got mugged?"

Crimson shot me a finger gun. "Yeah, so I tried to get wise to the lightning phoenix and take a taxi to get into a very different area of the dungeon to see if I could avoid it. Spoiler, all the taxis died horrible deaths about two months later, but that's not the important part."

***

The taxi kicked Crimson again and she curled around her gut. All she could think about was holding in the contents of her stomach.

"Don't die," he laughed, turning into a puddle and then shooting across the ground as he left her on the ground.

Crimson's idea had not turned out well at all. But she was still alive.

She clutched at her stomach and sat up, wincing at the bruises. "Gotta figure out the next step. It's two floors either way to a safe zone. Up is going to be easier, but that's closer to the damned bird."

She grumbled on for a minute about the damned bird as she focused on her breathing and eased herself to a sitting position. She might have lost her party, been denied by the bird in the dungeon twice, and just gotten mugged, but she was Crimson. One day, she'd be the best damned adventurer in existence.

She breathed heavily and pulled herself to a standing position. The muggers had at least left her with some armor. A weapon would have been nice, but she'd have to make do.

The taxi had taken her up and back down into another section of the dungeon. It was a level twenty-three, a few levels lower than her because she'd been hoping to solo anyway. Sometimes, other people sucked.

A growl caused her to freeze and turn slowly to see a lumbering bear made of stone approach her, huffing at the air. She rolled her shoulder, thankful that not all her abilities were dependent on a weapon.

The stone bear rushed forward far faster than a creature its size should have been able to move. The thing was made of damned stone! It should be dragged down by that kind of weight.

Crimson dodged to the right and snapped a kick, firing off an ability from her foot to take out a hunk of stone. The bear staggered sideways before surprising her and kicking out with its back foot.

Crimson spun with the hit, taking a graze from its stony claws but coming right back around with a punch to its rear and continuing to chip away at the monster.

It growled as she spun around, shaking her hand from punching stone and focused on using her feet. The heels on her boots were better weapons than she realized.

Well, probably not better than a longsword, but that didn't matter at the moment. She crushed the stone bear, and it turned to smoke.

"Let's hope there's a weapon." Crimson waved away the smoke and picked up the loot before making a face. "Huh?" She stretched out the whip and tugged on part of its length. "My lucky day." She grinned.

She always had a sword, it was just more versatile, but the whip was her love. It also wasn't that common of a drop. To get one so quickly was almost as if the dungeon were watching her.

Crimson tested the new weapon a few more times. It was a little stiffer than she'd like, yet she wasn't exactly swimming in options. Given that it was all that she had, it was about to be her favorite weapon for a while.

She rolled it up and held it in her other hand as she started walking.

To get away from the lightning phoenix, she had asked the taxi to take her to one of the 'dead' branches of the dungeon. The branching structure was so large that there were sections that didn't connect to any world.

They were out of the way locations, used to train. Even if she made it to one of the nearby safe zones, there wasn't going to be much. She might find a guild had set up shop in one of them to train, but it wouldn't be as built out as the main branches that came off Earth and had a heavy UG presence.

Assuming the taxi took her where she wanted, she was out on her own and would need to build herself back up.

Crimson frowned, wondering if her current situation was karmic justice for stealing Rick's CID. But regardless of the reason, it was time to persevere and fight another day.

***

"The rest is history." Crimson laid back in the bath. "I learned the whip, got strong, killed the damned bird, and got Limit Break from it."

I snorted. "Yeah, that sounds simple and completely normal."

She rolled her eyes. "It isn't normal at all. Remember, I've told this story to the UG. They searched the next couple floors up and down for another and never found it."

"Has there ever been anything like this panther?" I asked.

"Nope. Later when I got rather unfettered access to UG data, I dug around. There are a few accounts that seemed similar to mine, but they were always different monsters. Most people who have experienced something like this died or gave up adventuring."

"That's not about to happen," I snapped.

Crimson laughed, her chest bouncing at the surface of the water. "It better fucking not. No, what we need to do is push your training to the next level and then have you kill the panther. Charlotte is going to keep bringing you back from death until you are ready to fight it." Crimson punched her hands together splashing water everywhere. "Then, you are going to crush it."

Her splash tipped over a floating Bun-bun who came back up sputtering and squeaking angrily at her.

"Bun-bun, don't." Charlotte moved fast to grab the rabbit before it picked a fight with Crimson.

Crimson slipped into Charlotte's spot next to me and leaned against me. "We'll have such fun with training."

"Make sure to work on his stamina," Des added. "He needs improvement there."

"I agree." Crimson bobbed her head. "We should work on my Limit Break control while we are at it. I'm sure we can find a way to work on stamina at the same time."

CHAPTER 10

O ur party was drying ourselves off and getting ready to leave the bath when a familiar figure showed up. Ami, in her butler outfit, slipped into the room and handed me a letter before disappearing.

"Oooh. Secret ninja letters." Harley laughed.

"There is no such thing as 'secret ninja letters'. It is just a letter." I rolled my eyes and took out a knife to open the letter, never knowing if my grandparents poisoned it as a test. It would be stupid to run my finger through the paper.

Crimson walked behind me and read over my shoulder. "A job?"

"You learned the ciphers?" I asked.

"Duh. I'm your grandparent's ideal granddaughter-in-law," Crimson teased. "So, on the twenty-seventh floor there's a few Kaiming hold outs?"

"That's what it says." I tilted the paper to see the map on it before a portion of the letter caught fire.

"It's self-destructing!" Harley danced from foot to foot.

I read the letter again, making sure I got all of the relevant details before letting it burn up. "No, there's a chemical on it that reacts to oxygen. So after opening it up, the paper started to heat."

"Still sounds like it self-destructs, even if you explain it," Des pointed out.

Harley started singing 'secret ninja letter', which was a new song that apparently needed a flute accompaniment. She did a few rounds before she really hit her flow and got into it.

I ignored her, processing what I'd just read. We could take care of that issue while also pushing forward in the dungeon. My bigger concern was still on the panther monster.

Des could practically read my mind. "So, we need to talk about the panther."

We walked out of the locker room.

Crimson guided us in a direction. It seemed we were going towards the new Haylon tower we had spotted when we had entered the safe zone. "Yes, you said it sped up the longer it fought?"

"Yeah, I assume that is mostly a function of making it impossible for me to win with a purely defensive strategy." It was common for the dungeon to have soft timers in boss fights. Something about them often got more difficult as time went on. If nothing else, people started to run out of mana at a certain point.

"Then there's that thing where it teleports and shreds whoever is in front of it," Charlotte pointed out.

I nodded. "That's the biggest concern. I absolutely need a defensive cooldown to survive that attack."

"Or just a massive amount of stamina. The Harem Queen survived," Fayeth pointed out.

I deadpanned. "Yes, one of the strongest among humanity who is several dozen levels above me survived. I think I'd like a solution that was closer in reach."

"Point taken." Fayeth bobbed her head.

Crimson shifted where we were going. "Then off to the UG store we go. We can see what they have to offer."

"We have plenty of loot to sell too." I pulled up my CID and started to sort through some of it.

Anything metal would go back to the Nagato Clan for the trade deal with the elves. Beyond that, there were a variety of open requests from the clan as well. I had a lot of my brain space occupied with the various lists.

"So, what aspects helped you with the Lightning Phoenix?" Des asked Crimson.

Crimson shrugged. "Dodging. Lots of dodging. If you can dodge me, you can dodge a panther."

"Yeah, that's going to go over well," I said sarcastically, only to get a glare from her strong enough to make me look up from my CID. "I mean your full speed attacks. If I could dodge those, well I'd be able to go fight Naga, let alone fighting in the twenties."

My clarification mollified Crimson and she continued leading us into the UG store. Similar to the stores we'd seen before, the place was all pristine white floors brightly lit by magical items hanging on white metal shelves.

"Welco—" The woman froze as her eyes fixed on Crimson.

"Thanks, we are going to poke around," Crimson dismissed the woman's shock with a wave and moved through the aisles to find one appropriate for our levels.

Given where we were in the dungeon, level twenty through thirty took up nearly half the store. The UG knew their market.

"Did the monster do anything when you took a potion?" Crimson asked, glancing past the shelves to the racks of potions in the back.

"Haven't tried it," I admitted. "We'll try that on the next encounter."

"Chug some health potions. See if you can't train some stamina getting scratched up by the panther. Keep a buff potion on you, see if that helps. When I defeated the Lightning Phoenix, I chugged so many that I was violently ill afterwards. But I survived." Crimson stopped at the skill books and started to thumb through them on the shelves.

"See, that's the kind of detail we didn't get in your 'and the rest is history' storytelling," Harley sighed.

"Yeah. It's history. I'd rather not relive what I did in those weeks leading up to the fight. I'm pretty resistant to lightning now, and we aren't going to talk about that. We are going to talk about Ken working on his mana specialization if you need to keep up with this thing." Crimson pulled out a few skill books and put them to the side.

"Oooh." Des picked one up. "Defensive skills."

"I need one for the panther, that's for sure. If we are specially trying to build me up for the panther, then I should probably get a big defensive skill and maybe a smaller one that I can use more frequently and doesn't slow down my damage much." I played through the fight.

Something to help dodge or parry would be helpful as well. Those claws packed a punch and the act of dodging could be worked into my form a lot easier than some sort of shield or blocking spell.

I picked at the pile Crimson was making and quickly discarded a few of the options. Crimson saw what I was doing and finished going through that shelf before she blurred away and came back with an armload.

"Why not use your ability?" I asked, staring at her blue eyes.

Crimson scoffed. "I don't want to rely on it. That's only for when I'm either stumped or feeling lazy. I know what you need here."

The rest of my party was starting to pick through the shelves on their own. I spotted several pieces of gear that would be upgrades as well.

"Skills first." Crimson spotted my wandering eyes. "Gear upgrades are just a last-minute adjustment. Increasing your stats and working on new skills is the real challenge." She held up two skillbooks. One read Earthen Bulwark, the other Shadow Phase.

I could see why she picked the first from the stack of protective abilities. It was the largest modifier but only blocked up to a set amount of damage. "Maybe, but I'm not exactly throwing rocks around here. That feels more like something that would go with Myrtle. What about this one?" I picked up a spellbook called 'Mystic Defense'.

The spell provided long term damage reduction for a period in return for increased damage later.

Crimson wrinkled her nose at the spell, took it from me and put it back on the shelf. "Terrible ability. That's the kind that'll get you killed because it takes long enough you get screwed if you don't time it right every time. No, go with something short and high damage reduction." She handed me the other book that had been in her hand.

"Like this?" I grabbed and read it. "Shadow Phase, part of an attack will be cast off into the shadows rather than harm you. Reduces damage taken by fifty percent for three seconds. That's not a lot of time."

"The most dangerous abilities happen in an instant," Crimson pointed out.

She was right. That ability of the panther's where it teleported and seemed to hit its target a dozen times in the process was the whole reason I was looking for a skill.

My greater concern was that I hadn't yet seen a consistent time or trigger for it, making it harder to use an ability like Shadow Phase. I could always get more than one, but it was important to limit the number of skills I was actively trying to juggle in combat. Too many and I'd start to make mistakes, possibly lethal ones.

I thought back, dissecting the fight and looking for anything I had missed.

It took a moment, but I soon realized that the panther's eyes had flashed before it had used the ability both times. That could be enough warning for me to act.

I took Shadow Phase from Crimson. "At least this one matches my overall aesthetic. Might even find some benefit from my mana specialization."

Crimson had a giant smile on her face. "Perfect. Now for the easier to use one." She held up a simply titled spell book. 'Dodge'.

I didn't even have to check it with my CID. It was a versatile spellbook known to most adventurers.

"I didn't see this one?" It would have stood out to me on the shelves.

"Found it in the back." Crimson hooked her thumb over her shoulder.

"Wait, when you shot away, you went in the back?"

"Locks don't really stop me. Neither do doors really." She shrugged. "Sometimes they keep the good things in the back."

I took the spellbook and checked to make sure it was the real deal. Dodge was a short cooldown ability that shifted the user one foot to the side. It wouldn't stop some giant boss fist from hitting me or escape an explosive ability, but it might just be enough to stop a claw coming for my face.

With an ability like this, I could cut things a little closer with the panther and use it with dodging normally to avoid more attacks.

"I'll take it." I flipped it over to the back and nearly dropped it when I saw the price tag. "Oh shit." It was in the millions.

Crimson covered the tag. "Huh, pretty sure it shouldn't be that much." She grinned. "Let me go talk to the clerk and get it properly priced."

The way she sauntered off with a smile made me fear for that clerk's life. I also knew that it was properly priced. Even high-level adventurers still used such a versatile ability like [Dodge]. Many seasoned melee fighters pretty much had it baked into their martial forms. So the price was a reflection of the skill's value, regardless of the level and stat requirements.

There was a shout as Crimson startled the clerk, throwing the book down and pretending to get angry.

I palmed my face.

"What's Crimson doing?" Charlotte asked, seeing that our teacher had stepped away.

"She's 'correcting' the price on a spellbook," I sighed.

"Looks more like she is intimidating the clerk to get a discount," Charlotte snickered while Bun-bun squeaked out his own opinion.

"Yeah. I think she is." I shook my head.

"Why not just pay for it herself?" Charlotte tilted her head, and Bun-bun held on for dear life.

That was actually a very good question. After thinking about it for a moment, I thought I understood. Crimson was letting me buy it, or at least, she was letting me keep the illusion that I was the one buying it. She was very aware of the difference between us and didn't want to exert much if any dominance towards me.

The same was not true for the poor clerk who was cowering behind the counter as Crimson's voice rose. Several other adventurers combing the shelves booked it out of the shop the moment they realized who was arguing with the clerk.

I scratched my cheek awkwardly. "She has a reputation. Look at those adventurers run away."

"To everyone else, she's a level sixty floor boss wandering around," Charlotte said and leaned against me. "To the class, she's just a scary teacher and to you..."

"She's just another woman." I shrugged.

"Wait, you think all women are that terrifying?" Harley came up behind us, hearing the tail end of our conversation.

"Careful, Crimson might hear you," I said, earning a squeak from Harley as she slapped her hands over her mouth. "What did you pick up?" I glanced at the shopping basket in the crook of her elbow.

Harley pulled out a folded cloth that turned out to be a giant scarf. "Tada!"

I stared at it for a moment longer and then looked back at her eyes, patiently awaiting an answer as to what I was supposed to be seeing.

"It's a scarf with plus eight to magic!" She threw it on and wrapped it around her neck. "The scarf is the most versatile fashion accessory." Harley proceeded to demonstrate how it could be a head wrap, go around her neck in various shapes, or how it could be a shawl or even a belt.

"Nice scarf," Des interrupted her single-article fashion show. "I got a pretty dagger." Des held out a black, twisted blade like it was a piece of flame stopped in time. The hilt was gold with intricate inlay and a large red ruby on the bottom.

Harley stared at the blade for a long moment. "Are you evil, Des? Only evil people would think that is pretty."

"Don't be like that. It's nice." Des stroked the dagger. "Mostly it has plus five mana and plus five magic along with a modifier on damage over time abilities. They work five percent faster."

I nodded along. I agreed with Des that it was a pretty dagger. The bonus to her damage over time abilities was fairly significant.

"Okay, that's not bad at all." Harley played with her scarf. "What about you, Charlotte?"

Fayeth was heading our way after hearing Crimson arguing with the clerk. "Ken, do you need to save the worker?" The elf had a new glaive over her shoulder. The polearm had an ornate and large blade on the end of it.

"Nah. She needs them alive," I answered, much to Fayeth's horror.

Charlotte put Bun-bun in her arm and held a ring out as she slipped it on his ear. "I found something for Bun-bun. It's not like he can equip any armor, but rings work."

The rabbit fidgeted with the ring going over his ear and then turned his head about like he was testing the new weight.

"What's the bonus?" I asked.

"Six agility and two stamina along with a slight improvement to his speed." Charlotte pet Bun-bun's head.

The rabbit preened under the attention.

I looked at my own gear that sorely needed upgrades compared to what they were finding here at the shop. My CID was loaded up with plenty of money from the Nagato Clan, yet I couldn't quite bring myself to spend it.

Those funds were for improving the clan and paying out quests to the rest of the parties that had joined Silver Fangs. Frankly, I should have kept my own money separate, but I hadn't, and now I couldn't bring myself to pull from the guild funds for my own gear. I was already buying the two skills.

"Problem?" Fayeth got between me and my CID.

"Just feeling odd about spending money. I didn't keep what I was given for Silver Fangs separate from my own," I said awkwardly.

"Yeah, but it is your guild," Harley pointed out.

"What if Candice and the rest of the parties come and offload a ton of stuff on me when they get here?" I countered. "If I run out, the guild runs out, and that's more than a little awkward. Especially if I'm walking around with a bunch of shiny new gear."

I made up my mind with that to just get the skills, I'd have to focus on getting loot drops. That, and even with a 'discount', [Dodge] wasn't going to be cheap.

"Just keep your money separate in the future," Des said, taking my wrist and tapping at my CID. "I mean, you had to have about this much, right?"

I checked the screen after she tilted it back towards me. It seemed about right. Honestly, with everything going on, I had dismissed the thoughts about how much I'd had in the past and wasn't quite sure.

"So, buy the two skill books and then see if you can't get anything else," Charlotte agreed. "That reminds me about something else I wanted to talk about. Ken, you need to take my revive skill tonight." She blushed as Des grinned from ear to ear.

"Oh, he needs to take something from you?" Des leaned against me.

"Just think about it. Having the second revive in the group would help with safety in case something happens to me in a fight." Charlotte didn't back down from Des, but her face continued to flush bright red.

"That's actually a great idea." Fayeth bobbed her head, her new weapon dipping dangerously to the side as Harley danced out of the way.

"Watch it."

Fayeth turned and stuck her tongue out. "I'm completely aware of where my blade is, thank you. You were in no danger."

"So then you meant to scare me," Harley huffed.

I looked over at the clerk who was slumped over the counter while Crimson walked back towards us with a giant smile on her face. "Ah, did they correct the price?"

"Yes, someone must have pushed the zero too many times." Crimson handed me back the book reverently.

I checked the price. It had dropped from the millions to the single digit thousands. The spellbook was painfully underpriced, but I played along. "Thanks for helping me fix that." I tapped the book in my hand a few times. "With this price, maybe I can pick up a new weapon too."

"Wonderful idea." Crimson beamed, satisfied that she'd been helpful. "Let's go pick one out. I'll make sure the prices are right."

Her voice carried through the store, and I heard the clerk yelp.

I put a hand on Crimson's back. "It's fine. I have plenty of money; though, I want to check that you don't have any quests to turn in for Silver Fangs."

She perked up. "Oh, I didn't even think about collecting those." Crimson tapped at her lips as I froze at the idea of her coming back with thousands of turn ins. "I don't need the money, though. Maybe me and the new guild master can work out a different exchange." She winked.

I let out a sigh of relief. "Yes, I think the guild master can help you train control over a certain skill." I knew what she wanted.

Crimson's eyes sparked. "Yes. Yes, he can." She cleared her throat. "I will have to go farm after class tomorrow."

CHAPTER 11

O ur party ended up sleeping in the spire that the Harem Queen had built in the safe zone. It seemed that the one on the thirtieth floor wasn't enough and she'd had a second smaller one built on the twenty-fifth floor. I could only imagine what the one on the thirtieth floor looked like after being in this one for the night.

The area was pristine and more than comfortable enough for the party. Charlotte had convinced me that I needed to change over my skill, and we accomplished that in some privacy of our rooms.

Now, we were back in a classroom at the base of the spire, and I was fiddling with my new sword. I slipped it back into my CID when Crimson showed up.

"Alright. Everyone." Crimson smacked the metal lectern that sat at the front of class and it clanged.

Apparently, it was new enough that she rapped it a few more times to get used to the sound.

"Anyway, you all had fun getting muddy..." She trailed off and waved a hand in front of her nose. "Some of you chose not to get a bath... which is your choice..."

"I've showered like a thousand times." Taylor picked at her shirt. "This smell just doesn't go away."

"You need to bathe. Soak in hot water," Kendra sighed. Clearly, it wasn't the first time she'd informed Taylor of that fact.

"I told you. I'm not really a bath kind of person," Taylor huffed.

She wasn't alone. There was a particular muddy odor in the room.

"Isn't it more important to talk about the two missing students?" Penelope raised her hand.

The entire class turned to Felicity and her party.

Felicity stood up in an overly formal posture like she was reporting up the chain of command. "One of our members died and was revived. After said revival, they had difficulty facing monsters again."

The whole class was quiet. We were all glad that she wasn't dead. But for all of us that faced danger head on, it was odd to hear about someone suddenly turning tail after progressing so far through the dungeon.

None of us wanted to understand her situation because it was something we all dealt with in one way or another. We had signed up for being adventurers, going into that with full understanding of what we were taking on.

To see someone we might have had to rely on become a coward left us with no pity. Had she succumbed to pressure during a raid boss fight, it could well have killed us all.

"The other?" Candice pushed.

"Was her best friend. She wanted to see her out of the dungeon safely." Felicity nodded. "I'm frankly not sure if she'll be back."

"Over level twenty is a good spot. She can easily farm the lower levels for the rest of her life and live comfortably," Charlotte answered.

"If she can find it to get back in the dungeon at all." Helen was less than supportive. "The numbers say she'll probably stay on the surface and do something else. Those that lose their nerve in the dungeon aren't fit for it."

"Don't be so harsh," another of Felicity's team snapped.

"She should be harsh," I defended Helen, earning a scowl. I didn't speak out for her, though. "If she pushes herself to rejoin us, then she can have a shot, but it's when the most dangerous monsters are staring us down that she'd crack. That's the time we need everyone at their best. Look, I know we all want to be sympathetic to our classmates and cheer everyone on, but with the raid coming up, we don't have time to coddle anyone."

Crimson cleared her throat. "He's right. People die in the dungeon every day. Many of those deaths could have been avoided. Even more could have been foreseen because people went somewhere they weren't prepared to go. I want all of you to dive as far as you can go, but if you hit your limit, I'd rather you step out than push yourself to your death.

"On that note." Crimson perked up. "You all made it this far, congratulations. I want you all to kill the boss ten times before you move on. First, it is a wonderful boss as far as loot is concerned. Second, it requires the kind of coordination that you'll need in the raid. Third, I'm going to shuffle your parties so that you have to relearn the fight with different compositions."

The classroom erupted in conversation at her statement that she was changing up the parties.

Crimson fanned the air for us all to calm down. "I'm preparing you for the raid. There are workout facilities in this spire for adventurers, courtesy of Haylon. You are all going to work on your stats and fight the boss. Each of your ten times needs to be with a different party. This is also for Felicity and her two remaining party members to rotate around."

The class calmed down as she explained herself.

"Lastly, we are going to have classes on diplomacy, and to help us understand, I found a volunteer." Crimson gestured off to the classroom doors and they slid open.

Ami walked through with two UG members. Both held tablets, one of which was recording the final member of their group.

Felin walked in behind them. Her mane of white hair with blue streaks was pulled back while her white tail flitted back and forth. She'd traded out her tribal leather outfit for something far more human. She had on a white shirt that showed off her abs and a red leather jacket. Her pants were a dark leather that was stretched taut, showing off some of her muscles as she gracefully strode into the room.

"This is Felin. She's a shaman of her people." Crimson grinned at me.

I nearly smacked my forehead against the desk.

Des whispered to Charlotte while she jabbed the shy druid in the side. I had no doubt she'd collect whatever the 'standard bet' was from Charlotte before the end of class.

"Hi," Felin spoke. Her voice held a pleasant growliness to it as she stepped up to replace Crimson, checking with the older adventurer to make sure she was doing it right. "I'm Felin, and as your teacher explained, I'm a shaman. That is both a class and a position within the Nekorian society. Shamans are looked to as leaders, healers, and guides for The Great One. Crimson asked me to help you understand how to greet a Nekorian. I need a volunteer."

Several members of class raised their hands, but Felin put her arms behind her back and swayed in place as she stared at me patiently. The class paused, realizing there was something going on that they weren't clued in to.

Felin continued to sway, staring straight at me, waiting.

I sighed and raised my hand.

"Wonderful. Ken, thank you for volunteering. I also used you as an example for the rest of class. We Nekorians often sway and stare when we want something. My people are very good at waiting. Much better than humans." She held out a hand, and I walked up to the front of class, suddenly self-conscious that there were members of the UG recording the interaction.

"Felin, good to see you again," I greeted her and held out a hand.

She clasped my hand and pulled me into her. Her strength surprised me, and before I knew it, she had my head clasped with one hand and pressed her cheek to the side of my head.

"Nekorians have a really good sense of smell and we get a lot of information from that sense. This is an extremely friendly greeting, and I wouldn't initiate it if I were you." She continued to rub her face against mine, a low rumble of a purr coming out of her.

"Why don't we step it down and show them a basic greeting?" the UG member asked.

"Or step it up and show Ken your mating rituals!" Des cupped her hands around her mouth and called from the back of class.

I blushed and Felin kept a strong hold on me.

"Oh. We could do that." Felin smiled and I was unsure which she was about to go into. "When greeting a Nekorian for the first time, it is important to make sure they see you and then to stop and let them approach you. Honestly, the chances of a Nekorian coming over are low if you are just passing through. However, if you are occupying the same area for a period of time, I can guarantee that the Nekorian will become curious enough to introduce themselves. They will be fairly direct and may be a little assertive." Felin stepped back and stopped rubbing herself all over me. "We'll use Ken as an example."

I stood awkwardly for a moment as Felin feigned disinterest, looking at her nails and then pulling at her jacket.

After a few seconds, she started to wander around and then she fixated on me and marched right up to me. "See, that's fairly normal."

"So, you coming over and sitting next to me at that dinner was normal?" I asked.

"Yep. You made me curious and I came over. It was basic Nekorian behavior," she answered.

"What if they don't come over?" Kendra asked, stars in her eyes as she stared at Felin.

"Don't force it, maybe just give them more time. Or perhaps you had done or said something in their presence that offended them. We all have excellent hearing." Her ears twitched as she grinned at me.

She had overheard Fayeth talking about anime catgirls and how many men liked them. Then Yui had been talking about Grandpa's... collection. If that was what interested her, then this was a complete misunderstanding.

"What happens when they do come over and you don't want them to?" I asked.

The class seemed scandalized by the question.

"Typically, you give the normal human signs. Turn away, talk in short sentences, and generally show disinterest. Though, you can't lie to the nose." She tapped her very human-looking nose. It was hard to remember that it was so much better.

"Is there a way to show interest?" Des asked.

"Yes of course. Generally, physical contact is great. We are big on family, and a lot of that comes with touching." Felin used me to demonstrate as she pressed her hips to mine, ran her hand over my shoulder and let her tail play along me.

"What about the tail? Can I touch a cat girl's tail?" Harley asked, nearly vibrating in her seat.

Felin hissed at her. "Don't call my people 'cat girls'. I tolerate it, but many might remove the skin on your face for it."

Harley touched her face as if it were too precious to be lost.

"As for tails, they are delicate compared to the rest of our body. You really should not touch a Nekorian's tail unless you are very intimate." Her tail coiled around my thigh like a boa constrictor. "Even then, you should ask." She stared at me and waited patiently.

I was determined to wait her out. Though, when I met her gaze, I realized that her eyes were a soulful blue. And though they almost looked like human eyes, they were more of a football-shaped pupil rather than being perfectly round.

For a moment, I was lost in her eyes.

Felin pressed her thigh up harder against me, rubbing back and forth ever so slightly. I wasn't sure it was even visible for the rest of the class.

"Psst." Des hissed loudly from the back of the room. "She wants you to ask to touch her tail."

"Yeah," Crimson said from the side. "You need to help her with her educational lesson."

"It's for science," Harley agreed.

I sighed. "Felin, can I touch your tail?"

"Of course. You can touch any part of me," she said immediately, causing the class to chuckle.

I ran my hand along where her tail was squeezing my leg and it released. Soon my hand was moving over the full length as she flicked it back and forth.

Delicate, my ass.

It felt like I was holding a mid-level serpent monster in my hand. Something told me that her tail could break bones. But it was very soft.

Felin's tail coiled around my wrist and pulled my hand around her hip to hold her close. "See? A Nekorian's tail is very versatile. At high speeds, it is useful to help us balance when running and jumping."

One of the UG members raised their hands.

Felin stared at the gesture for a moment and then looked at me. "What is that?"

"He has a question," I sighed.

"Yes, please give me your question." Felin pointed at him.

"Are Nekorians more physically gifted than humans?" he asked.

Felin tilted her head making her unbelievably cute as her ears flopped with the motion. "I don't know. We haven't exactly studied the difference."

"Oh." The man was disappointed. "That makes sense."

"We are a physical people, both with touch and we like to stay active when we aren't resting," Felin said. "I'm unsure what physical differences there are, especially with different cultural practices in the mix as well."

Des spoke from the back. "Does your tattooing Ken mean anything?"

"Tattoo?" several people in the class asked.

Felin perked up. "Yes, I marked Ken here. Ken, please take off your shirt."

I stared at her for a long moment and turned around to the class before taking off my shirt. On the back of my right shoulder was the tattoo that Felin had given me.

"This is where Shamans are important to Nekorians. Rather than the technology that you all use to interpret The Great One's messages, we ask directly." Her hands ran over my back. "Shamans tattoo special ink from the dungeon into our adventurers and then perform a small ritual to show their stats and abilities."

"Can you demonstrate?" the UG documenter asked.

Felin glanced at me.

I shrugged. "Not worried about showing my stats," I spoke louder. "Can you blur or remove the video of my stats?"

"This video is for the upper level of the UG only," he offered.

Crimson cleared her throat. "You'll remove everything but his stat block. His class information and his skills won't still be on your device when you leave this room."

I didn't need to glance over my shoulder to know that the man was shitting a brick.

"Of course," he squeezed out.

"Go ahead," I told Felin.

She ran her hands all over my back and purred. "O' Great One, please show us Ken's power."

My back tickled slightly, and I realized it was Felin's tail brushing down my back for effect. No doubt it was leading the ink as it spelled out all of the details.

"Oh." The class was suitably impressed by the display.

"Wait, Ken is a Demon Lord?" Kendra blurted out.

I rolled my eyes. "Secondary class."

"It's an incubus demon too," Penelope said. "He used Charm on me during a fight once."

"Oh!" someone else blurted out. "That's why you were so clumsy in the tournament last year?"

I glanced over my shoulder to see Penny's face turn bright pink before it was hidden by her hair as she stared down at her desk.

"That's why Ken always gets stronger after sex in 74 wives?" Wendy asked and suddenly there was a flurry of discussions about the smut story.

I smacked my face. Of course the class decided to discuss the erotica of me on the UG recording.

Felin was staring at me with wide eyes. "You have 74 wives? That is a very large pride."

"I do not. It is a long story." I held my hands up in surrender.

Her tail tickled at my abs. "You do have several partners, correct?"

"A few," I said.

She nodded at that. "Yes, you have a pride." She spoke as if she was confirming something to herself.

And I wasn't an idiot. All of the physical contact she was displaying showed just how interested in me she was. Though, I had a hard time reading the Nekorian and was unsure if it was curiosity or more.

"Anyway. I'm putting my shirt back on." I didn't ask for permission. They had seen enough.

Felin's eyes lingered and then became slightly sad when I had put the shirt on. "There was something new there that we should talk about," she whispered.

I only nodded and stood there quietly for any more questions.

None came and she returned to the lesson. "As a shaman, I also have a role in my people as a leader. We are important to understanding the dungeon and often must memorize things about the floors."

"Do you have written records?" one of the UG asked.

"Yes, we have written records in each of the safe zones for the surrounding floors. We aren't barbarians, but we have never developed a dependency on technology. Instead, we use magic and the dungeon for much of our daily lives," Felin scowled at the UG man asking the question.

"What of your home world?" he followed up.

Felin went quiet. "I cannot discuss that with you."

He seemed disappointed but tapped on his tablet.

"Felin, will you be staying with us?" Taylor asked.

"Ah. Right now, I am going to be traveling with Crimson and will shadow your class," Felin said.

"You should join the Silver Fangs," Des said with a wry grin.

"What is that?" Her tail flicked back and forth with interest.

I stared at her tail, realizing it was giving me a lot of information about her mood.

"It's Ken's guild," Candice spoke first. "He's the new guild master, and we are all members."

"Oh. It is how he organizes his pride?" Felin's words made me jump in to correct the misunderstanding.

"No. Guilds are how humans organize themselves when diving into the dungeon. There are five-man parties, but guilds are made up of many parties and look out for each other, as well as offer rewards for collecting certain resources that then can be sold back to the rest of the guild at reduced prices. It's an organization built to have multiple tiers of adventurers all helping each other," I simplified when she tilted her head.

"Ah. Okay," she said, but I don't think she really understood. "Then I will join these Silver Fangs, if they are yours to command." Felin nodded sharply.

Crimson chuckled from the side. "Congratulations, Ken. I think your guild is the first to have a different race to begin with. And now you have a second different race joining."

I rolled my eyes. They were just people that looked a little different. "Let's continue with the lesson." I gestured towards the class for Felin and extracted my hand from her tail. "And I'll go sit back down."

CHAPTER 12

After an awkward class and being used as a demonstration for Felin, I snuck away to grab Ami before the class went down to exercise and prepare for swapping out groups.

"Did you find Felin or did she find you?" I asked the white-haired ninja butler. I grabbed her arm before she could slip away.

Ami turned and straightened up to me. Her face was impassive, but the mask made it especially hard to read her. "Ah. Apologies, Master. I ran into her while running errands for the clan. Do you have need of my services?"

"What errands?" I raised an eyebrow. She was my butler.

"Crimson had a few requests." Ami cleared her throat. "Building materials mostly, that she paid for but would use for the clan."

I had no idea what that meant, but I was sure I was going to find out later and likely regret not asking more questions.

Holding up my CID, I moved the items I had arranged for the guild. "If you are returning, here's a load of items." I had collected everything from the class as well throughout the morning.

Ami accepted the items with her own CID. "Perfect. I will deliver these to your grandparents when I return. Is that all? Do you need any assistance with the mission you were given?"

I hadn't forgotten about the mission. "No. I will handle that with my party."

"Do not delay. The information grows less correct by the day," Ami reminded me and then slipped away at high speed.

At least she was dedicated.

I thought about heading out on my own, but I had learned from the last few times I had attempted to be a solo adventurer. Instead, I caught up with the rest of class at the gym.

***

"Phew." I leaned against the shower wall, letting the spray come down over me. The facilities in the safe zone were top notch. I even had a full-sized men's locker room just for me. It only made me more expectant of the larger facilities on the thirtieth floor.

Exercises had been difficult, and Des was not helping my blood flow in the proper direction. After hearing from Fayeth about Elysara, Des had taken it as a mission to rile me up.

What was more interesting was the mingling of groups. Penny, Candice, Kendra, Felicity, and I had talked quite a bit about how we could rotate our groups so that everyone got the ten boss runs that they needed.

I appreciated that each of the party leaders was looking at the situation from a holistic perspective and not letting each of their members fight on their own to form teams.

They proposed a simple table and sliding some of the members through. Things got tricky with Penny's party, though. It was made up with two tanks, two healers, and only one damage dealer. However, that was quickly solved by rotating Taylor out for Penelope on the table before starting to cycle everyone.

Taylor was over the moon that she was a damage dealer for the exercise. She was already promising Kendra that she wasn't going to want to touch a shield again after being a damage dealer for a few days.

The door to the men's locker room opened, and I was pulled from my musings.

"Yes?" I called, stepping around the wall to peek out.

To my surprise, Helen was standing in the doorway in her black workout outfit. "Don't mind me. The line for the shower in the other locker room is too long, and we need to talk anyway."

"By all means, come on in. I'm not shy."

"Don't get any ideas, pervert," Helen scoffed, and despite her name for me, stripped before coming into the showers.

I did my best to keep my eyes up on her face. "Aren't you worried that I'm going to turn into some kind of animal if you show up naked?"

She stared at me for a long moment. "I could handle you." She came around the tiled wall in a bathing suit.

Ah, I see.

"Don't look so disappointed." She rolled her eyes and turned the handle for another of the showers, stepping in under the spray. Her unruly, red hair soaked up the water and stretched out, the weight straightening some of the kinks. "We needed to talk."

"Well, you have me at a disadvantage. I don't know what we need to talk about, but I'm listening." I offered her some of my soap.

She pumped some into her hands and sniffed it, finding it acceptable and then pumped a dozen more times before she started to work it all in her hair. "So, you and my mother."

"Let me save you some energy. I will never be anything with your mother."

"I've watched her twist dozens of men around her fingers. A pervert like you? You won't last a minute in her grasp," Helen scoffed.

I rolled my eyes. I had no doubts that the Harem Queen was quite capable when it came to flirting and romance, but she did nothing for me. I had no interest at all in the woman, but clearly Helen had been burned a few times and had her doubts.

"Crimson is fairly against her, add on to my lack of interest in your mother and I think it is safe to say I'll resist her charms."

Helen raised an eyebrow. "You can't even stop staring at my breasts, and I'm wearing a swimsuit."

I threw my hands up in the air. "I am not staring at them, unless they are on your face now. What do you want from me? You've done nothing but harass me from day one, and now you come in here while I'm showering. It seems like you are the pervert."

She blushed furiously. "I am not!"

Maybe I struck a chord. "Then why do you think me having a healthy relationship with several women my age makes me a pervert?"

"You are a boy in an all-girls school. That's a pervert's dream!"

"Crimson dragged me here when my class was 'Aberrant'. She saved me from not making it into a dungeon college at all because she saw some hidden potential in me. She had already promised the Headmistress that she'd teach," I shouted back at her.

"Then what about the rest? Hmm?" Helen crossed her arms as the shower rinsed the soap out of her hair.

"You mean the party with a drop-dead gorgeous woman interested in me, a cute druid, and an exotic yet lovable elf?" I blinked at her. "Finding them all attractive is pretty normal."

"No, I mean the whole class," Helen scoffed. "You have an incubus secondary class. I bet there are perverted little dreams of you dancing around with all of us in compromised positions."

I just laughed and laughed.

Helen was at a loss. "Stop laughing." She threw the soap at me, and I side stepped it.

"No," I continued. "This is just too funny. Let me guess, your mother and all her suitors are perverts too?"

"I pity the men. However, my mother? Yes. She is even going after a man who's not even half her age!" Helen scowled.

I wiped some tears in my eyes that had formed as a result of laughing. "Well, on that one we can agree. She's a little too mature for me," I put it politely.

Helen's face was pure horror. "You like litt—"

I dashed across the room and put my hand over her mouth. "Don't even say that. No. I was politely saying that your mother is too old for me."

Helen realized the closeness between the two of us and her face turned bright red before she shoved me across the room. "Get off me. I knew it. You can't even resist the temptation of me in a swimsuit."

"That wasn't it and we both know it." I pointed an accusing finger at her.

She crossed her arms over her chest even though it was already covered. "Pervert."

I rubbed at my forehead with the realization that I just wasn't going to get through to her. "Fine, I'm a pervert. What else did we need to talk about?"

She snorted. "You are giving powers out via sex. I hope you know that my mother is already spreading that around."

"It's not through sex—it's through love, you idiot," I sighed. "Elves believe in 'harmonizing their souls'. It's more like learning to love each other to the point that you are in sync. That's what is required for me to pass along my skills."

She frowned. "So you are saying that you love multiple women like this?"

"Yes." I paused, wondering if that would help her understand better.

Helen snorted and laughed. "You are so horny that you are deluding yourself. At least my mother is honest with herself. She just likes to have a different man each day of the year."

"Alright, I think you've overstayed your welcome in the locker room. Shoo or I'll call Crimson." I flicked my hands at her trying to shoo her out of the shower.

Helen huffed and turned off the shower, wringing her hair out as she walked. "Don't have to tell me twice. And don't stare at my ass."

"I'm not. Trust me, if I wanted to stare at someone, I'd just go find Des," I said.

"Because she's your type?"

"Because she likes it and I love her. Get out." I went back to the shower hearing the door open and close.

The hot water soothed out my mind. Helen was really a handful, and I think I understood her better. She didn't really see harems as legitimate relationships, just something for sexual pleasure.

It was a harsh point of view given how many harems there were in society now.

The door opened again and I growled. "Helen, I swear if—"

"Oh. You and Helen are having a secret rendezvous?" Des stripped and danced into the showers.

I sighed in relief. "No, quite the opposite. She came mostly to confirm that I'm a pervert. But since that's settled and my debuff is gone..." I pulled Des into my arms and then pushed her between the showers. "It's time to work on my stamina again and wear me out so that I can get to sleep early."

"Early?" Des asked, scandalized. "I thought we were working on your stamina."

"We have a job tonight." I pressed my chest to her back and whispered in her ear. "So, let's not hold anything back."

***

Des had no problem wearing me out and coming to bed with me very early. Though, my dirty clothes had gone missing in the locker room.

Now it was the middle of the night, and even if the Dungeon distorted our nights and days, most people kept roughly to their normal sleep schedule. The human body just did better with routines.

I walked towards the next floor of the dungeon with my party in tow.

Harley rubbed her eyes. "It's so late. Why do we have to assassinate people at night?"

"Just shout it from a mountaintop, why don't you?" Des sighed.

We walked down the stairs to the next floor, and immediately the scent hit me. It was like I'd just walked into a candy store.

Harley took a deep breath. "Fuck that smells good."

"Don't eat the snow," Des warned.

"I know, I know." Harley held up her hands. "Just because it smells good doesn't mean it tastes good."

"Oh, it tasted good. But it will kill you," Fayeth clarified.

"So, like sugar?" Harley quipped back.

"On steroids," Des answered.

"Keep talking like this and next thing we know Harley is going to make two snowballs and die happily with her face pressed between them." I glared at the party. "We have to get through this floor and down to the next one to find the Kaiming party."

"And kill them," Harley added.

"Yes, and kill them." I shook my head. "You know part of being an assassin is about stealth and subtlety."

"That's what Yui kept trying to tell me, but my way seemed to work just fine. Being loud with my flute fits my personality." She struck a pose and winked.

We all kept walking past her.

"Hey, I was supposed to stun you with my cuteness," Harley huffed and got back in formation as Fayeth carved her way through the dungeon.

"Save it for the monsters," Fayeth said.

Up ahead, several figures moved among the powdered sugar landscape. A chocolate bunny the size of a bear pulled its head from the snow, wiggling its little chocolate face.

Bun-bun screeched at the top of his lungs and rushed forward.

"So much for stealth," I sighed and put my head in my hand. "Charlotte, give him a hand."

"Growth." She buffed her rabbit so that he was the size of a horse as he fought the chocolate bunny with more determination than I'd ever seen out of the little white rabbit.

But the monster wasn't alone.

My eyes were drawn to three female forms that pulled themselves from the snow. The white powder clung to their transparent bodies like white dresses, and a pile on top that resembled a wide brim, pointed hat.

Harley started breathing heavily. "No... way."

I checked my CID. They were 'Gumdrop Witches' and their transparent red skin glowed as they gathered magic in their hands. "You gonna be okay, Harley?"

She swallowed audibly. "Yeah. Just going to have some interesting dreams tonight."

"They are quite curvy," Des agreed.

"Fayeth." I didn't have to say more.

The tank of our group charged forward, spraying her [Agitating Spores] over the monsters and cleaving through them. The witches shot sticky, red blasts.

Fayeth dodged one, absorbed another before getting splattered in the face with the last one. She cried out as Charlotte healed her. "It burns!"

I ducked under a wild swing of Fayeth's new glaive and started in on the Gumdrop Witches. The Gumdrop Witches swayed unnaturally as their bodies dodged and they continued to cast.

I slammed a foot down. [Earth Stomp] rippled under their feet, yet their bodies absorbed the shock and continued casting. Moving, I caught one of their spells with my own [Absorb] and quickly discharged to interrupt another.

Fayeth could handle the remaining spell as she swept her glaive back and forth angrily. The spells must have been particularly painful to annoy her so much.

Des' curses piled up and darkened the monsters, causing bits to harden and crumble off. I stabbed into those bits, searching for their mana crystals and dealing plenty of damage.

We dealt with the Gumdrop Witches quickly enough, then we moved to help Bun-bun with the chocolate rabbit.

He was dodging back and forth, striking out with furious attacks at the rabbit. He was moving so much that it was actually difficult for me to get in and assist him.

When the chocolate bunny dropped to the ground, Bun-bun jumped on top of its form and let out a screech of victory before it puffed into black smoke and Bun-bun thumped to the ground.

"Satisfied?" I asked the rabbit.

He walked out of the smoke with his head held high, chittering at Charlotte.

"He says he's the best bunny and these guys have nothing on him," Charlotte translated.

I shook my head and reached down to pick up the loot. It had dropped an actual chocolate bunny, one that we could eat.

Bun-bun, however, saw the candy and became furious, jumping up and snatching it out of my hand. Then he brought it low to the ground and destroyed it, covering his face in chocolate at the same time.

"Hey, I don't think rabbits should eat chocolate," Des pointed out.

"Pretty sure a dungeon creature isn't going to die from chocolate," I said, pointing at Bun-bun as he nibbled on his paws with a satisfied look on his face. "Besides, a real rabbit can't crush his foes like Bun-bun can."

He gave me an appreciative squeak.

Harley stepped up to the Gumdrop Witches and fell to her knees, picking up the loot. "I didn't want to kill you."

"You know, some of these floors have items to temporarily summon the monsters," Des said.

Harley perked up. "Really?" Her eyes lit up like two embers.

"Yeah, if we farm this floor enough, we might get an item to summon Gumdrop Witches," Des added fuel to the fire.

Harley's eyes became an inferno of passion. "Then we must farm this floor until there's nothing left! I could summon my own Gumdrop Witch."

"They are usually single use and don't last more than a few minutes," I said.

"A lot can be done in a few minutes." Harley turned to me and the passion she had was overwhelming. "If it isn't, then we'll just have to farm more."

I turned to Des, giving her a look that told her she should not be encouraging Harley so much. "Remember that we are pushing through this floor to go hunt a remnant of Kaiming."

"Right, of course." Harley cleared her throat. "We will also be coming back to get experience and levels though," she clarified.

"Of course," I agreed.

Harley had a giant, lopsided grin. "Then what are we waiting for? Let's go kill our way through this floor." She pumped her flute and led the way.

Fayeth grunted and hurried to get ahead of Harley. "Don't run off ahead. You are the support and I'm the tank."

"Sorry." Des shrugged as we walked next to each other. "I was just trying to motivate her."

"I can tell. But between her and Bun-bun, we are going to have our hands full," I said.

Bun-bun looked up at the sound of his name. The chocolate on his face wasn't cleaned off yet, and now there was a layer of powdered sugar on top of it.

I could already imagine Bun-bun layering those two substances until he practically had a candy helmet. "Come on. Let's go show all the chocolate bunnies that you are the true bunny king!"

Bun-bun squeaked and charged forward.

Charlotte sighed. "Careful. He's getting really worked up."

I held my hands up. "Just having some fun." I grabbed both of their hips and followed after the other three. "Assassinations don't have to be dull work."

CHAPTER 13

"Alright." Ken turned his CID to the ground and let it project on the white, sticky snow.

Des crouched alongside him, just wanting to be closer to him as he started to explain the plan for the Kaiming. Somehow, even though she was the temptress, she found herself completely smitten with him rather than the other way around.

At least, that was how it appeared to her. Ken focused on his CID while she stared at him.

"We are expecting three parties, all of which are level appropriate for this floor." He tapped at the projection on the snow. "They are holed up in this corner of the dungeon."

"What kind of resistance can we expect?" Des pushed him for more.

"They have high-tech alarms around their campsite. That means vibration sensors capable of going off if anything bigger than twenty pounds moves near them." Ken looked pointedly at Bun-bun.

The rabbit licked his paws and preened under the attention.

"Yes, that means you are going to help us disable them," Ken told the rabbit.

Bun-bun crouched low and started scurrying around their group.

"What's he doing?" Ken asked.

Charlotte sighed. "I let him watch too many spy movies this summer. He's currently singing the Bond theme song as he moves like that."

Bun-bun perked up and held a paw to his mouth before going back to 'sneaking' around their group. He used my legs as a corner, that he started peeking around them with bouncing eyebrows.

"I'm glad he's excited for his role." Ken went back to the diagram. "They'll have four men on watch. Two on each exposed side. They've set up tents for a larger group than was there last time we scouted."

"So, they are expecting more to arrive." Des nodded along. "Do we go in as a team?"

Ken shook his head. "It'd be almost impossible to silence all four guards at once. So..." He trailed his finger around the edge of the dungeon and into the back of the tents. "We sneak past, take care of the people in the tents first, and then finish the guards last. Otherwise, we might be overwhelmed."

"That's assuming we can get past them and do the dirty work before they notice," Des sighed. "We should split up, two and two." She pointed at herself and Ken, then Charlotte and Fayeth.

"Hey, wait," Harley scowled.

When Ken looked up at her, Des watched as he tried to control his face. Harley was wearing her pink yoroi, which wasn't stealthy at all.

"There are five of us. Six if you count Bun-bun," Harley continued.

The rabbit gave an indignant squeak of agreement.

"Yes, someone needs to keep an eye on the guards and possibly provide a distraction." Des smirked at Harley.

Ken frowned.

Des caught the look and put a hand on his shoulder. "Don't you even think of running off on your own." She pointed at his eyes and then at hers. "I'm watching you, Mr. Goes off on his own."

Ken rolled his eyes and smiled. "Not what I was thinking."

"I'm going with Ken." Charlotte crossed her arms. "Just in case the panther shows up. I have to stick with him to revive him."

Des winced at the mere mention of such a complication. "I can go with Fayeth."

"Agreed. Harley will be on guard watch, message us on our CIDs if you see movement from the guards. Bun-bun of course is going in early to destroy the vibrational alarms here and here," Ken settled the plan. "We'll go into a tent each and start clearing out the camp. When we are done, meet back at the very corner and we'll go take the scouts together."

Des bobbed her head and planted a kiss on Ken's cheek. "Wonderful plan, love."

He raised an eyebrow at the name. "I thought I satisfied you this afternoon?"

"I'm never satisfied." Des smirked. It wasn't just a joke. Ever since her class change, she was always interested in Ken. She stared into his eyes and reigned in her aura.

"I'll just have to work on my stamina." Ken looked back down at the map to confirm everything was in order and nodded. "We'll finish this up tonight and head back to the safe zone."

Des stood up from her crouching position. "Everyone take care of themselves."

Charlotte nodded and lifted her staff in a promise that she'd take care of Ken.

"Come on, Fayeth." Des pulled the elf along. She was slightly bitter that she wasn't the one at Ken's side, but she smoothed that concern out and instead pushed her focus for what was to come.

"He'll be fine." Fayeth put a hand on her arm.

"Of course he will," Des said as much for herself as Fayeth. "He ran off twice in the past to go kill people pursuing us. At least this time, I'm doing the operation with him, even if not at his side."

Fayeth nodded and crouched as they got closer to the camp.

Des hadn't used her [Demonic Eye] to do more than a cursory pass before the planning session. The eye unfortunately stuck out like a sore thumb in the snowy white terrain.

"Camouflage," Fayeth said, her body rippling and blending in with the surroundings.

Des followed suit and disappeared except for a ripple where the ability was a little slow to adapt to their movements. The two of them got into position as Bun-bun bounded over and started crawling forward as if to a beat that only he could hear.

Des shook her head at the rabbit's antics.

Despite him fooling around, he knew his objectives. He got up next to one of the sensors, balanced on a short little tripod, and struck with a flash of his claws. The sensor whirred slightly as it deactivated.

Bun-bun flashed Des a smug look before continuing to creep about for the other sensor in their way. He finished that one, and Des waved for Fayeth to move forward with her.

Des pulled up her CID and saw the all-clear from Harley, before she retrieved an older dagger that gave her three agility.

For a caster, Des was incredibly gifted in the physical stats, which was partially due to her demonic heritage and her new secondary class. It still had a focus on magic, but came with plenty of agility and strength.

She quietly cut through the side of the large tent and crept in, her eyes adjusting to the darkness with ease. Fayeth wasn't as lucky, and Des had to grab the elf's hand to steady her.

"Two there, and four here," Des pointed them out.

Fayeth nodded, dropping her camouflage and drawing her glaive. She raised the weapon over the two sleeping forms like an executioner's ax.

Des hurried to the other side of the tent and covered one form's mouth as her dagger drew a bloody line through their neck. The

Kaiming gurgled slightly through the new opening in their throat, but otherwise, died silently.

Des made a note. She'd have to strike a little shallower. She perfected the technique on the second body, cutting through the jugular but not the windpipe.

Fayeth's blade thunked across the tent as she just removed their whole head in one blow.

Brutal.

Des' next target jumped at the noise, and she leapt on him, making sure to finish him before he could raise the alarm. She buried her dagger into his throat as she held him down.

At that point, the last target was wide-eyed, staring at her in horror. His mouth was already open ready to shout.

Des shook her hair to reveal her second eye and hit him with the full strength of her aura. "Charm."

His eyes softened. "I love you," he blurted.

"Good," Des purred while feeling sick inside. Ken was the only one who was supposed to look at her like that. "Why don't you put on this blindfold and wait for a surprise?" She cut a sleeve off the man she was kneeling on and handed it to him. "I'll give you a reward if you are quiet."

The last man couldn't have been more eager.

Pathetic.

Des glanced over her shoulder as Fayeth finished the last one on her side of the tent. She switched the grip on her knife ready to end the last one.

Fayeth came over and put a hand on her shoulder. "Good job. You captured one."

Des nodded, remembering that they could use more information on what remained of the group.

Des played with the knife while she thought through what to do next. "Dear," she said to the man. "Lay down and let me put this gag in, so that we can be quiet." She ripped off a long strip from the bedroll and the man let her gag him and tie him up.

"Impressive." Ken poked his head into her tent.

Des beamed at Ken's praise, looking up from her handiwork. Her heart blossomed with his smile. "Thanks. Almost killed him, but Fayeth reminded me that we could always use information." She gave credit where it was due.

Ken chuckled and scooted closer to give her a kiss.

Des happily accepted the kiss and wrapped her arms around his strong shoulders, savoring the taste of him. "Perfect." Ken had washed away the unpleasantness of charming another man. "Now for the guards?" she asked as a pair of eyes glowed in the dark behind Ken.

"That's the plan," Ken said.

Des' eyes went wide as she watched the panther prowling out of the darkness.

***

It was Des' look of horror that clued me in that something wasn't right.

I spun around, my new short sword flashing out. It was a cool blue blade with yellow veins bleeding through the metal. The weapon was a little flashy for an assassin, but its stats were fantastic.

Before I had time to muse on that any further, I activated [Dodge] and slipped to the side to avoid a panther claw. "Again? Really?" I grumbled.

"We'll take care of the guards," Des answered.

"No, let me see if this guy can't prove a distraction." I leapt back, tearing a hole through the front of the tent and activated [Shadow Ambush], coming out beside one of the guards and tearing into him.

The man screamed as he fell and the other three were on their feet.

An arrow whizzed past me, scraping my cheek, but I turned and smiled as the panther came charging through him, crushing him to the earth. Its massive fangs removed his head in its attempt to get to me.

Another of the men on watch cut through the panther but did no damage. In his shock, a demonic Des came up behind him digging her claws into his arm and using her bulk to swing him around like a rag doll.

The last man charged me, rushing across the space between us with an ability. I barely blocked the two-handed ax and had to twist and turn it into a poor parry before he overpowered me.

The panther ignored him and swiped my thigh, making me stagger as blood rushed down my leg.

"You're arrogant enough to fight me and this monster?" He scoffed. "Men! Get up!"

I dodged away from the panther, noticing that it was already starting to speed up.

The man blinked when no one came running. Instead, Bun-bun screeched and jumped on his face, scratching it up as Charlotte buffed him and he grew to the size of a horse.

I laughed. "They are gone. Get fucked, Kaiming."

There was a moment of stillness as he escaped Bun-bun and reassessed me.

"Ken Nagato!" His tone was so bitterly cold that my blood slowed. He charged again, ignoring Bun-bun. He tried to skewer me with the corners of the ax before spinning opposite of the panther trying to force me to choose.

[Dodge] was invaluable as I slipped inside his guard and punched my dagger under his arm and through the gap in his armpit before I rolled under his swing. A hit like that and he wouldn't be able to swing that ax around so easily.

He screamed, barely getting out of the panther's path as he pulled something from his inventory, popping the cork and chugging the potion in one go.

The panther kept coming, and I had to focus on dodging its claws. I felt like I was getting into a rhythm that was steadily speeding up. I didn't have time to dance with the panther.

Where the man had been, a grotesque swollen monstrosity stood holding his ax. He rushed me with red glowing eyes.

Bun-bun crashed into him, driving him into the panther that disappeared into a puff of smoke for a second.

I activated [Shadow Arm] and [Mana Burn], latching the shadowy limb onto him and starting a flickering blue fire that burned away his mana. Whatever this form was he was using, the spell would either hurt him physically or at least increase the mana cost to keep it up.

He spun with his ax, moving faster than I would have expected of someone his size to move. Then he leapt into the air with a swing of his ax. The intensity of the hit felt like it would sever buildings and certainly sever me in two if it reached me.

[Dodge] was still recharging, so I activated [Shadow Phase]. It was a strange sensation as some of the ax's blade and force missed me like I was a shadow, while other parts sliced into me, opening a giant wound that went straight down my chest and splashed blood on my face.

I wasn't done yet, though. Knowing that I couldn't dodge, I thrust my sword into his gut while my dagger raked along his forearm and sliced open the leather bracers before drawing blood.

He staggered to the side, his ax nearly teleporting over his shoulder as he swung it back and then at me.

[Dodge] was back, and I slid a foot back, clearing his swing and the panther's renewed charge. I popped a potion from my inventory and gulped it down, paying more attention to the panther than the Kaiming soldier.

The panther was acting as expected, following the same patterns as our previous fight. Its attention was focused solely on me, and the Kaiming man had seemed to determine the creature wasn't after him.

I wanted to give the panther another good try, but it would disappear after I died and Charlotte would be able to bring me back easily if this man was gone.

He had to be the priority to protect my group.

Des must have thought similarly as curses popped up on his skin from her spells. I kept on dodging as the panther grew faster and the man more irate. Between the two, I had no openings to get much damage in and finish him.

When my [Mana Burn] flickered out on him, even with the shadowy limb still attached, I decided to risk it and stepped in quickly, activating my finisher.

"Mana Implosion." I put a hand to the mutated Kaiming soldier's chest.

Once again, a blue bead formed in his chest, drawing just a trickle of mana from him before it turned into a black hole that ripped out the flesh from the center of his torso and then pulsed a bright blue flare that tore his chest open and exploded over the panther.

The panther stumbled to the side, its shoulder torn off and black smoke trailing out of it. What was left of the man toppled over onto the dungeon floor, dead.

I brought my sword and dagger up, ready for the panther's attack.

Its eyes flashed, a key tell. I activated [Shadow Phase] again, knowing what was about to happen, yet the spell didn't activate as it was still recharging. If I'd been more prepared, I would have chugged a potion too, but I was out of time.

At the last second, I tried to activate [Shadow Ambush] to see if I could dodge the ability.

Yet, the next instant, my feet appeared out of the shadows ten feet away with bloody tops, and I fell down, with no legs to support me. I was gone from the hips down as the panther rounded on me, chewing on something.

The pain was blissfully short before everything went black.

***

It couldn't have been a minute later before I woke up in Charlotte's lap.

"You did a great job," Charlotte said, staring down at me with bright green, watering eyes threatening to spill over. "I saw you survive that big hit from him. If he hadn't been there, you would have taken that panther out."

Des was nearby, while Fayeth carried the bound man.

"You totally had it," Des agreed. "It didn't react to the potion."

"No, it didn't. Which is good news. I think I can at least see if there are other phases to the fight next time," I said.

"As long as it doesn't show up in the middle of a big fight again." Harley rolled her eyes. "That was a little spotty."

"I died, so I'd argue it was more than a little." Stretching my legs, I made sure they still worked the way they were supposed to.

I didn't doubt Charlotte's healing, but it was always a little weird to all of a sudden have limbs that were just lost.

"Getting comfortable lap?" Des teased as Fayeth dropped the surviving Kaiming soldier nearby.

He kept looking up at Des with eyes full of adoration as if he could see her through the blindfold. It rankled me more than I thought it would.

Des seemed to sense my annoyance and nodded at the man. "Wanna just end him?"

"No," I grunted and turned in Charlotte's lap, but I didn't leave it. "Go ahead and question him." I settled in to watch.

Des made a face and pulled out the gag, smiling at him. "I have a special game for you." Her voice caressed the inside of my head and made me curl my toes.

"Yes," the man panted.

"But first we should talk about the others. Are there any more of your group that might come up on us?" Des asked.

"Four guards," he gasped.

"What about others? Any more groups that might visit your camp tonight?" Des asked.

"No. The only other group we are connected to is on the thirty-first floor. Information is scattered. Mr. Ming is in hiding; I doubt they know where. A few of the groups moved to this area of the dungeon because Haylon comes up through here," he said.

Des made a noise of understanding. "And you are interested in Ken Nagato?"

"Yes! That rat bastard must die for what he did to us!" The man spoke with such passion. "He is at fault for the downfall of the Kaiming. First he dug out Gransmen Industries, then he foiled the arrival of our Naga superiors. It's because of him that the UG hunts us." Sense was returning to his eyes, the anger of talking about me was defeating Des' charm.

Des had a dagger out, clearly wanting to stab the man. "Did you find anything out about him?" She continued to push.

"Just that he's here and moving this way. Wait! You—" His eyes flashed with sudden understanding before going dull. He didn't get another word out as Fayeth's glaive dropped down like an executioner's ax.

"He didn't know much, that was clear." Fayeth justified her kill.

"I was going to kill him if you didn't." Charlotte was holding her gnarled staff like she was going to brain him. "He didn't seem valuable, and I was quickly growing tired of his hatred for Ken."

I patted Charlotte on the knee. "Thank you for wanting to guard me, but I can handle people wanting to kill me. It's just the attempts that become a problem."

Charlotte blushed. "Right. Well, that's what I'm here for. You won't die on my watch."

I kissed her thigh. "Let me spend a few more minutes recovering and then we can head back to the safe zone."

CHAPTER 14

I flipped through the CIDs of the downed Kaiming adventurers, clearing out the inventory and organizing it into mine. "Killing people is really quite lucrative," I observed.

They had everything they owned on them, we'd make more from selling their CIDs than the clan had been set to pay us. Des raised an eyebrow from where she leaned on my shoulder. Though, I was fairly sure she wasn't really watching what I did with the loot.

"What? It is." I shrugged and justified my comment.

Fayeth was passed out on the bed, and I was out in the main area sitting on the island. Each party had a suite to themselves; it was pretty incredible that the high-level harem members of the Harem Queen had made the building in just a few short weeks.

There was an even bigger facility down on the 30th floor safe zone now, which boggled the mind. Would those ones have their own workout rooms?

Charlotte flipped some pancakes to get us ready for the day. "Isn't there a code of honor for the Nagato Clan?"

"Yeah and we followed it." I rolled my eyes. "Now I have fifteen CIDs. These guys were on the run too, so they were carrying what they could." I continued to pick through, taking the loot and splitting it up for the party while also collecting any bounties on materials for Silver Fangs.

"Were we killing them as part of Silver Fangs or Nagato Clan?" Des suddenly asked.

"Huh? Nagato Clan," I said distractedly as I moved the loot around. "Silver Fangs is a guild and the dungeon focused side of things. The Nagato Clan is personal and also where the assassinations occur."

"Then why is Silver Fangs getting some of our loot." She poked at my CID and my organization.

"Because they are closely tied, and I need to fill those metal orders," I sighed and remembered Crimson saying she'd help, but I didn't want to rely on her too much.

As if summoning her, Crimson barged into our suite. "Did I hear my guild master needing metal?"

"Yes, you did." Des smiled. "Do you have quests to turn in for him?"

"I do." Crimson swayed and bit her lip, suddenly shifting her demeanor. "Though, as a delinquent member of the guild, I ask for the guild master's mercy."

There was a game afoot, and I knew that if I played my part, Crimson would be happier. It wasn't much work to join in the game.

I grunted like an upset guild master. "Let's see if you have enough to pay your debt."

Crimson's smile was brilliant as she knelt before me and pouted like a worried guild member. "Guild Master, this is what I was able to scrounge up. It isn't nearly enough." She looked up at me through her eyelashes. "But maybe I can make up the remainder some other way, Guild Master?"

I kept up the smug grin on my face as she pumped her CID to mine. I stiffened a little at the sheer quantity of materials she'd just transferred into my inventory.

It was a small fortune, and I nearly lost my cool.

I knew that Crimson didn't need the bounties from the guild. The best way I could repay her was to continue with this game she was playing and let her have the moment.

I grabbed her hair at the roots. "This isn't enough. You'll need to pay with something else." It was obvious what she wanted, and if I was wrong, she could certainly correct me.

Des licked her lips. "She's a pretty one. I think you could find a use for her, Guild Master. That way she can stick around."

Red sparks crackled at the edge of Crimson's eyes as she looked up at me. "Guild Master, I want to stay with the guild. If you have any demand, please say it."

Crimson pouted up at me, clearly enjoying herself. It wasn't often that Crimson prostrated herself in this way. And with Charlotte and Des nearby, I hesitated.

But Crimson's blue eyes bore into mine, and I decided that she controlled where she asked for it and this was what she chose.

"Des is right. You are a pretty one, and those lips look very soft." I ran my thumb along her face and played with her lips.

She sucked on my thumb, closing her eyes and slowly rocking on her knees as she took my finger into her mouth and played with it.

I didn't need much imagination for my pants to start tenting. "That's passable." I kept my tone cold. "You'll have to work harder if you want to make up the deficit for this round of requirements."

Crimson swallowed and let go of my thumb. "I just want to stay in the guild, Guild Master. Let me help you." She unzipped my pants and coaxed out my cock.

It didn't need much help before it sprang free of my boxers.

Crimson cupped it with her warm hands almost reverently. "Tell me what you need, Guild Master."

"Lick it," I demanded.

Sparks were dangerously flying out of her eyes.

"Cancel Limit Break." I had her by the roots of her hair still, knowing the control from me would help her control the power. With Des and Charlotte nearby, I needed her to stay in control enough that they would be safe.

There was something deeper in Crimson's psyche that latched onto the control. My command made the troublesome ability wink out as she closed her eyes and breathed over the sensitive head, her tongue playing along it.

"Take it."

She took the head of my cock past her soft lips, and I held back a groan as I softly closed my eyes and enjoyed the sensation.

Des had gone quiet to the side, watching with rapt attention. Unless invited, I didn't think she'd join. Charlotte was quietly still making pancakes as if I wasn't getting a blow job in front of her.

"Take it all," I demanded, feeling her lips play with the head. I wanted to feel the back of her throat take me.

Crimson gulped as she worked to take my full length. She wasn't one to back down from a challenge and swallowed it twice before she got it deep in her throat.

I opened my eyes and saw her happily sucking on it, with her eyes closed, enjoying the moment as much as I was. My attention must have registered because she opened her eyes, staring into mine and moaning as she savored it.

She was putting on a show for me, so I leaned back against the counter, holding her hair and rocking her onto me at my pace. Seeing the Mistress Crimson going down on me made me twitch in her mouth.

The corners of her lips quirked up knowingly as she worked a little harder, swaying her hips and chest with the motion. I couldn't help but get an eyeful down her leather suit, where it opened up and exposed part of her cleavage.

Crimson popped off and kissed my tip while talking. "Would you like me to use them?" She cupped her chest with her hands pushing them together.

They were bigger now that they had escaped the body suit.

"I am inexperienced there, Guild Master, but you may take what you want," Crimson continued the act.

"Do it." I tried to maintain the aggressive demeanor of an upset guild master, but that was difficult with what was in front of me.

Crimson unzipped her suit a little more and took out a little bottle from her CID before squirting it in one of her hands and oiling up her chest and my cock. She pumped it slowly, playing her fingers along the head as she oiled me.

"Up," I demanded, feeling slightly impatient at her playing with me.

"Of course." She rose to the right height and pressed me between her chest, adjusting further to get the right angle and then squeezed her breasts together.

The soft flesh pushed in around me and then slid easily now that everything was well lubricated.

"Is that better, Guild Master?" she asked bashfully. "I want to stay in the guild."

"Wonderful. Now use your mouth too." I pushed her head down as she smiled.

Her mouth opened just for the tip. She ran her tongue over it before it disappeared back into her cleavage. She bobbed up and down on her knees, coaxing me further. Her soft, inviting breast lovingly crushed me between them. It disappeared between her creamy mounds as she looked up into my eyes, watching for my reaction.

I held onto her hair as my nerves ignited with pleasure. "Wonderful. Now, keep going, and you might just stay in the guild."

"Yes, Guild Master. Please, let me stay, mark me as one of yours." She moaned and stopped using her mouth. She used the pressure of her soft mounds to engulf me repeatedly, bringing me to the peak and then beyond.

I could feel myself crest over the peak, my body filling with satisfaction as I shot rope after rope of seed onto her face and chest.

Crimson had a big goofy smile on her face throughout.

When I'd finished, she wiped some of my seed off her cheek and popped it in her mouth with a moan. "You didn't warn me, Guild Master, or I would have swallowed it all." A little spark of red lightning danced over her eyes again.

Damn.

"Maybe I don't want to warn a guild member so delinquent on their dues," I countered.

"Of course. I'll make sure to get some more and see if I can't make the next quota." Crimson pulled out a rag and hesitated. "Can I clean myself up?"

I cleared my throat. "Get presentable and join us for breakfast."

Crimson wiped herself off and joined us on the seat, her submissive posture fading back to the Crimson we all knew. "Phew." She let out a breath. "I needed that."

"Ken's the one that got the relief." Charlotte handed us both a stack of pancakes.

"Oh, trust me, there's something about giving up control for a little while that is just... satisfying in a way that's hard to explain. I'm having to hold back Limit Break on my own, but when I give him control and he just tells me to stop, it stops. I'm not having to clench a mental muscle that I've been using for too long." Crimson dug into the pancakes.

"Huh." Charlotte hadn't really expected the response, and paused for a moment before she went back to working at the stove. The green-haired druid was quickly opening her mind to more things in bed.

"That was hot. What did you think, Ken?" Des leaned on my other side. The temptress had a wicked grin on her face.

"I... liked it. Even if it was a little sudden." I glanced at Crimson.

She shrugged. "I went out last night to get that stuff and to use some of my nervous energy. You were out on a mission last night. I knew that and knew you'd be okay, but I was a little nervous."

"Aww. She cares," Des teased her.

"Watch it," Crimson warned; the woman who could strike fear into entire races was back. "Ken's the only one who gets to tease me, because he's my guild master."

I patted Des on the shoulder to get her to lay off, while I wrapped an arm around Crimson's waist to hold her a little closer and comfort her. "Thank you for being nervous on my behalf and also for not stalking us last night. I'd hate to become reliant on your strength."

Crimson grunted her agreement, even if she didn't like it. "You need a hand to eat?"

Both of my arms were occupied. Crimson cut a slice of my pancakes and held it up for me. I took the bite while keeping eye contact with her.

Des was ready as soon as I finished with Crimson's fork. "Say 'ah.'"

I opened my mouth, but I didn't make a sound.

Des pouted and stuffed the fork in my mouth. "No fun."

"Maybe I like being in charge," I teased.

"Oh, you certainly know how to take charge in certain ways." Des grinned and glanced at Charlotte, whose face flushed bright red.

"Don't tell bedroom stories," Charlotte admonished Des. "Some of us don't walk into a room with other people and drop down to our knees."

"It's a little more fun to act with an audience." Crimson shrugged. "Besides, I don't think I have a shy bone in my body left."

"Fair. Fame will do that," I agreed and switched topics. "If you weren't following us, then I have an update for you on the panther."

Crimson raised an eyebrow. "You had two cats stalking you last night?"

"Huh? Two?" My mind caught up. "Felin was tracking us last night?" She had said she wanted to talk, but I had assumed that was more of her wanting to flirt rather than something important enough to follow us last night.

"Yep. She's a curious kitty. She was following you when you left the twenty-seventh floor to the twenty-eighth," Crimson explained, which also meant she'd checked up on me at that point too.

"Well, she didn't show herself. We killed fifteen Kaiming, and we got a little bit of information. It seems they are all gathering in this path of the dungeon to target me. But while we were on the job, the panther interrupted us. I fought it and a Kaiming soldier. Also determined that potions don't set off the panther. I lasted longer this time, even with the other adventurer coming at me at the same time.", I explained.

Crimson nodded. "Good, then it has similar rules to my own encounter. Did you get a chance to try Shadow Phase against the ability?"

"No." I shook my head. "Had to use it on the Kaiming's big attack. I tried to Shadow Ambush my way out of it, but that didn't work."

"So it's instant. No delay at all between activation and damage," Crimson worked out. "Damn powerful ability. Might be tied to what it'll give you too. As I fought the Lightning Phoenix, it started to use something like Limit Break, and its stats scaled really high after it lost half its health."

I nodded, knowing that the panther would probably have a few tricks up its sleeves at some point in the fight.

"It almost seems to pick a fight when you are busy," Charlotte said before glancing at Crimson. "Was it the same for you?"

"Huh?" Crimson leaned back. "No, I don't really think it interrupted me a ton. Though it often came when I was worn down.

My final fight... I sort of taunted the dungeon and took on a bunch of monsters after I was prepared for it."

"It came when you did that?" I asked.

"Yep, I'd fought it no less than a dozen times by then and chugged like twenty potions during the fight to match its rising stats. Used four or five consumable items too. Worth it. Limit Break is an incredible skill, and because of it, I was able to go deep into the dungeon on my own, let loose and wake up with multiple levels gained." Crimson grinned.

"I'd like not to lose control of myself." I shook my head. "But the panther seems tamer than the Lightning Phoenix."

"You need to call it something more interesting than 'panther'." Crimson's food had been wiped out and she leaned over on the counter. "The Shadow Panther. Oh... I've got it. The Smoke Panther."

"Black Panther?" I asked.

Des wrinkled her nose. "It's a little bland. I vote for Smoke Panther."

"Me too," Charlotte agreed.

"That's it then." Crimson smacked the counter, and Charlotte gave her another stack of pancakes. "Thank you, Charlotte."

"Need to keep you fed or you'll eat Ken," Charlotte joked.

Crimson burst out laughing while Des shook her head.

I felt a blush burn on my face and hid it by eating some of my own pancakes. "Crimson, are you sure that you don't want the bounty from the guild quests?"

She waved her hand. "I have a stupid amount of money on my CID and in the UG bank."

"UG has a bank?" I asked, avoiding the topic of how much money she had.

"Yeah, for the high levels," Charlotte answered distractedly. "At a certain point, you really shouldn't keep everything in your CID. Your grandparents probably have one for the Nagato Clan or the Silver Fangs."

I nodded along. That all made sense. Us lower-level adventurers just kept things in our CID or in our homes. Someone like Crimson could lose her CID in a big fight and lose quite a bit. It was far too valuable to just leave lying around in a broom closet.

"Okay, well as guild master, I feel obligated to offer you something, Crimson," I said.

Crimson smirked. "Yeah?" She played with her food as a thoughtful expression came over her. "I'm walking a fine line. You and your guild are progressing. I don't want to come around with all of the solutions to your problems."

"You just filled several months' worth of quota to the elves," I pointed out.

She waved her hand as if swatting my comment away. "You would have gotten that anyway. Keeping up the trade deal with the elves is very lucrative, but ultimately, not super consequential to your personal strength as an adventurer."

I agreed with her on that. Most if not all of the money made from this trade deal was going to go towards improving the Silver Fangs, including training facilities and bulking up the guild store so it could sell items to members at a discount over what the UG would offer.

"Just say you want sex for it," Des huffed.

"That's not really..." I trailed off as Crimson shifted and raised an eyebrow. "I mean, it feels cheap to turn it into a transactional part of our relationship."

"Oh." Crimson nodded. "Yeah, I can see that. We need to untangle some of this."

I leaned forward and kissed Crimson on the cheek. "You are a beautiful woman, and taking a woman as powerful as you and making you kneel in front of me was fantastic."

Her eyes sparked.

"I enjoyed it, did you?" I asked.

Crimson bobbed her head. "Yes. Like I said, you taking control is a release in itself. Though more would be nice, I had some of the dinosaur leather turned into cord. We can play with that another time though. Maybe one of these days once I have Limit Break under better control, we'll flip roles."

I raised an eyebrow.

"I'm a switch," Crimson said without any doubt. "Not entirely sure if you are."

"When you can control Limit Break, we'll experiment," I promised. "Until then, play what games you like, but it is not a transaction."

Crimson grinned, her face softening and her eyes growing wider. "Yes, guild master. I'll do my best to meet the next quota, but please go easy on me if I can't make it. You've given me such demanding tasks, and my poor body might not make it." She winked at me as she ate another piece of pancake suggestively.

CHAPTER 15

Crimson tapped her foot as the mud troll pulled itself from the ground with all of the summoners still alive. "Understand that doing more damage is always better. Healing and tanking require damage to be taken. Less damage is always taken when things die faster."

As if to demonstrate it, she jumped up to the top of the giant mud troll and grabbed its head with a single hand that flexed. She crushed the boss' head in a single squeeze, and the boss collapsed back into itself.

We were all back in the boss' room.

"Thus, damage is king." Crimson rubbed her hands together.

"Yeah. We aren't all freaks of nature," Helen said, crossing her arms as we all watched from the back of the boss room. "I feel like you just brought us here to flex."

Crimson shrugged. "So what if I did." She glared at the Harem Queen who was also present with Class B, as well as a few scattered teams from the fourth year that had made it to the area. "I'm going to remind all students at Haylon that there is to be no fighting amongst the students or I'll solve it."

"She only really solves things one way," Charlotte added loudly.

"The only way damage dealers know how," Des played along and spoke loud enough to intimidate the rest of the students that didn't realize Crimson was deathly serious.

The Harem Queen huffed but didn't speak up. "Those of you who still need to level, please come with me to the twenty-fifth floor and we'll grind out experience while I keep track of your party locations."

It seemed the Harem Queen was helping her class by allowing them to be more reckless and being there to catch them.

"The next team to face the boss, stick around," Crimson said, tossing her long braid over her shoulder.

"Do you have a revive?" I asked.

Crimson grinned. "Of course I do. Just because I don't fling spells doesn't mean I don't have mana, and at a certain point, even DPS can meet the spell requirement. Bet I could cast your portal." She winked.

The rest of the class moved out except for my new group.

Myrtle's bangs hid most of her eyes and she hunched over like she didn't want to seem tall in front of me. "So, this should be an easy party, but maybe we should go over the strategy again?"

The parties had been split into their DPS components and their tank/support component before we started rotating through. We figured keeping healers and tanks together would be the safest way to do the rotations.

"Right, kill the shamans. Des does fantastically at that. You can save some time by letting her damage over time finish them," I explained. "When it comes to the boss' abilities, Des and I can block that mudball."

Candice blinked and turned to me. "By using the Absorb ability?"

I nodded. "Yep. So we can stop the boss' slow debuffs from stacking on us."

"No wonder you did so well." Selene came up next to me and stood very close. "With my added damage, you'd probably fly through most content. With Harley stepping out for her healer harem, you might even need a new healer." Her eyes were the brightest green and captured my attention as she smiled.

Des leaned on my shoulder and smirked at Selene. "Our testing is quite brutal. We have an elf who has this whole concept of soul harmony that you have to pass."

"That's for sex and getting to pass skills, yes?" Selene asked excitedly. "I'm pretty good with souls." She wove a ghostly blue strand of magic in the air.

"Cut it out and focus on the boss fight," Candice sighed, the blonde being the one to keep us on track. "Ken, you are going to cause trouble for our organization."

"It's his incubus secondary class. Must be it." Selene bit her lip. "Or we could just accept it..." She trailed off under Candice's withering stare.

"Alright, we all know the fight. I can handle getting Myrtle out of trouble," Candice said.

"If we go past five, I'm just not fast enough," Selene said. "My healing is fantastic for a single target or for a large number of targets taking continuous damage, but I'm terrible at managing bursts on multiple targets."

Candice nodded. "I'll pick up the slack there if needed but we need to do this cleanly to help her, not to mention she can do more damage."

"We always want to do it cleanly," Des agreed. "Manage your part; Ken and I will bring the damage."

Candice nudged Selene. "Let's get into position."

Selene gave me a finger wave and stepped to the side to get ready. Her dress flowed around her and her heels clicked on the stone.

The trolls had already respawned, and the groups that weren't sticking around had left.

"Let's hit this," I said, nodding to Myrtle.

The tank braced herself before she charged forward, swinging a familiar looking mace with a muddy ball at the end.

Des transformed, surprising Selene. And I used [Metamorphosis] after I appeared behind a troll and got to work, my claws flashing with dark light as I carved into the monster.

A fireball landed close enough that I felt the heat prickle the hairs on the back of my neck, followed quickly by a second and third. Candice's fireballs started dropping in different spots, coating the whole group of trolls in explosions. She was clearly trying to compete with Des.

Selene kept on my target and switched with me, letting me determine when the target was low enough. Overall, we worked together well on the trolls. Then again, Des was one of the best damage dealers for this part, and they were letting us take the lead.

I stopped and looked around to realize that the last troll had died before the mud hand slapped down on the ground.

"The best team!" Selene shouted. "We got them all."

"We've also gotten some upgrades since last time. Focus up," Candice shot back. The blonde was weaving more spell sigils in the air.

I spun my new short sword and got to work on the boss as Myrtle got into position and started smacking away at the giant muddy troll.

When the troll shifted and raised its fist high into the air, I got a few more slashes in before activating sprint and rushing out. Myrtle stayed even longer than me before turning and kicking the ground.

As she pushed off, the ground began to shift, and she rode a slab of stone out ahead of the wave of mud.

"Kick ass!" Selene shouted. "That's the new movement skill?"

Myrtle flushed bright red. "Yeah, it works well," she said modestly before she rushed back in and a ball of mud slapped into her.

"It was perfect." I gave her a thumbs up, and the tank hid her eyes to focus back on the boss.

I could respect the level of work and repaid it with my own focus, pushing my forms as fast as I could. When the boss went to send a wave towards the ranged group, I slipped to the side with [Dodge] and kept up my forms as best as I could.

"That wasn't bad yourself. Was that Dodge?" Myrtle asked.

"Yeah. It's new."

"Must have cost a fortune," she said, making conversation as we fell into a steady rhythm on the boss.

I was embarrassed to say that Crimson had helped, not to mention it would be completely misunderstood. "Actually, I just got that lucky." Lucky that Crimson was able to reduce the price, but I didn't need to say that. Myrtle would likely misinterpret the statement and think it was a drop.

"Oh. Wow." Myrtle smacked the boss' attack with her shield glowing gold. "Damn lucky."

"Yeah." I felt a little bad about the fib. "It was incorrectly priced," I clarified.

Myrtle nodded. "That's an odd mistake. But the UG is a big organization and there're always mistakes. Good on you for taking advantage of it. Let's get out," she switched topics.

I noticed the boss shift, and cut it twice more before rushing out with sprint. Myrtle surfed on her slab of stone again before turning around and rushing back. I absorbed another mud ball.

"By the way, what do you see for the future of Silver Fangs?" Myrtle asked while maintaining her focus on the fight.

"Uh... What do you mean?" I stalled. Truthfully, I hadn't given the future of the guild that much thought. It was a guild, and it would grow with its members.

"Are you going to push deep into the dungeon or will it be some sort of farming guild? My father is a senior member of the UG," she said by way of explanation for her question. The UG was by and large a guild for farming and making money.

I let out a whistle. Myrtle was connected, then. "My interests are in diving as deep as I can in the dungeon." If I got an ability to rival [Limit Break], who knew what depths I could go to. "Though, every guild has a farming group."

"Of course," Myrtle hurried to agree. "I want to dive deep too."

The boss telegraphed another round, and Myrtle didn't delay this time, starting to jog out before riding the slab of stone.

I noticed that the boss moved slower than last time.

"We got this," I encouraged everyone as I waited out the wave of mud. "One more big push?"

"Next wave, I think." Des gauged the boss. "Next one for sure. Get back in there."

I used [Shadow Ambush] to charge forward as soon as possible and start tearing into the boss. My mind was elsewhere, though, wondering if I needed to work as the Guild Master of Silver Fangs more than I was.

"Back out." Myrtle startled me into action and I sprinted out.

"Thanks."

"Could tell you were either in the zone or completely out of it." She smirked and rushed back in after the mud.

We all popped our abilities, and the boss collapsed into the floor.

"Phew." Selene dramatically wiped at her forehead. "That was easy, but an easy boss is still intense."

"Yeah," I agreed. "Until we are Crimson level, we have to take them seriously. I think this was one of the stronger combinations. That and we know what to expect. Myrtle even got that new ability to help her get out of the way."

"Agreed." Candice nodded. "But that's why we went first. Let's go." She picked at the loot and handed me some of the mana crystals and a muddy sword.

I wasn't interested in the rest. A set of rusty chainmail would go to the UG and the reagents as well.

"Great job." Crimson clapped, reminding us of her presence. "I'll go get the next team. Get out of here and farm as this party for a while."

I glanced around at the group and nodded.

***

We were having another picnic among the troll forest.

"So, this panther would kill you if someone helped?" Selene asked, curling her dark hair. "That sucks. What if I buffed you and the next second it appeared? Would it come for me or just insta-kill you again?"

"Good question, and I have no clue. Maybe it would wait until the buff expired before it would come?" I suggested.

"That would mean you could keep it at bay with finding someone to give you a long-term buff," Candice suggested.

I shrugged. "I don't know if I want to stop it from coming. As long as someone can revive me, I'll take the practice."

Selene shook her head. "Crimson made sure I got a revive before we went to the boss today. Still, dying is rough."

"It is just a really big wound that a healer fixes," I said. "Not any worse than the shit that tanks go through." I pointed at Myrtle. "Tanks deserve more credit. I'd have nightmares of giant things always trying to squish me."

"Helps when they fail to squish you while you are awake." Myrtle nibbled daintily on a sandwich. For how large she was and that she was a tank, she was very delicate with everything else.

"True," I could only agree with her. Tanking held little appeal to me. I tried not to look up at Selene, who was biting her lips and twirling her hair while she watched me. "What about you, Candice? Was this the class you always hoped to get?"

The stiff woman glanced up from her own meal. "I was trained to be a caster of some sort since I was young. There was almost no doubt from my mother and her sisters."

"What about your father?"

Candice blinked. "That's right. You don't know. My mother just found a sperm donor with high credentials. I only had my mother and her sisters in the guild raise me."

"You were raised in the Violet Citadel?" Des asked, finishing her food.

Candice nodded. "Yes. I even spent some of my youth in their dungeon territory."

"Dangerous to bring a kid down there," I commented, but knew that their guild could likely manage it. The Violet Citadel was an all-women guild which focused heavily on magic. They weren't the very top of progression, but they easily had several parties at the fiftieth floor.

Candice shrugged. "It wasn't like I was part of combat. Instead, I was just kept in their semi-permanent buildings on the twentieth floor safe zone."

Ah, that made more sense.

"What about you?" Selene pushed to hear my story.

I scratched the back of my head. "My mother kept me from the Nagato Clan, and they only dove twice a year from what I can remember. They died when I was in high school, killed by Kaiming."

Selene got real quiet, a strange intensity creeping into her gaze. "Kaiming killed your parents?"

"Yep." I nodded. The anger was still there, but it was distant enough that I didn't give any outward sign. "Good news is that I'll see the fall of Kaiming. They really fucked up when they pulled that stunt at the end of last school year."

Des snorted. "Everyone got to see the terror that is Mistress Crimson for themselves. Even if the Harem Queen still tries to struggle against her as a teacher, I'm pretty sure she knows she's solidly number two."

"Especially after the way Crimson thrashed her." Selene's eyes practically glowed. "Ken, about you and Crimson..."

"He's her guild master." Des pressed her lips together to keep from smiling.

I rolled my eyes. "Crimson has a way to tell potential, and sees enough potential in me that I could match her one day," I explained. "That's why she's so interested in training me and why she's interested in me in general."

There was also the help I provided for Limit Break, but I wasn't going to get into that in this discussion.

"Oooh." Selene bit her lip. "I see. Well then, we all have our work cut out for us. As the inaugural members of Silver Fangs, we need to stick together so that we can tackle those deep challenges together."

"With Crimson too," Candice reminded her.

"Even better." Selene bit her lip. "That whip and those leathers? We'd get along."

Candice rolled her eyes, and I wanted to change the topic. "What about you, Selene? I think this exercise is about more than doing the boss together. We are going to all raid together and should learn more about each other."

"Oh you know. Things." Selene didn't give a straight answer. "Does it matter where I came from? I'm here now. My hobbies include ripping souls out of monsters and using them to heal you." She made a heart with her hands. "I also knit."

Yeah... that wasn't not concerning at all. "What happens when you use your soul abilities on people?" I was curious what that meant about the soul.

"A debuff that reduces the target's total mana for a period of time." She didn't hide the ability. "It's long known that abilities that affect a 'soul' injure people's ability to use magic for a time."

Candice nodded along. "Many say that mana and magic stats are tied to the strength of your soul. You improve them prior to adventuring with meditation and learning."

I nodded, using [Shadow Arm] to pick up my sandwich. "After you get spells, using them is by and far the best way. You can restore mana a little faster with meditation."

Candice watched the shadowy arm and nodded, making a rune in the air to produce more hot water into a pot she had ready for it. "Starting to use magic for mundane things is a great way to improve." She then made a second sigil in the air that buffeted each of us, removing the grime from a day of hard work.

Des' eyes sparkled. "You have a cleaning ability?"

"Yes, I do. There's no reason not to make my party members more comfortable if I can," Candice said.

Myrtle cleared her throat after finishing her meal and starting to pack up. "If we get going, my stomach will have settled by the time we fight our first pack of trolls. No need to clean up if we are just going to get dirty again."

"It packs on in layers. Then again, you are a mud knight." Selene pursed her lips.

"I'm an Earthen Guardian, not a mud knight," Myrtle sighed, sounding like she'd made that correction multiple times. "Let's go." She picked up her shield and worked it onto her arm.

"Follow the tank," Candice said, quickly disappearing the picnic blanket and various items into her CID.

Selene rose and linked arms with me. "Lead on, Myrtle. Ken, sticking with this party is like a beautiful walk in the park. Don't you think the trees here are nice? Much better than that bog we started in."

"Just wait until you see the next five floors," I said.

"Vampire castles?" Myrtle asked.

"No, that's another area we could go," I corrected her. "No, this is a land of sugar snow and candy monsters."

"Does it drop chocolate?" Selene perked up.

"Actually, it does." I was unsure why that was a big deal because all of the ladies perked up.

Des filled me in. "Bun-bun destroyed most of the candy because they were rabbit shaped and he was insulted. However, those chocolates sell well. Dungeon chocolate is delicious."

"If there's something that heals the soul, it's chocolate. Doubly so for dungeon chocolate," Selene agreed.

CHAPTER 16

I made it back to the spire and broke with our group for the day only to find Felin loitering outside our suite. "Go ahead, I'll catch up." I waved Des away.

"Actually, can I come inside?" Felin asked, stepping up to me and getting close enough that her tail could play over my thigh.

"Let her in. What's the worst thing that's going to happen? She'll steal your clothes?" Des laughed and lingered in the doorway for just a moment to tease me before heading in.

I glanced at Felin. "All my clothes are in my CID."

"Are your bedsheets?" she asked, her tail flicking back and forth. I glared at her.

"Kidding." She held up her hands. "It's an honor among Nekorians for one to covet the other's scent."

Somehow, I thought my bedsheets might go missing still.

"Do you have a bunch of men stealing your clothes?" I asked.

"No. I keep them in my bag." She tapped the bag on her hip, which was only the size of her fist but held a lot more. "Many would love to get my clothes, but I am not interested. So I don't leave them out to be coveted."

I let her inside the suite, feeling like I was making a mistake on the level of feeding a stray cat. I had a feeling she would be back for more. Still, I continued, "You said during the class that you had something to talk about?"

"Yes." Felin plopped down on the couch and stretched out on it, her arms pushing over her head and her back arching hard enough to strain her shirt.

"Make yourself at home," Des said, checking the rest of the suite. It seemed we were the first ones of our party to return. "Want something to drink? Beer, water, milk?" she asked the last one as a joke.

Felin nodded rapidly. "Milk please. It is so curious that you drink the fluids for another animal's child. Yet I too find it delicious. You have a trade agreement with the elves for metal, maybe you could make one with my people with milk. Business agreements are how you build relationships as humans, yes?"

I gave her a funny look. "Not really, at least not romantic relationships. Actually, the prevailing advice is to not date those you work with, except in the dungeon." I paused as I realized the contradictory logics.

"So when they are replaceable, don't date. But when your life depends on each other, fuck it?" Felin's tail playfully danced between her legs. "Did I use that phrase right?"

"Perfectly." Des came from the kitchen with a glass of wine in her hand and a tall glass of milk in the other.

Felin sat up and greedily accepted the milk, drinking it in one go and leaving a milk mustache on her face. "Ah. That really is delicious."

"We'll keep some in stock for you. Thankfully, Fayeth cooks enough that we had that." Des settled into the couch and sipped her wine.

I glanced at my empty hand.

Felin handed me her glass as if that was the answer. "More please."

"Okay, but this time you have to drink it slower." I went into the kitchen and poured her a glass while getting myself some wine. "Now, you wanted to talk about something that probably wasn't a milk trade."

"Right. You had something I hadn't seen before on your stat sheet," Felin said. "I wanted to dive into it in more detail."

"The Smoke Panther?" Des perked up.

I came out of the kitchen and handed Felin the glass of milk.

She slurped it slowly. "I don't know what it was. Smoke Panther was the beast that attacked you last night and disappeared?"

"So you were there," I said, confirming it.

"I was curious why you left in the middle of the night." Felin's tail curled around her waist. "You killed your own people."

"Not my people," I corrected her. "They are people who betrayed humans and opened a portal to the Naga in another part of the dungeon."

Felin bared her teeth. "I have heard of these Naga. A human assisted them?"

"Assisted them in invading an area of our world," Des added. "The Naga were removed after some losses, and those who helped the Naga are being hunted."

Felin nodded. "Sometimes the pride must cut itself if only to remove weakness." She sipped her milk. "That is honorable."

"There are a lot of humans," I added. "We don't all get along in the best of times. My family takes jobs to remove those who cause problems," I explained in simple terms.

"Strong," Felin said before hiccupping and lolling on the couch. "We should look at your tattoo."

"You up to that?" I asked.

"That milk really relaxed me," Felin admitted, spreading her arms out on the couch to keep herself steady.

Des watched with a smile behind her wine glass. "I think she's milk drunk."

Felin hiccupped. "No, I'm not. Just very relaxed."

"Uh huh." I didn't believe her for a moment. "Let's do the tattoo thing in the morning when you are feeling better."

I regretted those words as soon as they came out.

"Agreed. I'll just curl up here." Felin dismantled the couch and surrounded herself with cushions before curling into a ball in the middle of them.

"Well... that just happened." Des pointed with her glass of wine. "Wanna go have fun?"

"Debuff," I sighed. "Going to have to put you in another room if you get too excited."

Des pouted at me. "We need to get you working on your stamina. Maybe Selene will help you with that?"

I rubbed my face. "She was quite assertive, wasn't she?"

"Another member of the pride?" Felin murmured.

"No," I said.

"Yes," Des answered.

I glared at her. "Selene is not part of my harem."

"Yet," Des shot back.

Felin yawned. "Listen to the lady. Besides, what's the harm in taking more? You'll grow stronger with the more you take."

"More skills isn't exactly strength," I countered.

Felin peeked an eye open. "You have more to gain than skills." She yawned again and smacked her lips before rolling over.

I couldn't help but notice that she had finished that second glass of milk already and the empty glass sat next to the couch with a white layer still on the glass. "Thanks for the cryptic answers."

Felin stretched. "If I gave you clear answers, you'd kick me back out on the streets like a stray." She pulled a blanket over herself and promptly fell asleep.

I ran a hand down my face while Des was clearly holding back a laugh. "Don't say anything."

"I said nothing." Des smirked. "Inquiring minds will want to know what a Nekorian is doing on your couch tomorrow though. Just imagine Harley's questions."

I groaned. "Let's go back to talking about Selene."

"Ha." Des sipped her wine. "She's very into you."

"Yeah, well she's also a little crazy," I countered.

"All adventurers are a little crazy, or they wouldn't risk their lives for treasure in a giant, living creature that might eat worlds," Des referred to some wild theories about the dungeon.

Leaning back on the last cushion of the couch, I thought about Selene. "She's a solid healer that does damage as part of her kit. Though, she either spreads a small heal to everyone or a big heal to one target. Three people taking damage at the same time is tough for her."

"Easily built around," Des said. "Besides, if Felin wasn't just bull-shitting you, maybe you could get some stamina from her. You should be like me and grow stronger with it from your demon subclass. I mean, yours is a 'Demon Lord'. Even if mine was a higher level in the dungeon, it feels like yours is stronger."

I shrugged. "With how I won, it is holding back," I admitted. "He asked for smut magazines at one point to give me a little more, but that was just some stats."

"He's probably jealous of your little harem." Des tossed her hair. "What was his name again?"

I deadpanned. "Anyway. I need some more levels before I can take on a level forty-five boss on my own."

"Or a certain panther's ability." Des swirled her wine. "I wonder what its skill is going to be."

"Something that we'll figure out when I get it. Who's tomorrow's party?" I checked my CID for the schedule.

Des smirked. "Helen, Meredith, and Dolly." When I groaned, she smiled. "You could ask for Selene again."

"No. Besides, maybe fighting alongside Helen will help her chill out. I wonder what her mother did to her to screw her up so much?"

"Nah. It wasn't her mother, at least not directly. I'd bet money that it was a boy that she dated. Probably her first crush," Des spoke with a knowing smile.

"Do you know something?" I asked.

"You should ask her tomorrow." Des sipped at her wine. "Or you might be able to get it out of me after wearing me out." She winked.

I drained the rest of my wine. "We'd better get some rest if we are going to have to deal with Helen tomorrow." I glanced at the Nekorian sleeping on my couch. "And with her." I hooked a thumb at her as I walked towards my bedroom.

Des was right behind me, joining me in the bed with the promise not to try anything. Although, it was always tempting with her next to me.

*　*　*

Felin had acquired several more articles of my clothing somehow over the night and incorporated them into her couch nest in our living space.

"She's kind of cute like that." Fayeth had an apron on and was making some sort of savory muffin.

"How did she even get eight pairs of my clothing?" I crossed my arms.

"Maybe offer to let her have them back after you wear them again and refresh the scent. Otherwise, I don't think you are going to get them back," Des teased and poked at the couch trying to see if the Nekorian was still asleep.

Felin's ears perked up, and she went from asleep to awake so fast that I would have missed it if I blinked. "These terms are acceptable."

"Were you not asleep?" Des asked. "Could have sworn you were passed out."

"I was, but one is always aware of their surroundings. If you are not, you die young in the dungeon," Felin explained.

"She's not wrong." Fayeth decided that the muffins were done and pulled them out of the oven. "Breakfast is ready."

Felin shot out of her nest, throwing the clothes at Des. "I leave upholding our bargain to you as the leader of the females."

Des raised an eyebrow but accepted my clothes. "I'll buy you more." She saw me watching. "Maybe some that really accentuate those arms?"

"Let's eat breakfast." I made my way over to the counter where Fayeth was serving up her still steaming muffins.

"Do you serve these with milk?" Felin asked.

Fayeth gave her a flat smile. "Is that where all my milk went?"

Felin snatched a muffin and stuffed it in her face to avoid answering the question. Meanwhile, her tail danced mischievously behind her.

"I'll take that as a 'yes'." Fayeth handed me a muffin. "Don't scarf it in a single bite like a certain greedy kitten."

"'M 'ot 'itten," Felin objected around the muffin in her mouth.

"Uh huh. Swallow first." I smirked.

"'Ould go ea'ier 'ith 'ilk." Felin grinned.

Fayeth took a moment to decipher the question before she was able to reply. "There would be milk if you didn't drink all of it last night." She served Felin a glass of water to wash down the muffin.

"This is good." I nibbled on my own muffin that had bacon and potatoes in it. "Quite tasty. Thank you, Fayeth."

Fayeth pointed at me. "That's how you eat someone else's food. You need to learn some manners if you are going to stick around."

"Wait a second." When did we get to Felin sticking around?

Des leaned on me and distracted me for a moment. "Gotta get your measurements for some new shirts." She pulled out a measuring tape from her CID.

I paused and stared at Des. "I know what you are doing."

"Are you going to resist?" Des whistled as she started to measure me.

Crimson came in. "Oh, look what the cat dragged in."

None of us laughed.

"I'd been saving that one," she grumbled. "At least give me a chuckle."

"I'm more interested in how all of you just seem to be accepting her. Also, there's the thing with my stats?" I urged Felin, desperately wanting a new topic.

"Right." She wiped some crumbs off her face. "We need to do the ceremony and see it again."

Crimson sat down and glanced at Des. "What are you doing?"

"Getting Ken new shirts. Could you run these measurements to the UG and get him something dark?"

"Red?" Crimson countered.

"Dark red?" Des hesitated.

"Please don't get me a bunch of shirts that look like dried blood," I sighed. "Dark blue or black would be best." I realized by agreeing to the shirts, I was agreeing to the deal Des had made with Felin. The Nekorian wasn't bad per se, but she had just kind of appeared and inserted herself.

"Perfect," Des said and winked.

"Oh, go a lighter blue," Felin said. "Can you get something that matches my stripes? Maybe it has a white element to it too?"

"No white," I insisted. "White does not make for a good night operation. Dark blue, maybe take Felin's color and go a few shades darker but keep it in the same color family." I gave in if it meant picking what color my shirts were going to be.

"I can live with that," Felin agreed. "Now take your shirt off. We were going to look at your stats again."

I took my shirt off and watched as it promptly disappeared into Felin's pouch.

She pranced around me and brushed her hands down my back. "Oh Great One, please reveal this man's strengths to me." She pawed at my back and I could feel the ink moving down my back.

"Interesting, interesting." Crimson watched. "So the dungeon gives you an ability to do this?" she asked.

Felin nodded. "The shamans of our people can call on the dungeon to advise us."

"Yes, but is it an ability? I have something similar where the dungeon tells me details about things I look at," Crimson continued.

Felin grinned. "The Great One Favors you too."

"I am pretty awesome like that," Crimson shot back. "You didn't answer the question though."

"Yes, it is an ability. One that we closely guard and I cannot explain to you," Felin sighed. "Please even keep that a secret. My people have learned difficult lessons in the dungeon and we do not trust others easily." She cleared her throat. "What interested me in Ken's stats was this." She brushed on my back and I felt the ink shift again.

"Huh." The ladies all seemed interested, and Crimson leaned in.

"Don't leave me hanging." I looked over my shoulder, but I couldn't see my back.

"Marked for Trial," Des read. "The dungeon will send another trial your way in fifty-three hours. There's a countdown."

"Wait, we can see the timer?" I perked up. "That would go a long way towards preparing for it."

Felin waved on my back again. "This was the panther monster from last night. I don't think the countdown is exact. You just won't get attacked again until the timer is up. At least that is my read on it."

"Anything else you can tell me?" I asked.

"From this? Nothing." Felin brushed on my back, and I felt my tattoo go back to the dagger on the back of my shoulder. "From Nekorian history? I can say you must kill this trial before it kills you."

"You have record of something like this?" Crimson asked. "For humans, I'm the only one who seems to have finished their trial."

Felin snorted. "Taking the trial blindly will only result in death. There are great rewards, but The Great One only offers such rewards with a suitable amount of danger."

"Why does the dungeon offer these trials?" I asked.

Felin shrugged. "It is not our place to ask. However, those Nekorians which have completed the trial are able to stand with or above the shamans and take roles of leadership otherwise unavailable to those who cannot communicate with The Great One." Her tail brushed along me. "I knew you smelled full of potential."

"I have to kill it first."

"It will grow with your own level," Felin warned. "In Nekorian history, those who had succeeded have done so close to the level it first appeared. Those who have attempted to stall it and level significantly before facing the challenge have always failed."

"He's gotten some skills to deal with its abilities and is fighting it with Charlotte present so that he can learn and she can bring him back," Des explained.

"Good, good. You can't directly help him, but that is a significant way to help." Felin nodded.

Crimson was tapping her chin. "If it only scales with levels, then we need to push Ken's stats and dig into his mana specialization."

I nodded. "I've been working on both of those." Holding out my CID, I showed Crimson the progress I'd worked to gain.

"You can use the CID to activate two nodes on the shadow tree." Crimson hummed to herself. "Why are you holding off?"

"I was wondering if I'd regret it after getting whatever ability beating the Smoke Panther provides," I admitted. "It feels like whatever it gives me is going to define my combat style in a big way, like your Limit Break."

"Let's look at the most universal options then." Crimson seemed to think that was reasonable.

However, as we went through the options, another fact occurred to me. The way Felin talked, the Nekorians currently had, or at the very least had at some point, people with Limit Break level skills. Most people considered the dwarves and Nekorians to be weaker than humans. If what she said was true, we could be very wrong.

CHAPTER 17

T he next two days went by smoothly, or at least, smoothly enough that I found myself walking the safe zone with Des as a way to calm down on a rare day off. With Felicity's party down two members, there were three people sitting out every day, and today was our day.

I was now aware that the timer on my next panther trial was about to run down. Somehow knowing when I could expect it to show made my anxiety even higher.

The center of the safe zone where the three races came together was a lively market full of all manner of goods. Dwarves stood under thick stone buildings with their arms crossed as if they were reluctant to even be selling to humans, like it was beneath them. They were what was expected of a dwarf. Most looked like stocky humans with thick, corded muscle showing for what little of their bodies wasn't covered in their thick beards.

I wondered if they were all male, or if the females had beards too. So far, I hadn't seen one that looked young or female. They were all wrinkled around the eyes, with beards that covered most of their face and chest.

"This says it will calm people. Think we should get Helen a truckload of it?" Des teased.

I chuckled and walked past the Nekorian herb vendor. "There's not enough herbs in the world to calm Helen." Our boss attempts with her had been rough.

Thankfully when it came to a boss fight, she was a consummate professional, but her attitude left something to be desired. There was a story behind her clear issues, I was sure.

Des avoided the dwarves and kept stopping at Nekorian stalls.

The woman in the current stall leaned over her fruits. "Well hello, little girl," the scarred Nekorian growled. "Are you interested in my fruits?"

Where Felin seemed more like a tiger, this woman had tawny hair that had gone gray years ago. One of her ears was heavily notched, and though she showed off her cleavage, it felt more like she was showing off the large scar that rested between her breasts.

"Those melons look delicious," Des said, meeting the woman's eyes. There was a spark of mischief in Des. She knew the joke wouldn't get across to the Nekorian who barely seemed to have a grasp of English. "I was wondering, if we had a Nekorian guest over, what would be something that they would enjoy? I want to make an effort."

"A Nekorian guest?" the woman asked and glanced at me with a huff in the air. "I smell her on him. Step up closer. My nose isn't what it used to be and there are plenty of stinking beards in this place."

A dwarf who'd been passing by jerked to the side at her comment. "Is a wet cat insulting our dignified selves?" It almost felt like he'd been standing there waiting for a reason to interject.

The Nekorian looked bored as she leaned on her hand. "Shoo, you are just pests. Don't you have orders to carry out?"

The dwarf puffed himself up to be taller; it had little effect. "You know nothing of the dignity of our people. It is an honor to serve your clan."

"Uh huh." The Nekorian smirked. "I know that you are infertile and make no decisions for yourself. Move along, little worker drone." She waved her hand.

The dwarf grew irate and grabbed a dagger on his belt.

The Nekorian didn't even seem to register him as a threat. Soon enough, the dwarf huffed and moved on after giving each of us a scowl.

"You called him a drone?" Des asked, batting her eyelashes. "We don't know much about the dwarves."

The Nekorian motioned for me to come closer. I stepped up, and she huffed over me.

"Felin?!" she said, her eyes growing wide before she squinted and made a sly smile. "That girl is a willful one."

"Tell me about it. I'm running out of clothes," I sighed. "Fruit," I kept us on topic.

The woman relaxed significantly and sniffed at me a few more times. "You do smell good. She's found a good one among the humans. If it's not too personal to ask, who are you among humans?"

"Ken Nagato." I held out my hand. "Guild Master of Silver Fangs, heir to the Nagato Clan and protégé of Mistress Crimson."

Apparently, even the average Nekorian knew of Crimson because the stall owner perked up at the name. "Hmm. Prestigious. Honestly, all of these fruits are just common fare that you humans don't normally see, and I make a steal on the novelty. You need quality to keep a lady like Felin content." She dug around under her stall. "Something like this." She held out a piece of fruit that looked like a star.

"I'm assuming that's not cheap," I said.

"Free for Felin's little lover." The Nekorian handed it to me. "Tell her Risha sends her luck for kittens."

I choked on the words. "No kittens please. I'm a young man."

"Oh. Do you not have them until you are old? Seems hard on the back, but not my place to judge another." She turned to Des as if talk of kittens was the same as talking about the weather. "As for the dwarves, we've come into conflict with them in the past. They are trouble."

"But to call him a drone?" Des prompted.

"There's a dungeon monster, a six-legged insect that builds large branching nests. They resemble a creature on our world," the Nekorian explained.

"Ants?" I asked.

"That must be it," Risha continued. "If they are anything on your world like they are on ours, they get into everything. No building is secure from them. Dwarves are much like them in that they get into everything, but also they have a hierarchy. Those you see here." She gestured at the square. "The lowest of the low. They are genderless infertile dwarves."

"Wait, like ants, so do they have a queen?" Des hissed, trying to keep her voice low and failing slightly.

"Yup, though they are organized into clans rather than hives. Felin can and would tell you more if you asked, at least judging by the scent she's leaving on you. The dwarves are split up into some organization I don't understand, but there are queens and soldier dwarves. All of them are bearded pests. Once they move into an area of the dungeon, they swarm it and you can't get it back," Risha explained.

"Huh," Des mused.

I had thoughts too, considering that humans had completely struck out in talks with the dwarves. The Nekorians were quiet about much, but at least they were present and willing to talk.

Now I wondered if the dwarves weren't just unwilling, but unable to talk to the UG. If their hierarchy was that rigid, humanity likely hadn't talked to anyone who could really negotiate or speak for their people.

"Thank you for the information," I said, smiling at Risha.

"Not a problem. Just keep Shaman Felin happy and it'll all be good." She winked. "A happy woman makes for a happy pride, doubly so for a shaman." She waved us off.

Des hooked her arm in mine and pulled me away. "You have some pull with the Nekorians now that you smell like a certain cat girl. Maybe I should see if she'll cuddle tonight."

"Paws off," I joked.

Des put her arms behind her back and skipped a step to catch up. "I'll be patient." She let out a put-upon sigh. "At least you picked your own shirt colors."

"Otherwise, Felin was asking for white. White, Des." I shuddered.

"Don't be a drama queen," Des teased. "We were never going to put you in white." She looked at me out of the corner of her eyes, and I caught sight of the heart-shaped pupil hidden behind her hair.

I slipped my hand around her waist. "The day is ours. What do you want to do next?" I gestured towards the view in front of us.

A voice grumbled at me, "Get out of my way."

I looked to find a dwarf. I really couldn't tell one from another, and had no idea if this was the one from earlier at Risha's stall or if he was just another grumpy dwarf.

"Go right ahead." I didn't think I was blocking the dwarf's way.

"No, you get out of my way," the dwarf demanded, planting himself in front of me.

Now he was just being unreasonable.

"The street isn't even that busy." Des waved the dwarf around.

At a certain point, I felt like the dwarf was picking a fight and actually stepping aside was just going to get me kicked in the shin when he started the fight anyway.

The dwarf glared at me, and the moment became a standoff.

At the same time, more dwarves seemed to flow from the surroundings until there were over a dozen dwarves glaring at me while I stood in front of the dwarf that unreasonably demanded I move.

"You are all welcome to pass me by." I gestured to the side. People were getting out of the way. Now, it was like we were standing out in the open. The dwarves could pass us by on either side with yards of clearance.

"Is there a problem?" a man in a UG vest asked, hand on his weapon. He clearly knew the answer to his question already.

I met his gaze with a hard determination of my own.

"This human will not move for us," one dwarf said.

The UG man raised an eyebrow at me. "Seems like there is plenty of room. Besides, he's not someone you get to demand things from."

The dwarf eyed me, and I was growing more sure that it was the same one from Risha's stall. That was the only reason a dwarf had to be upset with me. A knife appeared in his hand as he squared off against me.

"Hold on now." The UG man was backed by other UG representatives who had appeared to reinforce him.

The dwarves didn't care and threw themselves at me with hollow eyes of people prepared to kill at the ultimate cost.

I stepped back, parrying his knife, my own appearing in my hand as my sword appeared in the other, and I cut him deeply in the shoulder before snapping a kick into his knee. The knee was supposed to give, but instead it felt like I'd kicked a brick wall.

Using the force, I pushed off him and created more distance. The other dwarves all pulled simple weapons and attacked the closest person to them.

"Let me." Des' pulled back her hair and tried to [Charm] the charging dwarves, but it had no effect.

It was suddenly like we'd kicked a beehive. Dwarves were throwing themselves at anyone and everyone within reach.

I used [Dodge] and avoided another strike from the lead dwarf before countering and cutting into the dwarf with [Dark Strike]. My blade cut into him, but it was like trying to cut through boiled hide rather than skin. Even then, it was like steel wire instead of muscle once I broke through.

The dwarf continued after me as if he didn't have a nasty gash on his bicep.

I paused for a second, wondering if I was just about to start a large-scale incident between the dwarves and humans, but the knife nicked my cheek and the pain brought clarity.

This guy wasn't going to stop until one of us was dead. He'd been aiming for my throat.

Des hit him with a flying tackle. He didn't go down at first, but she threw her weight to the side and took him down to the ground where her dagger appeared, and she found the same difficulty piercing the dwarf that I had.

I noticed that each of the dwarves had gone for melee weapons.

On a hunch, I activated [Shadow Arm] and [Mana Burn], latching it onto the dwarf in front of me. It burned for just a second before the dwarf was out of mana.

I activated [Mana Implosion] on the dwarf. The blue bead didn't find any mana and immediately ripped into the center of his stomach before exploding out. The shockwave caught me, and I jumped to ride it out as it tore the side off a dwarf next to him.

Des rolled to her feet. "Were we supposed to kill them?"

"He had a knife aimed for my neck." I shrugged and watched as the UG representatives piled on, cutting down the dwarves as the

Nekorians looked on with feigned disinterest that only reminded me of a housecat.

It was oddly clinical as the UG wrapped up and the other dwarves in the area continued to scowl.

"Ken Nagato?" The UG man who had intervened at the beginning stepped up to me and held out his hand. "Kyle with UG security."

"Well, Kyle." I shook his hand. "I think I need a crash course in Dwarven diplomacy because it felt like that guy had it out for me and I don't even think I looked at him wrong."

"Yeah, we can—"

He was cut off as a boom sounded above us, and I didn't even have to look to know that Crimson was falling through the air. Sure enough, she landed hard, blowing away a few of the corpses and a nearby stall.

Kyle swallowed. "Crimson. We were just wrapping up."

She didn't even look at him, instead scanning the area with bright blue eyes and then her gaze flickering to a nearby dwarf. "I will end your clan if you try something like this again."

The dwarf only stared back at Crimson for a long moment before turning back and disappearing into one of those stone buildings.

She turned back to me and Kyle

"I'm afraid that we need to take Ken in for a debriefing." Kyle fidgeted under Crimson's gaze.

"Alright, he's my guild master, though, and I'm going with him. That's his right."

Kyle didn't know what to say to that. No doubt me being Crimson's guild master seemed ridiculous to most adventurers. A level twenty-something student at Haylon being in charge of the Mistress Crimson. His eyes were slowly getting wider; I was afraid they were going to fall out of his head.

"It's a formality," I tried to get his eyes to go back into his skull. "But I think regardless that we can accommodate Crimson's request, can't we?"

"Yes of course." Kyle nodded. "The recent memo... uh... never mind."

"Smart man," Des commented. "Let's go question Ken." She inserted herself into all of this. Not that I thought she'd let herself be left behind.

The man turned around to lead us and moved quickly. The rest of the UG vested adventurers made way for him and then scurried to the edge of the street when they saw Crimson.

I wondered what was in the memo he'd started to reference, but decided it didn't matter.

Kyle led us over to the UG area of the safe zone, into a shop and then into a back room that had thick steel plate walls. "Alright. Here's the Zone Director."

He gestured at a woman in the room. She had blue hair that was pulled back in a tight ponytail with a pair of spectacles on her face as she tapped on a laptop. Otherwise, she looked like a typical businesswoman in a gray blazer and white shirt.

But as I studied her more carefully, I got the feeling she was no slouch when it came to the dungeon. A person didn't get put in charge of a safe zone without a fair amount of strength. Especially not a safe zone that connected to two foreign races.

She looked up from her laptop. "Pleased to meet you." At the very least, she didn't let Crimson intimidate her. "This is regarding the situation with the dwarves?" She took her glasses off and crossed her legs while she sat back in the office chair.

The room was fairly bland. The only decorations were a single picture frame facing her and a succulent that looked like it was fresh from the store.

"They initiated an altercation with Ken Nagato. The situation was cleared prior to Crimson's arrival," Kyle reported swiftly, standing at attention.

The Zone Director glanced at Crimson while playing with her glasses. "I'm afraid I need to have this conversation with Ken."

"He's my guild master." Crimson smirked and sat down across the table from her. "Guidelines say a guild master is allowed two members to accompany him to any meeting."

"For safety purposes. There is no need to be concerned for his safety," the Zone Director replied calmly.

"That's just what a Kaiming assassin would say." Crimson smirked. "I think I'll stay and ensure his safety."

"I see." The director put her glasses down, coming to a decision. "Your concern is valid." She shifted slightly in her office chair to focus on me. "Please, have a seat." She gestured to the seat next to Crimson. "This might take a moment."

Des leaned against the wall next to the door and stayed quiet with Kyle.

"So, the dwarves?" I asked.

The Director steepled her fingers. "Yes. You are in a delicate situation, and we are keeping track of you, Ken. Currently, you are a bridge to the elves, and I understand a Nekorian shaman has been staying with you the last few days?"

"It's more like I fed a stray cat and it now sleeps on my porch," I deadpanned.

"Either way, your relationships with two other races in the dungeon is of interest to us. It is also a delicate situation, because to reach your full potential, we cannot swarm you with guards, but we are watching you in this safe zone, for reasons you've probably already surmised."

I raised my hand. "Actually, I have not understood why the dwarves attacked me, assuming that is what you are referring to."

"To put things lightly, the attack means you've been marked by a dwarf," the Director said. "What do you know of dwarves?"

"That they are apparently like ants?" I hesitated.

The Director frowned at me. "Like ants?"

"That's what a Nekorian said. Those on the streets were the lowest caste. She called them drones and said that dwarves were organized like ants," I quickly repeated some of what Risha had told me.

The Director steepled her fingers and leaned back, swinging from side to side in her chair. "Truthfully, we have only come into minor conflicts with the dwarves while making little headway diplomatically. There have been several instances of humans being marked through means unknown to us. The dwarves then start to act irrationally without heed for themselves and attempt to kill said marked person."

"Wonderful." I rubbed my face. "So you know nothing except that I'm in danger now? Does that about catch me up?" I didn't need all dwarves to want to attack me on top of everything else I was dealing with. I was already on my guard with Kaiming; this was just more fuel for the fire.

"There is no need to become upset. We will monitor the dwarves closely and ask that you refrain from engaging in any activity that would bring you close to them," she stated calmly.

"Like diving the dungeon?" I grumbled.

"No. The dwarves thankfully stick to their own areas of the dungeon and only connect to humanity on two safe zones. We would ask that you refrain from public spaces in the safe zones and certainly avoid Dwarven areas. My daughter said that you would understand logic," the Director continued.

I raised an eyebrow. "Who's your daughter?"

"Selene," she replied, making me look her over more closely. She showed some of her first real emotion, smiling as she noticed my eyes. "Selene takes after her father more than me."

"Oh. Where's he?" I asked politely.

"Prison," the Director didn't miss a beat.

Well, now I felt like a dick. I cleared my throat. "Anything else that you need?"

"Actually," the Director continued. "We would be very interested in understanding your current engagement with the Nekorian Shaman Felin. And we have a few other questions for you as well."

CHAPTER 18

I had not been aware that 'a few other questions' would end up taking hours. After talking to Selene's mother, I felt like someone had wrung my brain dry of information and then continued to twist and squeeze it for more in frustration.

The class was now gathering back up for the night. It was determined that we should embrace the idea of mixing our parties and go out as a group tonight to the UG tavern on the safe zone.

Penelope blushed as she stepped up to Des and me. She folded her hands in her lap. "Please take care of me for the evening." The woman wore a silver dress that shimmered slightly, and she had done her hair up.

"No problem at all. We'll go do the boss tomorrow, so we should really mingle before that happens. Otherwise, it would be like when Helen used Ken as a target for her ability and got him hit by mud." Des was wearing a rather thin dress at the moment.

As we stayed within the UG area of the safe zone, there was no need to be prepared for anything other than a good time. We were going to be taking on the boss with Penelope tomorrow, and she was determined to spend some time tonight to 'forge bonds' among our temporary group.

However, Meredith had disappeared with Harley, and Dolly was currently teasing Regan about something from their earlier fights.

So I was left primarily with Penny and Des.

"So, uh. What do you drink?" Penny asked as our group sat down at the tavern.

Selene came rushing over, drawing my attention. "You met my mother today! She didn't do anything untoward, did she?"

"No?" My answer came out as a question because of how ridiculous her phrasing had been. "She was rather stiff."

Selene sat down and pushed Penny aside even if the blue-haired frost knight was a head taller than Selene. The soul weaver's personality engulfed her. "That would be most people's first impression. Mom's a bit of a wild card sometimes. At least, that's what dad would say."

At the mention of her dad, it got awkward.

"Ah shit. I know that face. Everyone gets weird when they know he's in prison." Selene sighed and rested her cheek on her hand. "Now I have to tell the story, don't I?"

"No." I waved my hands. "Please if it is private."

"Do tell." Des grinned. "Was it a financial crime?"

Selene bit her lip. "It would be wonderful if it was so mundane. No, he burned down a guild and killed all of their members in a very public display."

Penny sat forward. "It's really hard to send high-level adventurers to prison. It must have been very public."

"Oh yes. He impaled the whole guild beside the highway for one of them spitting on my mom for doing her job." Selene nodded. "He agreed to go because my mother forced him to prove a point. It's okay though because he won't serve too long. Just long enough for it all to leave the public discourse and he can be set free without making the news. I don't want to talk about it, and don't give me that look again."

I held back a shudder as I knew exactly who her father was, the world called him 'the Impaler'. Suddenly, I was more than a little wary of Selene and the father that lurked behind her.

"Selene, did you see the latest chapter of 74 wives?" Des leaned in with a giant smile and thankfully shifted the topic.

"Oh my god yes." Selene bounced in her seat and pulled out a bottle of wine. "That was the first time my character got a chance in the story and it was fantastic." She blew a chef's kiss. "You seducing Ken and then him lining me, Candice, and Myrtle up to go through one after the other was just perfect."

"You know, if the writer is going to do scenes like that for each of these new parties, some characters could get their first. Like you, Penny." Des pointedly watched the frost knight's reaction.

"Ye-yeah," Penny stuttered and fidgeted with a dress that clung to her in all the right places. I'd never seen her out of armor before. "The author seems to overlook our group quite a bit. It probably won't happen."

"Not with that attitude," Des shot back.

"You had all those notebooks in your room. If you wanted to tell a different story, you should." I smiled at Penny.

She blushed all the way to the tips of her ears. "Yeah..." Penny said noncommittally.

I guess I shouldn't put her and those notebooks on the spot. She must be shy about whatever she writes or she would have shared it with the world.

"Yeah, Penny. You should write something," Selene encouraged her.

"Don't push her if she's not ready," I admonished Selene. "That's how you wind up in prison."

Selene gasped and covered her mouth.

For a second, I thought I had really fucked up with that joke. She had an interesting sense of humor and I'd hoped to hit it.

But then she started laughing behind her hand and couldn't hold it back. "You made a joke about my father being in prison?!"

"You wanted me to not be bothered by it. What better way to demonstrate that than to make a joke of it?" I asked, relieved that I hadn't crossed a line and didn't have to sleep with my eyes open tonight.

"Perfect." Selene made an okay sign with her fingers. "So, what about you and the kitty cat?"

"Which one?" I asked.

"Oh, not the Nekorian. That would be offensive, right?" Selene checked with Des.

"Yes, though Felin is pretty chill if you want to make a joke about it," Des explained. "So you mean the panther?"

Selene nodded emphatically. "Everyone wants to know what sort of crazy skill Ken would get. My mom already put together all the research that Crimson has done in the past to guess this is something like how she got Limit Break."

I blinked, not quite realizing that the UG was so on top of the recent events.

Penny seemed to relax as the topic shifted further away from her writing something and into adventuring. "Yeah, it seems to be a difficult monster."

"You might get to see it again tomorrow. The timer is up. It'll attack again soon." I leaned back in my chair as Des went to get us drinks. "We will see what the conditions are for it to attack, but it tends to come while I'm busy."

"Such an interesting thing." Selene leaned on the table. "That it just comes and attacks only you. I think you'll get it soon though."

"Thanks. We are working on some strategies, but my goal this time is to survive and see any additional phases to the fight," I set my own expectations.

The doors to the tavern banged, and I glanced over my shoulder as several upperclassmen stormed in and scowled at our class.

"Trouble," Selene - sing sang.

Des came back with an armload of drinks. "Do we drain them to get ready, or hold them at the ready to throw in their faces?"

"Neither." I made eye contact with one of the upperclassmen and didn't back down, taking a slow sip of my beer. "They don't get to cause us problems. It isn't as if they are stronger than us. Normally, they'd be double our level, but we pushed hard this summer. They might have done some extra, but they weren't getting drilled by the Silver Fangs this summer."

The girl I was keeping eye contact with motioned to the ladies behind her as she moved over to our table. "You must be the infamous Ken." She held out her hand. "Ren, Class President of the Seniors."

"Nice to meet you. I think Candice is our class president," I said and sipped my drink.

She pulled up a chair. "We can agree that it doesn't matter much. You're Crimson's protégé, so you get to make decisions too."

I shrugged. "My focus is on diving the dungeon. Talk to Candice." I searched the tavern and pointed at the blonde. "That's the one. She'd love to talk about any class-to-class politics."

Ren held her hands up in the air. "Fine. Just wanted to say watch your back. There were a few locals that we know that warned us someone's looking for you."

I nodded. "Thanks for the tip."

Most likely, it was Kaiming. And most likely, they already knew exactly where I was. If they hadn't already, the earlier situation with the dwarves would have made plenty of commotion.

"You guys got a raw deal," I talked about the elephant in the room.

Ren raised an eyebrow. "The requirement to graduate? We were pretty pissed at the announcement, but several pointed out that if we don't push ourselves, then we'll just end up joining a guild and getting passed by the next year and the year after that."

The other seniors nodded along.

The logic was fairly reasonable of them and quite possible. If they didn't stay ahead, the guilds might not kick them to the curb, but they'd certainly get shoved into low-tier groups in the guild, if not just sent to low-level areas to farm valuable gear as sort of a newbie tour.

And that would only push them further behind.

The one great thing about all of the class joining Silver Fangs was that we'd all be on the cusp of progression for the guild. Meaning, we'd be pushing as deep as we could go from the beginning. We had no reason for the nonsense like doing farming duty for a few years that some guilds would put their fresh recruits through.

While I was thinking, Ren was watching me closely.

"So, me and some of the girls were wondering if Silver Fangs is still recruiting?"

Her question caught me completely off guard.

"Oh," I stalled. "Sorry, I wasn't expecting that." I almost deflected, but then again, I was the guild master. "I don't see a reason why we wouldn't take quality members into the guild. We are all pushing deeper, though, and we don't have the foundations that most guilds have today."

"Sort of skipped a generation," Ren agreed. "Besides, don't sell your guild short. Crimson has joined it, and that's enough to immediately compete with the highest-level guilds out there. Except you don't have any intern bullshit."

The other girls nodded along with her.

"If you can put in your applications through the UG, I'll have someone review them." I raised my glass of beer. "Tonight, though, I'm off duty."

Ren nodded at that and uncrossed her legs, signaling for the others to back up. "Alright, see you later then. I'll talk to Candice about the school stuff."

Des watched them go, leaning on me possessively. "You know, if you keep just letting in girls to the guild, people are going to start making funny assumptions."

Selene chuckled. "Let them. Maybe he'll make 74 wives a reality one of these days." She tried to clink her glass to Penny's, but the taller woman was too busy blushing and looking into the middle distance. "Earth to Penny?"

"Sorry." She shook her head. "Just imagining how wonderful Silver Fangs will be in the future. It also isn't all girls. There were a number of men from the clan that were part of the guild."

"Yeah, but they are in the background. Not here drinking with Ken." Selene sipped her beer, her green eyes growing brighter in the light of the tavern. "To Ken." She clinked her glass to mine.

"To Silver Fang's future." I tipped my glass in her direction and took a tiny sip.

Selene pouted. "Des, it's your turn. And, Ken, you need to take a respectable drink and not something like you're afraid to get drunk."

Des raised her glass high, shouting to the whole place. "To Silver Fangs and our fearless Guild Master, Ken Nagato. Come on over and give him a toast." She grinned over her glass as she clinked it to mine and took a long drink.

I matched her. "You are trouble."

***

The next morning hit me like a truck.

"Uggg." I tried to roll over and failed, but the room decided to spin for me. As I moved, I found myself wrapped in several warm limbs.

Last night had gotten a little hazy. First, Selene and Des had goaded everyone to come toast to me, which included taking a drink with each one. My beer almost magically refilled itself, seeming full every time I looked back down.

The night fled past in a hazy blur of drinks and laughing. Selene had gotten handsy and Penelope had eventually pulled her away. Des had brought me back to our room, and I vaguely remember Charlotte healing me before I passed out.

I was on the couch with cushions piled around us. Felin slept on top of me with Des, Charlotte, and Fayeth.

"Awake?" Crimson asked, coming out of the kitchen with an apron over her leather bodysuit. "Guild Master, you should really go easier on the celebrations." She held a hand out for me.

I took it and she pulled me out of Fayeth's snuggle and put me on my feet. "Thanks." I held onto her for support.

She handed me a steaming mug. "Tea with a poison resistance potion mixed in."

The first sip hit me and washed away much of the next day's grogginess. "Should have taken this last night."

"Where's the fun in that?" Crimson sauntered back into the kitchen, and I followed behind her. "Though, you could have taken it before you went to sleep and slept a lot better. With how dangerous adventuring can be, it is good to take the time and have fun some nights."

"Just keep poison resistance potions stocked?" I asked.

"Duh. I'll hand some out to the rest of the class. Last thing I need is for you all to die because you decided to be college students for a change and have a party." Crimson clicked her tongue. "I mean, most of the kids staying on the surface are getting a level or two so that they can do keg stands with the extra strength and stamina."

I sat down at the counter while she went back to chopping up various ingredients. "Well, it was a nice night. I think we all sort of needed that."

"Compared to my time at Haylon, you guys are pushing hard. I was at this point only a year after graduation, not my second year at Haylon." Crimson started the process of her cooking where she took out a large carton of eggs and started cracking them two at a time into the skillet.

"Not like we have much of an option," I stated. The Naga attack had changed everything.

Crimson shrugged. "You do have an option. You've chosen to step up and ready yourself for the challenge. Don't go pretending that you don't have the determination that you do." She raised an eyebrow at me and held my gaze until I answered.

"You're right. I want to dive deep in the dungeon, to revive my grandparent's guild, and live up to the potential that you and my party see in me." I met her gaze head on.

She smirked and leaned forward enough for me to see that her suit was heavily unzipped behind the apron. "Guild Master, I'll follow you to the bottom of the dungeon, just take good care of me, okay?"

I stood up, catching her chin with my hand and planting a firm kiss on her lips that made sparks dance out between her closed eyelids. "Thanks for pushing me, even in this way."

"You aren't some person being carried by the wind. You are the wind. I'd say it's all the ladies in the class that are being carried by your drive. Just remember that and let them let loose from time to time like last night. Invite me next time." She winked.

I thought about Crimson showing up at the tavern last night and getting tipsy enough to start showing public displays of affection. Gosh, the whole place would become a rumor mill of epic proportions if that happened.

"Oh, by the way. That reminds me. Bellaire contacted me asking where we were in the dungeon now." Crimson was mixing everything. She'd filled it to the point that the pan was nearly overflowing.

I blinked at the name of the pretty influencer that we'd met on the seventh floor. She'd been getting power-leveled by another guild when we had run into her. "What does she want?"

"We've been messaging on and off. She's really looking to make a career change." Crimson started another pan of her egg creations. "She wants to apply what she's learned as an influencer to a broader scale and try to do PR for a guild. I told her there was a fledgling guild master who could probably use her services."

I deadpanned. "Besides the fact that I probably can't afford her services, why would I agree to this?"

"For one, she's hot." Crimson pointed a spatula at me. "For another, she actually seems pretty damned good at what she does. I know most just sort of see a pretty face when they look at her, but she's done a hell of a lot to get as far as she has. If she could apply half of that to Silver Fangs, I bet she'd be a huge boon."

"I'll take point two as the valid one."

Crimson nibbled on a carrot that fell out of the second pan. "Well, she's power-leveled to forty and we are two students down. Felin will take one spot. I was hoping your favorite princess would take the other, but I need a backup. A good portion of her payment will be helping her level."

I rubbed my face. "Is she already coming?"

"Yep. I really thought you'd be more excited." Crimson took the lid off the first pan and emptied her calorie laden creation that was just a two-inch thick disk of vegetables and meat encased in a heavy layer of egg.

"It's more work. I have enough going on between school, the panther, Kaiming and now the dwarves." I leaned back in the chair. "I'm taking half of this one."

Crimson narrowed her eyes, but didn't stop me as I took half of the first pan. "Welcome to the life of a guild master. Things will be busy. Again, take the joys when you can. Like my cooking."

I took a bite and smiled at her. "It's superb. Not everyone can claim that Mistress Crimson cooks for them."

"No one can claim that except for you." Crimson smiled.

I pointedly lifted another piece and ate it. "Which is why this tastes so damn good. Now, let's talk about the details and figure out what I can use Bellaire for if she's already on her way."

CHAPTER 19

Penny cut through the chocolate bunny as it burst into black smoke. "More chocolate." She picked up the dropped candy greedily.

I soon learned that the ladies in my class would quite literally kill for chocolate. Kill dungeon monsters, that is. Without Bun-bun with us, we could actually collect them too.

We'd managed to defeat the boss as a group, and then Penny had led us straight into the 26th floor.

"You know, I bet Ken would like some of the chocolate." Des leaned on me.

Penny stiffened. "Ken, would you like some of my chocolate?" I noticed that while she asked the question, she had a slight death grip on the candy.

"No." I wasn't sure why Des was so interested in teasing Penny, but I wasn't going along with it. Just mentioning her notebooks had frozen her up the other night.

Dolly picked up some of the loot from the candy cane men. Dolly currently had her pink hair in two big ponytails and flounced around in a frilly black dress. She turned to face me, and I looked away. The time she'd asked me to tie her up was still in the back of my mind, and I didn't want to give her any false ideas.

Dolly looked around. "You two clear areas pretty easily. So much faster than with Helen."

"Don't say that too loud or she might hear," Meredith teased.

Dolly only grinned wider. "What's the worst she could do? Punish me?" Dolly held herself and squirmed.

Penny sighed. Clearly that type of talk happened often in their party. "Keep moving. We still have most of the semester, but I'd like to reach the raid before winter break."

"To push the thirty-second floor, we'd probably want to at least be level thirty. Even then, it might not be the best idea to enter the raid at that point," I pointed out. Having a few extra levels didn't change the content of the raid and only made it easier for everyone.

Penny nodded. "Yes, but then we'll have a starting point and we can gauge the competition. I hear there are powerful adventurers among the other schools. The Royal Academy is notorious for having their people power-leveled."

I rolled my eyes. "To what end? So that they can stall in lower levels and work on their stats? Feels like putting the cart before the horse."

"It's a strategy." Des shrugged. "They get access to better gear."

"Bought with their parents' money," I tried not to sound bitter. "Pendulum is a better school."

"Not better than Haylon," Meredith added.

"Of course," I corrected myself quickly.

Truthfully, I had been looking to go to Pendulum from the start, but as a guy, Haylon hadn't even entered my thought process. Now that I was here, I wouldn't dream of being anywhere else. Trusk was full of oddballs, and I didn't have a parent sponsoring me for The Royal College.

"When we get to the thirty-second floor, we'll prove Haylon is a head above the rest," I promised them all.

Penny froze as she looked into the sticky snow landscape. "Ken, your friend is back."

My weapons were at the ready a moment later as the Smoke Panther prowled towards me. It comically stuck out in the white landscape.

"I have a revive," Meredith reminded me. "Crimson made sure we all had one."

"Give him some space." Des held her arms out to urge the rest of the group back.

I shifted back and forth, making sure I was loose and ready to move quickly. When the panther was in striking distance, I struck first, thrusting my sword forward and scratching its cheek as it flowed around me.

It moved with a fluid grace, coming from my side with its massive paws. The claws peeked out and looked relatively harmless, but I knew better. The second the paw would hit me, those claws would shoot out and rake across me like a set of daggers.

I dodged one paw before catching the second on my sword and diverting the momentum while going in with my dagger. After the past several encounters, I knew its rhythm well. I wasn't going to let it box me in with its rapid strikes.

The next swing came and I ducked, activating [Dodge]. I slid underneath as I activated [Dark Strike] along its flank, tearing up its side and sending curls of smoke into the air around us.

The panther growled and tried to reposition to get me in front of it again, but I kept close to its side. I got several more heavy blows in before it backed up and came at me again.

This part of the fight was the easier part. I knew that, with each swipe, the Smoke Panther would grow faster and faster. The time I could make with [Dodge] grew smaller with each use, and the time I had to counter shrank until it was almost non-existent.

It wasn't long before I started taking damage and slugged back three potions to improve my odds and heal.

I gained more ground, dealing back plenty of damage.

"You got this, Ken!" Des shouted through cupped hands. "Kick its ass!"

"Yeah!" Penny rattled her sword as the other two shouted encouragement.

It seemed I had gained a cheerleading section. Strangely, that bolstered me more than any potion. I couldn't let the girls down; they were rooting for me.

I picked up speed again, fighting tooth and nail against claws and fangs. There was no room for error as it became a blur of paws flying at me. Its eyes flashed, and I activated [Shadow Phase]. Dozens of strikes cut into me as the panther disappeared.

"Potion!" Penny shouted at the top of her lungs.

I didn't need the reminder, but her concern was heartwarming as I chugged down another potion. Potions were wonderful, but drinking too many was toxic. Frankly, I was amazed that Crimson had drunk as many as she had and survived.

The panther slowed down, not to its original levels, but enough for me to let out a sigh of relief as I managed to keep up. It was like the ability used its speed in a burst of some sort.

Purple lightning danced along the panther as it built up speed once more.

I felt like I was in a race against time. I pushed out as much damage as I could, taking two more potions as I took damage in order to dish it back out. The fight continued on, and I was barely keeping up, but I wasn't dead yet.

A few more hits into the battle, the dungeon around us seemed to shift as the panther leapt back. The fabric of reality split and shattered, leaving the panther and me in a dark space, fragments of reality floating in a circle around us.

I glanced at the rest of my party, but they were frozen in time. Des was mid-cheer, pumping her fist in the air while she blew me a kiss with the other.

The panther let out a low roar that rumbled through the strange new space we inhabited.

"Okay, not sure what this is. But admittedly, this is cool as fuck." There were all sorts of effects that the bosses or the rooms in the dungeon could do, but to freeze time was incredible. "Guess it is just you and me."

I rushed the panther, and when I struck it, a little purple lightning danced over my arm. It attacked twice, already moving quickly, purple lightning dancing over its fur.

Curious, I tried to check my CID to see what was happening, but the device was non-responsive in this space. Instead, I had to focus on the fight and just beat this panther, which seemed even more difficult as the monster grew faster at an alarming rate.

And as I attacked, more and more purple lightning was racing across my body. Hit after hit continued, and it wasn't long before the panther was purple with how much lightning was racing across its fur, and it was far too fast for me.

I could have chugged a few more potions and tried to make up ground, but as I processed the current moment, I realized that the best solution was to let the current fight end and come back even more prepared the next time.

Although, it wasn't much of a choice. I was about to lose.

The panther was moving side to side so fast that it was like fighting multiple enemies, and its claws quickly got past my guard tearing into my side, thigh, and finally a deep cut down my back that made everything blissfully numb as I fell and darkness enclosed me.

***

I jerked awake, taking a deep breath.

"He got you with that ability the second time," Des said, patting my shoulder. "I didn't see its eyes light up either."

I had a huge grin on my face. "It wasn't that. It was a new ability." I sat up. "The panther froze time, and everything sort of split apart. We fought in this little area where the world had frayed."

Des looked at Meredith. "Did your revive come with hallucination warnings?"

"Stop that." I excitedly pushed her off me and stood up to see that everything was the same. "Look. It was about this wide." I paced the area. "Everything inside this space was dark, like we were somewhere different. There were edges, like the world was shattered, and you"—I pointed at Des— "were stuck like this." I mimicked the pose I'd seen. "Then I fought the panther, and I think we were both speeding up."

"Both speeding up?" Penny took me seriously.

"I'm more concerned about the time stop." Des shook her head. "If the 74 wives writer finds out about that, she's going to go down that erotica path."

I deadpanned at her. "Not the point. The Smoke Panther was already so fast, and it outpaced me. Both of us were speeding up as we attacked. If it continued, it would go parabolic."

Penny's eyes went wide. "There was no stop?"

"Nope." I grinned like a loon. "I wonder how fast we were going at the end. It outpaced me, and I didn't see it at first, but as more purple lightning surrounded me and the panther I noticed my cooldowns were taking abnormally long to recover. It took a bit, but I realized that it wasn't the cooldowns. I was just going that much faster."

"This has you excited why? Speed is good?" Meredith asked.

"No, it's because he knows how to fight the last stage." Des grinned back at me. "He needs to find a way to build up more speed than the panther. That's really all it is. If he can get ahead, like he said, the acceleration will outpace the panther, and once he's faster, it's over."

I nodded. "It has a head start, but that's workable. I need to fix my fighting style to build up as many stacks as I can in a short amount of time or some gimmicky ability that can do it for me."

I felt great because I saw an end to the panther fights. And the deaths.

***

"WHAT?!" I shouted at Felin, not that it was her fault.

"Eight days," she said, crossing her arms as her ears went flat. "Don't yell. The trial is going to come slower and slower. Remember that it will get harder as you level too."

I grit my teeth. "So I should stop leveling for a week and just focus on stats." I had already informed the people present about my latest fight with the panther and my ideas for solving the next stage.

Crimson sat perching on the back of the couch. "Could be worse. Just eight days."

I knew she was right, but it still felt like a win was within reach, only to get pulled further away.

"You aren't too close to the next level, so you could do the boss fights with several parties. We should really speed that up and finish so that we can all move on to the next set of five floors and farm." Charlotte rubbed Bun-bun's head as he, for once, behaved himself.

Though, that was probably due to the carrot rather than a rare celestial event.

Felin rubbed her chin and nodded. "Still, a very interesting fight. It froze time? That is very powerful, even in small areas. I'd love to check your tattoo when you had this buff going, but there is nothing for me to look at now. I cannot tell you anything about it except to agree with your assessment. Abilities that build off attacks are an interesting study." She fished around in her pouch.

"Got something?" Fayeth asked.

Felin pulled out an old looking scroll. "Just wanted to refresh myself on this one. It's a copy, but we've had shamans look into on-hit abilities. You said you were getting faster when you hit or he blocked, but not if the panther dodged?"

I nodded. "That seemed to be it."

"Then it is likely the same for the panther. I hesitate to call the Great One 'fair', but it is logical," she explained. "If the second phase had you two sharing the ability, then it is likely connected to what you'll get from it and also a hint to its own abilities."

"Odd for you not to call it fair," Des said.

Felin tilted her head making her ears flop. "We revere the Great One not because we love it, but because it could crush us and our world like an ant under its boot. I thought humans and their god was the same." She pulled out a bible. "It talks about god flipping tables angrily."

"Uh." I scratched my cheek. "I'm not the most literate there, but I think he becomes a kind god in the latter half."

Felin now seemed more confused. "That makes no sense. But maybe it isn't about making sense. I just wanted to understand you better." She threw it back into her pouch.

"More importantly, the scroll?" Crimson urged.

"Right right." Felin glanced through it. "These kinds of skills aren't unheard of. In order to trigger an on-hit effect, most need the intent to deal damage and to be done with something that is considered a lethal weapon. It goes on to describe horrible events that could happen without such restrictions, such as a friend punching another playfully or someone reprimanding someone with a switch."

I raised an eyebrow in question. "Corporal punishment fell out of style a while ago for us."

"How else do you teach soldiers?" Felin blinked.

"Never mind." I waved the thought away.

Des burst into laughter. "He thought you were talking about children."

Felin made a wide mouth as she understood. "No. That makes sense. Anyway, you could try simply lighter weapons to fight the panther at a faster pace."

"A short burst of stabs might be possible too," Crimson added. "You might get mauled for standing still and trying it, but if you have some potions ready, you could get a big burst to your speed and then recover."

Charlotte pumped her fists to mime the action. "It might work. I'm more concerned about Kaiming closing in and the situation with the dwarves. Those aren't related, are they?"

I blinked, not even considering the thought, but after replaying it, I dismissed the thought. "Doubt it. Unless the Naga are secretly aligned with the dwarves?" I turned to Felin who might have additional information.

"No. The dwarves are stupid. Well, most of them are. The queens might be smart. Never talked to one, though." She looked up, realizing we were all leaning forward. "Right, you guys haven't fought them. We have. They make up for their shortcomings with large numbers." She snickered at the joke.

"It isn't nice to make fun of someone's height," Fayeth pouted.

"It is when you already hate them." Felin winked. "Nekorians and them have had three great wars in our history. Basically, what you heard from Risha are the broad strokes. Imagine a hive animal like a bee or an ant. Dwarves have a queen; she's like eight feet tall and an extremely strong caster."

"Wait, does she give birth to all the dwarves?" Des blurted.

Felin shrugged. "I have no idea how they reproduce. I only know the records on how to kill them. Basically, a 'clan' is a hive, and there are three main castes. Queen, soldier, and drone. Soldiers have genders, drones do not."

I raised my hand, feeling like I was in a classroom again. "How can you identify a soldier?"

"They have life in their eyes," Felin deadpanned. "Once you see a soldier, you'll know. They seem so much more... alive compared to the drones. They laugh, they get angry, not just murderous. You might see one. The dwarves no doubt can tell you have the dungeon's attention, meaning that you have high potential. So they'll try and kill you."

"Wait, it's because of the trial?"

"They'd kill more than just people undergoing a trial." Felin pointed at Crimson. "They'd go after her if she wasn't so terrifying."

"Wonderful." Crimson had a smug grin on her face. "Maybe I could go put some fear into them. Or I could take my energy out on training Ken." She eyed me.

"They don't have fear," Felin said. "The drones are just that, an endless swarm of physically adept dwarves. They can probably handle monsters on this floor but not much deeper. The soldiers farm the area of the dungeon that they control and are much stronger."

"Can I expect them? The soldier dwarves?" I asked.

Felin shook her head. "I have no clue. I'd have to ask some of the elders for their opinions. But I'm not leaving until you finish your trial." Her tail flicked mischievously behind her.

"Uh huh. Why do I feel like you won't leave after that either?" I asked.

"It's likely I'll keep coming back. After all, I have a nice bed here, and Fayeth feeds me."

I glared at the elf, who shrugged and answered my look. "She's a guest and she compliments my cooking."

"Alright." I smacked my knees. "Anything I can do to get the dwarves off me?"

"You could spend some time with the Nekorians; they won't come after us. If they do, we murder another of their clans." Felin shrugged. "Once the queen dies, the soldiers and drones go into a frenzy and kill anything they see. It is a very costly and bloody endeavor to fight a clan, but it can be done."

Crimson cracked her knuckles. "Sounds like fun."

"Except for the part where they come into the safe zone and murder tons of people," I tried to calm Crimson's bloodlust down and strategize. "After I have the next panther fight, we'll see if they calm down. If they can't, then I'll just have to put them down."

CHAPTER 20

The next several days went by without issue. I had stuck around the boss room and was helping multiple groups from my class, as well as advising several groups from Class B.

I was in the dungeon, watching yet another fight, and trying not to roll my eyes as the Harem Queen chose that moment to once again try to seduce me.

"Really?" She held my arm lightly, not exerting any pressure but letting me know she was there as she pressed her soft chest against me. "I am so excited for what this monster means for you. If this is even half of what propelled Crimson forward, you are going to shine bright among humanity."

The room roared as mud splashed everywhere but stopped short of us. The party shouted as they got hit. Things weren't looking so good for this group. Thankfully, I had gotten [Revive] from Charlotte.

The Harem Queen wasn't really paying that much attention to the fight. Her eyes were locked solely on me. "You know, my daughter would make a wonderful tank. She's so nurturing and protective."

"The tank position in my party is taken," I tried to rebuff her.

But my statement didn't even faze her. "Oh, don't be like that. You'll need several in a raid setting, and even then, you'll probably need a rotation so that you don't get bored. Trust me, I understand you better in that regard than most." She winked. "But Helen is such a kind girl."

"You realize that she hates me, right?" I faced the Harem Queen. The party had gained on the boss; they were going to win.

"Really? She writes that lovely story about you."

I deadpanned. "You know as well as I do that she's not the one writing that."

The Harem Queen sighed. "Yes, and that she's only using you as an excuse to escape me, but a mother can hope that her daughter gets into a good relationship. Heaven knows that she's been so angry about everything since that boyfriend of hers freshman year."

Hearing a gap in Helen's armor, I pushed. "She hasn't told me about this."

"It's her story to tell, not mine." The Harem Queen waved away the topic.

I wasn't done yet. "You slept with her boyfriend?" I asked incredulously.

The Harem Queen became legitimately angry at that question. "No, that would be absolutely hideous of me. I would never do such a thing, and to drop accusations like that without proof to high-level adventurers is how you end up never coming out of the dungeon."

I raised an eyebrow. Her reaction had been far more intense than I had expected.

"Oh, don't look at me like that. I have every right to be upset when you make an accusation like that. Look, I didn't sleep with him, but he was an asshole from the start."

"So he tried to sleep with you."

"He came into my room, calling me a whore and offering himself. I quite literally kicked him to the curb. I had to pay some hospital bills because he broke his pelvis and had a daughter who refused to talk to me for a year because of it. When he was in the hospital, he went on and on about how it was 'worth it.'" She rubbed at her forehead.

I couldn't help it. I burst out laughing.

"You think that's funny do you?" The Harem Queen glowered.

"Yes. Yes, I do," I wiped at the tears in my eyes. "It just makes so much more sense."

"I shouldn't have told you that."

"Probably not, but I won't spread it around. I don't think Helen would take kindly to it, and I value my life."

"Smart man." She patted my cheek. "Now if you were a really smart man, you'd figure her out and lock her down."

The party wiped, and I used that as an excuse to escape Helen's mother and go revive them. Des was right, though: some boy had fucked her up.

***

"Faster. What, do you want to be fighting this panther for the rest of your life?" Crimson egged me on as I stabbed her as quickly as I could.

Not that my hits did anything. The level sixty dinosaur leather that made up her newer outfits was tougher than steel. The scratches I was making could probably be buffed out with some polish.

My shirt was off, and it was just the two of us in the gym. I had stayed back to continue training with her.

She dodged to the side and her knee flashed forward. I threw myself to the right, keeping both daggers in reverse grips, much in the same stance a boxer would take, with my arms up only to duck back in and pump those daggers at Crimson and dulling their edge against her armor.

Crimson was modulating her speed and strength, keeping me light on my feet and dodging as I worked on the motions of my new technique.

"I'll get the panther next time," I promised as I used [Dodge] to duck one of her swings. In the same motion, I stabbed at her thigh before trying to move behind her.

Crimson hip checked me hard enough for me to slide back and then came around and hooked my leg to break my stance. She twisted to pull me down. I had to shift all of my weight to my other foot and let her pull my leg free.

Something coiled tightly around my back foot, and the world turned upside down as Crimson laughed and landed on me, straddling my hips.

"You didn't see the whip." She smiled.

"Pretty sure you knew that." I rolled my eyes. "Besides, I didn't even know the whip was in play."

"There still might be a surprise or two from your real opponent, so stay on your toes." She swayed her hips on top of me, her face softening. "Guild Master, are you all right?" She leaned over and touched a hand to my forehead. "Let your favorite guild member help you."

I chuckled as she lifted me to my feet. "Are we done practicing for the day?"

Crimson pouted. "Guild Master, I've—"

"This is an interesting sight," Neldra's voice made Crimson snap to attention, and in a blur, she was leaning against the wall, eating a bag of chips.

"I was just teasing him." Crimson rolled her eyes. "Don't elves have the decency to knock, or does that require a sword? I seem to remember you having a habit of breaking yours."

Neldra scoffed. "If you are going to tell me no weapons in the house again"—she pointed at my daggers—"then you are just full of shit."

"How's Ely?" I asked, not seeing the princess with Neldra.

"Her butt is getting sore sitting on the throne. At least, that's what she says. We need to work on her stamina if that's real." Neldra picked at the weapon rack. "What are you two doing?"

"Training," I answered, pulling Crimson off the wall and to my side as I sat down on a workout bench. It had only been a few weeks since I had left the elves, but it felt like far longer. "There's a unique monster that keeps showing up to try and kill me."

"Huh." Neldra didn't comment further, rather her eyes lingered on Crimson behaving as I moved her. "That was some interesting training when I came in."

"That would just be Crimson being Crimson and changing the rules mid training," I admitted. "Are you here for some metal?"

Neldra ran her tongue along the inside of her cheek. "Officially, that's the plan. Unofficially, I also have a pile of letters from Ely for you. And I'd like to go up to the surface and talk to Mr. Lyntean."

I tapped on my CID a few times and held it up.

Neldra bumped her Elven CID to mine. Thankfully, the storage function on the two devices worked the same. Both were developed from items in the dungeon.

"I've deposited the letters. I'll be back for dinner; you two try not to have too much fun," Nelda said.

I glanced to my side, and Crimson angrily broke off a chip while glaring daggers at Neldra. "We'll do our best."

The Royal Censor wisely disappeared after that.

Crimson blurred to the door, locked it, and then just to make sure no one would disturb us again, bent the handle.

She turned back, and I had a raised eyebrow. "Getting interrupted upset you that much?"

"It's... ugh," Crimson sighed and returned to my side, picking up her bag of chips. "Sometimes it can be really hard to get the mood right with you."

Running my hand along her waist, I coaxed her to scoot closer until her hips were pressed against mine. "That's fair. We do stay quite busy, and oftentimes you are being either Crimson the badass or Crimson the teacher."

"Right." Crimson nodded. "It's rare for an opportunity for me to be 'Crimson the guild member.'"

"I hope you being a guild member is more than just a sex thing," I admitted.

She shrugged. "It's the one relationship we have where you are in charge." She popped another chip.

I knew she was being careful. It was easy for her to be intimidating to most men, and honestly there were times when Crimson was terrifying. Yet the more effort she put in, the less I worried about those parts. Because if she was trying that hard, it would work out in the end.

Glancing her up and down, I reached over and grabbed her chips. "Are you eating chips in the guild facilities?" I played my part. "When you are behind on your guild dues?"

Crimson's eyes poured out red lightning as I took away the bag of chips. I wondered if taking the chips had pushed her too far.

"Cancel Limit Break," I demanded.

The red lightning stopped, and I took her chin in my hand and made her look me in the eyes. I ran a finger through her choker, the one she had me put on her. Sitting down, I easily was taller than her and used that to loom over her.

"I'm sorry, Guild Master," Crimson breathed. "I just needed a break. Do I need to be punished?"

"Is it a punishment to be with me?" I countered and kissed her. "Maybe I've grown to like my delinquent guild member." I kissed her again.

Crimson leaned against me and looked up through her lashes. "No, I'm glad. I have a secret: I might not be making my dues so that you can force me to pay them another way."

I wasn't looking to tie her up in the training room, but a break that involved kissing her, playing her games was easy enough.

"Is that so?" I eased her down on the workout bench and hovered over her, taking her lips again for another sweet kiss. "Well, I came in here to get a break, but I don't want chips." I used my weight to push her down on the bench and kissed her.

Her legs wrapped around my waist and smashed our hips together. "Anything for you, Guild Master."

I captured her lip and played with it between my own as we kissed, then shifted slightly, pressing our lips to each other again and again like we were trying to see what position worked best.

Our arms were wrapped around each other, and it was just a comfort to be in each other's embrace as we kissed for what felt like hours. I couldn't get enough of her lips.

When I finally pulled back I noticed that even at her high level, her lips were swollen from all the kissing.

"That felt good," she said with a smile that I knew was as goofy as mine.

"Yes, it did," I said and kissed her neck.

She bent her head to the side, opening up her neck to me and moaning. "Ken." She ran her hands through my hair.

"Crimson." I wasn't going to strip off her clothes, and she didn't seem to be in a rush to do so either.

There was something like refreshing an intimate connection in just reveling in each other's lips and bodies that didn't require us to have sex right then and there.

This was something that I'd been missing with Crimson. It was always like we were moving at a thousand miles a minute and we'd skipped some of the earlier steps. Then again, it was like Crimson to skip all the steps and jump to the end.

I cupped her leather clad ass and pushed down hard on her, rubbing myself through our clothes.

"Are you just going to tease me?" Crimson moaned, her pink lips parting, and she licked them with a wet smack.

"Maybe. You are delinquent on your dues." I kissed down her neck and unzipped the top of her bodysuit.

Crimson pushed my head down into her chest. "Too cruel. I love it."

I chuckled and pulled a breast from her bra to play with it. For how hard her armor was, her skin was still incredibly soft. I let my lips and fingers play over it while Crimson groaned in satisfaction, holding my hips to hers and bucking lightly.

Red lightning danced out between her closed eyes. "Fuck yes."

I didn't comment that [Limit Break] appeared to be active; she seemed to still be in control.

"Yes. Ken," Crimson moaned. Her legs had me like she was trying to ram me into her through both of our clothes.

God, she smelled incredible as I teased her breast. "Crimson, you are amazing."

"Damn right." She shifted and her heels locked around my neck as she pulled me back up to her lips with an impressive feat of flexibility. "Kiss me." There was a haze over her blue eyes as she said it, and more lightning continued to pour out around her face.

I was happy to oblige and continue making out with her. The red lightning of [Limit Break] didn't affect me at all.

Things were getting hot and heavy when the door handle jiggled. Crimson groaned, "Ignore it."

I was happy to comply. I was more interested in her lips than the door or whoever was behind it.

But the person on the other side apparently wasn't willing to wait. After a few more wiggles of the doorknob, the door exploded inward.

Crimson went from being under me to standing at my side, her hand catching the door as the metal shrieked. She crumpled the door up in anger.

[Limit Break] was still pouring red lightning out of her eyes as she threw the crumpled-up door to the side, and spoke slowly through gritted teeth, "You are a second from dying, but I want to know what was so goddamn important that you busted down the door."

There were three people on the other side of the door. Two of them were wearing UG vests while the last was wearing Haylon colors, but I didn't recognize any of them.

"Uh..." the lead said stupidly, staring at Crimson as red lightning continued to build up on her body.

Her eyes glowed bright blue. "Famous last words."

Crimson grabbed him by the face and lifted him up before squeezing with such force that his head exploded and it tore him apart all the way down to the middle of his chest.

"You two can die as well." With a wave of her hand, she turned all three of them into a smear on the ground.

Then she turned back to me. "Where were we?"

"Taking a shower," I deadpanned. She was covered in blood. "Also, you do realize that Limit Break is active?"

Crimson touched her face and saw the red lightning dance off to her hands. Her face lit up in excitement. "I'm doing it! I'm in control." She danced around. "Alright, the key is sexy time with you. I'll go find some high-level iron skin potions so that I don't break anything."

Her smile was infectious as she danced around the door and looked in the mirror to see herself. "I look pretty badass."

"Your ass looks something special. That's for sure," I teased.

She wiggled it at me. "Alright, since the mood is ruined, I have to tell you that those were idiots looking for a bounty." No doubt she'd gleaned it when she had activated [Eyes of Wisdom] earlier.

"On me?" I pointed at myself, suddenly dumbfounded.

"Yup," Crimson sighed. "We need to look into where it came from. I didn't get more than that they were after you for a bounty, but there's really only one group that would put a price on your head."

"Kaiming," I sighed. "Makes a certain sort of sense. They can't get at me directly, not without going through far too much of the UG, not to mention you. Their personnel are ravaged, but maybe they have enough money to do something like this. So, those three were just idiots?"

"Idiots who were going to kill you for money." Crimson stepped away from the mirror and a sly grin crossed her face. "Let's go take a shower. You should join me, you know, for your safety." She winked at me as she walked out the mangled doorway smeared with blood.

CHAPTER 21

F ayeth cuddled up on my side. "I can't believe you were attacked here today."

"Neldra defeated several of the systems," I said, glancing towards the dining table.

The Elven Censor sat there with a frown. Crimson had laid into her once it became apparent. "You should have told me you were in such dire straits."

"Well, I didn't really know someone put a bounty on me until those guys showed up. Yes, I'm aware of an organization that has it out for me, but..." I trailed off as Crimson walked back into the suite.

"The groups you told me about have been taken care of." She dusted off her hands. "Idiots to think they could hide out remotely near me. You should have told me sooner." Crimson was feeling protective and sat down next to me.

"It's under control." I patted her thigh. "My focus is on the panther. You deal with Kaiming in the relative area, and we let the UG deal with the dwarves."

"What about the Nekorians?" Des glanced at Felin.

"We are a problem?" Felin huffed.

"I don't know. At this rate, we are going to learn your people are going to kill Ken for you playing with him," Des explained.

The shaman huffed. "Please, don't lump my people in with the dwarves or these Naga worshipers. We are reasonable. Though, if one of my suitors wants to kill Ken in his sleep to impress me, I can't be held liable." She held her hands up.

I stared at her.

"It was a joke," Felin laughed. "None of my suitors would come near Crimson's protégé."

I let out a weak chuckle. Did that mean if Crimson wasn't here that they would try and kill me? "Alright, then the Nekorians aren't a problem and we can focus on our own issues. Namely, the panther."

"Two more days," Fayeth reminded me.

"We'll be back together as a group by then." Charlotte gave me a soft smile.

"Yes, we will be." I reached over and squeezed her hand. "Otherwise, I'm doing training with Crimson for the most part and doing a few boss runs to finish out my ten."

"I've already hit my ten," Des said.

Of course she had. So far, she'd been vital to several groups because she was fantastic at the first phase with the shamans.

"Maybe I should get a try?" Felin asked as she greedily accepted a glass of milk from Fayeth who narrowed her eyes at the Nekorian. Felin gently sipped the milk and put it down with her ears pinned back.

"You want to do the dungeon boss?" I asked.

"Sure. Why not? I'm level twenty-eight. I can do damage, or support." Felin grinned.

Des stretched. "Ah. Do I hear the beautiful sound of a day off? I met a Nekorian merchant that said she sells the best bubble bath."

Felin frowned. "I'm pretty sure it's full of hallucinogens."

Des' jaw dropped. "Really?"

"Yep." Felin nodded without an ounce of hesitation. "Better give them to me for safe keeping."

My temptress narrowed her eyes. "I'm onto you, Felin. When you steal Ken's clothes, that's okay, but don't you dare steal my toiletries. Here in the dungeon, they are a woman's sacred artifacts."

Everyone but me nodded around the table.

Must be a girl thing.

"So, Crimson, was sex with Ken good?" Neldra asked.

There was the sound of metal shattering, and Neldra jumped to the side as her scabbard exploded.

Crimson broke a potato chip between her teeth as red lightning danced over the chip. "That was a very bad question."

I sighed and pressed my face into my hands. "Crimson, she didn't even draw it." Though, I knew Crimson was upset enough at all the interruptions that Neldra's question had hit a sore spot.

"She might as well have drawn a verbal weapon!" Crimson huffed.

"She was clam jammed." Fayeth patted Neldra on the shoulder as she stared at her broken sword. "Don't take it personally."

"It's fine." Neldra scooped up the remnants and stuffed them in her CID. "I brought multiple spares and several decorative swords that I wouldn't mind getting shattered." She pulled out another scabbard and slid a sword into it.

"That's good thinking," Des commended her. "Back to the topic of Felin joining the fights, what exactly does a Nekorian Shaman do?"

Felin tilted her head thoughtfully, making her ears flop. "We can throw around a few different elements or use said elements to buff someone. For example, I could use lightning to make Ken faster, or fire to make his strikes explode with each hit. I can use ice to shield Fayeth for each hit she takes, or wind to make everyone run faster."

"And as damage?" I asked.

Felin shrugged. "Mostly calling lightning in various forms works best. Fire does some damage, or ice is nice to support other damage dealers."

"Can you heal?" Charlotte asked.

"I have a heal, but it is pretty weak. Mostly, I have shields to prevent damage." Felin glanced up as Fayeth paraded out several large casserole dishes. The Nekorian had her fork out in a flash and ready to dig in.

"Felin, how do you keep ending up in here by the way? Have you left?" I asked.

Her tail twisted back and forth. "Well..." The Nekorian looked away.

Charlotte sighed. "I keep coming back and she's waiting outside our door. She gives me these pathetic eyes and I let her in."

That made... all too much sense. It really was like we'd picked up a stray.

"I'm glad she lets me in and then Fayeth is kind enough to feed me." She was happily scooping some of the casserole onto her plate.

Neldra watched the Nekorian. "I thought your people were famously proud and standoffish."

Felin scooped some of the casserole into her mouth and talked around it. "Oh we are. I'm just trying to get into Ken's pants."

I choked on my water.

"Oh." Neldra made a sound of understanding. "Are you interested in one of his skills or his Trelican status?"

Felin shook her head. "He's just gonna be strong enough to tame me."

Crimson nodded along with that. "Especially once he can kill this panther."

"Maybe it would be a good idea for you to try running the boss with one of our groups," I tried to bring the conversation back on topic.

Felin nodded hard enough that her cat ears flopped around and her white hair danced on her shoulders. "I would be very interested in seeing you fight."

"Otherwise, I think we are just doing the boring work of grinding out in the dungeon, Neldra," I tried to make it all sound casual and not like I'd been attacked several times.

She nibbled on Fayeth's food. "What are you going to do with all the funds you got from this trade deal?"

I really hadn't glanced at my CID since accepting it. At the time, I had been a little distracted by Crimson.

My eyes popped out of my head. "Uh... I don't know." I sounded like an idiot, but was trying to do the math on how much I'd given away when people had turned in scrap metal. Still, this was enough to fund a small guild for a few years.

"Well, I'll be back next month." Neldra shrugged. "It's not that much in the grand scheme of things; you should see the operating costs of a global empire."

Right, she'd be back next month and I'd give her this much again.

I could probably take half of it and set it aside so that I didn't have to worry about people coming for turn-ins, and then possibly expand the quests for the guild a little. Then the other half, I could send back to the surface for my grandparents to dump into recruiting.

My line of thought was all on using this for the guild rather than myself. After all, investing in it would pay dividends down the road if I did this right.

"I think you stunned him with money," Des teased, poking my side to bring me back to the table.

"Sorry, just doing some math. I'll have to get Ami down here to run some errands."

"I like Ami." Felin nodded. "She has pretty white hair like me."

"And she bargains with my clothes," I grumbled.

Des perked up at that. "It reminds me, when she comes back, she should have your new clothes so that we don't have to recycle them as quickly."

"I'll get to have more?" Felin perked up, her tail whipping back and forth.

"You live with me, doesn't it all already smell like me?" I asked.

"It isn't the same," the Nekorian pouted, her tail snaking behind Des and smacking me lightly before trying and failing to curl around me due to running out of length.

"Well, let's enjoy dinner," Fayeth prompted everyone. "Thanks for visiting, Neldra."

"Not a problem." The older elf smiled. "Maybe in the future I'll get to bring the Lady with me."

***

Ken was off with Felin to go play around with her at the boss fight.

Crimson cracked her neck as she stood behind Director Amato. "So you think there'll be plenty that took the bait?"

The blue-haired director looked up from the tablet she was working on. Crimson knew she was in the mid-forties for levels, but her strengths seemed to lie in organization and analysis rather than direct combat.

Sometimes, those could be the best allies for her.

"I tried to organize a meet up through the same channels that have been discussing the Kaiming bounty. Why have you stepped up at this juncture when we've asked for you to deal with the Kaiming before?" Director Amato asked.

Crimson shrugged and ate another potato chip. If she said that it was because they had interrupted a wonderful time with Ken, people just wouldn't understand. "They pissed me off. Besides, I think it is healthy for Ken to have some challenges coming his way and for the Nagato Clan to get an opportunity to strike back at Kaiming. However, this is a step too far, and all that really matters is that I'm here now."

They both stood at the edge of the thirtieth floor safe zone.

"Will you participate in a conflict with the dwarves?" Amato asked.

Crimson somehow felt that this woman would get Ken mixed up if it meant pulling Crimson to help with that situation too. "Ken will probably help you if you ask him. Better to give those on the floor some experience and then let the higher levels like us look after the overall situation, no?"

The Director nodded, but let that topic die as she tapped away on her tablet for a moment.

Crimson looked her up and down again. This woman didn't have the same fear that so many people had around her. "You aren't afraid of me."

"No, I am not," she said without looking up. "Is that so odd?"

"A little. Everyone seems to be a little afraid of me," Crimson admitted. "Like I'm just going to go crazy and start ripping heads off. It has been worse since I came back." She ate another potato chip, enjoying the salty, oily flavor that reminded her of simpler times.

"Well, I'm not a threat to Ken. In fact, I'm helping Ken. Thus, I firmly believe that you will not only not harm me, but assist me in my endeavors. Also, my daughter is smitten with him, please provide her your support." The Director sighed. "She could use a good man in her life since her father."

"The Impaler." Crimson already knew about it. She looked up and watched as a crowd started to form. It wasn't time just yet for her to make a scene, but the time was growing closer.

"Yes, well. He has his mission. Infiltrating the organizations that these criminals make in prison is not such an easy thing. Often times, it requires time most of all. However, you have him to thank for many dead Kaiming. He's been vital in understanding that side of their organization," Director Amato talked about her husband in prison like it was a slightly rainy day.

Crimson couldn't imagine letting Ken get himself put in prison for the UG or really anyone. It took a certain kind of person to be okay with justifying the means with such ends.

"It's time," the Director said. "I think this is enough."

Crimson put away her potato chips and pushed off the building. "Okay, just stay back—I get to be scary for once."

She let her anger at these people out and red lightning sparked at the edge of her vision. Yet she remained in control with a singular focus. She was going to put the fear of Crimson into these people for trying to come after Ken.

In just a flicker, she was among the throng of would-be-assassins who'd mistakenly gathered in a hope of working out the contract as a large team. [Eyes of Wisdom] confirmed that they were all who she needed them to be as she grabbed the first by the throat and lifted him in the air.

She scanned the surroundings and let her ability mark several others who had been watching. Those would be the more professional hit men. She would take care of them after or maybe mark them and let Ken deal with his own problems.

Holding the man by the throat got their attention.

"Welcome to the group that wants to kill Ken. I'm your host, Mistress Crimson. Ken is my protégé, thus under my protection." She crushed the man's throat and let him fall to the ground, choking as his windpipe no longer worked. "You see, it would be an incredible insult to me if my protégé died under my nose, no?"

One at the edge turned back, and Crimson's whip lashed out, catching him by the ankle and flinging him towards her. Another flick of her wrist and her whip snapped in the air loudly, followed by a wet splatter and the man exploding.

"So, that's about it. I don't need to explain things to dead people." Her whip made a full circle and destroyed over a dozen people in a single go. She didn't need to kill all of them. In fact, letting a few go would let it spread that this mission was a death sentence.

Her whip lashed out and killed a few more in gruesome and gory fashion to send the message clearly. It wasn't like on the surface where everyone would scream and panic as they ran away. Many of the adventurers who weren't involved, watched from the sides, concern etched on their faces.

"If you come to fuck with my protégé, you die," she said loudly enough for it to reverberate off the walls of the nearby buildings.

Director Amato was there suddenly with a megaphone. "These criminals were working with the defunct organization Kaiming. According to the agreement with various countries, they will be stripped of their citizenships and full criminal penalties will be held posthumously."

The surrounding crowd made a sudden noise of understanding. It was quite clear that Kaiming was universally hated at this point. Nothing like a common enemy to unite humanity.

"Fucking Kaiming, traitors to humanity," a man grumbled. "I saw a few get away, should we report them? I recognized their party."

"Happily," Director Amato addressed him individually. "We'll take anything we can get to clear them from the table."

Crimson nodded and moved away, those that she'd marked she was going to investigate them and see if they were part of any larger groups. Since they had been so kind to gather up for her, she was going to clean house.

***

Felin stretched her arms over her head and swayed her hips as we waited for the other group to leave the boss room.

The rest of the party was staring at her.

"Hi. I'm Felin." She held out her hand to Penny.

"Penelope, but my friends call me Penny. My father said that your people are unfriendly," she admitted.

Felin nodded. "There are lots of rules. Easier to just shun everyone rather than worry about the rules, right? That, and honestly, we've come into conflict with several other races."

"Like the dwarves?" Selene asked curiously.

Our group would be a good one. I didn't want to fail with Felin, and I was unsure of her actual capabilities. Bringing Candice would offer plenty of flexibility.

"Most likely," Candice commented. "Though, does your world connect with the elves before the fifties?"

"No." Felin shook her head. "We haven't dealt much with the elves. Though, I do enjoy Fayeth's cooking." She reached into the bag on her side and drew a staff out hand over hand. It was a gnarled thing with a big bulbous end and a gem embedded in it. "Let's do this. I have to impress Ken."

She started to smack the butt of the staff on the ground as a storm cloud grew overhead, lightning roaring in the boss room.

Penny nodded and moved to engage the trolls.

I watched for a moment as lightning struck Felin's staff, gathering static around it before she pointed it at the trolls. A thick cord of lightning tore out of the staff and hit one of the trolls before losing some strength and bouncing to the next and next until it petered out about three quarters of the way through.

I couldn't stand around and do nothing, instead rushing in and joining Penny in tearing down the trolls. Felin continued to fling lightning around, burning through several of the trolls with Candice.

The big muddy hand of the boss slapped down and pulled himself from the ground.

Felin switched tactics, and a shield of ice swirled around Penny before Felin started throwing blasts of cold air. "It makes the boss more brittle," Felin shouted.

I followed through and punched my dagger into an icy patch of mud, it sheared off more than I had expected, and I continued to work on the area that Felin had weakened.

When it came time for us to rush out, Felin stood there holding her staff as wind curled around her and then shot over to push at Penny's back to speed up the slowest member of our party.

Honestly, she had quite the variety of abilities and was using them well for the group. Candice hadn't touched healing or any support from what I could tell. The Spell Weaver was just standing behind a battery of three sigils that were pumping out fireballs into the boss' face. Likewise, Selene seemed focused but not stressed as she kept Penny alive.

Everything was going smoothly. I could tell that we wouldn't have any trouble.

CHAPTER 22

"Oh my gosh. Do you want to join our group?" Selene asked.

Felin had just used an ability that cleansed us of the smell from the mud boss. "It isn't that expensive of an ability. Nekorians have sensitive noses, and we can't be stinky unless we want to annoy everyone."

Selene made grabby hands at Felin. "You could make so much selling them."

"Back to grinding trolls?" I asked, trying to change the topic.

I wasn't successful.

"Would you trade milk for these spellbooks, Ken?" Felin asked, her bright blue eyes boring into me. They seemed even more intense with the blue tiger stripes on her skin.

"I don't know if that's an equal trade." It was one thing to sell metal to the elves, but milk? That just seemed like I was taking advantage of Felin.

Her tail swished behind her as she held her chin thoughtfully and looked up at the ceiling. "I think milk is valuable, but with most things, the source is more valuable than the product. Can we trade cows?"

I raised an eyebrow. "Getting cows down here would be very difficult."

"Increasing the cost and value." Felin nodded as if her suggestion had become a success.

I wasn't so sure. And getting the cows down would be more than difficult; it would be an absolute pain in the ass. "Maybe we just sell you milk and other things. We'll have to work out a value for the milk."

I made a mental note to have my grandpa start a farm.

Felin twisted her lips. "I can accept that deal."

Candice looked completely dumbfounded. We'd ended up back at Felin's original suggestion.

Whatever. "We can talk about the deal in more detail later. I'm assuming some leaders of your people will need to be a part of it?"

Felin blinked. "I am a leader of my people."

"But like more senior leaders..." I trailed off as Felin's scowl grew.

"I'm not some spring kitten! I am a full grown Nekorian Shaman," she huffed and puffed her cheeks out. "You bear my tattoo!"

"She's got you marked," Selene laughed.

"Don't you start. I only need one Des in my life or I'll find myself in bed for all eternity." I rolled my eyes. "Let's go farm."

"The twenty-sixth floor," Penny added.

"We can do that." I led them down the stairs.

I had one more day until the panther could show up again, and I was ready for it. I wasn't close enough to a level to hold off farming. They were really starting to slow down.

I wondered if once I finally stopped tormenting both Crimson and myself, we'd be able to hop around the dungeon for a few events and speed leveling up.

With that thought, my mind began wandering far from thoughts of the monsters.

"What's got you blushing?" Felin tilted her head with genuine curiosity.

"I bet it was Des," Candice offered.

"It is always Des," I cleared my throat.

"He was too quick on that one. Not Des," Penny said quickly.

All of us raised an eyebrow at how confident she sounded.

"Do tell how you knew that?" Selene teased.

Penny blushed a dark red. "N-nothing. I just pay attention to Ken."

Selene pointed at Penny. "You need to be careful of the quiet ones, Ken. They become stalkers."

"Or write smut about you," Candice offered.

Penny waved her hands in the air. "No. No. That's not me. Definitely not me. It's Helen, remember?!"

Penny was getting pretty flustered, and I had to admit, it was a little fun to watch her get shy and rosy cheeked.

"Lay off Penny. Helen said it was her." Even if we all knew it wasn't true. "And the writer hasn't come forth, so let them stay anonymous."

As soon as Penny turned away, I stopped schooling my face. It really couldn't be more obvious.

"Sooo..." Felin dragged out the word. "If it wasn't Des, who was it?" Curiosity was painted on her face as she scooted close with her hands clasped behind her back.

"Do Nekorians hate water?" I asked.

"We drink water. And we do swim, if that's what you are asking. I quite enjoy swimming." Felin narrowed her eyes. "Des made a joke about spraying me in the face with water. You wouldn't be thinking of something similar... would you?"

That was a trap. Abort.

"Oh look! Dwarves!" I commented on the first thing I saw, then suddenly tensed.

Dwarves seemed especially abundant at the moment, and more than a few of them were following me with their eyes.

"They don't look friendly," Felin stated the obvious.

Many of the human adventurers were standing tense, and more than a few of them had their weapons drawn. The dwarves were far too present in the human area of the safe zone.

Not that there were any actual rules and intermingling was common, but this felt like an invasion.

"You don't say." Selene leaned against the Nekorian. "Don't suppose you have a solution to this? Like do you know how to make us all invisible? Because a lot of them are looking at Ken."

"Then let me draw them away."

Penny, Candice, Selene, and Felin all snorted and started laughing.

"What's so funny?" I frowned at their sudden reaction; this was no time to be laughing.

"Des said you'd say something like that. Nope, we are in this together. Today, we are your party." Penny put a hand on my shoulder. "Let's head to the Haylon building and get Crimson before anything breaks out."

"Yeah, pretty sure Des would curse my soul if we left you alone to 'lead them away'," Selene added.

"We'll just get to the Haylon building then," I said.

A woman screamed around the corner.

My sword and knife appeared in my hand.

"You had to jinx us. I thought Des was the one with curses," Selene sighed, but she kept up with me as I hurried to see what had happened.

Several adventurers were trying to get through a dozen dwarves as they captured three women. But the dwarves wouldn't let them through.

I didn't hesitate and rushed forward. "Shadow Ambush." I appeared behind the dwarves carrying the women and thrust my sword into the closest dwarf's face.

My blade blinded him in one eye, and I grabbed the woman, twisting at the hip and hurling her over to Penny. Dwarves cut at my side before an expanding shell of ice protected me and rebuffed them.

I had two more women to save.

A fireball exploded among the scuffle followed by a second and third. Candice buffed me, and I felt reinvigorated. It was like I'd just downed a line of espresso shots and pushed through the chaos as healing washed over me.

I reached the second woman and stabbed the dwarf. [Dark Blades] helped me cut through them easier than just using the edge of my sword. Two other dwarves tried to pin me down while she struggled to her feet.

That's when I recognized her. "Bellaire?" I blurted out.

She pulled her dark hair away from her face and blinked at me for a second before she punched a dwarf in the face as hard as she could. The dwarf rocked back on his heels, but he didn't take a step back.

Penny's longsword cleaved into the crown of the dwarf's head before coming out with a wet slurp. "Get out. Get to them." Penny pointed to the three supporting us from behind.

I pulled myself into the other dwarf and stabbed my dagger in three quick strikes. It felt like I was trying to put a hole in a brick, but I chipped away before the dwarf pushed me away, blood running through his beard.

Penny blasted him with frost and mowed him over as she charged with her shoulder.

"Great work." I came after her.

The situation was devolving. All around us, dwarves were grabbing people and fights were breaking out on every corner.

"Last girl." Penny was still focused on saving them. "We get out together with her."

"Clear. I'll take the dwarf. You take the girl." I went low, swinging my sword at the back of the dwarf's leg, cutting deep into their hamstring, assuming they had one or something similar. We were all roughly the same shape, and I had to assume so as the dwarf buckled on that side.

Penny came in next, roughly grabbing the woman and shoulder checking the dwarf. With one leg not working, they went over into a dwarf next to them, and Penny grabbed my forearm as if she was my mother. "No running off into danger."

I stuck out my tongue. "Not planning on it. Let's get her clear."

Candice lobbed several more fireballs into the mess over our heads.

The UG security had now shown up, and with them healing and beating back the dwarves, the situation was clearing up quickly. I was just happy we'd gotten the chance to save Bellaire and the two ladies before anything had happened to them.

We pulled behind an advancing line of UG guards, and I handed the last of the ladies off to Bellaire. I recognized them now as the two camera women that had orbited around her the last time we had met.

"So—" Before I could get another word out, a spear launched itself free from the fray, taking me by surprise.

Penny jerked to the side and took the spear in the shoulder. It tore through her armor and the tip poked out her back, glistening in blood.

Candice's eyes were wide and lit up by the purple lines she was drawing in the air to heal Penny.

A dwarf with blonde hair and fire in his eyes rushed through the UG's line, heading straight for us. He had heavy leather armor that was mostly hidden by his beard and mane of hair flapping in the wind.

Felin grabbed the spear in Penny's shoulder and spun with a grunt of effort, ripping it free and then smacking it towards the dwarf. He came up short to parry the wild spear strike down to the ground. Felin let the spear hit and used it to spin and send a kick, connecting with the dwarf's jaw.

"Damn. She's got moves," Selene shouted.

I was pretty impressed too. Wasn't she supposed to be a support?

The dwarf must have had a jaw of diamond though because he just took two steps back and wiped his beard. "I'll kill you for that too." He ripped the spear out of Felin's hand and forced her back with several expert jabs.

Penny came back with a vengeance, her sword gathering frost as she came at him with an overhead swing. I gripped my weapons, ready to time my attack.

The dwarf swung his spear up to block Penny. As soon as he did, the ice on her weapon shattered and sprayed over him in dozens of razor-sharp shards.

While he was dealing with the shards, I slipped up behind him with [Shadow Ambush], coming out of his shadow and stabbing into a gap in his armor.

The dwarf stepped back into me and snapped a kick backwards. The hit was a little low for my knee and hit my shin, but at that moment, I realized he was at a much higher level. My leg shot out from under me.

I swung my sword as hard as I could at the back of his head, but he stepped back into Penny, where his spear clashed with her sword. He checked her with his full weight and strength, sending her sailing backwards.

"He's a soldier dwarf," Felin called out, her staff back out of her bag.

"Ah. A shaman." The dwarf's English was a broken thing. "A dead one as a bonus to the marked."

I jumped back just in the nick of time as he swung for the fences and nearly ripped my head off with the shaft of his spear. Instead, I just got a cut across my collar that would be healed soon enough.

"Poor decision," I taunted the dwarf, remembering the others hadn't had much mana. "Shadow Arm, Mana Burn." I launched the combo and it stuck to him, burning off bright, blue flames.

Selene hit me with a heal, closing up the wound on my chest.

The dwarf paused, considered how much mana he was losing, and shrugged. "I expected more."

He twisted, pulling something from his pouch and throwing it hard at Selene. Selene swung her staff to meet it and when she did, it exploded into a thick acrid cloud of smoke that hung in the air.

The dwarf chuckled and closed back in on me.

"Over my dead body!" Penny came roaring back in, buffeting him a step to the side with icy winds and swinging for his back the next second.

The dwarf was fast, blocking her and then swinging back to stop my advance the next second. That spear of his really helped his lack of reach in keeping us both away.

Penny, however, was more determined than he expected, taking a blow that made her shoulder plate crunch in order to get a solid swing at him.

I couldn't let her sacrifice go and swept in as well. Unlike the other dwarves, this one had enough mana that my burn wasn't flickering out.

I activated [Metamorphosis]. The current fight was clearly a moment that I could use the extra strength as I crashed into the dwarf. As soon as Penny finished her attack, I used all my extra bulk to swing.

Hitting the dwarf felt like I was trying to move a car, but his feet gave, and I redirected my force to push him rather than trying to get him airborne.

My plan worked.

He stumbled towards the line of UG guards, and his feet carried his momentum right into one of the higher-level humans.

With all the other dwarves, likely drones, dying so easily, no one seemed to think we needed the aid. But with the soldier dwarf crashing into the UG guards, they turned on him.

The soldier dwarf managed to injure two of them before he was taken down.

I released [Metamorphosis]. "Penny." I turned away once the danger was gone. "Let's look at that shoulder."

A retching noise caught my attention, and I realized that Candice was holding Selene's hair. Both of them had snot dripping out of their nose and their eyes were red. Felin was encased in a bubble of wind and slowly blowing a breeze that dispersed the thick, black smoke.

Whatever they'd been hit with, it had lingered like a heavy blanket on the area and clearly was not pleasant. Felin gave me a thumbs up and pointed to the three ladies that we had saved protected behind her.

"Get Candice and Selene ready. Penny's gonna need some healing." I focused back on Penny. The blue-haired girl was blushing. "We need to peel this off." I worked at the armor around her shoulder. The dwarf had hit it hard enough to warp and pinch it around her arm.

She'd need it off to get healed.

"Thanks." She glanced at me with watery eyes. "That was a close one."

"Nah," I joked. "That was a pretty standard day for me." I pulled a dull practice blade from my inventory and worked it up under her armor while I cut the straps that had held it in place. "This is going to hurt."

Penny nodded and put one of the leather straps in her mouth. I used the dull blade as a lever and pulled the armor off.

Penny whimpered into the leather strap as her arm crackled again. It wasn't just the armor that had been battered; her bone was broken and I'd just shifted the injury enough that it was threatening to rip through her skin.

I cursed.

I reached around the ruined metal plate and dug in with my hands. Parts of the metal pierced my skin, but I ignored the pain. That pain meant I could stop from pushing a broken bone through Penny's skin.

Once I had a strong grip, I pulled with a foot on Penny's thigh and ripped the armor off of her.

Selene had snot on her face and tears kept streaming down her eyes. It looked like she'd just had the worst breakup of her life. "Don't stare," she grumbled and put her hands over Penny's arm.

Her light blue magic seeped into Penny, and the tank's arm crackled as the bone reset itself and started to heal. Penny closed her eyes and grunted. She was a tough woman.

"I'm so sorry." Bellaire came back. "If I'd known."

I waved away her words. "Not your fault. This was probably coming for me if you'd been involved or not." I glanced at Felin. "We need to talk after this, but for now, let's get clear of this and meet up with everyone at the Haylon building."

Felin nodded. "I will meet you later. I need to go check in with my people."

I met her bright blue eyes. "Come back."

Felin smiled from ear to ear. "Of course." She nodded vigorously and bounded off towards another part of the safe zone.

She'd be fine on her own if she stayed clear of the conflict. I had a feeling she could get out of any trouble if it found her anyway.

"Come on, Bellaire, you too. Crimson invited you, so there's no reason to put you out." I waved the influencer over and took Penny's arm to make sure she was stable as she started walking.

Penny winced and leaned on me for support.

"Huh. I thought I healed you," Selene said, casting another heal on the tank.

"I don't know. My side still hurts and Ken's support is helping." Penny blushed all the way to her ears.

"Uh huh," Selene sounded unconvinced. "Whatever. You deserve a little support," Selene said. "But I call dibs next. That smoke was nasty."

Candice nodded in agreement. "It was like some sort of tear gas. Very effective at preventing us from casting."

The assassin in me perked up at the idea, and I wondered if I could find a similar ability to use. The human in me also saw how bad the two ladies looked and realized it was something that should be saved for mortal enemies.

CHAPTER 23

"Well, welcome to the new training facilities at Haylon." I gestured Bellaire into the lobby. The space was all the same polished, white stone that mirrored the architecture of Haylon.

I'd learned by that point that the Harem Queen didn't do anything that wasn't over the top. It felt like we were staying in a several thousand dollar a night penthouse.

"It's nice." Bellaire blinked, apparently neither impressed nor disappointed.

"It was a rough welcome and Crimson or the Harem Queen will probably come storming in with lots of questions soon. I can wait to hear the story until they are also listening. I'm glad Felin protected you from that smoke."

"What about us that weren't?" Selene looked at me, her mascara had run all down her face.

"You should fix that. Here." Bellaire pulled out some makeup remover and a small mirror from her CID.

Selene took one look in the mirror and snatched up the items before sprinting away.

"Sorry about that, Selene," I called. "You fought well."

"Idiot," Candice muttered.

"What?" I frowned at her.

"It's okay." Penny pat me on the shoulder. "It is part of why we all find you attra—" Penny froze. "I mean, just keep being yourself and don't worry about it."

I wanted to tease out what had caused the issue, but the door slammed open and the Harem Queen came charging in, ushering her students into the lobby.

"In. In. Once you are all safe, I can go deal with this." The Harem Queen spotted me and scowled. "You."

I pointed at myself. "Me. We are safe, but we got into a little tussle, and Felin went back to the Nekorians."

"Stay put. The UG Director will probably be by shortly to check to make sure you are alive. Which means you will stay here where she knows to find you and I know you'll be safe." The Harem Queen huffed and pulled her dress up as she rushed back out.

"I heard the rumors, but I didn't believe them," a woman from Class B murmured to another.

"They are totally knocking boots," the second agreed.

"Don't listen to them." Penny pulled me aside.

"Honestly, it doesn't bother me. What bothers me is that if Helen overhears that, I'm going to find myself waking up with a spiked mace beating my face in." I shrugged. A pissed off Helen was more annoying than it was worth.

"Helen's just..." Penny trailed off. "Confused. She's very confused and doesn't know what to do with her feelings."

"If you could tell her that, it would be great." I sat down at the table that Penny had brought me over to.

Bellaire and Candice followed, but Selene was still missing.

Bellaire was turning more than a few heads as she sat down with me. "Ken, I was wondering if we could discuss my employment."

It was poor timing, but there really wasn't any better timing right now. I nodded at her. "Crimson said you wanted to move to PR."

She nodded. "I'd like to utilize what I've learned and my brand to make the move."

"Tired of being fawned after?" I joked. Bellaire was stunning as most influencers were.

Bellaire frowned. "I want to be more than a pretty face to sell things."

"How is PR being anything different? You are still a pretty face, but you are selling my guild rather than a perfume," I countered, finding myself pushing her away.

I wasn't sold on us needing a ton of PR, and I also wasn't entirely sure that we could afford her rate.

Rather than argue, Bellaire gathered herself rather professionally. "There is a major difference. I don't believe in the perfume they have me sell. I don't think it is going to solve anything. Your guild is a small startup with a recognizable name. Yet with the Haylon class that is making headlines and Crimson among its roster, there's so much potential for more. I believe that helping you grow will help protect us from the Naga or the dwarves or whatever other conflict awaits us in the dungeon." Her voice grew in strength as she spoke until she ended quite passionately.

"And what do you intend to do to help us?" I pushed.

"Improve your standing in people's minds. Use my brand to talk about how incredible Silver Fangs is, how you saved me from dwarves, or are building peace between the Elves and Nekorians."

She held my gaze for a long moment.

I nodded. There was a passion in what she said, and I honestly could see some benefit to having her help. Crimson certainly saw it if she extended an invite to the woman.

"There's a matter of payment..." I trailed off. "A small guild like ours..."

Bellaire scribbled on a piece of paper and handed it to me.

I schooled my face as I lifted the paper and looked at what she'd written. The number wasn't so bad. "This is for?"

"One year salary," Bellaire clarified. "Though, I'd like to become a member of the guild, with full standing."

I glanced at the number and then back at my CID where the funds from the elves sat. We should be able to afford her after all. It was going to hurt though.

In the end, I trusted Crimson's judgment in setting this up. Marketing was not my strong suit, killing things was.

After a moment, I held out my hand. "Welcome aboard."

The beautiful influencer clasped my arm with a rich smile. "Thank you. You won't regret this."

"Sure. We'll talk more about what you can do when we aren't regrouping from an attack from another race." I grinned. "Though, you might have to get used to that level of chaos. That seems to happen in the dungeon."

"There's more than normal dungeon things happening around you," Penny pointed out. "Nice to meet you, Bellaire. I don't think I formally introduced myself last spring."

"Pleasure." Bellaire was all smiles as she greeted Penny and Candice.

"I'm back." Selene reappeared, this time without dark makeup dripping down her face. "What'd I miss?"

"Not much." I shrugged.

Bellaire cleared her throat. "I've joined the Silver Fangs, though mostly in an administrative role. I'll be doing your PR."

Selene grabbed her hands and bounced in place. "That's so incredible! I bet the world will be gushing over the guild and everyone will be trying to join it with you helping promote it."

"That's the plan." Bellaire flashed a smile.

More of our class filtered in and saw us, coming over and pulling up chairs.

Charlotte saw me and came over, pushing Penny aside as Bun-bun bounded into Bellaire's arms. "Bun-bun, what are you doing?" Charlotte accused the rabbit.

He squeaked several times indignantly.

She sighed and gave up on the rabbit to focus on me. "I'm glad you didn't get into any fights with everything going on out there."

"About that," I chuckled and scratched the back of my head. "There might have been a small scuffle with some of the dwarves when this all went off. A few of them were trying to take Bellaire and her two camera women."

Selene's mother came in; the woman glanced around the room once before homing in on our group. "Daughter," she spoke sternly.

Selene shot to her feet. "Mother, this is Ken." She stood a little too close. "Ken, this is my mother."

"Director Amato." I held out my hand.

Her mother shook it briefly, but her eyes searched the room for someone else.

"Crimson should be here shortly," I said.

"No. I was looking for the Nekorian Shaman," she corrected me. "Crimson just turned several city blocks of dwarves into red smears on the ground. She was encouraged to do as much damage as she could and seems happy doing so."

I nodded. Crimson liked to let loose and had made a promise to the dwarves if they went after me again. I wasn't sure if she was going to exterminate an entire clan like she promised, but she was going to put a dent in one. "Felin was with us when we were attacked, but has gone back to her people to discuss the incident."

The Director nodded sharply. "As long as she wasn't injured and wasn't a risk here. It is best for her own people to have the opportunity to protect her. When Crimson returns, I'd like you to accompany me to visit the Nekorians."

I nodded, Felin would probably make a scene, but I could live with that if it meant keeping everyone safer.

"Wonderful." The Director went to leave.

"Sorry. She's like that," Selene apologized for her mother. "Dad says she often doesn't see anything but the thing she's working on. Very focused."

"She doesn't seem so bad," I added. It seemed that most of our class had gathered around me. "Let's do a headcount and make sure we have everyone. I think we are done adventuring for today and can relax. No drinking though, in case this becomes something bigger."

I eyed Selene.

She crossed over her heart. "Promise."

***

I walked with Crimson as she used a towel to get off the last of the blood. "Looks like you had a bit too much fun."

"Oh, just playing around. Someone attacked you and I had to send a message. It felt like the rest of it was some sort of dispute that had overflowed, but the one that went after you was personal," Crimson said.

"You didn't go kill one of their queens or something, did you?" I asked.

"No. At least, I haven't met an eight-foot-tall dwarf yet. Met a few of those soldiers, the ones that have a little more intelligence in their eyes and actually have decent gear. Well, decent by their level standards," she corrected herself when I looked a little worried. "They were chumps."

Director Amato sighed. "Don't call other races chumps. We need to be diplomatic."

The three of us walked up to the Nekorian encampment. The more permanent structures were made out of stone, but the Nekorian area changed quite often as their people came and went, setting up various levels of homes. Some just had hide tents, while others built small wooden structures.

We were headed to the largest stone building.

Felin spotted us and skipped over. Many eyes followed her as she bounded up to me and wrapped me in a hug before rubbing her face against my cheek. "I talked to the old shaman here and she'll let you guys come and talk to her. Well, Crimson can talk. She's passed a trial and we'll respect her words as if she were a shaman. Some might listen to Ken, but he won't be very respected until he passes his trial."

"What about me?" the Director asked.

"Would you let a foreign person come in and tell you how things worked if they didn't have qualifications that you recognized?" Felin asked the Director sternly while still cuddling against me.

"No," the Director deadpanned.

"There's your answer. We respect those who've gone through trials at the same level as a shaman. You are neither. Crimson is one, and Ken is very likely to become one." Felin pulled herself off me and took my hand. "Let me show you both in."

Crimson raised an eyebrow at me, and I could only shrug as I followed Felin in.

"This is a place for gatherings," Felin explained.

The rough stone exterior didn't do the building justice on the inside. Someone had painstakingly carved intricate reliefs into the stone telling stories of their people.

"What's this?" I pointed at one.

"The second Dwarven war." Felin waved away any more discussion. "Come inside." She pulled me into a room with six other Nekorians of various ages and appearances.

The one that they all glanced at was a woman whose hair had gone gray, only a few tufts of orange still remained on her tail.

"This is him?" the elderly Nekorian asked. Her voice held some gravel but was strong.

"This is him." Felin clung to me. "He will pass his dungeon trial shortly."

The shamans in the room huffed to smell me.

"So it may be," another shaman spoke from the side. "But we don't give a child a sword because they may be a fighter one day. So I deny his voice because he may one day be worthy."

Felin growled at the Nekorian and spoke on equal grounds. "You may not give a child a sword, but would you not grant a weapon to one on the cusp of warriorhood? How else will they learn to wield it if not given a chance."

The oldest one chuckled at that. "Felin shows you her claws for him."

"Out of respect for Felin, I will allow him to speak. Though the weight of his voice is up for each of us to decide. Besides, we have a more important guest," one of the shamans spoke and looked Crimson up and down. "The famed Crimson."

Two of the shamans were men, and they sat up a little straighter in front of Crimson.

Crimson put an arm around my shoulder and leaned on my other side, trapping me between her and Felin, while also giving me support. "I'm actually this guy's subordinate, but I'm happy to be the one asking the questions. First off, what the fuck happened today?"

"Language," one of them growled. "You will show respect here, human."

"I could turn you into a smear against the wall," Crimson shot back. "But I won't because that would probably upset Felin and Ken by extension. So, let's talk and not just sit there judging everyone's worth, aye?"

I put my face in my hands. "Crimson, lay off."

She grumbled.

Felin spoke up, "She's being crude, but that is her way. Like some of our own who've passed the trial throughout history, she has few equals and is allotted much leniency among humans."

Many of the shamans nodded in agreement. "Then what would you ask of us, Felin?"

"The truth. What happened today with the dwarves?"

"They were expunging weakness from their nests. We've seen it before where a clan queen reaches new heights and is able to produce stronger drones. Her old drones are pushed to the edge and enraged. Rather than continue to expend resources on them, they are used to injure an enemy," the oldest Nekorian said.

"So the closest Dwarven queen has broken through some threshold?" Felin asked for clarity. "Does that mean conflict is near?"

The old shaman took a puff of a pipe where she sat in her chair. "Dwarves are always filled with ambition and greed. Conflict is always near if they sense weakness. With how Crimson went out and fought, she perhaps evaded larger conflict."

"Or perhaps not. The dwarves are not well known for their sense either," a shaman barked a laugh.

"No... they are not," the oldest echoed those thoughts.

"What of a soldier dwarf being among them and aiming for Ken?" Crimson asked.

I remained silent, letting the two ladies fight for me.

"That was likely a plan already set in motion. The expunging of weaker drones was likely just a good cover. He should pass his trial quickly so that he has the strength to defend himself." The eldest eyed me. "What do you think of your trial?"

"Difficult, but not impossible. I have died several times already, but I think victory is now within my reach. My last attempt was close, and I've trained with seeing the final phase of the fight in mind since then." I nodded to the shaman.

She waved her pipe and glanced at Felin.

The Nekorian at my side nodded. "He knew not what to expect last time. This time he is fully prepared."

"Then I wish you the best of luck." The shaman smiled at me. "Hopefully next time you are in my presence, others don't object to your voice." She pointedly glared at the other shaman who'd spoken out against me. "Maybe they will learn to respect those that will soon become great before they fall into difficulties and have no one to help them."

The second shaman looked away with an angry flush on her face.

"Or he could die," one of the men spoke out. "If that happens, please find me for comfort, Felin."

She scoffed at my side. "I sense and respect his strength. He will return, and you will not feel so comfortable mocking him next time."

The Nekorian dipped his head. There was no heat or anger in his expression, just a subtle touch of loss.

"Thank you all for your guidance," I finally spoke. "It seems the dwarves are a growing concern if their queen, filled with ambition and greed, has grown stronger. I appreciate your wisdom and will keep it in mind for my future decisions."

"HA!" The elder barked a laugh. "He'll go far. Good nose, Felin."

Felin's ears went straight up at the praise from the old shaman. "Of course. I have learned from the very best, even if I have sought my pride in different pastures. Thank you all for your words. I have heard them and we will return more prepared for the future." She gave only a sharp nod at the room and turned back.

I frowned, but stayed silent, knowing that their hearing was superb.

Only once we were most of the way back did I speak. "We didn't really get that much information."

Felin grinned. "No, we got plenty. And maybe I just wanted to show you off a bit."

The Director nodded. "Knowing that they are increasing in strength is good to judge their near-term actions and gauge if they are preparing for war. Excuse me, I have work to do." She shot off.

"You need to get some rest and prepare yourself for tomorrow." Felin poked my chest. "I'll come with you to see you defeat the panther."

CHAPTER 24

We were out on the twenty-sixth floor, clearing chocolate rabbits and collecting the loot before Bun-bun could destroy it. The rabbit still had it out for the chocolate imposters.

The band was back together, and I was enjoying having our dynamic back. It had been good practice to fight with other classmates, but it definitely wasn't the same.

Here, the landscape was the everpresent rolling hills of sugary snow and candy cane trees dusted with frosting.

"... and of course Harley missed it all because she was chasing skirts." Des was picking on Harley yet again.

Harley huffed. "To say I was chasing skirts implies that I didn't catch any. I certainly caught some."

Des chopped at the top of Harley's head, but Harley ducked out of the way. "That's not the point."

"Been working on my agility just for you, Des." She danced away playing the flute.

"Well, you should have been around for the fight."

"You weren't there either. Ken had Penny, though. I heard she took a spear for him," Harley teased me.

"She did. It was pretty impressive, as was Felin. The woman has moves," I said.

Harley held her cheeks. "To see a cat girl flip out over me getting attacked." She faked swooning and barely caught herself before she fell into the sugar mounds.

Fayeth grumbled to herself.

"What was that?" I asked.

"I'm tired of this whole splitting up of the party. Nothing good happens when you split the party. Your world has entire jokes about not doing it, yet Crimson broke us up," the elf mumbled murderously.

It was adorable.

"I'm fine, and we all have our ten boss kills, so we are back together until we get to the raid. Then we'll be folding in a lot more, and we will be glad for the practice we got with the others," I said.

Fayeth nodded happily. "Yes. I look forward to staying in front of you. If I were there, I would have blocked the spear too, but taken less damage."

I rubbed the top of her head, ruffling her perfect golden strands of hair. "I love you too, my Adrel."

Fayeth blushed all the way to the tips of her ears. "I love you. It is frustrating being unable to help with the panther. And then beyond that, I missed you being attacked by the dwarves. I am meant to be by your side."

"Hopefully, we can finish the panther today," I said, following Fayeth as she started weaving through the mounds of sugar in search of our next prey.

"Didn't Crimson say that she taunted the dungeon to get her last fight to show up?" Charlotte asked.

I groaned. "That feels less than ideal. The dungeon has already given me enough trouble. I don't need to go looking for more."

I was ready for the fight. I'd prepared plenty of potions and trained for it with Crimson. This time, I was going to kill that panther and see what sort of ability it had for me.

And once I had finished the trial, I was definitely tempted to go rub my new status in some Nekorian's noses. A few of those shamans were downright rude. Somehow, my ego was salved by the fact that she'd come back to our place once everything had settled. It wasn't like she was mine, though.

"Too bad Crimson can't solve this for us," Harley groused.

"She's back at the safe zone, along with the Harem Queen. The UG begged them to watch over the dwarves," Des said.

I nodded along, though I knew in Crimson's case that it was less begging and more pointing out that her killing spree had put everyone in a precarious position and she had a responsibility to protect everyone from the backlash of her actions.

For someone who ran around and did what she wanted, Crimson did still care about her actions affecting innocents. So, she'd planted herself visibly in the safe zone for the moment. And with her in the safe zone, there wouldn't be dwarves slipping past her to chase after me.

"Well, this is a me thing anyway. We'll just keep grinding through the dungeon floor for training."

I glanced at my CID.

Ken Nagato

Class: Emperor

Secondary Class: Demon Lord
Level: 26
Experience: 78%
Strength: 68 (+6)
Agility: 133 (+24)
Stamina: 98 (+9)
Magic: 91 (+6)
Mana: 101 (+6)
Skills:
Dark Strike, Earth Stomp, Charm, Metamorphosis, Sprint, Absorb, Discharge, Dark Blades, Shadow Arm, Camouflage, Shadow Ambush, Elemental Shield, Portal [Special] [Restricted], Mana Burn, Hydra [Elysara], Cleave [Fayeth], Spell Mirror, Dungeon's Blessing, Blades of Shadow, Mana Implosion, Shadow Wave [Desmonda], Revive [Charlotte], Shadow Phase, Dodge

My level hadn't made much progress, but it was expected to slow down. And we were only a month into the school year. It was my stats that had gone through the biggest improvement, and I was on my way to catching back up and getting ahead of the stat curve compared to my level.

My gear was better, but that wasn't saying much. It had been lagging behind for a while.

"More chocolate bunnies up ahead," Fayeth warned.

We all snapped to attention, dropping any lingering thoughts. Bun-bun jumped off Charlotte's head and growled.

"Yes yes," Charlotte sighed. "I will make you big again, but you need to stop destroying the loot."

Bun-bun bounced back and forth, growling and squeaking at the chocolate bunnies ahead of us.

"You have to wait for me," Fayeth reprimanded him. "Or I'm going to stop feeding you while I cook."

Bun-bun's ears stiffened and he looked pleadingly up at Fayeth.

"Good rabbit," she said as she marched forward towards the already alert group of candy monsters with her new glaive ready to cleave into them.

* * *

Des laid down on a pile of snow. "I don't think your panther is coming today." She looked over at me.

"Maybe you should shake your fists at the dungeon and do lines of the sugar from this floor in defiance," Harley said.

We all looked at her.

I suddenly began wondering what she'd been doing the last few days.

"What? Don't tell me none of you have been thinking about it? Really?" She looked around the group as we stared at her.

"Never even crossed my mind," I said.

"Damn, this place has just been begging for some booger sugar jokes from me this whole time." Harley sat down and stretched her neck.

"I'm surprised it took you this long to use it then." Charlotte took some carrots out of her CID and handed them to the bunny who looked like he'd just walked through a massacre of chocolate. And, he had.

And despite Fayeth's protests, he'd still destroyed more than a few pieces of chocolate loot.

I sat down on a stump that looked like a giant candy cane had been felled. My pants stuck to it to the point I was worried they were going to rip when I got up. "Crimson said that her test always came at a bad time for her."

"So we are supposed to get ourselves in a bad situation?" Des frowned. "Can't say I much like that concept. Maybe you should start shaking your fist. Don't worry, I'll get the line ready." She picked up a little of the sugar and sprinkled it on her breast before using a knife to neatly put it in a line.

"If you aren't going to do that line, I just might." Harley eyed Des' chest.

Fayeth's glaive fell down in the space between Harley and Des. "Careful."

"It was a joke." Harley held up her hands and almost painfully pulled her eyes away from Des' cleavage. "You really are one lucky mother fucker."

"Don't I know it," I sighed. "Des, clean yourself off." I dusted off my pants and looked up at the ceiling of this floor. It was an illusion of a sky above, but I knew if someone jumped high enough, they'd hit it. "Hey dungeon! I'm here and ready to fight, so why are you chickening out?"

We all braced, but nothing happened.

"Ken, you can do better than that," Harley huffed. "Tell the dungeon about all the vile nasty things you do to it if you got it alone in a room. Oh, and tell it about how you plan to find its mother and repeat those things."

I deadpanned. "Does the dungeon even have a mother?"

"I don't see you coming up with better ideas." Harley put her hands on her hips.

Instead, if the dungeon was some god-like being, I didn't need to shout at it. I didn't need to insult it. I needed to challenge it.

Raising my fist, I thought of the most defiant gesture I could make and put in my all as my middle finger sprang up like a defiant pillar to the heavens. *I accept your challenge unless you are too cowardly to send it again.*

The ground rumbled.

"Fuck, you did it now." Harley clung to Des. The warlock immediately tried to strip the clingy bard off of her.

"Ken, you got this. Focus on the panther." Des' eyes locked on something over my shoulder.

The panther prowled out of the snowbanks.

Once again, the dark, big cat had faint sparks of purple lighting dancing over its form. Small trails of smoke curled off its side. The monster was the size of an SUV as it came closer, watching me carefully.

It seemed slightly bigger this time, its eyes fixed on me and glowing faintly.

"This is the time, Ken!" Charlotte bounced up and down, waving a disgruntled Bun-bun around like a pom-pom.

I steeled myself, rotating my shoulders and re-adjusting the grip on my weapons. We'd been grinding all day, and I was tired, but an adventurer needed to not be so weak as to let something like 'tired' stop them from performing.

Opening my inventory, I popped a potion that made it feel like I'd just downed a dozen coffees, and I bounced in place, warming up. I was both reviewing the strategies and also trying to get out of my own way and let my training take over.

[Dark Blades] activated on my weapons, giving the edges a thin purple sheen. My CID was organized and ready. Health potions were in the right spot and so was the selection of enhancement potions I'd settled on.

I was ready.

The Smoke Panther came in fast, its paws swiping at me. I parried and dodged, focusing my efforts right now on damaging the beast as much as I could.

[Metamorphosis] might add plenty of stats, but it made me too bulky. The extra size would only get in my way. If Felin was right, every dodge was worth its weight in gold because it prevented the panther from building up its stacks of the buff that sped it up.

Even before I knew that, dodging was too important. This made it critical.

I worked my rotation in between avoiding attacks and using the ability [Dodge] to open enough space to attack in a flurry of blows. When the panther's eyes lit up—a tell I'd grown to recognize—I activated [Shadow Phase]. Sure enough, the monster teleported behind me, leaving me riddled with shallow wounds.

I chugged a healing potion, spinning around to face the panther and resume our dance. There was a concern in my mind. Given that the panther slowed down after using that ability, I weighed the decision of either drawing out the fight for it to use it again or pushing to the next phase.

I quickly determined that I was accruing enough damage that the simplest solution was to push forward and rely on everything I'd prepared to beat it in the next phase.

Pushing hard, I took damage where I needed to in order to get the monster over to the next phase. Sure enough, the panther leapt back, the world shattering around us.

This time, I didn't gawk. Instead, I used the brief break in fighting to open my CID and slam back potions like my life depended on it.

And I was ready.

I quickly chugged a potion for agility, one for stamina, another for movement speed. Finally, I threw back one that would boost my agility by 25% for six seconds. The early boost would be vital.

Putting my sword in my CID, I pulled out a simpler knife with a weaker +4 to agility. It wouldn't matter in the long run, I just needed something lighter to work with. All of them together, mixed with my nerves, made me queasy, but I gritted my teeth and pushed through it.

I didn't let the panther start the next hit. Instead, I stepped in, activating [Hydra] and [Triple Strike] to start things off. The three cross slashes had purple lightning dancing off the panther and onto me as I picked up speed.

My knives came up in a boxer stance as I rapidly punched them into the panther, using [Dodge] to avoid its first strike and focus on building my speed buff as quickly as I could.

Purple lightning raced down my arms as my focus was locked on the panther. Its side was torn up in a matting of smoke tendrils, and I sidestepped the next swipe, feeling like I was getting an advantage in speed.

The short duration potion fell off, and I felt the drop in speed as I had to take a swipe on my forearm after dodging the other. My daggers kept up as the panther's speed increased. Yet I could feel my acceleration pulling ahead.

Slowly at first, my pummeling with daggers grew more frequent as I was able to sidestep the panther's claws more easily.

My strategy was working!

In my excitement, I looked out past the battle towards my party to join them in their cheering. But what I saw made my blood run cold.

When the panther had frozen time, he had frozen not just my party, but several of what I could only assume were Kaiming assassins mid-ambush. They were about to attack the rest of my party.

And I recognized one of them as the mage who had fought my grandparents after the plane crash. They had called him Mr. Ming, and from the intel that had been shared with me, he was the highest remaining member of Kaiming. Level-wise, he was in the mid-forties.

The rest of my party would die if I failed this attempt with the panther. I didn't know what ability I would receive, but it was clear I was going to need every advantage.

I faltered, and the panther whacked me across the shoulder hard enough to make me fumble.

Glancing at the panther, I realized a few facts. One, the dungeon really did like to present the challenge at difficult moments. Being stalked by assassins was certainly one of them, even if I hadn't known it at the time. Two, there was even more pressure this time to not fail. Because I couldn't rely on Charlotte's revive.

The panther came at me, and this time, I felt anxiety.

The safety net had been torn away from me, possibly by the dungeon's own design. Knowing that I needed to focus on the fight, I cleared my mind, using techniques my grandparents had taught me. My worry, my anxiety, it was nothing but fuel for me as I stepped back in with my daggers, punching as fast and as hard as I could.

My muscles burned as I chugged a potion and pushed myself to my very limits. Everything faded away as I performed at my peak and maybe a touch beyond as I tested my very limits.

The panther, however, had a surprise for me.

Its eyes flashed, and I activated [Shadow Phase], yet it wasn't instant. Instead, the panther's speed easily quadrupled as it came at me.

I took the hits. [Shadow Phase] reduced the damage as I pumped my daggers into the monster. My best hope was that this was temporary and that I could come out the other side faster.

After what felt like an agonizing eternity, its speed cut off and purple lightning pulsed more densely around the monster than before.

I was battered and my body wanted to give up, but I pushed through the exhaustion. Seeing the end of this, I felt my speed pick back up to stay on pace with the panther and steadily surpass it.

First, I was able to duck below the panther and get one, then two strikes in before dodging another. Quickly, I was at three and then four with the same maneuver.

Before I knew it, I was tearing into the panther's side between swipes.

This monster was insanely durable. There was no way that I could have killed it in a straight up fight. But that was why this second phase existed. It was about being faster than the panther and dodging all of its attacks to build up speed faster than it. A unique challenge—like it was tailored for me. It required me to retain intense focus for a prolonged period of time.

It excited me the faster I went and the more I shredded into the panther. Part of me knew that this would be part of the power that was in the ability I was going to get, which only made me more excited. Something like this could help me save my party beyond the shattered space and the frozen time.

And it was the type of ability that I needed to keep up with Crimson.

In my excitement, I nearly missed the panther's eyes flash once more, but this time, no ability came. Instead, the panther puffed away into black smoke like every other monster in the dungeon.

There was a solid smack as a spellbook hit the ground.

I looked around quickly, worried my party was about to fall. But the space around me was still frozen. Unsure how long it was going to last, I chugged a healing potion and picked up the spellbook, reading the title just before I used my CID to learn the new ability. Purple lightning still raced over my body as I turned and faced the next problem at hand. Only this time, the lightning would stay past the boss fight.

Bracing myself, I took one step forward, moving out of the frozen world and directly into my next fight.

CHAPTER 25

"You can do it!" Charlotte shouted. She was so excited, Ken seemed to have this in hand.

Yet.

One second, Ken was squaring off against the panther; the next second, Ken was alone and wreathed in crackling purple lightning.

Ken glared at her with anger before he disappeared in a sudden boom of movement. For a second, Charlotte didn't understand. Had the skill clouded his mind? But less than a second later, the sound of a dozen blades clashing rang out behind her.

Ken hadn't been glaring at her, but the people behind her. When she turned, over a dozen assailants were stumbling back or stopped in their tracks as Ken reappeared for just a split second.

"He's *fast*," Des breathed.

"I could still win," Bun-bun grumped.

"Not even close," Charlotte chided the rabbit.

Ken blurred back and forth, fighting all of the attackers at once.

"Harley, hit him with haste," Des demanded.

"Even if he's an ally, how the fuck do I hit that?" Harley didn't wait for an answer, still dutifully trilling on her flute and buffing Ken.

***

I was pure speed.

The buff from the panther hadn't left me. Instead, it had continued over onto the ability. Or at least, the first half of it.

Rather than dwell on that, I focused on the Kaiming assassins. There were over a dozen of them all garbed in similar red and black outfits that were mostly cloth with leather over their vitals and a metal circlet around their head.

It was a simple, lightweight armor; though, I didn't doubt that the leader of this group would have cloth that could potentially even stop a blade.

As soon as I stepped out of the space of frozen time, the area around seemed to be moving like it was stuck in molasses. I shot forward, knocking an arrow out of the air, and then striking every assassin rushing forward with as much strength as I could muster before shooting past the front line to attack the several archers in the back.

My blades raced along their bodies, tearing through their armor's weak spots and then their skin. [Liminal Speed] was an incredible ability, but I also knew that I had built it up on the panther before the current fight.

I left two of the archers in absolute ribbons. Their reactions and attempts to throw me off of them were laughable with my speed.

The Kaiming assassins quickly shifted their focus from trying to attack me to forcing me to defend my party as they threw knives and spells in an abundance at the others. I appeared before one of the spells, using [Absorb] to suck it in before I was off, knocking knives out of the air and deflecting the weapons back towards spells that were still in the air.

A Kaiming assassin drew near Fayeth, and I appeared between him and his target, kicking his knee sideways with a wet crack and spun, landing my boot in his face and sending him spiraling off to the side.

Harley hit me with a haste buff, but it felt completely unnecessary.

I still used it, though, shooting between two of the assassins and dragging my blades across their hamstrings before blasting over to deal with other attackers.

My mind struggled to keep up with all the inputs that came with moving at this speed. I overshot my next target and had to land behind him, stabbing him three times before racing off to the next one.

While my current goal was to get rid of the assassins, the real target was still hovering in the back shouting at his men and casting wide area spells. After watching Kai Ming fight with my grandfather, I'd never forget his face. Leave it to zealots to name their child after the organization.

I dodged out of a wave of acid and let it dissolve a man that was going to bleed out in a minute anyway. He sent out rapid pulses of deathly green energy in a full circle around him.

I didn't see a way towards my target immediately, so I raced off to deal with several more of his men, stabbing the closest one in the thigh twice and cutting through the back of his neck.

With each strike, I was growing faster and faster.

My CID displayed the buffs now, and the stack was ever growing. As far as I could tell, if I kept attacking, the stacks would climb. I was pretty sure they would go away if I stopped and stood still for too long.

So, I didn't stop.

Instead, I decided I would use the second part of the ability only when I saw a chance to finish the fight.

Fayeth had caught two of the assailants and was stopping them from getting to Charlotte, while Des had already used [Metamorphosis] to grapple a third.

I jumped on the back of Des' target and buried my daggers repeatedly into him before speeding around and planting a kiss on my favorite warlock. Then I took out the two men fighting Fayeth.

Soon all of them were dead but Kai Ming.

The caster glared daggers at me and continued to surround himself with magic. "Ken Nagato. I will kill you."

I bounced between my feet, grinning like a loon. "Not a chance. Your organization fucked around, and it's time to find out." Purple lightning crackled around me, giving me an ominous glow.

He grabbed several potions and downed them at the same time. Wave after wave of magic burst forth from him.

I gritted my teeth and raced through them, feeling the dark green magic burn at my skin like acid as I reached Kai. He was slow to react, his eyes dropping down to me as my daggers punched into his armor. Unfortunately, his armor was high level enough that my daggers didn't penetrate more than a hair's breadth.

Kai Ming tried to grab me, but I ducked out of the way, and snakes rained down on us.

I smacked the closest one away and stepped back out of melee as he unleashed more of the area attacks. If he couldn't hit me with a single target spell, he was just going to blanket the area and force me to weather it. As much as I hoped he was an idiot, he adapted to my speed quickly.

For a moment, I thought about retreating, but then a heal hit me.

"You got this!" Charlotte shouted and twirled her staff as she healed me again.

Des started to fire hexes at Kai Ming rapid fire.

The last of the Kaiming organization, for which he was named, growled and ignored me, throwing waves of that deathly energy at my party.

[Absorb] didn't work well on large attacks either. Instead, I used Charlotte's [Heal] to push back through the abilities he was throwing out to keep me away and pulled out my new sword to try and hack through his armor.

Kai wasn't a stranger to fighting and shifted, drawing a blade of his own. He abandoned parrying my strikes, instead swinging to limit the damage I could inflict and defend the weak spots in his armor.

I pushed harder, cutting the sleeve of his armor off.

Kai must have sensed the end, because he pulled out a bandoleer of flasks and threw them all high into the air towards my party while he grabbed a spell in between both hands.

It didn't take a lot of deduction to know that whatever Hail Mary he was throwing out was not going to be good.

Sensing it was time, I activated the second part of the ability. "Liminal Space."

The world around me fragmented, peeling the dungeon back around me and freezing the potions flying through the air, as well as Kai.

I checked my CID. As I expected, all the stacks I had built were rapidly declining. Even with all the stacks that I had built with the panther and against these assassins, I only had a minute.

Luckily, a minute would be plenty.

I jumped up into the air, gathering the flasks and putting them in my CID before returning to Kai. My blade flashed over the collar of his armor, peeling it back and revealing his throat.

My sword bit into his throat, and I used the back of my dagger like a hammer to drive it into his throat before twisting it and pulled it back out.

I stepped back out of the effect to end it early. My stacks were greatly reduced. Everything didn't seem quite so slow now.

Kai dropped his spell in surprise as he reached for the gaping hole in his throat.

"This is where you found out that you aren't my match," I said, watching the last of the organization that killed my parents fall to the ground and choke on his own blood.

There was a long-forgotten anger that bubbled up from my teenage years. It rose, and to my surprise, it dissipated as if a ghost that had been haunting me for years left, and I felt my shoulders relax.

"He's not going to eat us or anything, right?" Harley asked.

Des didn't have that hesitation and jumped on me, giving me a big hug and pulling my lips to hers. She sucked them before her tongue invaded my mouth. She felt like a bubble of passion ready to burst.

"My turn." Fayeth grabbed my collar and pulled me away from Des to kiss me, her blue eyes shining bright as she searched mine.

Charlotte wasn't far behind. But rather than being so bold, I had to step away and wrap her up in a hug to kiss her. Once I initiated, she showed me just how happy she was to return the kiss, going as far as jumping into my arms and wrapping her legs around me.

"So, you didn't go crazy when you used your new ability?" Des asked.

"Nope." I shook my head. "Kind of hard to adjust to the increased speed at times, but it is damn useful."

Harley approached Kai who had died kneeling, his eyes still full of grief, even if the life was gone. "So, how did you just, you know." She made the sound of an explosion and her finger blossomed at her neck as she stared at the gaping wound.

"Oh. I can stop time."

Harley looked up at me with a strange passion in her eyes. "How long does it last?"

"Not long enough for the things you are thinking of." I narrowed my eyes. "Besides, I have to build up stacks by attacking many, many times."

"We should experiment." Des smirked. "Because if we can get you going that fast before a boss fight..." She trailed off.

"What just happened was an extreme example. I had built up a lot of stacks against the panther. But longer fights, I'll put out the kind of damage that Crimson might have been capable of at my level." I had a sudden realization that made me smirk.

This ability would be a huge gap closer between me and Crimson. Before, I think a part of me always knew that, even if I met her level, [Limit Break] was such a game changer that I'd always be chasing after her shadow.

Yet...

I stared down at my hand as a little purple lightning still jumped between my fingers. This new ability would change everything.

"Congratulations." Des kissed me again. "Also, I'm happy you aren't going crazy and trying to kill us."

"Yep. We don't need that plan then," Fayeth said, nodding.

I raised an eyebrow. "Plan?"

"Well..." Fayeth looked away.

"We had a whole plan of how to escape if you went Crimson crazy on us." Harley spoke up.

"You know, just in case," Des placated me. "We can't be too careful."

I hugged her back. "Glad you all were thinking ahead because I wasn't. I was just trying to kill the panther. Then I saw the assassins in the frozen time zone while fighting it." I shook my head, remembering the fear that had briefly coursed through me. "Let's get back to the safe zone. First round of drinks is on me."

"All of the drinks are on you," Harley teased. "We should invite the rest of the class. Everyone is probably waiting for the good news." She tapped at her CID as we started heading back to the safe zone.

**

We reached the tavern just down the street from the Haylon spire.

"Surprise!" Crimson shouted along with the rest of the class. Our teacher pulled out a kazoo and blew loudly in it.

I took a step back, reaching for my daggers.

"He doesn't do well with surprises." Des kissed my cheek as she placed a hand on my arm that was ready to strike and lowered it down.

"Fair." Crimson shrugged, giving the kazoo another puff before putting it away. "Not many adventurers do."

We didn't have the whole tavern to ourselves, but the celebration certainly had many of them turning their heads in our direction. It wasn't every day you got to see Mistress Crimson blowing a kazoo.

"How was everything back here?" I asked, trying to awkwardly continue the conversation. I really didn't like surprises, yet this was nice of them to do. Logically, this was great, but it would just take a moment for my body to stop getting ready for a fight.

"Pssh." Crimson waved her hand. "Dead dwarves. Not much else to say. I killed all of them that entered the safe zone as a warning. They stopped coming around noon."

"More importantly, what ability did you get?" Selene shot out of the group and clung to my arm.

"It makes him fast as fuck," Des simplified.

"Oh?" Crimson raised an eyebrow. "How fast are we talking?"

"I could probably match you while you have Limit Break active if we do it right," I said. I didn't mention that it would probably take a long time to build up the stacks. I could get there.

Crimson had a look of disbelief. "Tomorrow we are going to the zone director, and you are going to work with them to run some tests. I want to see this." She broke open a beer and took a long drink before handing me my own.

"Oh and I killed Kai Ming." I dropped casually.

Crimson paused mid-sip and lowered it slowly, a faint spark of red lightning dancing out of her eyes. "They attacked you?"

"Later." I put a hand on her arm. "When we aren't celebrating." I turned to the rest of the class who were all eager to greet me and held up my beer. "This new ability is going to destroy the other schools at the raid on the thirty-second floor."

The class cheered.

"You guys have to see it to believe it." Harley mingled in with the group, putting an arm around Bonnie and taking a pink bubbly drink from Meredith. "He beat the panther and was all scary, covered in purple lightning.

"I about pissed myself thinking he was going to go Crimson on all of us."

Crimson was pulling me down into a seat next to her when she cleared her throat.

Harley coughed into her hand. "You know, be all bad ass." She tried to salvage her statement. "Anyway, then he fought like a dozen assassins on his own. He moved so fast that he was able to block them all and knock arrows out of the sky. Then he went all shwing shwing, and they all fell apart like fish on a sushi board." She swung her glass around as if it were a sword, sloshing little bits on the table.

The crowd laughed, while Meredith made appreciative noises.

"It wasn't like that. I didn't slice through them all," I countered, all of us sitting at one big table.

"But you fought a dozen of them at once?" Penny asked and echoed 'a dozen at once' to herself much quieter with a thoughtful expression.

I had a feeling her smut story was going to take an interesting turn.

"Something like that." I took a sip of my drink. "Kai Ming was tough, though. He decided to just cover huge areas in magical attacks."

"That's one way to deal with an opponent that is far faster than you." Helen nodded in understanding, more interested in the fight than anything else.

Felin burst through the door and saw I was already inside. "Ken! Sorry I'm late."

"Join us." I waved her over.

She bounded over and took a big huff of my scent before her eyes went wide and she latched onto me with a big hug, rubbing her face on mine.

"Down, girl," Selene joked.

"Sit down," Des clarified and pulled Felin off of me. "We were just getting a recount of the fight."

"Oh yes." Felin's face became serious. Then she pulled out a small scroll and a primitive pen. "I should document this for my people."

"Okay, well if I have to tell the story. So, we had been at it all day..." I got into recounting the situation.

"You did what? To the Great One? Lucky you are alive," Felin scowled when I got to the part about angering the dungeon to summon the panther.

"So cool. It froze time when you were being attacked?" Taylor's eyes were big. "So then you had to beat it to save everyone?!"

"As you can see, he did." Fayeth waved to the rest of our party and shooed me on to continue the story.

There were ohs and ahs as I got into the detail of fighting Kai Ming and the assassins.

"To Ken!" Selene threw her drink in the air, and I raised my glass while fighting down a blush as all of my classmates clinked their glasses to mine.

"Any one of you would have done the same," I asserted.

Helen tipped her glass in my direction. "No, that was good work. Glad you used your new skill for something useful."

Was that... a...a compliment from Helen?

The world might freeze over tomorrow with an omen like that.

I tipped my glass at her and took another heavy drink as if this was going to be the last night of the world. That and I was totally stealing one of Crimson's potions before bed.

"We are going to kick Royal Academy's asses." Kendra threw back her drink. "Those assholes won't know what hit them."

"I think Pendulum is the greater threat," Penny said.

"No, you can never count out Trusk. They are weirdos, but they manage to do incredible things." Leah sipped out of a stein far too large for the small woman.

"Doesn't matter," I said over my drink and met Crimson's eyes. "Because we are a step above them all. After all, the Mistress Crimson is our teacher," I spoke smugly and then in a low voice for Crimson only I added, "and I'm going to show you how fast I am tomorrow. As an agility-focused fighter, I hope you don't take offense."

Her eyes sparked. Not just because I had challenged her, but because of my tone.

I felt it too.

With my new ability, I felt confident that I could match, if not pass Crimson one day. And that confidence suddenly made me take her off the pedestal I'd put her on and brought her down to my level.

Maybe after we trained tomorrow, I'd even put her beneath me.

CHAPTER 26

I stretched my legs in the UG building as a number of technicians in green vests busied themselves around the room. Everyone else had gone off, and Felin had filled in for my spot in my party. I was going to take a day testing the limits of my new ability.

"Alright," Director Amato had a tablet in her hand as she orchestrated the testing personally.

The entire time, she was clicking around on her high heels to check in with each group. I was getting a feeling that this was a bigger deal than I'd given it credit for.

"I wanted to thank you for your assistance in these tests and the opportunity to see another skill of the same caliber as Crimson's Limit Break," she said.

"No problem. I'm excited to see exactly what I can do." I shifted my weight from foot to foot, eager to get started.

"We all are. As a reminder, this building is made out of stone quarried from the fiftieth floor in the dungeon. It serves a few purposes, but right now, it's a place that even Crimson isn't going to shatter if she goes all out," the director explained.

I glanced at Crimson for confirmation. She was in her standard red leather bodysuit; her long, black hair was braided down to her hips.

"I'd have to really try and break these walls, but as for fighting you within them, they should hold up even if I use Limit Break." She was holding a bag of chips, shoving them into her mouth at a record pace.

She caught my gaze, her blue eyes flashing with amusement. "What? I burned a lot of calories yesterday against the dwarves. Gotta refuel." She licked the salt and oil from her lips.

"You might need more food too if your explanation of this ability is correct," the director continued. "While we are here testing, this device attached to your CID will give us live feedback to analyze." She tapped at the dongle that had been attached to my CID with a second band. "And these cameras are special equipment used by the UG and high-level guilds." She pointed to the cameras scattered around the perimeter of the room.

My eyes went wide. "Those are damage meters!"

"Precisely." She smiled. "Do I need to explain those?"

"No, ma'am," I said, looking at the devices. They were small cameras on tripods, but the real magic happened in the fortified boxes behind them.

The box contained a computer that ran a complex algorithm. The cameras watched every participant and assigned accurate damage calculations per attack. At the end, they would spit out graphs and charts to help the participants hone their abilities and understand where they stood compared to other members.

At the top end, the damage meters were what guilds used to measure their members and hone in on what did the most damage.

My shifting from one foot to another became more rapid as I grinned.

"Now, to start, we are going to run through a few fairly standard exercises. I want to assess how exactly your stacks trigger and what might affect that." She pointed to the other side of the room where various objects were being lined up. "You are going to go down the line and perform three attacks on each. The first, a casual attack, the second with more determination, and the third, I want to you imagine that you are stabbing your mortal enemy."

I raised an eyebrow.

Crimson answered, "The dungeon is smart enough to recognize the difference between friend, neutral, and enemy. I'm guessing there are severe restrictions on what you can attack to build up stacks."

The director picked up her comment. "Otherwise, you'd be able to just stab a wall until your stacks were through the roof and then start a fight. The dungeon is not keen on gimmicks."

I nodded. That logic made sense when it came to keeping the dungeon a challenge. This ability might be powerful, but there was no reason for the dungeon to give me something that would let me cheat to that extreme.

I had to admit, the thought of building up thousands of charges and then blitzing down a raid boss in a snap of a finger had come up last night over drinks, and my buzzed mind had latched onto the dream. In my sleep, I had killed the dinosaur spawn that Crimson named Fred.

That was just what they expected. The UG was here to test that theory.

"Alright, go ahead and get started." The director tapped on her tablet.

The little device on my wrist chimed, and I walked over to the first target. I looked at the big stone block and then struck it with a training knife once. Gritting my teeth, I gave it a real slash with a second hit before I overlayed Kai Ming's face on it in my mind and struck as hard as I could.

No purple lightning raced up my arms, and a check of my CID showed that I hadn't gained any stacks.

Next up was a wooden dummy, which ended up acting the same as the stone.

"It was sent down here for slaughter anyway. Kill it with a fourth blow. Don't let it suffer," the director said for my benefit.

There was a cow tied to a post, looking around like it was disappointed there wasn't any grass.

I gritted my teeth and struck it casually enough that I didn't even penetrate its hide. No lightning. The second attack gave me nothing too, but the third gave me a stack before I got a second when I finished it with the fourth blow.

"Good." The director continued to tap on her tablet. "We'll assume most strikes meant to inflict harm will work on a monster as well. The final test is..."

Crimson appeared in front of me as the techs hauled away the other targets. "Me." She posed. "Let's see how fast you really are." She played with her short sword.

"Careful what you wish for." I struck casually.

Nothing happened.

The second attack caused purple lightning to spark along my hands, and the third, she blocked, but that didn't matter, another stack built.

"This is all?" Crimson taunted me.

I went into a flurry of attacks, all of them mundane as my stacks built up and more purple lightning gathered on my body.

"Good. I want to see you use all of your skills," Crimson pushed me, matching my speed and strength as I continued.

I activated my skills one after another, while the UG techs collected the data.

Some adventurers would try to hide more of the information about their abilities, but Crimson didn't seem concerned. And I figured that, by the time I was at a level where it was a concern, most of my skills would have changed.

Crimson stopped matching me and stood back with a bag of chips, lazily blocking my strikes with a chip before she popped it in her mouth and pulled another one out.

"Are you mocking me?" I huffed playfully.

"I thought you said you were going to be stupid fast. Not feeling it." She shrugged. "Bet you couldn't even steal one of my chips."

I met her eyes, and we were both smiling as I kept at it, picking up speed. The challenge was made.

Crimson eventually stopped being able to grab a new chip between every hit, and I could see it when her brow pressed down in focus as she continued to block my attacks. A thrill raced through me. I was still getting faster.

Rather than continue a smooth curve up in speed, I modulated my own speed, slowing down fractionally each strike for several dozen attacks before I exploded in speed and snatched the bag of chips out of her arms.

The way her pretty blue eyes snapped open in alarm was so pleasing.

I'd found myself even more attracted to her today. I knew it was because my own attitude had changed, but I found my eyes drawn to her curves in that tight leather bodysuit more as we fought before shifting back up to her lips.

She had a smirk on as she caught me staring and exploded in a flurry of slashes with her sword.

"You think you can steal my chips and get away with it?" Her sword stabbed out so quickly that I could have sworn there were ten of them.

I used [Dodge] to slip to the side and strike back at her.

She almost seemed shocked that I had been able to react so quickly, and we started to trade attacks more evenly. She still wasn't using her full strength behind the attacks, but I could tell that she was closing in on her max speed.

I stuffed the bag of chips into my face for a second as I stepped back and pulled it away with a mouthful of them. I crunched them messily in my mouth.

"Wasteful!" Crimson exploded, moving even faster, and the two of us kept speeding up until I started to exceed her. I found myself able to slip past her guard on more than one occasion and nick at her high-grade armor.

"Well, at least it's better that I eat them." I flashed to her side and pushed her back on the defensive.

The look in her eyes was a mix of astonishment and delight with those hits. She let me hold the advantage for a minute, chasing her around the room as she was repeatedly forced to disengage.

"You want to play it like this?" Red lightning was already teasing its way out of her eyes, and I could tell that, if it weren't for her new found control, her heart rate would have already pushed her into [Limit Break].

"Give me your worst." I threw the bag of chips to the side and pulled out a second dagger as Crimson stopped holding back.

Red lightning poured out of her eyes and wreathed her entire body in explosive jags of energy.

If I thought I had the advantage before, I was very wrong.

Crimson's sword nearly teleported next to me, and I was forced to use [Dodge] to escape and tag her twice in the side before rolling to avoid a snap kick.

But the fact that I just dodged two of her attacks while she was in [Limit Break] hit me suddenly. I was on her level, at least in terms of speed.

She came at me hard with eyes full of intensity.

I wasn't afraid though. I was excited. How many people could spar with Crimson? Maybe a handful could, but after she activated [Limit Break], she had beaten the utter crap out of the Harem Queen.

Yet here I was dodging her attacks.

Crimson sliced hard enough to gouge the incredibly hard stone floor, and I swallowed, remembering that she might not have perfect control of her strength at the moment.

I struck her three more times and worked to focus myself. It would only take one slip up to lose. I was certain that there was someone with revive on staff, but my pride wouldn't let me lose to Crimson, not after she'd let me build up the stacks to get to my current speed.

I desperately wanted to defeat her.

My daggers beat out a rhythm on her armor as I picked up even more speed. She drew her whip and tried to keep me off of her, but where the weapon had always been something terrifyingly agile, I could see the paths it drew in the air.

I hopped over it like a game of jump rope and got in her face, grabbing her ponytail and kissing her deeply before zipping out of range of the whip.

She tried to catch me. I could see where the whip coiled around where my leg would have been, but I reappeared and tapped her several more times with my daggers and snagged her choker, snapping it on her neck.

It was a game of teasing her now.

She knew it, her eyes held a warmth in them as I played my games, toying with her as we fought.

When the fight had gone on long enough, I prepared to move to the next phase. If I didn't, I had a feeling I'd soon be naked on the floor with Crimson right there and then in the UG room.

I activated [Liminal Space] and froze time around Crimson and me.

I paused and walked up to her, taking her CID, and leaving a long kiss on her lips before thumbing through her CID and hurrying out of the circle so that I didn't lose all my stacks.

Crimson stopped mid-strike and touched her lips before glancing down at her wrist where her CID was now missing.

"Really, you got quite slow." I leaned against a far wall, eating a bag of her chips. "You should really fix that." I crunched down on one and dangled her CID in my hands.

The red lightning around her retreated as she stared at me. She wasn't mad. She actually looked like she was about to drag me off to bed and show me just how happy she was.

Crimson licked her lips. "You are fast. you aren't *too fast*," she teased.

"We'll have to see." I winked, feeling the lightning around me start to fade with every second I wasn't attacking.

"We will." She gave me a smoldering look that told me we were only seconds from stripping down here and now.

"Incredible," one of the techs breathed and broke the sexual tension roaring between Crimson and me. "It doesn't seem that there's a limit to his ability."

"No. It seems quite boundless." Crimson cleared her throat and marched over to me, her heels clicking on the floor and the leather of her thighs swishing with each stride. "Though, how long was our fight?"

It seemed while she enjoyed giving Des and the others a show, the UG techs weren't going to get one.

"Twenty-five minutes," the director said, swiping on her tablet, the blue reflection of letters off her glasses hid her expression. "The last minute of fighting, we actually lost attacks with the damage meters. You both exceeded the frames per second."

She pushed up her glasses, and I could see her eyes full of earnest praise. "The most impressive thing, however, is Ken's stat gains. He gained two agility and one stamina during that fight."

I blinked. "What?" Training stats took time. I would typically be training for the bulk of several days before I saw the improvement of a single stat point.

"Well, by the end, you were moving well beyond the camera's ability to track you. It isn't impossible to say that you were essentially doing several hours' worth of training every minute there at the end." The director flashed a smile.

Crimson's own smile became predatory. "Wow, that's one hell of an improvement on training time. I'll have to put you to the grindstone."

My stomach growled despite pounding down chips.

Crimson walked over and took her CID away from me.

"Hey, you have plenty in there. I saw how many you keep on hand," I teased.

"A lady needs to have some secrets," Crimson warned and handed me one of her culinary creations that was an inch-thick disk of eggs with all manner of vegetables and meat stuck in it. "Also, there's a reason I keep these on hand."

I bit into it, my body sighing in happiness. It tasted like heaven and calories. My body was catching up with what I'd just put it through, and if I didn't feed it, it felt like it was going to devour me from the inside.

"So, what about the results of the testing?" I munched on the disk.

"We'll need some time to go over all the data. The timestamps of so much of it are so close together. We'll probably need to use some software to make these graphs even readable and do some calculations based on your increased speed to really dig in." The director swiped a few more times on her tablet and looked over to the techs who were hurriedly nodding in agreement. "Thank you for sharing this ability with us."

I was gnawing on the rapidly disappearing food that Crimson had given me and nodded my head, swallowing before I could speak. "Not a problem. Help me understand it better and how I can optimize some things like my mana specialization and abilities. That'll be worth sharing this information with you."

"Of course." The director pushed up her glasses and they caught the light. "We'll run a full analysis and assessment."

"Great. Now, I need to be somewhere else." I grabbed Crimson's arm and pulled her along with me.

She cocked an eyebrow at me. "Feeling bold?"

"I mean, I was able to steal your potato chips not once but twice. I'm feeling beyond bold. I'm feeling dangerously confident. Also, there's a delinquent guild member of mine that I think I need to settle up with. You wouldn't believe it. She's missed her dues for the entire time since she joined the guild."

Crimson's eyes sparkled with barely contained lust as we walked out of the UG building. "Oh no. What's going to happen to her?"

"Well, I'll be blunt with you. She's damned attractive, and I happen to know that she's desperate enough to do just about anything to stay in the guild."

Crimson swallowed audibly and breathed out heavily. "Yes. She is. You should be rough with her. Very rough."

CHAPTER 27

C rimson slammed the door behind us as we made it into the suite with a boom like she used too much of her strength in her eagerness.

I shoved her up against the door, the wood cracking as I claimed her lips and kissed her with passion that I'd buried deep inside of me.

"Fuck," Crimson moaned as she started to kiss and nibble at my neck. "You were so incredible."

Her soft hands ran along my shoulders and down my back, sending tingles to my head and then all the way down to my pelvis.

I groaned as her wet lips played against my sensitive neck, making goosebumps of excitement pepper my skin. "I'm going to do a lot more than steal your chips."

"You'd better," she mumbled between kisses, her voice becoming throaty and her breath heady. Reaching down, she tore my shirt to get at my chest. Her long lashes fluttered as she looked up at me with those soulful, blue eyes. "Because your delinquent guild member owes you more than she could ever repay."

She licked her lips and planted a slow soft kiss that smacked with wet suction. She was reminding me of our little game.

It was time to get into character. Despite how much I wanted to rip the leather suit off of her and plow her against the door, I should make this fun for both of us.

My cock was protesting that logic every second it wasn't buried deep inside of her. It might have been the toughest moment of my life to stop kissing her and step back.

I grabbed her by her choker and pulled her along with me like a misbehaving dog. "You missed your dues again."

"Yes, Guild Master. I'm sorry. There was this group in the dungeon that caused issues and I just... I couldn't make the dues this month," she pleaded with pouting lips.

"Again," I added.

"Again," she agreed and looked down, but dutifully followed me into the bedroom.

I sat down and crossed my legs, my pants shifted uncomfortably as a part of me fought its confinement.

She closed the door behind us and fell down on her knees. Crimson's expression was one half excitement, the other half struggling to stay in character for the scenario she'd created.

"Guild Master. I've given you what I have, I don't have anything else to give you." She licked her lips. "Unless I could make it up like last time?"

I kept a stern face even as my member attempted to shove my one leg off the other and expose itself to her. "Do you really think that you can keep doing that for every time you've missed your dues?"

"Yes?" she asked shyly, getting back into the game again and crawling forward on her hands and knees until she was waiting for me to uncross my legs and give her access to her prize. "I know you might need more. For someone with stamina like yours, once might not be enough."

"Your mouth isn't enough," I growled, and damn did I mean what I'd said. I wanted to break the bed with her underneath me screaming my name.

Crimson struggled to keep her smile down. "Of course, Guild Master, but I don't suppose I could take the edge off before we do more?" She gently put a hand on my knee that was almost pleading for me to uncross my legs.

I grabbed her chin and held her face as I moved my legs and the tent in my pants became apparent. "Crimson, you'll become mine tonight. Do you understand that? You have a path out—"

She grabbed me through my pants and breathed heavily. "Not a chance, Ken, my Guild *Master*," Crimson panted as she started to stroke me through my pants. "Guild Master, this one just wants to satisfy you."

She captured my thumb in her mouth and suckled on it as she nuzzled the tent in my pants. Heavens above, I wanted to throw her down and break her right then and there.

Yet I kept to the role, knowing that it would be all that much sweeter. I unzipped my pants and let my member spring free, eager to feel Crimson's warmth.

She didn't disappoint, cradling it in her soft hands. There was something about someone else's touch that relaxed a muscle in me that I didn't even know I had.

I groaned as she did a few preliminary pumps to ensure I was primed and ready.

Crimson kept eye contact with me as she kissed the shaft, slathering her tongue over it. "Guild Master, relax. This one will take care of you. Afterwards, you can decide what extra is needed to make up the deficit. Oh!" she started. "There was one more thing I found. Maybe this could help?"

She bumped her CID to mine. If I didn't know this was part of the game, I wouldn't even bother to check. Instead, I grabbed her braid and forced her down on me, eager to feel her swallow me.

Using it to guide her with one hand, I checked my CID. Crimson had transferred several leather straps, likely scraps from her new armor as well as some oil.

I swallowed. Knots were within my wheelhouse. Grandma Yui had taught me how to tie someone up for interrogation, but I wasn't entirely prepared to tie a person up *pleasurably*.

Then again, I doubted I could hurt Crimson and would just do my best.

"Yes, this a wonderful start," I groaned as I pushed her down until I sheathed myself in her flexible throat and rolled her over the head.

Crimson took me with excitement, her eyes shining with anticipation as I got more dominant. I pushed her throat down over my cock, using her braid as a convenient hand hold to control her head.

She gulped over me, her nose flaring as she worked to breathe.

"That's it. You feel good." I slowed her down, dragging myself through her throat. Her slick flesh gave every inch for me as I throbbed, rapidly approaching my peak.

When her eyes sparked, I wasn't worried or even concerned.

I enjoyed knowing that her heart rate was spiking as I used her throat. "It's coming. Oh, this'll pay off some of your debt," I groaned and shoved myself all the way and held her to the point her nose was buried in my pelvis and felt myself twitch before I shot ropes of my seed down her throat.

She moaned and swallowed, eager to get every last drop.

I pulled from her throat that clenched, like it wanted to seal me in there for eternity, but she relented and I came free with a wet suck.

"Good girl." As I passed out of her lips, I left a drop of cum on her lips. "It looks like you didn't get it all." I wiped it away with a thumb.

Crimson was on me in a flash, grabbing my hand and taking that thumb past her lips, kissing, suckling, and licking it until there wasn't a trace of it left. "Did I do good, Guild Master?"

"Very good." I cupped her chin. Her lips were a little swollen and she looked demurely up at me through her lashes, her blue eyes locked on me, pulling me in deeper.

"I know that my debt is quite severe. Perhaps I could do more for someone with your... stamina?" She unzipped the front of her suit a little, her finger teasing the zipper.

I leaned back to watch. "Strip, slowly." My cock was still free and softening, but I doubted that would last for long. Not with the look that Crimson was giving me.

Crimson teased the zipper a little more and stood up, but she didn't step back. She was still standing between my legs as she swayed in place, slowly pulling the zipper down right in front of me. My eyes were locked on that piece of metal as her fingers slowly pulled it lower and lower.

The tight red suit parted with every half inch, revealing more and more of her tantalizing, creamy skin beneath. Her bra was a lacey black thing that would be removed soon enough.

My eyes raked over her as she peeled the suit off her shoulders and down her arms.

The top half fell down to her waist and she covered her chest as she blushed to match her name. "G-guild Master."

I grabbed the suit and pulled it down over her waist until her ass popped out, the two perfect globes jiggling in their freedom. "Step through."

I unzipped a little at the ankle, and she stepped out until she was in nothing but her underwear and heels.

Crimson had the kind of body that filled teenage fantasies. Her long, toned legs went on forever, and just where they ended, the swell of her cute bubble butt started. Past that was her toned abs and finally her two breasts that swelled far more than you'd expect with someone so fit.

"Sit in my lap," I commanded.

Her face was soft at that moment, with the stark contrast of her eyes that were always filled with such intensity. Any of her intensity was all in the heat of her gaze as she stared back at me and crawled into my lap.

My flagging member was finding his second wind and perking up in hopes of finding its way inside of her.

She slowly ground herself on my lap, and I could feel the wet heat already pressing through her thong. "Guild Master, what will you do?"

"You need to be punished." I held her chin and kissed her softly on the lips. "But I need you to know that you deserve this; you need to do this willingly."

"I know I deserve this," she panted and curled up against my chest.

"Do you? Then why do you keep missing your dues?" I forced her eyes into mine.

Crimson licked her lips. "Because... maybe I hoped my Guild Master would do something like this." Her hot breath tickled my nose; we were only inches apart. "That he'd take me, mark me, fill me."

I kissed her again. This one was a long, lasting kiss as she excitedly ground against me, and her hands searched for the edges of my shirt to rip it off and wiggle at my pants. I kicked off my boots and rolled back onto the bed before rolling on top of her.

"Yes, Guild Master," she breathed. "Punish me. Tie me down and use me. Fill me up, cover me in your seed and fuck me." She groaned as she writhed under me.

Any weakness left in my cock vanished as it begged to be thrust into her.

But I couldn't yet.

Throwing my pants off in a hurry, I pulled out the leather cord and looped it over her wrists quickly wrapping them in a bind before looping it over the headboard of the bed.

Crimson put up a token struggle as she gasped and writhed.

"Not so fast. This is your punishment for your missed dues." I spread her legs, eager to dive right in, but also knowing that doing this slowly would be more exciting for her.

I peeled her thong off and revealed her ready and glistening slit.

"Guild Master. Please, punish me, take me." She pulled at me with her feet, it seemed she was out of patience as well.

I was happy to move things along.

I lined myself up and pushed in slowly. Crimson's eyes rolled up in her head, and she came as red lightning coursed over her face and down her body, jumping at me through our union.

"You were so pent up?" I broke character.

Crimson gasped for breath like it had just rocked her whole body. "I've gone years with everyone so scared of me. Ken, don't you dare stop. Fuck me senseless, cum all over me, and then hog tie me and paint my face and back."

I rocked into her steadily and she clenched up again gasping as she came again.

My confidence skyrocketed, and I leaned over her, grabbing her wrists to remind her that I had her held. "You will not cum again until I have my satisfaction."

"Yes, Guild Master, this greedy woman just wants everything. I want you to give it all to me."

I bottomed out, and she tensed her body to stop from having yet another orgasm.

Damn, she was sensitive.

More importantly, she was almost too tight. I slowly worked myself in and out of her, picking up speed and slamming into her.

Crimson squeezed me with her thighs, trying to stop another orgasm from rolling through her. But she failed.

"I'm sorry, Guild Master," she cried as she let loose again, her pussy flooding over me.

With a scowl, I picked up her hips to find a new angle and give me access to her ass as I slapped it hard.

"You dare disobey me during your punishment?" I slapped her again and she came.

I struggled to not laugh as I plowed into her and her eyes rolled up into her head with another release. Her eyes fluttered closed as she rolled into another.

I grabbed her choker and snapped it as I pushed myself harder to the end and buried myself to the hilt before I came hard enough to see spots in my vision.

Crimson came down panting. "That was incredible."

"We are just starting," I laughed and rolled her over. "Legs up."

I produced another of the leather cord and tied it around her ankles before threading it through the bind around her wrists and pulled them until Crimson was unnaturally stretched.

"Ken, go easy on me."

I slapped her ass and then paused. "We probably need a safe word."

"Yes, we probably do." Crimson's eyes flashed hungrily as she saw my wet cock. "But I can't think straight enough to come up with one. Just put that big boy back inside of me and let's see what sort of limits we both have."

With her hogtied on the bed, I pulled her knees apart and slid her to the edge of the bed. "Well, there's one way to find out."

I had recovered and thrust myself back into her as she cried out.

***

"Absorb," I said.

After we were both thoroughly covered in sweat and other fluids, I regained enough sense to remember this part of our time together.

Red lightning gathered below my hand, and rather than suck into my hand, it exploded, singeing my chest and sending me flying back and through the bedroom wall.

The drywall crumbled around me as two studs were broken and sticking out into the kitchen of the suite now. Charlotte, Des and Fayeth were in the middle of dinner and looked up at the blast.

"Oh is it that late?" I said before picking myself up off the ground and groaned in pain.

"Heal." Charlotte waved her hand in my direction, casting a soothing green light over me. "Yeah, we finished up diving for the day about a half an hour ago."

Des creeped out of her chair to peek through the hole in the wall. "Hello, Crimson. Want me to help you with those?"

"No. Ken has to come in and finish. We aren't done catching me up on my dues yet," Crimson said from inside. "I'm guessing Limit Break didn't transfer over?"

I used the counter and the broken wall to pull myself back over to the room. "Nope. That fucking hurt like hell, too. Not doing that again. How about you?"

Crimson's eyes fixed on a point behind me, and a portal opened there and on the other side of her in the bedroom before she started laughing like a maniac. "It worked."

"Well, I'm glad you're happy. Now I'm going back in for another skill since Limit Break didn't cooperate."

"Come back in, baby. Come all the way in and all over," Crimson coaxed me back over to the bed with a wiggle of her hips.

Des was still leaning on the edge of the broken wall. "Do you two mind if I watch?"

"Not at all." Crimson's voice was breathy.

I flipped her around so that she was on her back, her arms were bound behind her now, and I adjusted some of the straps to lash her shoulders to the side of the bed before I opened her mouth with a thumb and tilted her head back.

"'An't 'alk 'ow." Crimson swallowed me as I pushed myself into her mouth and saw the bulge in her throat move as I started to fuck her mouth while she was upside down on the bed.

"Yeah. Keep going, Ken, make her choke on it." Des slowly crept into the room until she was right behind me, whispering in my ear. "Take her harder," she breathed into my ear.

Des was like a devil over my shoulder telling me what would feel better.

I rammed myself down into Crimson's throat, but she didn't choke, swallowing me like a champion. Crimson refused to be bad at anything.

Her eyes lazily closed as she slurped on me.

"Damn." Fayeth came in, dusting her hands off on her apron. "I'll have to work on my knot tying."

"Ken seems to have it in hand," Charlotte said, putting down a sleeping Bun-bun. "So, if he can't get Limit Break, does that mean his ability is off the table?"

"Likely," Felin appeared. "Oh." Her eyes went wide. "Is this what you like, Ken?"

"No, this is just her initiation to the pride," Des tried to explain in words Felin would understand.

I was having trouble speaking as I steadily reached my own peak in Crimson's throat.

"That makes sense," Felin said, her tail lashing excitedly behind her. "It is a very strong pride, and as its leader, Ken should assert his dominance. For someone like Crimson, he should be very firm."

CHAPTER 28

I downed another whole casserole dish that Fayeth had kindly left out for me.

While the rest of the class was doing their physical training, Crimson took me to a room and helped me pick up speed. I kept the speed up with Crimson and trained for about two hours at top speed.

After that, I was starving, and I moved the casserole dish to the side and used the spatula as a spoon to start devouring the next one.

"You might even have it worse than me." Crimson's smile was frozen on her face all day with a morning afterglow.

"Well, your body has adjusted, and a lot of your mana channels are doing the work. I don't know how it all works, but it seems my body is doing a lot of it under the buffs, or I wouldn't be so damned hungry." I shoved another scoop of some chicken and cheesy casserole into my mouth.

"Well, the Zone Director sent over an analysis of your ability along with their recommendations." Crimson showed me her CID.

I frowned, checking my own CID for it. "I should have that."

"You will. She asked me to check it over before she sent the official one. Pretty sure you are going to start getting some premium treatment. I mean, they asked me to check it before they sent it to you."

"You're also my teacher and my trainer," I said around a mouthful of food and read off her CID.

Ken Nagato's [Liminal Speed] may be one of the most powerful abilities documented to date. It is classified on par with Crimson's unique [Limit Break] only because of its limitation in activation time.

The ability builds up upon Ken striking a living creature with the intent to harm or kill. Many other abilities follow this trend, and we will assume that Ken's is not unique in this regard and thus far has not shown itself to be.

After a period of ten seconds without striking, a decline begins in the ability's stacks, but the stacks do not decay if the period is interrupted with Ken adding another stack.

This allows for an uncapped maximum for the potential speed that Ken can generate using this ability. The fact that many bosses will die before he starts breaking the light barrier with each step is a blessing.

Abilities do trigger additional stacks, and it is our recommendation that Ken Nagato equip himself with several abilities that generate multiple attacks. [Flurry] is the highest commonly available ability, and generates seven attacks. Other temporary increases to agility will also help him best at the onset of a fight.

At present, his largest limiter is getting those initial stacks built up. Once his speed is increased, his cooldowns are not. Thus, the best ways to multiply his damage are through low mana cost on-hit abilities. He currently has [Dark Blades], but the recommendation is that he acquires several others to give himself a variety of elements should he encounter monsters that are immune to physical and/or shadow damage.

I nodded along with the assessment. What they'd determined made perfect sense to me. [Liminal Speed] would shift my focus on which abilities I needed; it was a build-defining ability that needed care.

Additionally, we've charted out what we believe to be the optimal use of his mana specialization for the near term, mid term and long term. Given his current focus on agility and shadow damage, there is a specialization [Shadowed Strike] that has a small chance to generate a second shadowy limb to strike as if the attacker took an extra swing.

Other assessments show that this would likely add an additional stack, and the ability as a whole would both increase his rate of acceleration and scale with the additional speed as well as other abilities.

It is our recommendation that Ken seek this specialization before moving onto agility fighting and, finally, sharpness where it would open him up to get the prerequisites for multiple abilities that provide more than one attack.

In conclusion, this ability will give Ken the potential to become a top-tier adventurer alongside Crimson, or one day surpass her.

I felt a chill run down my spine at the last part and glanced at Crimson.

She shrugged, that smile still plastered on her face. "I would love for you to catch up and give me something to chase after."

"One day," I promised her and checked my CID. A fire lit inside of me.

Our day's training had already paid off in several improvements on stats. If I kept up my training like I had today, I'd be making incredible progress. But sadly, not all strength was built in training. Much of it, including levels, needed to be forged in fighting dungeon monsters.

"By the way, did you gain any stats today?" I asked.

Crimson grinned. "One agility. Hey, it's good training for me too. When you hit that ultra-high speed, it forces me to adapt more than most things I try."

I nodded and leaned back, checking my CID and my mana specialization to see how far along I could get to what she suggested. Before I could get far, the rest of my party came traipsing in with towels over their shoulders.

"Penny was so obvious today," Des laughed and saw me digging into the food in the kitchen. "Hungry much?"

"Starving." I purposefully stuffed my mouth full with the next spatula scoop of casserole.

Fayeth raised an eyebrow. "I'll make more tonight. Are you at least gaining stamina when you train with Crimson, and Crimson, you are keeping him focused on training?"

Crimson slapped a salute at the petite elf. "That I am. With how his speed builds, we were doing long sessions."

"I got three stamina today." I swallowed my food.

Des purred at that and walked over to me, draping her arms over my shoulders. "That's wonderful. Eat up, we need to get enough food that you can push yourself like this every day."

I kissed her before going back to eating. "Going to destroy any food budget I had planned."

"Maybe we should see if we can't do some organized farming for you. Draw monsters in so that you can keep that speed buff going, like the event we had done as a class," Charlotte said.

Crimson glanced thoughtfully at the ceiling. "I have portal now, so... that's not out of the question. While you guys are out today, I'm going to go through the UG records and see what I can pick out for the class. I tried to teleport to the Elven world yesterday, and it didn't work. I'll have to go run to wherever we want to do this so that I can open the portal. It seems my prior experience isn't enough to just start portaling around."

I nodded, following her logic. "We'll be fine if you want to go this afternoon. With Kaiming put down and the panther gone, it's really just focusing on leveling and avoiding the dwarves."

Crimson grunted. "The Harem Queen has the safe zone protected. And I won't be gone long."

"Did you get the reward for Kai Ming?" Charlotte asked, pulling out a small snack for herself so that she didn't go on a dive after this on an empty stomach.

"Director Amato will give it to me with a formal analysis on my ability," I said.

"I forbid you from spending it on the guild." Crimson pointed at me. "You need to spend it on yourself. Take the analysis and the money and give yourself a solid boost forward."

Sighing, I wanted to refute her just because of her tone, but she was right. "After I split it with the rest of the party."

Des raised her hands in the air. "I did nothing. Smacked one guy around for about ten seconds before you cut him apart."

"You deserve most of it. If you insist on giving us something, make it proportional to our efforts, not split evenly." Fayeth gave me a look that told me not to even bother arguing with her.

"Fine, we'll see," I answered noncommittally. "Are we going to get ready to dive?" I scooped up the last of this dish, and Fayeth picked it up and put it in the sink to soak. "Thanks."

***

Our party was off diving, searching through the twenty-seventh floor. We were looking for an area denser in monsters so that I could keep my stacks rolling as we went.

"Alright, Bun-bun." Charlotte tossed him lightly on the ground.

The rabbit landed on his feet and looked up at her like she'd betrayed him.

"No, your job is to go find another pack of monsters and lead it back here," Charlotte tsked at the rabbit.

He folded his ears and snuck a peek at the chocolate bunny in the group we were about to fight and then pinned them back further as he let out several squeaks of protest.

"No." Charlotte's tone was firm. "Go get more monsters."

Bun-bun dragged his feet as he took several steps and looked back at Charlotte.

I was proud of her as she crossed her arms and slowly shook her head.

"I'll give you glazed carrots tonight if you do a good job." Fayeth decided to sweeten the pot. "You are still banished from the kitchen, though."

Bun-bun perked up and bounded off before Charlotte could say anything to stop her.

"You spoil him," Charlotte said.

"You've become harsh to him," Fayeth countered.

"Yeah, well you don't have to hear his sass all day." Charlotte waved it off. "We are here to grind."

I watched the whole exchange, feeling like things had changed while I'd been busy elsewhere. "Alright, let's do this and work together," I championed for the group.

"We are fine," Fayeth said, marching forward and spraying her [Agitating Spores] over the group of monsters.

"Of course." I used [Shadow Ambush] to appear behind the Gumdrop Witches, and my blades started to carve into them.

I followed the Director's instructions and had [Dark Blades] active, and watched as purple lightning raced up my arms and I sped up. The first Gumdrop Witch felt fairly normal, but with the second one, I pulled aggro from Fayeth and had to taunt it off me.

"Careful," she chided me.

I switched targets, splitting my time between the two remaining Gumdrop Witches before Bun-bun came barreling over with a pack of chocolate rabbits chasing after him.

"Bun-bun. Circle around." Fayeth bashed her shield into one of the witches and stepped up like a batter at the plate and swung a [Cleave] through the trail of mobs behind Bun-bun.

"Ken, pick it up," Des warned, switching her tactic to area of effect attacks.

"He's going to pull aggro." Charlotte was chanting, casting a more powerful heal on Fayeth every few seconds.

"We can keep this up. Charlotte dishes out the health and I'll dish out the mana." Harley took a break from her flute for a moment.

"Except Bun-bun is already getting more," Des pointed out.

The rabbit was off gathering more of the chocolate bunnies and making a big loop back this way.

"That's what we get for encouraging him," I chuckled and focused in, picking a chocolate rabbit and pushing my speed as high as I could.

The monster turned to me, but I ignored it and activated [Metamorphosis] and [Dodge] to slip the first attack and started really going at it with my claws.

The chocolate bunny only got two more attacks on me before it went down and I switched to another. This one peeled away from Fayeth, and I only had to [Dodge] one more attack before it puffed into more black smoke.

"Keep 'em coming!" Des shouted at Bun-bun. "Actually, Harley, give Bun-bun haste. He needs to start pulling faster."

The last Gumdrop Witch died, and I started to carve through the rest of the chocolate bunnies as the next pack came rolling in following Bun-bun. This time, it was a marching troop of candy cane men.

I noticed that he was avoiding pulling the Gumdrop Witches, likely because their spells would hit him as he led them on a merry chase.

My feet pushed off the ground, and before I knew it, I was behind the Gumdrop Witch pack. My blades tore through the three of them in seconds, and I moved back to the party and their new foes.

"Damn," Harley gasped seeing me move so quickly. "If we can get him wound up enough, can we just release him on the floor and follow around picking up loot?"

"Ask Des the best way to wind him up," Charlotte chuckled.

"It's all in the eyes," Des laughed. "Ken, go get all the witches you can. We are going to keep a few of these alive so that you have something to keep your stacks up on."

I nodded, shooting off to the side and tearing into several witch packs and bouncing through the dungeon, until I ran into one of the upperclassmen parties I knew well.

Ren met my gaze as I appeared and destroyed a pack on my own before exploding away in another direction. I ran into a few other scattered groups, and realized I needed to be organized with how I went about my next moves.

I quickly came up with a plan. I would search in a spoke and wheel pattern, with my party at the center and a point I could reach if I needed to restore my stacks while monsters respawned.

As soon as I saw more, I was off again, tearing through the dungeon like a mad man. The whole time I had a giant grin on my face.

I realized my current elation must be what Crimson had experienced as she used [Limit Break] to level for the first time.

I mowed through the dungeon in wide passes, killing everything in sight and then zipping back. My speed started to get so fast that I was clearing the whole wheel and spoke model before they were regenerating, so I decided to zip much farther away and passed the upperclassmen again. I avoided stealing too many of their monsters as I shot through the whole dungeon floor, going from group to group.

Finally, I returned to my group and did several more clears before all of the movement and fatigue hit me like a boss monster punch in the gut and my stomach roared.

I came to a halt by my group, looking like a miniature lightning storm, and grabbed bag after bag of chips from my CID. I started pouring the greasy goodness down my throat, chewing as quickly as I could. The stacks faded quickly, and I stood in the middle of them, devouring chips.

"Well, that's the limit on it," Des said, laying out a picnic blanket.

I glanced around. "Harley?"

"She went that way to start picking up loot."

I looked around, noticing that the ground was absolutely glimmering with loot all over the sugary snow banks of this floor.

I blushed. "Maybe I'll pick up some of the loot next time."

Des shrugged. "This time, it is going to be an absolute blast to collect all of this. By the dozenth time, I doubt we'll be so amused." She couldn't keep the sly smile off her face though. "That was pretty incredible. We'll need to figure out a better plan going forward."

I nodded, my mouth too full of food to speak at the moment. After they helped me build up my speed, they could shift to helping pick up loot. It seemed I didn't really need that much help with gathering more monsters, not with how fast I got going.

"Well, we'll talk after you finish devouring everything in your CID," Des laughed. "There's plenty of chocolate and candy droppings on this floor."

I made a face. There was no way I was going to stuff myself with candy to fuel myself.

"Okay, we'll stop by the store when we are back in the safe zone and you can get Fayeth to make you heaps of food. She'd love it actually." Des kissed my cheek. "She and Charlotte miss you. You've been a little busy lately, and with the group swapping, time has been limited," she reminded me.

"Thanks," I said, finding a moment to swallow everything and speak. "I was picking up on a little disharmony with those two. They are both Adrel. I'll have to spend some time with them to try and bring us back in tune."

"Good man. I'll distract Crimson and Felin if it comes to it." Des winked. "Now, let's get you stuffed and back at it. I think we'll blow through the levels at this rate and maybe make it as the first party to the thirty-second floor." She clapped her hands. "Bring it in, everyone."

CHAPTER 29

As our party got back from our latest dive, I watched as Des pulled Crimson away, both of them disappearing out the suite door while having a conversation about 'important equipment'.

Whatever that was.

I started to browse the kitchen, tempted to use [Eyes of Wisdom] to locate a snack, but that just seemed like a silly use of it.

Fayeth bopped my hand with a wooden spoon, interrupting my thoughts. "Hang on." She grabbed an apron from a hook on the wall.

Even if we were only in this safe zone for a while, we'd turned it into our living space in small ways. It was an important part of staying sane as you dove the dungeon. There was no fridge, but there was an interface that the UG could upload with food when you ordered any. As a result, the cabinets had a variety of items for me.

I moved to help Fayeth put on the apron rather than continue to browse. My hands slid on her smooth dress and through the gaps in it to get a taste of her supple flesh.

Touching her again ignited something in me that I realized I missed. I slipped my hands into her dress rather than tie the aprons to pull her close. But rather than doing anything untoward, I just wanted to feel more of my skin on hers and the weight of her against my chest. "Missed you."

Fayeth's lips tugged into a brilliant smile as she held my arms around her waist and leaned into me. "My Adrel," she breathed.

We stayed like that for a long minute, just feeling each other.

I was sure there was some powerful hormone thing happening, because the longer I held her the happier I was becoming. Truly, I hadn't given her much attention lately and I was worse for it.

This was better than any potion at restoring my energy.

"Alright." I pulled my hand out and she dragged her fingers over my arm like she wanted every last touch she could soak up. "I think I have my own apron in here somewhere." I poked at my own CID.

Fayeth's eyes glimmered as I pulled out my own apron and turned around for her to tie it. "Going to join me in cooking tonight?"

I leaned down to kiss her petal soft lips. "Yes. Mostly because I want to spend time with you, and a smidge because I feel guilty with how much I've been eating."

She chuckled a laugh and went over to the interface, tapping on it and pulling out item after item. "Tap your CID here. Because you are paying for all this food."

I clenched my chest playfully and tapped my CID to it, knowing it would be expensive, but worth the benefit of using my new ability to train as quickly as we could.

"Are you breaking Ken's heart?" Charlotte pulled her hair back into a ponytail. It hung in loose wet curls from her shower where even the hot water hadn't been able to straighten where it normally curled with the braids.

"Making him pay," Fayeth chuckled. "That, and putting him to work. Get the cutting board and knife out for him."

Charlotte was familiar with the kitchen and pulled out what Fayeth had asked for while humming to herself and sticking Bun-bun in front of a small TV on a chair in the living room that started to play a spy thriller TV show.

"He's not allowed in the kitchen," Charlotte explained.

The rabbit melted into a puddle as he became transfixed by the show. His little nose occasionally twitched excitedly.

"Wow, he just..." I waved my hand around him, trying to distract him. But his eyes were glued to the show.

"He loves spy shows and movies, but I'm running out. I don't think he'll mind when I start to replay some of the older ones, though." Charlotte put on her own apron and focused on Fayeth. "What's on the menu tonight?"

"We'll do Hemi's cheesecake and some of that breakfast casserole. Ken seemed to like that. And then we'll make a bunch of boiled chicken and turn it into something," Fayeth rambled off. "That's just to start."

Charlotte pursed her lips and glanced at me.

"What? The skill makes me hungry." I held my hands up innocently.

"And very lucky," Charlotte said with a glimmer in her eyes.

I decided that I needed much the same as I'd done to Fayeth to her. Wrapping my arm around Charlotte, I pressed our chests together and just hugged her. Charlotte's body softened until she was plastered against me, hanging off my shoulder.

"Then maybe we'll work on some..." Fayeth glanced at us and cut herself off, going back to pulling more food out.

"This is nice," Charlotte murmured in my ear and went on her tiptoes to snuggle her face into the crook of my neck and breathe me in.

I slowly swayed back and forth with her doing much the same as an idea popped into my head. "Fayeth, get two bottles of wine. Nothing goes better with cooking than wine."

"For the chicken?" she asked.

"No, for us," I chuckled and squeezed Charlotte once more before letting go of her.

She seemed reluctant to let me go, but left a kiss on my cheek before she settled down on her feet solidly. "I'll take some wine. White, please, something sweet."

Fayeth nodded and pulled two bottles out, and after a pause pulled a third. "It's on Ken, so why not splurge," she teased.

"My money will never be safe." I played along and positioned myself in front of the cutting board, pulling out one of my dungeon knives.

"Eww. Put that away," both of them scolded me.

"What? It's sharp."

"And it has been stuck who knows where." Fayeth shooed at the blade until I put it away.

"I do clean it," I told her.

"Yeah, with oils, I bet. Use the kitchen knife." She placed an armload of celery, carrots, and some onions in front of me. "I'm sure you are just as good with a kitchen knife."

Technically, the kitchen knife didn't have any stats to make up for the ones on my gear, but I supposed that was a moot point. I started in on the carrots as a glass of wine appeared by my cutting board.

Charlotte started several pots boiling and worked at cleaning some chicken breasts. Fayeth set herself up across the island from me and pulled down several half full bags of powders that she pulled from the cabinets, eggs and cream.

I knew who to butter up for desserts. "Fayeth, you look just divine right now."

She eyed me, a light blush dusting her cheeks. "Keep chopping. There's more where that came from." She pointed behind me.

I took a glance over my shoulder to see a whole pile of vegetables as well as several cartons of eggs. "You want me to chop the eggs?"

"No, you'll crack them all into a large bowl and beat them. Do you have no idea how to cook?" Charlotte began filling the pots with chicken and pulled out a pan to start browning some sausage.

I chuckled before I took a sip of my wine and kept on dutifully chopping. "So, Fayeth, send any letters back with Neldra?"

The elf blinked. "Yes, yes I did. To my parents and to Ely. She really should hurry up before a certain cat girl sneaks into your bed."

Charlotte chuckled. "I think we are a little late there." She gestured out into the living room where our couch had become the Nekorian's nest, complete with my pillowcases and an old bed sheet.

"As long as she replaces the bed sheet, I have decided to allow it," I sighed heavily. Some battles weren't worth fighting.

"Don't look so put upon. She's gorgeous," Charlotte teased me.

"Oh. Trust me, I'm aware." I mulled over some of my resistance and found my current situation to be part of it. "Like with you two this week. I was clearly spread too thin and didn't spend as much time with either of you as I'd like." My knife blurred over the carrots reducing them to little orange coins as I talked.

"That's sweet." Charlotte kissed my cheek and left me grinning like a fool. It was very nice to reconnect to both of these lovely ladies.

"Yes, but the point is I don't want to spread myself thinner," I argued.

Fayeth stuck her finger in the batter and tasted it as she thought over my words. "Is it such a problem if she replaces Harley? You'll stay with the group."

"There's the whole issue of Selene or even Penny. If I say okay to Felin, what does me saying no to them mean?" I felt like I was balancing the whole organization of our class and the budding Silver Fangs on my romantic life.

Both of them shared a look filled with meaning that I didn't understand.

"Want to clue me in? Or is this about Penny's writing?" I asked.

"Des told you?" Fayeth asked.

"I understand advanced facial cues for interrogations. It doesn't translate one for one, but all someone had to do was talk about the story in front of her and me. It is blatantly obvious that it's Penny. I really should have put it together sooner, honestly," I sighed.

"Okay, so Penny has it hard for you. Selene certainly wants a cut," Charlotte admitted. "But I think we all understand what's happening. Both that you'll spend more time with the party, and secondarily, that more girls seem to want in despite the fact that those in your party will get more time with you."

I paused mid-chop. "Wait. Is this a common topic of conversation when I'm not around?"

"No. I wouldn't say that." Fayeth glanced at Charlotte to continue in a way I'd understand.

"It is more like a mutual understanding we all have. Harems are common enough; it's not like the dynamics are a secret. We can tell they want in, and we aren't stopping them. Yet the reality is that you'll be diving primarily with us," Charlotte tried to explain it.

"Like that." Fayeth gestured with a batter covered spoon. "We all know the score, and yet they are still playing the game."

"A sports metaphor from an elf," I gasped.

"I have spent too much time with Taylor this week," Fayeth sighed and went back to mixing. "Don't distract us from the topic at hand."

"Never," I said playfully, moving onto the eggs. I found a large bowl and started cracking the eggs carefully into it.

Charlotte was busy manning the stove, but she wasn't too busy to push the topic further. "If you aren't interested in them at all, we should probably let some of them know. They will probably leave Silver Fangs after graduation."

I nearly choked. "Because I'm not interested?"

"Yes. Well, it sort of became a movement to have the whole class join. Even Helen did it," Charlotte explained. "But the first few were lured by your grandfather promising them... uh... how did he put it?"

Fayeth paused, remembering the exact phrasing. "Join Silver Fangs for a ride on Ken's prized serpent."

I smacked my face. "He didn't."

"He did," they said in unison.

Then Charlotte added as if it would be helpful, "more than once."

I wanted to strangle my grandfather. "Okay, so where does that leave ones like Helen?"

"She's confused," Fayeth said without even missing a beat.

"Very," Charlotte echoed.

Penny had said the same thing. How many conversations were these ladies having on this topic?

But I also had to acknowledge that mixing up the parties had probably given a lot of time for those conversations. They were all adults. We talked about all sorts of things while traveling in the dungeon, and while there was a lot of fighting, there was also a lot of downtime in diving.

"Okay. So, they are all options, is what you are telling me?" I asked.

"Except Harley's healer harem. It would be rude to steal," Fayeth clarified.

"Great," I sighed. At least there were only twenty-five women in the class. Harley and her harem would take up to five of them. But there was no way I wanted twenty women, even if the other women were okay with it. I was still trying to balance my current love life.

"Let me ask you, are you less committed to Elysara now that you haven't seen her for a month?" Fayeth got right to the heart of the matter. "Here, I need you to whip some cream."

I stared at the cream and stuck my finger in it before wiping a dollop on her nose. "No. I'm not less committed to Ely, and I know exactly where that question is going."

Fayeth stared at her nose, going cross-eyed. It was quite possibly one of the cutest expressions I'd seen on her. "My point, exactly." She wiped the cream off and stuck it in her mouth. "Not whipped enough. Chop chop."

"I thought you wanted me to whip? Now you want me to chop?" I teased. The cream wasn't whipped at all, but I got a whisk out and went to work.

Fayeth went over to the oven and put two cheesecake tins in before standing up and wiping her hands on her apron. "Well then, if you understand that, then I don't understand why we need to have this conversation. You need to stop staring at all the monsters and gear to look at the lovely ladies from time to time."

"Yeah?" I grabbed her, letting my eyes linger as I roamed her body. "There are some ladies that I could stare at all day." I kissed her.

She melted against me and wrapped those thin but deceptively strong arms around my neck, and hoisted herself up until she wrapped her legs around my hips and deepened the kiss.

Charlotte moved silently behind us, cleaning up the counter. The druid had grown far less shy as everything had progressed.

Fayeth's soft lips pulled my attention back to her as she breathed and broke the kiss with a soft smack. "I love you, my Adrel. Tonight, you'll take me to bed?"

"Sure," I said with a grin as she slid off of me. Not leaving Charlotte out of the moment, I hooked her hips and pulled her to me in a side hug that ended up with her lips pressed to mine. "I could split my time?"

"Or just include me." Charlotte pecked my lips again. "Not particularly interested in Fayeth, but I wouldn't mind putting a show on for you," she amended.

"Similarly," Fayeth agreed. "But it would put us both in his arms for sleep, which I could certainly use." She raised her wine glass to Charlotte who clinked hers in turn.

"Yes please." They both took a sip before Charlotte turned her attention to the boiled chicken breasts. "These look about done. Ken, you'll need two forks to shred it all."

"That's a lot of chicken." I stared at them while Fayeth sipped her wine and went back to the device to order more food.

"Glad you are here," Fayeth said without looking up. "I'll make you a treat while you work."

I raised an eyebrow, but then I decided that any treat from Fayeth was worth its weight in gold. "Alright, let's get this started, Charlotte. You get me a big bowl to empty my cutting board into."

"Put it in three different dishes and we'll mix them up differently so that the glutton has some variety," Fayeth teased.

"Did I mention how much I love you?" I grinned.

"Hmm. You can show me later. Des is distracting Crimson and Felin tonight." Fayeth winked.

I hummed as I started shredding the chicken. Charlotte moved the chopped pieces into a bowl and also started lining four baking dishes. Three for the chicken and one for the now-browned sausage.

We worked like a well-oiled machine, Fayeth starting to feed me tasty morsels as I finished the chicken and started on the potatoes.

The wine flowed freely, and we found ourselves curling up on the couch after we finished, kissing and playing with each other. Our hands found their way through our clothes as we just enjoyed touching each other.

We spent hours reconnecting until we fell asleep on the couch.

CHAPTER 30

T he world erupted into fire as a pentagram burned before me, revealing a horned man in a loincloth flipping through a small library of magazines, each one more depraved than the last.

"Oh, hello there!" Demon Lord Snu Snu lay on the floor with his head propped up as he thumbed through the magazine in front of him. "Bring me any more?"

He didn't look up from his reading. The Demon Lord was the picture of arrogance.

"Uh, no?" I looked around, not entirely sure why I had arrived into his space, but since I was, it provided an opportunity. Having seen Des' transformation told me he had been seriously holding back.

Snu Snu moved, and manacles jangled on his arms as he shifted to better see me over the smoldering lines of the pentagram that bound him. "Well, you've been having some fun out there. Can't blame you for being a little confused. Want me to recap?"

I moved to the edge of the pentagram, knowing that, despite binding him with a trick, Snu Snu was a level forty-five boss. Apparently, he was one that the UG prevented people from visiting because it was so difficult. He had a [Charm] ability that rendered many adventurers useless, or worse, made them fight their allies.

"A friend of mine bec—"

"Yes, yes. She became a little temptress. Is that why you are here? I bet she's insatiable. Can't keep up?" Snu Snu flipped through the book in front of him and seemed to find a picture he liked based on the way his expression shifted and his eyes lingered on the page.

"You have a lot more stats. You could give me even more skills, couldn't you?" I pressed.

The Demon Lord yawned. "Want to come in here and defeat me in a real fight?" he taunted me.

I was half-tempted to do just that. With the new skill, I felt invincible at times. Yet the more logical part of my mind reined the other half in. A level forty-five boss was not something I should even think of trying to solo. Crimson wasn't rushing off into the seventies to kill bosses. And there was the same degree of gap between me and Demon Lord Snu Snu.

I focused on Demon Lord Snu Snu and asked my newest skill if I could beat him. [Eyes of Wisdom] activated and there was a glowing outline around the demon lord before it turned bright red and a little danger symbol popped up.

Well, that confirmed that it was a bad idea.

"No. Just checking in on my tenant and seeing if I can't shake you down for rent," I joked.

"You! You dare ask me? A Demon Lord for rent? The name Snu Snu is feared throughout Hell and galaxies beyond, and you ask me for rent?!" He sat up and puffed himself up. The pentagram around him flared with hellish flames as if they were restraining him.

I scoffed and stood outside the pentagram with my hand out, palm up. "Rent's due, and since I can't kick you out, I'll see if I can't take away your... fun." I glanced at the shelves of smut magazines.

Snu Snu's flare disappeared in an instant as he threw his body over the nearest shelf. "No. You can't. They are all that keep me sane."

"Well, then do you think after you go insane, you'd be more willing to bargain?" I asked thoughtfully.

The Demon Lord glared at me. "You are a truly evil man to deprive another of his pleasures. And this is coming from me, a Demon Lord. Thus you know you are truly heinous."

I focused on the shelf behind him. This was my space even if I didn't want to enter the pentagram.

The shelf wobbled under my thoughts, and Snu Snu clutched onto it, snagging a magazine that shot off. "Look. Wait. We can talk about this."

"We were talking about it, and you refused to pay rent."

Another shelf shook, and Snu Snu was torn between the one he was already protecting and the other shelf. A certain, very used magazine rattled out of the other shelf, and he jumped to put it back in and hugged that shelf with all his strength.

The first exploded as all the magazines danced into the air and away from Demon Lord Snu Snu.

"NO!" he screamed like he was dying. "Not the Baywatch editions!"

"Well, you are going to have to make sacrifices," I chided the demon, trying to keep my face schooled. I hadn't expected the negotiation to be so easy. The demon was truly hooked on his smutty magazines.

"Fine, return my... err... sacred artifacts and we'll have a civil conversation about what you want." Snu Snu held out his hands for me to return the magazines.

Nodding, I made a neat stack just outside of his pentagram prison. "Let's talk specifics first." I sat down on the stack to prove a point.

The Demon Lord leaned against the closest shelf as if his strength had left him. "Fine. What is it that you want?"

Unfortunately, I didn't really know what exactly I was missing. "How about a list of what you can give me?"

"Sure." Snu Snu waved his hand, and a paper burned into life and flew over to me.

I snatched it and read over it. The whole thing was just a list of sexual positions. I made a face before schooling it to an impassive mask and stared back at him. The Demon Lord held his belly while he started laughing.

I threw the paper to the side, and with my mind, made all of the shelves of magazines rattle and begin to dump their contents to fly over to me.

"It was a joke! Can't you take a simple joke!" The Demon Lord snatched several of the magazines out of the air with such speed that I had to commend myself for not crossing the border of the pentagram. In fact, I would wager that he wanted me to do just that. "Alright, alright. How about I give you something to keep that temptress satisfied in bed?"

I pulled the magazines faster and jerked one of them out of his hands. "I don't need more positions."

"No. No, a skill!" The Demon Lord held onto a particular magazine with a pleading expression. "A really good one too."

I paused and relented my removal of his magazines.

Snu Snu put that magazine carefully on a shelf. "Alright, so. I *am* an incubus-type demon. I have a few tricks up my sleeves, and honestly, it's insulting for you to get so drained by her."

I nodded along and prepared to butter him up. "Of course it is. That's why I'm here, clearly a Demon Lord is far above some temptress. But she clearly has full access to her demon."

"She is a demon," Snu Snu scoffed. "It's in her blood, not some idiotic seal borrowing my beautiful power." He put a hand delicately on his chest. "You'll give me all my things back when I give this to you, though."

I stared at the stack next to me. There was nothing I could really do with any of the magazines anyway. And it was in my best interest if he stayed busy and didn't try to break out of the seal. "Sure."

"Wonderful." He waved his hands and a little disk with a pentagram floated out away from him but stalled at the edge of the pentagram.

I rolled my eyes and grunted as the magazines flew back in and surrounded him.

Snu Snu let out a pent-up sigh and the pentagram flew all the way to me. "Glad the deal has been struck."

He quickly grabbed everything and sank back into his prison like he was afraid I was going to steal more of his prized possessions.

***

The dapper man in a bowler hat braced against the wall as gunfire exploded around him, and he checked his gun, readying to fire back. His cover was blown, but it was okay because the spy would end up killing the bad guys and come out ahead.

That's how it worked, how it had to work. It didn't make it any less exciting to see the conclusion.

Bun-bun's eyes were fixed to the little screen as it grew dim sharply and the video stopped before the whole thing winked out. The rabbit monster frowned and smacked the television once with his little paw, eyes becoming larger when nothing happened.

Not sure what to do next, Bun-bun smashed it repeatedly with his little paws. Not hard enough to break it, though. He would never break the sacred object that gave him spy movies.

Bun-bun perked up and looked around, only to realize that Charlotte, Fayeth, and Ken were in a cuddle puddle on the couch.

The thought of disturbing Charlotte for the charger occurred to him. But she wouldn't be happy if he woke her up for that, and Ken was fidgeting a lot in his sleep. It would surely wake Ken up which would decrease the chances of Charlotte helping.

In fact, it would make Charlotte quite angry.

He stretched out, kneading his paws into the chair and arching his back. Maybe he should go to sleep. But what happened next in the movie? It was like an itch that he couldn't quite scratch.

There had to be something to distract him.

Looking around the room, his eyes landed on several leftover carrots in the kitchen. Bun-bun's eyes slid back to Charlotte and then the terrifying warden of the kitchen.

The elf might look smaller than the rest, but she was far more terrifying and had banned him from the kitchen after he had stepped in her pasta dough, leaving behind just a few tiny, little hairs.

It hadn't seemed like a big deal to Bun-bun, but it had set the elf off. Really, they should be honored to consume some of his fluffy, soft fur.

He checked the group again to confirm that they were sound asleep. Glancing back at the television, an idea occurred to Bun-bun, and he smiled to himself as he rolled off the couch and braced himself against the leg of the chair.

It would take a truly skilled operator to sneak past the fearsome kitchen warden. This wasn't a job for just anyone; it could only be done by the best.

Agent BB was the only man for the task.

Bun-bun, now known as Agent BB, slipped into his best secret agent stance and mimed putting on a pair of sunglasses. If he couldn't get to the kitchen and nab the carrots out from under the evil kitchen warden, then the whole world was doomed.

It was up to him and him alone.

Agent BB was on the case.

He slipped to the next chair leg, glancing around it to ensure that the alarms hadn't gone off, and then tiptoed across the open space to a pile of discarded— He meant his secret armory.

Bun-bun pushed a spot next to the basket of odds and ends and tipped it over while making a whooshing noise. The rattle of its contents sounded deafening to him, and he braced, glancing over his shoulder carefully to make sure that no one had woken up.

"Step one of the plan to save the world, complete." Bun-bun wiped at his brow before picking up a pencil, a measuring tape, and a paperclip.

A true spy could do just about anything with a paperclip.

He eyed the high counters and then back at his tools. They'd have to work; it was the world's only hope. Bun-bun rolled to the side for effect and fell over as his armory 'exploded'.

"Phew, they are onto me," he spoke with his rough Jersey accent. "They blew my glasses off." It wasn't exactly spy material. He sounded more like a mobster, but that was just the voice he'd been given.

Agent BB pretended to put back on a pair of sunglasses, and casually strolled towards the kitchen, keeping his eyes up and his stride casual. The trick to blending in was to act like you belonged and keep moving.

Agent BB was the best of the best as he kept his cool even under the pressure of the world near the tipping point of its doom.

It was up to him and him alone.

As soon as he was in the kitchen proper, he flattened himself to the wall and checked his 'watch'.

"It's o' six hundred. Right on time, as the best spy in the biz always is," he muttered to himself and went over to the counters, pretending to fiddle with the open space under the cabinets.

He had no idea why they put this space here, except maybe so they didn't bash their toes when they swung the doors open? Anyway, he fiddled with his paperclip until the 'grate' for the 'air vents' came loose.

Agent BB rolled into the 'air vent' and flattened himself to the floor as he crept one inch at a time, double checking that none of the alarms had gone off.

He had his tools of the trade. He just needed to get over to the correct counter. Then he would use the measuring tape and the pencil to scale the cabinets to the counter. Every spy needed a grappling hook.

Agent BB touched his ear and nodded several times. "Understood. Send me the schematics. I'm a little busy here." He flattened himself to the side and held his objects close like he was being quiet for a passing guard before continuing. "I was almost caught. You didn't say anything about the patrols," he huffed.

His analyst once again made a mistake and was rushing to find a new updated plan. Agent BB didn't have time to wait. The world was at stake.

He hurried through the air vents until he was at the right spot, and rolled out of them looking up at the counter and a carrot leaning off the side. "I have a visual on the target. Over. There's no way up. I'll have to use the grappling hook."

Agent BB knew that the world was relying on him, but he kept his cool under the pressure. He was a top-tier agent; he didn't get rattled easily.

Agent BB tied the tape measure around the pencil and gauged the distance with his tongue sticking out to the side. "I have one shot at this or the world explodes." He pulled on the knot with his teeth for good measure.

If he could get the pencil up through the handle and to brace, then he could get up there and get the carr— save the world. Yes, save the world.

He could see the perfect shot, lined up the pencil and threw. It clinked four inches off of his intended target and fell back down with a loud clatter.

Agent BB cleared his throat. "I have one shot." He picked it back up. "One shot to make this work and save the world."

He threw it again and once again missed. Bun-bun picked up the pencil and looked around the kitchen before hopping up and looping it around the handle before landing again.

"Got it in one shot," he said with a smug glint of his eyes. "That's the best for you. Take notes, young analyst."

Agent BB grabbed the tape measure with his front and back paws, starting to scoot himself along it.

"What do you mean there's an issue?" Agent BB spoke into his ear piece. "A what? You're cutting out. Anyway, time to save the world."

Bun-bun reached the top of his tape measure, and there was still a gap. Most importantly, there was an overhang that he couldn't quite get over.

"This wasn't on the schematics, but don't worry. I am the best." He hopped against the cabinet, and it swung open slightly only to close with a bang.

Agent BB froze, but there was no sign of movement. He tried again, this time successfully swinging open the cabinet door. He crawled on top of the door and lined up his jump.

This was it. Agent BB would be a hero.

He wiggled his little butt, preparing the jump to the counter of carrots.

"Time to save the world." Agent BB jumped.

There was a whoosh and a giant blade nearly took his ear off.

Agent BB was skilled and performed a spy aerial maneuver to kick off the glaive blade to flip backwards and land on the floor. The Kitchen Warden loomed over him like a behemoth of epic proportions.

Agent BB wasn't a coward, but sometimes the situation called for a tactical withdrawal. This was one of those times.

"Abort mission!" Agent BB screamed into his earpiece. "We've been found! Abort, requesting immediate extraction!" His long ears flapped in the wind as he made a speedy retreat.

"I've warned you not to come into the kitchen." The pointy eared devil glowered down at Agent BB and raised her executioner's glaive high into the air.

"They have a bazooka!" Agent BB dodged the next swing, but it shaved off some of the fur on his little tail. "They almost got us. Extraction. Where's the extraction?!" He raced through the kitchen as Fayeth's glaive tried to make him into mincemeat.

"I'm going to put you in a stock pot. I warned you." Fayeth jabbed several times.

Agent BB wasn't sure if he was going to make it out of the firefight, but there was one hope.

The analyst gave him the extraction point, and Agent BB glanced at the couch to his groggy green-haired master who was waking up with the commotion.

"I see the extraction point. It'll be a close call, but I'll make it."

He dodged Fayeth and swung around the side of the couch, using it for protection before he leapt up into Charlotte's lap. Being in close proximity to Charlotte slowed down the Kitchen Warden's next attack.

"Base, come in. This is Agent BB. I wasn't able to get the device. The world just might end if I can't get it. What? The agency sold us out? Why?" He pinned his ears back as he sat safely in Charlotte's lap. "That long-eared rat bastard. He was out for himself this whole time. I never did trust him. No matter, the world's safety comes first. I'll settle my score with him after this is done."

"Huh?" Charlotte rubbed her eyes. "What's going on, Bun-bun? World's safety?"

"He was in my kitchen." Fayeth glared daggers at him, but right now, she couldn't get to him.

"Base HQ, this is Agent BB. It is of the most vital importance that we get those carrots; otherwise, the world is doomed!" Bun-bun pinned his ears back and made his eyes wide at Charlotte.

She rubbed her face. "Bun-bun, you aren't allowed in the kitchen. You know this."

"I'm Agent BB, and I'm on a mission. If I don't get those carrots, the world is over." He made an explosion noise. "Kaput, kablooie. Everything is done, Toots, if we don't get those carrots away from the evil Kitchen Warden."

"Can he have some of the leftover carrots?" HQ had to at least play nice with the foreign government.

"No. Not after I found him sneaking around in there."

"Sorry, Bu— Agent BB. Looks like you are out of luck on this one."

What they didn't know was that Agent BB never gave up. "It's okay. Thanks for trying, Toots." Agent BB played along and let his ears droop.

Ken fidgeted in his sleep like he was having a nightmare and that drew both of the ladies' attention.

Agent BB rolled out of HQ and pressed himself to the side of the couch as the Kitchen Warden dropped her guard.

Agent BB smiled. He saw his opportunity. As the best agent in the biz, he knew that would happen, and snuck around back. There was always a back door.

Agent BB managed to evade multiple traps as he reapproached the base with the world-devastating weapon. The Kitchen Warden had been pulled away by his previous plan; it had worked like a charm.

He avoided the air ducts. They were now booby trapped. His best chance was now using speed over stealth. Enemy agents came from every direction, and Agent BB had to duck, roll, and fire back as he raced back to his grappling hook.

Even if they'd caught him before, they hadn't had the time to detach it. Under enemy fire, Agent BB scaled the rope, swinging onto the still open cabinet and finally making it onto the counter.

He put his hand on the carrot and glanced over at the couch where his mortal enemy had laid back down to sleep.

"Perfect. The world is saved." Agent BB snagged the leftover carr— the doomsday trigger and bounced off the counter as he saved the world, feeling high.

A 'good job' from the analyst was all the thanks he'd get. Being a secret agent was a thankless job. Even though he had already saved the world multiple times, no one was going to throw him a parade.

Agent BB ferried the doomsday triggers off into Ken's unused room and curled up under the bed, where they wouldn't hear him disarm the bombs.

Bun-bun nibbled on his carrot with little crunches.

Until next time.

CHAPTER 31

"Why are there carrot chunks all over my floor?" I asked no one in particular as I went into my room to change my clothes.

No one heard me. They were all in their own rooms getting ready for the day or in the kitchen.

I peeked under the bed to make sure there wasn't a larger mess waiting for me and scooped the shreds of carrots into my hand. Then I brought them into the kitchen to throw away.

Last night had been odd. I'd made the deal with Demon Lord Snu Snu, and it seemed that Bun-bun might have had his own adventures. But I'd managed to get a new skill, even if it wasn't exactly what I'd been expecting.

[Delirious Pleasures] - Give your partner such intense pleasures that their mind might struggle to keep up. +1 Mana on successful use for caster and +1 magic each time the target survives.

I swiped on my CID and stored the skill quickly in the hidden view, along with Demon Lord. I didn't need anyone to casually see that. It wasn't exactly a pile of stats... yet.

If I showed it to Des, she'd likely beg for me to use it, and I probably would.

The bonuses were just too good. Though... my eyes lingered on Crimson for a moment. She would be willing to test it, right? After all, I doubted it could harm Crimson.

And it was her fault that I'd gotten that Demon Lord put inside of me anyway.

"So, did you find a place for us to level?" I asked Crimson, peeking into cabinets to find something to eat.

"A few," Crimson admitted. "There's this one on the twenty-eighth floor in a dead branch of the dungeon. Seems like high density, but it has humanoid monsters. Vampires." Crimson bobbed her eyebrows.

"Oh no. Are they going to suck my blood?" Des teased.

"They actually do have a move like that. They latch on and immobilize you from behind." Crimson nearly teleported behind me to demonstrate as she kissed my neck and sucked on it. "Then they drain you and recover health."

"Ooh," Des said appreciatively. "Sounds fun."

"They are also humanoid monsters, so they are quite different to fight," Crimson explained. "I'd be a little concerned about sending you all off to deal with that one if my class didn't have a certain new secret weapon." She released me and put a hand on my shoulder with a wink.

"So, when are we going?" I asked.

"After I show off my portal a few dozen times to the Harem Queen," Crimson answered with a straight face. "So, we'll do morning class and training before shipping you all off for the afternoon."

"Right. Class." I had sort of forgotten about that part. We'd been spending a lot of our time farming and working on our stats.

"Yes, class. That thing where I as the teacher go up front and you ogle me from the back while I try and stuff knowledge that will keep you alive into your head." Crimson played with my hair and dodged as I tried to smack her hand away.

She was in a good mood. A fantastic mood. But I wasn't surprised. We'd had a good time together, and she'd gotten a much-needed release.

"Well, I hope you enjoy rubbing the new skill in the Harem Queen's face. Make sure she gets absolutely zero idea of trying to get the portal for herself." I eyed Crimson.

She pouted. "It's no fun if she doesn't want what I have."

"That's what I was afraid of," I sighed and wanted to change the subject. "So, what are we going over for class today?"

"How to properly analyze adventurer performance," Crimson said. "Knowing how you'll be evaluated helps quite a bit in performing correctly. It's a little bit of a song and dance, but that's just how things work."

"We are learning how to interpret damage meters and survival scores," Des explained.

That sounded like quite the diversion from how to kill monsters, which was usually Crimson's topic of choice.

"What were you three up to last night?" I asked, moving around the stove and starting to make some eggs for all of us.

"Things," Crimson answered a little too quickly.

Des glanced at Crimson and nodded. "Things," she said with a thick sense of mischief.

"Really? I could have never guessed. How do you want your eggs?" I asked Des.

"Deviled," she joked.

I raised an eyebrow and opened the fridge to find what I needed.

"It was a joke." Des splayed her hands pleadingly.

"Do you at least like deviled eggs?" I asked.

"Yeah, I mean they are tasty, but too much work for breakfast," Des said.

"Let me worry about that. I'll get it done before class. Besides, Crimson wants to show off her portal, so she's going to portal us to the Harem Queen's class by accident to taunt her," I said.

Crimson's eyes sparkled. "That's perfect."

I wasn't sure if she was humoring me or if she hadn't thought of the idea yet. It seemed like the perfect way to go about rubbing the new skill in the other woman's face.

Either way, I slipped on my apron and got the whisk ready as I started boiling a dozen eggs.

"Ken's cooking." Charlotte's tone was half disbelief, half shock as she came out for breakfast.

"Oh, don't make a big deal out of it." I decided to add another dozen eggs to the pot. There was no such thing as too much. Worst case scenario, I'd just end up eating them later.

"Did I hear you right? Ken is treating us to breakfast?" Fayeth came out.

I pulled out another pan. "I'm taking orders for your eggs."

"While they are fertile, I think I'd like to adventure a little longer before settling down," Fayeth joked and sat down.

I blinked, unsure how to even respond to that statement.

"Sunny side up," Fayeth ordered with a snicker seeing my stupefied face. Kids hadn't even crossed my mind.

Crimson took her own seat. "You know how I like my eggs, scrambled and stuffed to the brim."

I quickly filled the stove with pans and started going through the fridge to get everything ready.

Managing all the tasks might have been difficult in the past, but with all the bonuses from adventuring, it was trivial to manage all of the pans and keep up a conversation with my ladies.

"So, class today?" Charlotte asked.

"See." Crimson pointedly looked at me. "Some of you are decent students and don't forget about class. Adventurer evaluation," Crimson answered Charlotte.

"Oh. Damage meter assessments. I did those for my father as a summer job for a while," Charlotte said as she accepted her scrambled eggs with cheese. "It's not too hard. You just need to take into account how much they buff the rest of the party, take those averages, and then attribute some of that damage to them as well as looking and balancing the difference between single target damage dealers, multi target and then area of effect damage dealers. And most importantly, you need to consider how they do during their weakness because it isn't ever just one type in a dive." She picked at her eggs as I stared at her.

"Or Charlotte could teach the class." Crimson waved a fork at her.

The druid blushed and hid her face slightly behind her braids before pursing her lips and fighting the urge. "No. I think the textbook probably covers some things I'd miss."

Crimson watched her for a second but said nothing more as I handed her an omelet that was more filling than egg. She dug into it with a big grin.

Finally, I took a moment to smear some extra whipped filling for the deviled eggs on a plate and made a few drops of hot sauce around the plate. I delicately placed each of the finished eggs.

"Stop." Des was blushing at how I was overdoing it.

"No, it's too fun seeing your reaction," I teased and then turned to Fayeth who wanted to try them as well and made her a similar plate.

"Oh, these are good." Fayeth munched on one. "Feels like I could eat dozens of these before getting full, though. Which is odd because they are eggs and should be heavy."

"I think it's a trick that happens with whipped food. Somehow, it makes them less filling." I shrugged and made my own plate with a smattering of all the other ones I'd made before taking a carrot over to Bun-bun. Then I brought a plate over to Felin's nest in the couch.

I waved a plate of bacon and a glass of milk by the pile of cushions.

Felin's head popped out between several articles of clothing, my shirt hung off her head. "Mmmm," she moaned and reached for the plate with her eyes still closed.

I stepped back and she crawled forward, her tail swishing behind her. She almost fell off the couch before her eyes snapped open as she tottered precariously off the edge of the sofa. I thought for sure that she'd still fall but her balance was impeccable.

Felin's tail lashed behind her, sticking as far back as it could to try and balance her body before she toppled.

"What are you doing?" She angrily glared at me before she saw the milk and bacon. Then her expression turned to one of joy as she tumbled off the couch in a neat roll before she popped up and snatched both.

"Thank you." She was already scarfing down the bacon and washing it down with milk.

"She might eat faster than you," Crimson chuckled.

Felin looked at the rest of the room and realized they were all having eggs. "Oh." She glanced at the bacon. "You didn't have to make something special for me."

"What was the last thing you said about eggs?" I asked the room.

"Slimy," Des answered.

"No, I think it was 'why would you eat unborn chickens when their meat is so much better'," Fayeth played along.

"Pretty sure she just stuck her tongue out and ran away last time you offered her eggs," Charlotte piled on.

Felin's ears drooped and her cheeks blushed bright red. "Well... all of those things are true. The meat *is* better," she grumbled to herself and then perked back up. "So, what's on the agenda for today?" Felin moved the conversation off her embarrassing regard for eggs.

"Class," I said, walking back to the counter and finishing my own plate. "Which we will be late to get to if we don't leave soon."

Des checked the time on the CID. "We have like ten minutes, and Crimson is going to teleport us."

I pointed at Crimson, but I wasn't talking to her. "You think she's going to gloat for less than ten minutes to the Harem Queen?"

Crimson snickered, no doubt already coming up with one liners for the Harem Queen.

"This is an odd game. In my people, it would be like Crimson is trying to entice this Harem Queen to join you all at this rate," Felin said, setting down her empty plate and licking the bacon grease off her hands.

Crimson froze, horror struck at the implication. "Absolutely not. She's a diva and a man-eater."

"There's a younger form of her. I think she might even be prettier if she tried half as hard as her mother," Felin pointed out. "What's her deal?"

"Confused," everyone but Felin and I said in unison.

"Huh," Felin said, done cleaning her hands. "So, then are we portaling? I'm excited to see something that can portal in the Great One's realm."

"Your people have no record of something like this?" I asked.

Felin shook her head. "Nope. The Great One is always changing what is possible. What this means is beyond me. The other shamans would have opinions, but we rarely see everything the same way."

Crimson put her plate away and threw her hand into the air with a giant grin. "Portal."

A portal ripped open in our room, and Crimson marched her way through with full confidence.

I was close behind.

"Wh-what are you doing?" The Harem Queen was at the front of her class and half her students were in the room as she tried to maintain her composure.

"Huh." Crimson looked around, confused. "Did you steal my classroom?"

"No. I did not steal your classroom. This is my classroom."

"I swear this one is a smidge bigger than mine." Crimson continued to find fault with Helen's mother.

"It is." The Harem Queen's lips twitched. "A foot in both dimensions."

"Ha!" Crimson pointed a finger; the two of them were acting like bickering children in front of the whole class.

"I don't know her." Des hid her face as she came through the portal.

"She's Crimson. You were just eating with her," Felin helpfully supplied. "Did the portal damage your head?" She looked at Des, concerned.

I chuckled.

"No. It's a human thing, Crimson is embarrassing for her, thus she's breaking association," Fayeth explained.

"Oh," Felin said with a drawn-out noise of understanding. "I don't know her either."

"Since this is the bigger room, it must be for the leading class, though," Crimson continued to argue, hand on her hip.

The Harem Queen smirked. "It is for the best class, thus the extra room."

She was totally doing this on purpose.

Why the two of them suddenly had a rivalry was beyond me, but I knew that this was more than coincidence. The Harem Queen had made her room just a little bigger than Crimson's to make a point.

Crimson narrowed her eyes. "Well, then my Portal ability must be confused." She shrugged. "Maybe we'll just make another." She waved the first away and made another.

"Oh no," Crimson said in completely fake surprise as it came out at a safe zone in the fifties. "Looks like I just go wherever I want, after I get this ability down of course. Let's try that again." She waved her hand and another portal appeared, this one to a tropical paradise. "Oh, that looks nice."

"Stop this and go to your class. Class will begin momentarily," the Harem Queen spoke between gritted teeth.

"It's more fun to do it with portals. Don't worry, I'll get this down." Crimson played with her ability, faking making them to the wrong place and just showing off how easily she could traverse the dungeon now. "There!" She finally made a portal to the room next door.

"Now get out. My class is going to have trouble settling down and paying attention because of your stunts," the Harem Queen shooed us.

"Don't you want to try it?" Crimson gestured to the portal. "You know you want to. After all, you chased Ken until an Elven ambassador had to stop you."

The Harem Queen glowered. "You hated me before that."

"True, but that made messing with you so much juicier." Crimson stopped pretending and grinned from ear to ear. "Maybe if you ask nicely, I'll ferry you and your class to the same area that we are going to start training in. It's an event on a vampire floor."

The Harem Queen frowned for just a flicker of a second to think. "I know the event. We could be there in... two weeks."

"Or instantly." Crimson waved her hand, dismissing the portal to the next room and made one to the event in question. It looked like a haunted mansion.

"Crimson, what do you want?" the Harem Queen sighed.

"Well, that's no fun." Crimson frowned and dismissed the portal. "I'll take all the Haylon students that want to go after classes today," she spoke to the broader room.

"Thank you," the Harem Queen said. "Now, please leave. Class is starting."

"Sure." Crimson walked out of the room rather than use the portal and several of the onlookers nearly fell over. Crimson did like to make a show.

"Crimson. Why do you dislike her?" I asked, hearing that it had started before the Harem Queen chased after me.

"Oh. It's pretty simple. Her hair color," Crimson said offhandedly as we walked back to our classroom.

"Her..." I closed my eyes for a moment of understanding of both why and how stupid it was. "Because her hair is red? Because it is crimson? You've got to be kidding me."

"People used to confuse us a lot," Crimson pouted. "This one time, someone actually gave her my award. Everyone expects me to have red hair." Crimson pulled at her pitch-black hair. "Stupid last name."

"It's fine." I shook my head at the absurdity of the grudge. "I can't imagine you without black hair at this point. Let's get class done."

CHAPTER 32

"That is one way to view it," Crimson agreed as she led class. "But while damage is important, survival is as well. There are very few classes that can go out with a big enough bang to make their death viable for damage. For most, staying alive will always be the strongest tool in their damage dealing kit."

Crimson tapped on the chalkboard where she had drawn up several records of damage meters. "Now, let's move on to tanks and how those are evaluated."

Crimson looked out at the class for a volunteer. Normally, she would pick on me, and her eyes did linger on me, but then she surprised me and moved on to Helen. "Why don't you help the Silver Fangs guild master understand. He'll have to make these decisions himself one of these days."

Helen glanced back at me with a scowl and returned her attention to Crimson. "Tanks have different specialties. It's important to have variety; though, their damage still matters."

"Yes, it does. Especially at the high level, when you push content, the difference between a tank's damage and say—"

There was a loud thump against the window that interrupted the class.

A clunky spear had hit the surface, but it had failed to punch through the glass. I stood up and moved to see what was happening, activating [Eyes of Wisdom] and asking the skill for who threw the weapon.

A dwarf lit up blue in my vision. "A dwarf threw that."

Smoke started to drift up from the fallen spear and billowed over the window, blocking our view.

I turned away from the window with the realization that we were under attack. "Candice, Myrtle, block the windows. Get something that's air tight up behind them. Helen, take your party and go check on your mom's classroom."

"Who put you in charge?" Felicity barked even as Helen was pulling her party together.

"I did. Got a problem with that?" I stared down at the shorter woman. Even after the week of changing up parties, I'd never gotten a chance to get to know her better.

She sat there with her arms crossed in a baggy cloak. "If I do?"

"Then I'll put a fist in your face so you can sleep on the ground while we deal with this situation," Taylor threatened. "Now isn't the time to argue. Work your shit out later. Ken, what are we going to do?"

"Check to see if the other classes need help, and help them. After that, we can figure out how to fortify the building against the attack. The UG is going to crack down hard on them. We just need to weather this out." I glanced at Crimson who'd been surprisingly quiet.

She was staring at her CID. Then her eyes lifted and met mine. "The UG has been hit hard. It seems that the last issue with the dwarves wasn't as benign as we thought. They measured our responses. There were teams ready to strike the UG response team the second they stepped out."

I quickly processed the new information.

"There's enough of us to hold this building. Go help the UG get back on their feet." I knew that a lot of lives would be saved if she could go untangle the UG first.

I could tell that she agreed, but she still hesitated.

"We'll be fine. The cheap knockoff, I think you called her the Harem Queen?" I joked. "She'll do fine against a few lousy dwarves."

Several more impacts hit the windows that were now mostly covered in stone. One of the windows cracked, and Felicity made an air elemental that kept the smoke out while Candice finished up.

"See? We've got this. Go," I shooed Crimson and turned back to the class. As she left, I felt the breeze of her quick exit on my back.

Over the last few weeks, I had learned quite a bit about my classmates, both how they operated under stress and their strengths that had nothing to do with their classes.

"Alright, with the windows sealed, let's move down the hall and seal the rooms off." I waved the class forward. "Myrtle, take the rear. Healers in the center. Fayeth, we are following you."

The class was quick to organize themselves despite our school being attacked. We were adventurers, and we dealt with life-or-death conflict every day. We had to always be prepared for anything.

A safe zone was safe from monsters, but never people. This was a valuable lesson.

We entered the hallway, and immediately, the sounds of conflict were echoing down the hall.

"Move down only as quickly as we can seal the doorways behind us. Rushing does us no good if we get pinned between enemies on four sides," I gave the order and we moved.

Myrtle and Candice were working on the right, sealing off the doorways with mud and stone while Leah and Felicity were using ice to seal the doorways on the left.

Fayeth kept glancing over her shoulder and moving forward.

Helen shot out of a doorway, thick, acrid smoke clinging to her as she coughed and covered her eyes. "This way. Follow my voice."

I glanced at our group. "Healers, stay back. Melee damage. Let's get in there. Felin, can you cleanse the air like you did before?"

"Yup." The Nekorian gave me a salute and chanted while banging her staff to summon winds that blew back into the room, pushing at the smoke.

The Harem Queen was coughing lightly into her hand as she came out of the smoke with a sword burning with blue fire. "Everyone, this way. Move slowly."

The room was filled with hacking and coughing. Even the Harem Queen was blinking out tears and clearing her throat.

"We are sealing the doors behind us and moving down the hall to collect the other classes," I informed the Harem Queen. "The spear bounced off our window. It must have been a lucky angle."

She grunted and waved her sword at the ceiling. The blue fire jumped from the sword and ate at the cloud of smoke. "Whatever this is, it is quite potent."

The smoke burned slowly from her sword, and she focused, the flames intensifying and burning more of it. The smoke parted for several students rushing out and stumbling forward.

The healers in our party were quick to start casting heals, only for another spear to come out right behind one of the students, hitting the back of their head and exploding next to the Harem Queen.

Fire roared and knocked us to the side as the Harem Queen took most of the blast while shielding her class. She skidded back several steps, her dress singed and her eyes filled with a burning anger.

"Fight back," one of her students coughed.

"She can't," I said, understanding the situation. With most of her class in the smoke, she was hobbled. Any attack she threw out would be blind.

But mine wouldn't be. [Eyes of Wisdom] located the enemies in the room.

Two stocky red outlines appeared in the smoke, as well as a number of crouched over green ones. Several of the green forms were already fading to a dimmer color.

"Shoot where I do," I shouted and took a throwing knife, hurling it into the smoke.

"Ken!" The Harem Queen glared at me, but the rest of my class didn't hesitate.

Des threw a shadow bolt while Regan fired an arrow. Their hits were quickly followed by the rest of my class. The barrage knocked down the dwarf that we must have caught by surprise.

I turned to the Harem Queen, knowing my eyes were glowing like Crimson's. "I can see through it, and several of your students are bleeding out." I wasn't positive that was what the more dull coloring meant, but it was a fair guess.

The Harem Queen pointed her sword as I threw another dagger. Her sword glowed blue for a second as the energy gathered at the point and a thin beam of blue sliced through the smoke. I watched the outline for the dwarf explode.

"All targets down. I'm getting the students." I braced myself and rushed into the smoke.

Immediately, I regretted entering the room.

I made a note to carry a gas mask in my CID in the future. And given the way my body reacted to the gas, I wasn't too worried I'd forget that lesson.

It suddenly felt like the saliva in my throat had thickened to concrete and angry hornets were racing up and down my sinuses. They might have even been equipped with little daggers at the damage it felt like I was incurring.

Everything told me to close my eyes, but I kept them peeled even as they burned. Tears raced out of them to find the dimmest of the outlines.

I scooped my fellow student up and raced back through the smoke. As soon as I cleared the dark haze, heals hit me in rapid fire before landing on the woman in my arms.

She was covered in blood. A nasty gash went from her throat down between her chest.

"Point me to the ones that need it." The Harem Queen grabbed my arm.

Several casters were pushing wind into the room to try and blow the smoke back out the window, but the progress was slow.

"This way." I took her arm rather than let her drag me. The classroom wasn't large, but navigating the tipped over desks and the students that were struggling to breathe made it seem like a trek.

"Here's one." I pulled the Harem Queen's hand down to the girl crouching under the desk.

"Injured?" she asked.

"Not that I can see," I answered.

She grabbed the student and lifted her, knocking the desk over in the process before flinging the student towards the doorway with uncanny accuracy.

My class crumbled backwards but caught the other student.

"Wait, are you going to..." I hesitated as she grabbed another of her students and flung them clear of the smoke. "... throw them all?"

"Not the injured ones," she huffed, reaching out to hold my hand to keep us together. I couldn't see her through this thick smoke.

"What do you think this smoke even is?" I pulled her along to the next student.

"Who knows. It's clearly designed to deal with mid-level adventurers," she answered, following my hand down to the next student. "Injured? You know what? Just save the injured ones for last."

"Already on it." I saw her move in a flash and throw the next student clear.

It felt a little much that these students were panicking or had dealt so poorly with this attack, then again, they had been surprised by the smoke and more than a few of them appeared to be incapacitated more than I'd expect from the smoke alone.

The two intruders must have acted quickly.

"The dwarves were functioning in the smoke. When we clear the room, I want you to show me their bodies." The Harem Queen must have been thinking along the same lines as me.

"Let's finish up." I pulled her to student after student.

The smoke finally started to thin as we wrapped up clearing the room and our casters managed to clear half the room. We pulled the last of the students out of the smoke to see the situation.

Most of Class B was groggily holding their heads. More than just the smoke had disabled them, which made me feel better. At least they weren't incompetent.

"Alright," I wheezed as I was hit by multiple heals to recover.

"Your eyes..." Kendra stared at me with worry.

"Huh?"

"They are glowing blue, and your sclera are pretty much entirely red. It looks awesome," Selene told me with a grin.

I blinked and it felt like I was rubbing sandpaper over my eyes. It was probably due to the heals that I wasn't bent over throwing up by how irritated my throat had become.

"We are going to seal off this room and keep on going," I spoke through the pain.

Several of the groggy Class B students glanced at me and then at the Harem Queen.

The high-level adventurer crossed her arms. "Consider this a test. Survive. Anyone who I consider to have failed will get an F. Everyone else will be graded on performance."

"If we don't survive, uh... will we be dead?" a student asked.

The Harem Queen deadpanned. "What do you think?"

I knew that she didn't want to tell them that she'd cover them, that would only lead to complacency.

"Move it, unless you want to waste time arguing." I chugged one of the potions that Crimson had given me to prevent hangovers, hoping that whatever was in this smoke counted as a poison.

"Where's Crimson?" the Harem Queen asked.

"The UG called on her," I said.

My answer made her check her CID and nod to herself as she followed our class out.

"There's nothing on these dwarves like gas masks that I can find." Des was rifling through the one dwarf whose body was intact. "Either we got very unlucky, or the smoke just doesn't bother them."

"Could be a difference in anatomy," Candice offered. "Though, to find something that works on us and Nekorian but not themselves seems..."

"What?" I asked.

"Like it was either designed by them, or the dungeon is encouraging conflict." Candice stopped holding back.

Felin burst out laughing. "Of course the Great One wants conflict. It eats our scraps."

Her view on the dungeon was interesting, to say the least.

"Will the Nekorians fight?" I asked.

"Only if we are attacked, which they might be wary of because of our peoples' shared history." Felin shrugged. "Doesn't mean I can't help you."

Before we got to the next room, two dwarves walked out of billowing smoke looking confused before their eyes locked on us. Then they turned to run back into the smoke.

"Not so fast!" Regan jumped in the air with an acrobatic grace and fired two arrows. Both of them missed and hit the door frame, but tethers snapped into place, locking both of the dwarves from running and pulling them back.

The tanks hit them like cars on a highway, slamming into them with various movement abilities and throwing them against the wall. The two dwarves were crushed and stabbed brutally before being thrown to the ground.

"What are your plans?!" Helen demanded and put her boots on one's throat.

The dwarf wheezed something.

"What was that?" Helen lifted her boot only for the dwarf to froth at the mouth and spit something at her.

Penny was next to Helen a moment later, her blade intercepting the glob that sizzled on her sword.

Helen's boot came back down like a hammer. She crushed the dwarf's chest and Penny's blade made quick work of the second. She glanced up at me after with a blush like she'd made a mistake.

"No, they weren't going to talk," I agreed with their actions. "We'll keep moving. I think it's safe to assume that the upper floors weren't broken into. Classes were on the second, so we'll head down and clear out the first floor. Did anyone see the upperclassmen today?" I asked no one in particular.

"Yeah, I saw some of them in the cafeteria," Taylor answered.

"Right, let's go." I moved through the hall and we sealed off the doors.

No new dwarves lingered in the second floor, but several other rooms had been hit by the horrible gas.

"Candice, work with Felicity and come up with a way to deal with the gas." Those two would be perfect at working through the problem.

Both of them looked at each other before nodding and stepping closer among the class.

"Meixie, check the stairs." I motioned forward.

The quiet assassin shot into the stairwell and scanned upwards before coming back down. "Clear."

"Let's see what's downstairs for us. Fayeth, take us down." Part of me wanted to lead, but I knew having the tanks do so was for the best.

The elf moved down the steps and held up a hand for us all to stop. I was close enough to crouch and see down into the common areas. Dwarves were everywhere, and many of them were carrying unconscious Haylon students over their shoulders.

"What do we do?" Both classes turned to me.

"Save them. They are Haylon, and despite our differences, not one of us will let someone else, much less a bunch of stinking dwarves, fuck with Haylon."

My brief speech set a fire in the rest of the student's eyes.

"Anyone with stealth, move to the front. I want you to get down there and prepare to cut off that line carrying students." I set my jaw and activated [Camouflage].

CHAPTER 33

T he cafeteria was silent except for the stomping of the dwarves and the occasional grunt from their captives.

More dwarves marched single file out of adjacent rooms, each of their stocky bodies surprisingly strong for their size as they deposited more girls into a pile. As soon as they finished dropping off one, the dwarves walked single file back to grab another.

It was eerie as it was all done in total silence, and the dwarves were so uniform in their movements that they felt unnatural.

I glanced over at our group of adventurers hiding in the stairwell, waiting for their chance and then back over to those of us who had snuck down and positioned themselves around the cafeteria.

We'd save the upperclassmen and move on from there.

Fayeth was the first to attack, coming out of her [Camouflage] with a strike that severed a dwarf's foot. The dwarf staggered, losing his balance along with half his foot.

The rest of the dwarves in the line drew weapons and charged.

I broke away from the wall, and the others followed my cue. Together, we crept down. Arrows, spells, and blades dug into the marching dwarves. It was an oddly quiet battle. There was no screaming as the dwarves moved in unison. And we were going for stealth.

Yet nothing was as loud as ringing steel in the quiet, announcing to those in the stairwell that the battle had begun.

The rest of the class came pouring down to meet a troop of dwarves marching out from the rooms where they'd been retrieving the upperclassmen.

My sword rang out against a dwarf's hammer as I fought. Our surprise attack had taken many, but now it was a brawl. The dwarves kept coming.

I smiled. Where in the past a constant stream of enemies was annoying, I knew it gave me a chance to build my stacks the longer the fight went on.

The dwarves fought like cagey veterans. The dwarf in front of me swung his hammer hard enough that I could only dodge rather than block or parry, and his other hand held a small knife that he constantly jabbed towards my gut.

I couldn't take my focus off it for a moment or he'd have it buried in my liver before I could blink. The only saving grace was that I had a good foot reach on him with the sword, and I was getting faster the longer this drew out.

My sword slipped past his hammer and cut hard into his bicep, making his arm sag. That was the start of the end for him.

"Ken, watch out!" Des shouted over the sound of a dozen weapons ringing.

Trusting her, I used [Shadow Ambush] and startled my opponent by appearing behind him with a [Dark Strike] to the back of his neck that would put him down.

A heavy maul slammed down where I'd been. The giant bronze weapon cracked the floor and told me all I needed to know about its wielder.

The drones we'd been fighting all had hammers, knives, and a few swords. Only the other soldier that had fought us before had carried a real weapon.

I quickly assessed my opponent. This soldier was fast for how big of a weapon he swung around and whipped that bronze maul up from the shattered floor towards me.

A flash and red hair fluttered in my face as Helen appeared, a skill igniting on her shield as a white cross appeared. She caught the mace and reflected the damage back at the dwarf, launching it across the cafeteria and into a crowd of dwarves.

"Thanks." I smiled.

"Don't get yourself killed," Helen snorted.

"It almost sounds like you care." I blocked another dwarf drone and slipped inside his guard to thrust my sword through its beard and into what I hoped was his throat. With how thick their beards were, I wasn't even sure.

Helen smacked a charging dwarf's hammer with her shield and introduced his face to her spiked mace. "Don't get it in your head that I'm like the rest of these girls simping after you."

"There's the woman I know," I laughed, flowing around her to finish the dwarf.

"Yeah, well, at least you saved my mom's class and are working to save this one. Even if you probably use that thick cloud as an excuse to grope my mom," Helen scoffed. "Pervert. I bet you are saving all these ladies so that they fall in love with you."

She covered my back and blocked a thrown knife before blasting a blazing, white fire back at the dwarf.

"Yep. Nothing's changed. Phew, for a second I thought you hit your head too hard." I side-stepped her, our hips brushing as I snapped a kick to stop a low swing from another dwarf and slashed to push him back from Helen.

The two of us worked well together as we danced around each other, covering each other's backs. Purple lightning was racing down my arms as the stacks began building up.

"You good to take him on your own with that speed?" Helen asked, her eyes tracking across the room as the soldier dwarf charged towards us.

"Wouldn't say no to you stopping him for a moment," I joked.

Helen tucked her shoulder and pulled up her shield as she shot off with an ability. She rammed her shield into the dwarf's chest, and I teleported behind him with [Shadow Ambush]. My blades danced off the armor on his back, barely scratching the hard leather.

"I thought you could actually do damage," Helen grunted as the shaft of the maul crunched down on her shoulder and she battered the dwarf with her shield, her mace hanging limp in her other hand.

She was trying to stay close enough that he couldn't leverage the huge weight of that maul to do any real damage to her. Yet the weight of that maul was enough to ruin her arm.

With an unguarded back to strike, I was quickly accelerating. That speed wouldn't do much good if the attacks weren't landing, though. I activated [Dark Blades], and my blades started to cut through the dwarf's leather armor and drew a trickle of blood.

"Hurry up, why don't you," Helen grunted before the dwarf threw her off and spun around with an ability.

I ducked low, stabbed his ankle and rolled away as the dwarf activated something like [Whirlwind] and spun in place, using the weight of his maul to keep himself spinning.

"Not touching that for you." Helen rolled her shoulder as heals hit her and she winced.

"Well, thanks." I shrugged.

The spinning dwarf made me step over into Taylor's fight and stab a few dwarves to keep my stacks up. The second I stepped away, the soldier dwarf stopped spinning and used all the momentum he had built up to throw himself, maul first in another direction.

He was fast, faster than the student from the other class could react. She was barely able to bring the guard of her sword up to catch part of the blow.

The woman's arm crumpled like a wad of paper before the maul and the dwarf spun, the weapon crushing her leg bad enough for bone to stab out through her skin in two places. She screamed and fell, only for the drone that she'd been fighting to cut her off with a wet crack of his hammer to the side of her head.

"Get her out of here!" I shouted at the students around her.

Helen was there a second too late, fire in her eyes as she battered the dwarf soldier with her shield.

Still, it split the line that the Haylon students had made, and dwarves were pushing hard to get to our back line of healers and ranged damage dealers.

Two other girls pounced, one quite literally, as she jumped and turned into some sort of bipedal bear. She tried to crush the dwarf. Charlotte and a buffed Bun-bun appeared, and the girl was loaded on the giant rabbit's back as they pulled her out of the melee.

The fight was growing chaotic.

I cut down another dwarf before zipping over to the soldier dwarf, my blades dancing along the tough leather armor that covered his body.

I tore ribbons out of his armor to get to his skin and plunged a dagger as deep as it would go.

He spun and tore the dagger from my hands only for Helen to spot the move and swing her mace back. She grabbed her mace with her shield hand and slammed down with her full weight behind it like she was trying to drive a railroad spike.

The dwarf coughed up sticky yellow blood as the dagger's tip punched through the front of its chest, yet incredibly, the dwarf didn't stop fighting.

"You've got to be fucking kidding me. Why won't this thing die?" Helen stepped back and redirected the next attack.

The girl who was currently a bear growled angrily as she reared back and her hands slammed down on top of the dwarf, who was forced to block with the shaft of the maul.

I wanted my dagger back, and shoved my sword in the same hole before activating [Dark Strike]. The ability tore up his insides as my hand tried to perform the maneuver, and his guts were far less durable than his skin.

The dwarf staggered, more goo running down his beard.

Helen's mace smacked his chin hard enough to snap his head to the side, and he crumpled to the ground.

I reached in, finding a hilt and pulled out my dagger covered in what was more like bug guts rather than blood. It was easier to understand why the smoke might have had a different effect on dwarven anatomy than humans. At least elves and Nekorians had red blood.

"Ken, you better put that speed to use and help clear this place up," Helen growled as she smashed another dwarf.

It took me a second to see that we were being overwhelmed. The drones had kept coming from the back room, and the soldier had broken our line so that the rest of the students were being pushed back in different directions.

Even though we'd taken down the soldier, we still needed to reform the line.

"Push down the center. We need to stop that wedge." I shot forward, my blades faster than any of the dwarves could react to and they found throats with ease.

My sword did most of the work, being heavy enough to deal more damage to the tough race. Stacks built up, and I started to mow through the dwarves, purple lightning dancing off my body.

***

Penny blocked a dwarf and spun with her blade low to throw it off balance. She followed up the move with a heavy slash that left a jagged frozen cut on her opponent.

As soon as she finished, she winced as another stupid hammer bashed into her shin and made her wince. *Fighting humanoids is much different, even worse when they are a bunch of ankle biters.*

There was a flash of envy when she saw Fayeth's shield and her shorter stature helping the elf protect her from another low blow. At least Myrtle was facing some of the same issues, but largely because the Earthen Warden had waded too deep into battle.

"Push," Penny demanded of the damage dealers behind her as she stepped forward to fight the next dwarf. There were so many of them. It was worse than walking through a swamp, each step had to be fought over.

Penny could see the battle clearly; thankfully, the short dwarves made that part easy. Yet what she saw was that both her line and Fayeth's were being driven steadily apart by the press of dwarven drones.

Helen was off behind her, with Ken fighting the more powerful dwarf.

For a brief moment, Penny was distracted, the thought of Helen letting Ken take her as thanks for saving her life flashing through her mind. That would make a good chapter down the line.

Penny let her [Frozen Armor] take a hit so that she could get a clean kill and stabbed her large sword into another dwarf that had its back turned to her.

The swing still jarred her, and a rush of healing came soon after because the healers paid attention to the tanks. More than a few of the damage dealers were going down, and Charlotte had supersized her bunny to pull them out and heal or revive them.

Penny kicked a dwarf in the chest and sent him sprawling back so that she could take another solid step forward.

A moment later, Ken appeared. One second she was facing off against a line of dwarves, the next she saw a purple flash with Ken wrapped inside of it.

The next half a dozen dwarves fell over, and Penny didn't need to be told what to do. She took two steps forward, and with the space clear, swung a wide arc.

"Frost Wail," she shouted. Her blade shivered in her hands, letting out a sharp keening noise as she swung it. Blue magic poured off her blade and froze the beards of the dwarves in front of her before her blade came just after and shattered some of their chins.

"Push!" Penny tried to rally Taylor behind her, but the rest of her line was slow to react and didn't move in time for her to close the gap. Penny could only step back to not get surrounded.

When this was over, she was going to write a kickass chapter. Maybe she'd even put on that maid outfit and serve Ken for the afternoon.

Her cheeks dusted bright red at the thought. Ken knew her interest; he had to. Yet he hadn't said anything about it. She had been so bold, to try and seduce Ken with her short skirt, only to chicken out at the last minute. However, Ken came and saved the day. That maid outfit still sat in her CID under a special tab.

Penny fell into a rhythm fighting the dwarves, and her focus was split almost on purpose. It was easier than focusing entirely on the task at hand. Her muscle memory rose to the surface, and her situational awareness heightened as she stopped paying attention to any one thing.

Ken reappeared and cut down more of the dwarves, pausing just long enough to look into her eyes before disappearing.

Penny flushed a little and gritted her teeth in both amusement and disappointment. What would it take for him to use that [Charm] ability on her again?

"Pushing forward!" she shouted behind her and trudged into the dwarves with wide swings, knocking their weapons back and holding the space that Ken had created.

***

"Toots, we got another." Bun-bun was currently eight feet tall at the crown of his head, with another few feet if you counted his ears. The rabbit dropped a student that had fallen to what seemed to be a dozen stabs.

Charlotte put her hands over the girl, calling on her [Revive] to bring her back from death. Charlotte's mana strained and she felt light-headed.

Harley's music was a soothing melody against that pain and forced it back as Charlotte's mana restored. All of the revives were taking a toll, not to mention it would be so much better if they could just get ahead and keep healing people.

There were too many dwarves, and the healers had fallen behind, forced to spend time and mana reviving instead of keeping adventurers on their feet.

Bun-bun shifted as an arrow pierced his hide and the rabbit squeaked in pain. He was such a baby. "Toots, it hurts. Pull it out." He turned to give her access and wiggled in distress.

Charlotte put her hand around where the arrow pierced him and pulled. The giant bunny groaned in pain as she pulled the arrow out and patted the wound with a glowing green hand.

"All better," she promised. The arrow wasn't more than a splinter to him at his current size.

"I'd rather not turn into a pincushion if that's alright." Bun-bun had, however, used his bulk to protect her. "There are archers now."

"Ken will get them." Charlotte had absolute faith in her man.

"I still think you could do better," Bun-bun huffed his disapproval of Ken. "Really, you deserve a man all to yourself. You are such a wonde—" His eyes shifted to look at her and cut himself off mid-sentence as he saw her look.

"You know the answer to that. I love Ken, even if I have to share. Besides, sharing isn't all bad. After seeing how he handled Crimson, his tastes might be varied enough that I could use the help." The thought made her blush. "Now, get back out there and carry that girl who just fell back here."

Charlotte slugged back a mana potion. The flavor of the last one still lingering on her lips, but it was up to her and the other healers to keep everyone alive. The fight wouldn't last much longer.

Ken was a purple streak at that point, leaving spots in her eyes as that purple lightning shot around the battle. It didn't take long for it to zip behind to the archers and for them to all start falling over while spraying goo into the air.

Charlotte took a deep breath and cast another [Revive], healing the latest adventurer Bun-bun brought back.

Chapter 34

Haylon managed to gather together once again, and we pushed through the dwarves until the cafeteria was an absolute mess of dwarven corpses.

No one from Haylon died. Well... not permanently. The Harem Queen even stepped in twice to save her students and then give them a teacherly glare that gave me the shivers knowing that they were going to pay for that.

The dwarf drones were tough and plentiful, but they weren't actually that dangerous. Most of the people who went down had gotten themselves surrounded.

We weren't exactly soldiers, and though we had the strength of adventurers and the discipline of fighters, we had little experience fighting shoulder to shoulder in a line.

I came to a stop, purple lightning around me starting to fade as I stared out several of the broken windows. The same thick smoke was everywhere outside. Each direction was the same; it was like the dwarves had blanketed the whole safe zone.

A clap got my attention.

"Great job, everyone." The Harem Queen strolled through the mass of students.

We weren't done yet, not in my opinion. "Seal off the windows." I told the casters. "Melee, get a little rest. Healers, work your way through the group. Let's make sure everyone is okay before we help the upperclassmen."

The older students were thrown in a pile and barely stirring, but there wasn't much blood. It seemed that the dwarves had used the smoke to disable most of them. They could wait until we had everyone fully healed. It was best to be prepared for any further attacks before helping them.

I glanced over at the Harem Queen. "We should leave anyone behind who doesn't feel they can make it, and push out into the rest of the safe zone."

She glanced at the smoke and walked out with her sword. The sword swung back high before she stepped with the swing and blew smoke away for twenty feet with just the wind pressure from the swing.

Even that seemed to disappoint her.

"Why didn't you do that back in the classroom?" I frowned.

"Because then I wouldn't have had a handsome man like you leading me around." She batted her lashes, but at my frown gave me the real answer. "And because the smoke didn't have anywhere to go; it isn't like I could push it directly out the window very easily."

Ah.

The smoke started to reclaim some of the lost ground, but outside the building, it would be easier to clear it with the mages in our group too.

"You and my daughter fought well together." She raised a red eyebrow.

"Let's get the other classes on their feet. Maybe we can use some of the casters to generate enough wind to make some headway," I said, ignoring her comment and heading back inside.

Truthfully, I did fight well with Helen against the soldier dwarf, but that wasn't really a conversation I was going to get into with her mother. I knew she was just going to try and push the two of us together.

And we were still in the middle of battle. I needed to keep my mind on the task at hand to keep others from suffering as a result. They were looking to me to lead.

"Felicity, Candice, I need you both to help clear the smoke away from the building. Tanks, let's get some protection for them while the healers work on the upperclassmen."

There was no time to waste.

***

Crimson jumped out of a cloud of heavy smoke with her eyes glowing blue. "Director, that building is also cleared out."

She wasted no time as she landed in front of the woman on top of a UG building. The roof was being used to organize the troops. The normally playful Crimson was gone. Instead, she looked like a woman on a mission, which she was at that moment.

The dwarves had made the fight as difficult as possible. The smoke was heavy and took far too much effort to move out of an area. Yet those short bastards moved through it without a problem, and their ambush had crippled the UG.

From the top of the three-story building, the human adventurers made themselves targets, but it wasn't like the director was helpless.

"They were far too prepared. How are your students?" The director was swiping on her tablet, her eyes gleaming and text reflecting in her glasses.

"Ken's leading. I only checked on them twice. But they were doing fine. The Harem Queen can keep them alive if the worst comes. The soldiers so far haven't been too difficult." Crimson shrugged with a goofy grin now that the subject had shifted back to Ken.

A dwarf jumped out of the smoke to attack them.

Crimson didn't move.

It was the director who glanced up, and in that single glance, she seemed to understand everything about the dwarf before she threw a single needle made of mana that pierced right through the dwarf's beard and out its back.

The dwarf fell back down lifelessly.

Crimson raised an eyebrow at the one-hit kill and stayed quiet. The director was an interesting woman that was born for administration and paperwork. She was also capable of pushing more than paper.

She was also the reason that Crimson wasn't just trying to blindly kill her way through the smoke.

"There's a weak point behind the beard." The director pushed at her glasses and went back to the tablet. "I've been assessing the situation, and I believe I now understand their direction of attack and their objective." She turned her tablet around for Crimson to see the results.

On the screen was a map of the safe zone with far too many details for Crimson to take in at a single time. It was like when you zoomed too far out on a map that still had all the zoomed in details competing for space.

Crimson sighed at the headache forming as she even tried to make sense of it. "Just give me the CliffsNotes."

"They most likely have sent their primary force into the twenty-fifth floor behind us while leaving enough to combat and stall us here. I believe that they are aiming to take this branch of the dungeon."

Crimson blinked. "Fucking idiots."

She glanced in the direction the director had indicated. She knew the next thing that the director was going to ask was for her to stop their expansion, but she didn't want to be that far away from Ken.

Call her clingy, but she had just managed to break through that last barrier between them. And she was not about to lose him now; he'd just gained an ability that would bring him to the level he needed to be able to dive all the way to the bottom of the dungeon with her.

What they had was worth protecting.

"I've contacted the UG and informed them of my assessment." She stabbed her tablet with a finality. "What I need is for you to make sure that this doesn't get any worse. Go up to the twenty-fifth floor and plug the leak; we'll deal with the safe zone."

Crimson's eyes sparked red that wasn't too far from Ken. "I can do that. Do I go all the way and kill the queen behind this?"

"The UG would prefer that we don't. We aren't sure of the dwarves' strength now more than ever, and would like to understand more before antagonizing them."

"Right." Crimson shot off towards the human entrance to the safe zone and crossed the small distance in a flash before somersaulting to get the right orientation and kicking out with her heel.

She activated [Pierce] and crashed down like a meteor, knocking all of the smoke away and revealing a steady stream of dwarves that disappeared into splatter as she spun her whip over her head. She began to force her way up the stairs against the steady flow of dwarves.

***

I glanced back, noting that the healers were wrapping up rousing the upperclassmen. We had fortified the building and the casters were clearing the smoke outside the building. Felicity and two students from Class B were throwing around wind magic and peeling the smoke back.

I stood in the doorway, listening beyond the howling gales produced by the mages. There was a slow steady marching beat echoing through the dungeon. I actually felt the beat more than I heard it. It sounded like thousands of boots pounding the ground in unison.

I had heard the sound of giant monsters; this wasn't that. The feeling was slightly prolonged, like whatever was pounding was slightly out of step.

"What are the dwarves doing?" I glanced over my shoulder to Felin who had been attracted by the sound as well. I had a feeling she would have some intuition about their aim.

"They are pests that invade. Like ants, they always find a way into your territory and try to gobble up resources... but I think this is a little more than that." Her ears flattened. "I think the displacement with the drones the other week was a queen throwing away her old drones to prepare for an invasion."

I raised an eyebrow, noticing that the Harem Queen also perked up as she came to join the conversation.

"Then I should just kill this queen," the Harem Queen insisted.

Felin shrugged. "It would have to be a weak queen for you to take it on your own."

The Harem Queen scoffed, "You underestimate me."

"I do not. I am well in tune with the strength and potential of those in the dungeon." Felin glanced sharply at the powerful adventurer. "If Crimson weren't here, I'd probably suggest that we run, but I think she can probably kill the queen if she shows up. Again, I'm making guesses. This attack seems to be far more aggressive than trying to take resources."

"Would your people fight them? If they set up in this part of the dungeon, won't that just mean you are all next?" I asked.

Felin shook her head. "We have rules. The shamans are the leaders, but we are so fragmented that there are certain rules we all agree to adhere to. The dwarves don't attack us, and in return, my people won't fight."

"Sounds like a great way to get ambushed," I said.

She shrugged. "It also stops a lot of fighting if we all stick to the agreement. When someone does attack, then the claws are out and we crush them with overwhelming force. It works pretty well to keep everyone civil." She bared her teeth.

I nodded. "So, it's a rule born of consistency and also your biggest threat." It was certainly a different way to be diplomatic, and honestly far simpler.

"That doesn't help us right now," the Harem Queen said, staring out into the clouds of billowing smoke. "We have incoming."

I blinked and activated [Eyes of Wisdom], looking for hostiles. The outline of red stocky figures moving through the smoke lit up. And they were moving in our direction.

"Shit," I cursed under my breath before shouting over my shoulder. "Incoming. All tanks up front!"

With four classes now up and ready, a hundred Haylon students scrambled to get into formation for another fight.

I played with my weapons, eager to take the fight to the dwarves. But I needed them to move out of the smoke. Luckily, it was slowly thinning. The dungeon ate dust, and as the smoke slowly settled, I would imagine it would be no different and disappear with everything else.

A moment later, the first dwarf stepped out of the smoke, a small buckler on his arm with a short sword in the other hand. More poured out of the smoke. All of the dwarves had the exact same equipment and marched in unison.

I noted that these dwarves felt different than the ones we'd fought inside the building. Even if they were drones, they were made for war.

Our tanks did their best and formed a tight arched line at the front of the building.

"Hold the line." Helen smacked her mace on her shield. "Ranged DPS let loose."

There was a pause of those behind the tank. They'd expected the command from me, so I quickly nodded agreement. A moment later, arrows, along with spells, started flying over the line of tanks.

My biggest problem was that there weren't easy gaps for melee damage givers like me to use to get access to the attackers.

"Melee, get behind the tanks. Tanks, sub out if you get tired," I gave an order for what I thought was best, but I was an assassin not a general.

The dwarves rushed in after my words and drowned out any more comments as shields and steel clashed together.

"Like tanks get tired," an upperclassman scoffed. "There's no such thing."

"That's an ill omen," another said. "We'll take the help when we need it, but it might be a while."

I wrinkled my nose. She was right. I'd seen Fayeth hold out for a long time.

Instead of worrying, I flicked open my CID and pulled out a crappy spear that wasn't much more than vendor fodder, and stepped up behind Fayeth, my spear jabbing over her shoulder and stabbing a dwarf.

Purple lightning crackled along the weapon and raced up to my arms.

I smirked.

"Stay over my left shoulder. It gives me good coverage with my glaive on the right," Fayeth called out to me.

I adjusted and stabbed again. The hits weren't doing much damage, but it kept the dwarves off Fayeth a little better while the real damage came from the back line.

Fireballs, lightning bolts and small blizzards were raining down on the dwarves. And each stab added another stack for me, even if it was slower than using my blades. I smiled, glad for a way to prepare for the eventual soldier dwarf by building up stacks.

As if my thoughts summoned them, several dwarves with more intelligence in their eyes stepped out of the receding smoke. These dwarves held ranged weapons and tilted their crossbows up. As one, they began firing over the tanks towards our back line.

Several of the arching bolts were bulky, and my attention snapped to them. I knew what they held, and we needed to get rid of them.

"Get rid of those!" I jumped, lashing out with my spear and knocking two off course, but there were still another two heading towards the healers.

Bun-bun caught one while Reagan caught the other.

"What ar—"

"Throw it in your CID," I shouted, grabbing the two and stuffing them in my CID, unsure if they would go off without an impact.

Reagan acted fast, but Bun-bun didn't have a CID to use. The bolt he caught exploded into a thick cloud on him.

"Gale Force!" a student shouted, and the cloud pushed right over our melee and tanks.

There was a wet squish a moment later.

Two dwarves were amid our tanks and had run two second years through in our moment of blindness. Weapons were going straight through the two adventurer's skulls.

I lashed out with my spear in a flurry of blows to try and drive them back to reform our line. Several others joined me, jabbing their weapons at the two soldier dwarves.

Both of the dwarves barreled forward with enough durability that they were able to ignore some of the hits.

As we continued to focus our efforts, the drones began expanding the gap behind the soldiers, pushing through our line. One of the soldier dwarves was decked from head to toe in black armor with a shield even bigger than he was, and he seemed to be able to take quite a bit of damage without having any visible impact.

I sighed. The last thing I needed was a heavily armored opponent.

My spear glanced off his glossy armor, but at least the hit built up more stacks. I jabbed as fast as I could while a student from Class 2-B joined me, using her halberd to smack the leading dwarf and stall his advance.

Penny shouldered her way in front of an upperclassman and met the armored dwarf. "Dolly! On me."

I smirked.

They were going to try something tricky for the heavily armored opponent.

Penny pushed too far forward and caught a number of stabs from the dwarves while her long sword came crashing down on the armored dwarf again and again, frost growing on the armor and making it brittle.

I shifted my target and tried to clear space for her while continuing to build stacks of my [Liminal Speed].

Penny's wounds vanished and goo splashed out between the joints of the armored dwarves.

"Don't fuck with me," Penny growled as she kept hammering away at him to the point her weapon chipped. She didn't even seem to notice as she used her sword more like a hammer striking an anvil.

The dwarf stabbed her several times, only for the wounds to vanish in a flash of light.

"Brutal." An upperclassman noticed what was happening. "Turning a tank and a healer into two damage dealers."

Dolly was an unconventional healer. Rather than heal the tank, she transferred wounds from one target to another. Penny's recklessness was backed by her high stamina so that she could hold out until Dolly removed the wound and applied it to her opponent.

It wasn't something I could do with my stats. My health was far too low to risk taking that much damage just to deal more to my opponent.

My spear landed with a lucky squish in the throat of a dwarf, and I struggled to pull my spear out. The tank in front of me shouldered the dwarf for me, and I was able to pull the spear free and keep on helping.

"What's the lightning?" the upperclassman asked.

"Speed buff," I grunted, thrusting forward now twice as fast as I normally could.

"Nice buff," another melee commented.

"Oh, you've seen nothing yet." Taylor barked a laugh. "He trains with Crimson at full speed."

Her comment got all the upperclassmen around me to turn in surprise.

"Focus forward," I demanded, instantly upset at the commentary during the fight.

I pushed myself and thrust the spear into several dwarves in time to see the armored dwarf collapse before a Penny with ragged, torn clothing. She turned to see me and blushed. With a forced expression, she gave me a thumbs up.

I sighed. "Head in the game, Penny, unless you want to talk about your writing."

She went from a slight blush to being as red as a tomato. "Don't talk about silly things while we are fighting for our lives."

"I want to know about this," a Class B tank said.

"Later," I barked and pushed my way between two tanks. My spear was now flying so quickly that I was able to create a gap in the dwarves even though the spear wasn't my weapon of choice.

Once I broke through, I threw the spear into the mass of dwarves and drew my sword and dagger, blocking a dwarf. Before it even realized what was happening, my dagger pierced his beard and the soft flesh behind it.

Another dwarf died by my blade soon after, then another as I cut a swath through the army of dwarves. Purple lightning raced up my arm with each strike, and soon the clouds of smoke around me lit up purple with how bright I had become.

"Push out!" Fayeth shouted, practically reading my mind. "My Adrel will slay them! Casters, get up here and disperse the rest of the clouds. They look thin."

I smirked and continued to move through the area, mowing down dwarf after dwarf. As soon as a dwarf was dropping, the one behind him was just realizing he was dead as well.

CHAPTER 35

I soon found myself alone among the dwarves, my blades making short work on any that stood between me and my goals. Dwarves pressed in around me, but that only made what I needed to do that much easier.

I spun, knocking swords aside, and my dagger punched out, grievously wounding the dwarven drones one after another. They had always been fodder, but now they had entered the grinder as I tore through their ranks.

The several soldier dwarves that had appeared to fire bolts past our tanks had disappeared once again into the smoke, but I wasn't discouraged.

The smoke was thinning. At first, I thought it was just me being hopeful, but now it was clear that the smoke was in fact settling. Above my head, the air was clear enough to see for a hundred feet, and soon that would settle down further.

I activated [Eyes of Wisdom], searching for those still interested in attacking me. Several red outlines appeared inside the smoke, and I dodged as a bolt whistled past me.

Soon, I'd have access to them.

In the meantime, I turned myself into a dam, halting the flow of dwarves against our tank line. Each time I struck, I was getting faster.

It got easier as time went on. My speed more than made up for the countless number of dwarves coming. One versus three could be hard, but it was so much easier at triple the speed. At five times the speed, one versus three became trivial. I was able to step in and out of range with ease, and they had trouble countering any of my moves.

The three enemy weapons became far less dangerous when I was this fast.

I pushed forward, favoring my sword for its reach as I pushed the dwarves back to the heavy smoke. Wind picked up behind me, and several casters from Haylon were pushing the thinning clouds back.

This time, the clouds moved far easier and exposed more and more ranks of dwarves. It felt like an endless horde, but I only grinned as I got to work. I hoped that, when all was said and done, the UG would give me a nice reward. Or maybe the dwarven weapons would sell well.

The ground was soon littered with dwarven corpses and more were piling on as we cleared the smoke back, continuing to reveal more masses of dwarves ready to attack.

I zipped back to Felin. "How many of these are there?" I attacked the nearest dwarf to keep up my stacks and returned to her.

"More than you can imagine. They are described as 'endless' to my people. Queens can produce dwarven drones continually." Felin made a face.

I kept my stacks up by finding another dwarf and returning. "That's like a cheat ability."

Felin glanced at me with a blank face.

"Point taken."

"This is why it is extremely difficult to push into a dwarven-occupied area. It is like fighting your way upstream," Felin scowled as she twirled her staff and threw lightning at a nearby dwarf. Thankfully, she had joined the Haylon students in fighting the dwarves saying that she could defend her pride.

I knew if I waited too long to continue attacking, I'd lose my stacks, so I ended the conversation there.

I moved around the edges of the area we had exposed and cut down as many drones as I could. Meanwhile, several heavily armored soldier dwarves exposed themselves and drew the attention and fire of the Haylon students.

Out of the corner of my eye, I spotted a number of drones sprinting out of the smoke. I looked away only to look back. My intuition had felt like something was off.

It took me a second to figure out what had caught my attention. This group of dwarves didn't have weapons, only shields. With our push out, the back line was exposed, and these dwarves were rushing towards them.

"Des, to your left!" I shouted and crossed the battlefield, cutting down several more drones on my way to stop the weaponless dwarves.

There was a flicker of confusion before recognition flashed in Des' eyes, and she pulled a mage next to her to redirect their attack. Wind buffeted the charging dwarves enough to slow them down.

I was among them a moment later, my sword piercing two of them before they even knew what had hit them. That was enough, though. The hits triggered something and the dwarves exploded.

Fire washed over me, and the force hit me like an enraged boss, tossing me up into the air.

Charlotte's green healing light washed over me as I landed hard enough to drive the wind from my lungs. Selene was next to me a moment later, grabbing my hand and picking me up.

"Get up, we got you. You don't want to lose those stacks, do you?" she teased, and with Candice's help, I found myself on my feet, my purple lightning already starting to wane.

Realizing they were right, I rushed forward to the nearest dwarf, hacking into its side and feeling the speed stabilize, even if I'd lost a good chunk of my stacks.

It wasn't until I started to climb in my speed again that I let myself deal with what had just happened.

Those dwarves had been suicide bombers.

I shuddered in realization that if the queen could mass produce those drones, then the equipment on them was probably more valuable than their lives. If they had the equipment, it would be easy for them to send wave after wave of bomb-strapped dwarves to soften us up.

Felin had said that the dwarves were difficult, but I was really only starting to get a clear picture of just how dangerous the dwarves could be.

"Is the queen here?" I asked as I activated [Eyes of Wisdom].

Far off in the distance, probably through several buildings, a red outline appeared.

"Fuck," I cursed as I buried my dagger in a drone's face. "This isn't going to be over quite so simply." My eyes shifted over to the Harem Queen, and I stepped away from the dwarves for a moment to get her attention.

She was standing in the middle of battle, her sword balanced on the ground while her hands rested lightly on top of it. Her eyes tracked me as I approached and then flicked back out to watch her students.

"Yes?" She didn't have the time to be flirty.

"The Dwarf Queen is out there." I pointed in a direction.

She glanced at my eyes, her head tilting for a moment before she pieced it together. "Same ability as Crimson?"

"Yep." I would reveal that if it made her more confident.

She lifted her sword, the tip sliding out of the ground before she slung it over her shoulder. "You are in charge of the students. None of them are to die while you are here, understood?"

"Completely. The queen is in that direction, maybe five hundred yards." I pointed where I'd seen the red dot.

The Harem Queen sank slightly before launching herself up into the air in the direction that I'd pointed. She was putting a lot of faith in me, both trusting me about the Dwarf Queen and also protecting the other Haylon students.

But at the moment, I had enough stacks that I could move through the battlefield with ease. I slashed through another dwarf to keep the stacks before using my ability again.

"Eyes of Wisdom, tell me which students are in the most danger." Several of my allies' outline lit up, and I went back into the fight.

***

Wind whipped at the Harem Queen's hair and pulled at her dress as Heather, The Harem Queen, flew through the air above the smoke that stopped not only the Haylon students but many of the adventurers from putting up a counter offensive.

The smoke was truly an abhorrent weapon.

She gauged the distance from what Ken had described and drew on her lovers' [Bonds of Love]. Pink veins of magic shot towards her and gathered in her chest as her stats exploded.

For every man that loved her, she was gaining a small percentage of his highest stat. It wasn't comparable to Crimson's ability, but she gained around thirty percent more in most of her stats.

It would have to be enough.

That damned Nekorian had underestimated her abilities when she'd indicated that the Harem Queen wouldn't be enough to take on a Dwarf Queen. She might not be Crimson's match, but since the humiliation last summer, she hadn't been slouching either.

Her sword blazed as she activated another ability and launched herself down at the spot she'd chosen. She landed like a blue meteor. This time, she didn't have to hold back to keep anybody else safe. As she landed, the explosive force blew the cloud away enough to clear a space.

The area also filled with blue fire, burning away dozens of weak dwarves before several stepped forward. They curbed her fire before it could reach the mound of humans behind them and the woman who stood even taller than the mound.

Heather blinked as she took in what must be the Dwarf Queen. She was huge.

The queen stood at least nine feet tall with muscular arms and legs. She wasn't dressed to impress; instead, she had hard, dark armor that was practically glued to her body.

What caught Heather's attention most were the egregious beach ball-sized breasts on the front of her. Really, that was just ridiculous. Was she feeding an army with those things?!

The Dwarf Queen tilted her head slightly at Heather. "You will make a good resource."

That comment caused Heather to frown.

She glanced at the bodies in horror as the Dwarf Queen reached out and grabbed one of the unconscious humans. The other queen's magic wrapped around the man, warping his body in seconds, and she set down a dwarven drone with blank eyes that ran off to battle.

The horror in Heather's face must have shown because the queen smirked.

"The ones made from flesh aren't as strong as I would like, but you work with what you are given." The Queen stared at her, challenge in her eyes.

Heather brought her sword up to fight, feeling a renewed sense of purpose. She would not let some heartless monster use her as a 'resource'. Crimson had knocked her down a peg, but she wasn't going to fall any lower than that. "There's only room for one queen here."

She shot forward, her sword a brilliant, blue flame as she attacked those stronger dwarves in front of the queen.

The Dwarf Queen didn't even flinch, but she didn't need to. One of the soldier dwarves blocked Heather's attack and stepped back two steps before he stabilized himself.

Heather cursed as she dodged a spear with a twirl and hacked down hard enough to bite into the shoulder of another soldier dwarf before her heeled foot came up and kicked off the first's leg to gain some distance. The five powerful soldier dwarves surrounding their queen were trying to encircle her.

"Bring her to me," the Dwarf Queen ordered without looking up. She was now working on the next body in front of her, picking up the person's CID and frowning at it as she held it up to her face.

Heather didn't have time to worry about the Dwarf Queen making more drones. The five soldier dwarves in front of her were going to give her some much-needed practice.

Among the five, they were differentiated by weapon. With a start, she realized they resembled a dungeon party: shield, spear, bow, maul, and staff. The last was the most interesting to her because she hadn't seen any dwarf besides the queen use spells yet.

Arrows whistled through the air at her, and she could immediately see the maul-wielding dwarf move to the opposite side to catch her.

Rather than take the easy dodge to the side, Heather ducked the arrow, going low enough that she had to drag her sword on the ground before coming up and narrowly dodging a spear thrust at her heart.

She used the shift and turned it into a full spinning swing. [Tempest Blow]. Her sword slammed against the shield and wind rushed around the blade, feeding the flames and expanding them around the shield dwarf.

The dwarf stumbled back from the impact. The explosion allowed Heather to slip past to her real target.

The archer had another arrow nocked and pointed at her face. She stared him down right until he released at almost point-blank range. [Dodge]. She shifted a foot to the side and went for the staff-wielding dwarf.

This dwarf was different. There was no beard on its chin; instead, it had pudgy cheeks and a rounder face. Heather thought for a second that it was young, but then she realized it was a female dwarf.

Not that it mattered to her.

[Cross Slash]. She swung her sword as the ability accelerated her, and she flashed past the dwarf, leaving the after image of two slashes in a perfect plus sign with a slight tilt.

Fluid splashed out, and the flames flared hard on the dwarf, but Heather wasn't done. If that was all it took to kill them, these soldiers wouldn't be enough to protect their queen.

Heather spun around, her hair flaring out behind her as she activated her class's namesake and one of her most powerful abilities, [Mythic Flames]. She stabbed the back of the healer dwarf as blue fire encompassed both of them in a raging inferno of heat hot enough to melt steel in seconds.

As a Knight of the Mythic Flame, the flames didn't harm her in the slightest. Instead, the blue fire healed her as it danced along her hair. It restored her energy along with it, and she put it to good use, hacking down on the dwarf several times even as an arrow managed to punch through her flames and bury itself in her side.

Her flames parted as the maul-swinging dwarf caught up to her blitz, and his giant, black hammer crashed down upon her. Heather angled her blade for it to glance off and add to the momentum of her dodge before jumping back and letting the force of the blow carry her away.

She'd used multiple abilities in a short timeframe, and important ones like [Dodge] were still on cooldown. But when fighting multiple enemies at once, she knew better than to hold anything back. She needed every possible advantage.

Thrusting everything you had forward in a play for the healer was basic one on five tactics. Now it was time to see how the strategy had worked out for her.

The tank was covering the healer, while the spear- and maul-wielding dwarves were forcing her away. The healer had fallen to their knees and their head was still back. A massive gash on her face and terrible burns showed that the attack might have worked.

However, what happened next was outside Heather's expectation.

The Dwarf Queen lifted her hand and muttered something.

The healer jerked up right like a marionette being pulled by her strings and her flesh shifted to cover the burns. Next, the wounds pulled closed on their own.

"That was an impressive display," the Dwarf Queen spoke slowly, like she barely had a grasp of English.

Heather had forgotten that, despite the queen's indifference to the battle, it didn't mean that she couldn't interfere. It was one on six, not one on five.

Two healers changed the game considerably.

"Here I thought you weren't going to fight," Heather scoffed.

The queen tilted her head. "But we were fighting. You were fighting my soldiers; they are an extension of me. I have forged each one of them, spending great care on the soldiers. They are not as disposable as the drones, and I will not allow you to simply destroy these ones as you wish. Rare materials went into them."

Heather looked at the pile of bodies, rare materials indeed.

Was that why the dwarves were attacking? What did they make all of these other ones out of? She frowned, imagining the horrors that were the dwarves. This queen seemed to craft out of flesh.

"Will protect Queen to the end," the maul-wielding dwarf spat with broken English.

Heather thought about her next move, dropping her sword slightly. "Where I come from, I'm a queen too. Do your people not have a way to resolve differences? You've stepped on my territory, and I refuse to allow it."

The Dwarf Queen was quiet for a long moment before she waved her hand and the soldiers backed up. "I find myself interested in you and will claim the resources of your body myself."

The large woman tapped something, and the contents of a CID spilled out onto the ground. Her eyes went wide with greed seeing all of the mana crystals and gear. "Ah. There are even more resources hidden inside. Yours must be even better to compensate for your strength."

Heather huffed. "It is so much better. That was a weak human. Mine has resources all the way down to the fifty-fifth floor."

"Interesting." The Dwarf Queen moved faster than Heather expected, exploding forward with a palm strike that pushed her sword aside and landed directly into her gut.

Heather jerked back, blood spraying out of her mouth.

Unceremoniously, she tumbled backwards over the ground until she was able to stab her sword into the dirt and clutch it with all of her strength to stop herself from rolling further.

The Dwarf Queen strolled slowly towards her. "Interesting. You are sturdier than the softer humans. Do human queens also toughen their exteriors?"

Heather blinked and realized that the Dwarf Queen wasn't wearing armor. The dark area was more akin to chitin rather than skin to protect her.

"Something like that." Heather wiped the blood from her mouth and raised her sword. "We also draw strength from those who care."

She loathed to overuse the ability, but she activated [Bonds of Love] again. This time, it would draw dangerously from her harem and weaken them for a time, but she needed every ounce of strength that she could get to fight the monster in front of her.

Her CID chirped, and she opened the call without looking.

Director Amato's voice came over. "Would you like me to recall Crimson?"

"I will find you and shove my sword down your throat if you bring her to solve my battles," Heather spat.

There wasn't exactly a grudge between them, but every time someone mistook Crimson as The Harem Queen, it pissed Heather off. She was clearly the better looking of the two. A woman who came in second when it came to strength had to at least win on other battlefields, after all.

"Understood." The Director cut the call, and Heather focused forward. She had a fight to finish.

CHAPTER 36

M y [Eyes of Wisdom] was unbelievably helpful as I moved through the ranks of the dwarves. As I used it more and more, I got better at using the information it provided while killing. I was spared having to assess each fight.

The ability identified who was in the most danger, getting me to them faster to support them and move on to the next person.

Even the soldier dwarves were much less of an issue now as I wove between the dwarves. I was learning where they had gaps in their armor, piercing into them with swift strikes from my dagger.

The weapon had chipped, though, from all of the impacts, but for now, it was good enough. Soon I'd replace it with something new.

I spun around a tank and found Taylor struggling with two dwarves. One of her legs was weak from where she'd been stabbed, and no healer was nearby to help her.

My daggers made short work as I supported her. As soon as those dwarves were killed, I looked up to see the next person I could help.

There were no glowing targets among my allies, and to make things even better, the smoke had finally thinned to the point that we could see more clearly. Finally, after what felt like forever, the dwarves were almost out of reinforcements.

I let out a breath of relief, only to realize one glowing bright spot remained. Off in the distance, my [Eyes of Wisdom] had the Harem Queen glowing like a spotlight in the dark.

I moved through the dwarves, cutting down the now petering marching line. I realized part of the slowdown in dwarves might have been from the Harem Queen engaging the Dwarf Queen. The Dwarf Queen couldn't make new drones to attack us, however she did that.

"Des, you're in charge while I'm out." I surprised my lover with how quickly I appeared behind her.

She twirled, knife in hand, only to stop short and flash me a smile. "Ken, pleasure to see you."

"Going to help the Harem Queen." I didn't wait for a reply, zipping along through the trail of dwarves back to the explosive battle going on in the distance.

The number of dwarves that I could move between to get there was thin, but I managed to keep up my stacks as I approached the battle.

I arrived, taking in my new opponent quickly.

The Dwarf Queen was huge, about half again as tall as me. She had dark armor that reminded me more of the exoskeleton of a beetle rather than armor; it hugged her body so tightly that it barely even moved as she fought the Harem Queen.

Another explosive exchange blew me back a step. The Harem Queen oozed blue fire that had burned the surroundings. Her large sword clashed with the queen's armored fist.

The heat stopped me from getting closer, and I was sensitive to any pause in fighting. I needed a target to keep up my stacks if I had any chance of being helpful in the current fight.

I'd have to find a more opportune time to intervene.

Five powerful soldier dwarves stood nearby, watching the battle. If that was odd, the two combatants didn't seem to mind the audience.

I appeared behind the one with a staff, wondering if it was a female. My sword cut into her throat before she even noticed. The cut wasn't deep, so I slashed twice more until the goo started to flow from the wound.

The delay gave enough time for the dwarf to react and swat me away with her staff. The air pressure from the swing pushed me back as several arrows tried to pepper me. The other soldier dwarves standing around the fight moved to engage me.

I dodged the three melee dwarves, noting that if I had barely cut what appeared to be the caster, there was no reason for me to fight those with stronger defenses.

My chipped dagger was worse for wear, and a thin crack had started next to where the blade was missing its chunk. So I favored my sword and slashed the archer's wrists before avoiding an ability from the spear-wielding dwarf.

"Ken!" the Harem Queen shouted after another explosive exchange with the Dwarf Queen. Her red hair was flowing behind her, lifted by the fire that outlined her body. Her dress was split up the side and ragged at the bottom, and there was dried blood on her chin. "Watch out and kill the healer."

She charged after the other queen, who at least from what I could see, appeared no worse for wear. As they fought, and the dark chitin armor cracked and repaired itself, the larger woman created gaps in the fighting for her armor to heal.

But I left her to the battle, knowing that I needed to keep focus on the more powerful soldiers, who were now chasing me like hounds with a scent.

Thankfully, I was fast.

But I had noticed through the battle that the level disparity made it difficult to do appreciable damage to these dwarves. With each failed attack, doing something about penetrating higher level armor was quickly rising on my list of things to do until it couldn't wait.

"Throw me a weapon; mine is about to break," I shouted at the Harem Queen. She tapped at her wrist and threw out a short, flat gladius in my direction.

I grabbed the weapon, a tingling sensation in my hand as I felt my arm swell with power and my reaction times increased. I cursed, realizing she'd given me a weapon that was far too high of a level. The time I could hold it was limited, but I couldn't distract her again. I needed to make the most of the situation.

I was fast enough that I had the stacks to spare, but not the time. Closing in on the healer again, I activated [Liminal Space]. The world shattered around me, and the healer dwarf was frozen like she was trapped in amber.

The borrowed blade had started to feel like I was holding something fresh out of the oven, yet I clenched harder as the tingling raced up my arm. The pain and potential damage was worth settling the current fight.

Sadly, the frozen world didn't seem to stop the blade from harming me.

I pressed the weapon against the dwarf's throat. It sliced cleanly into her neck, and I cut the dwarf's throat all the way to the bone. Jumping back, I threw the weapon away from me and exited the ability, seeing my stacks had dropped severely.

It would be close, but I was fairly sure I still had enough to dodge and weave through the remaining dwarves.

"Ken!"

For a moment, I thought she was shocked at my success, only to feel an immense pressure behind me. I used [Sprint] as well as [Dodge] to get away as soon as possible.

My instincts served me well.

The Dwarf Queen crashed down where I'd just been. The explosion from her ability sent me stumbling, and the air pressure was so thick that several grains of dirt cut my cheeks.

"Great work!" The Harem Queen doggedly pursued the Dwarf Queen, smashing into her with her large sword and stopping her from whatever she'd been about to do to the healer.

It was then that I put together that the queen could heal too. The Harem Queen had been stuck between two healers. It was no wonder she'd been getting worn down.

The Harem Queen's attacks cracked the dark chitin once again as she pressed the Dwarf Queen away from the healer's body.

***

Heather was sweating with exertion. The fight with the Dwarf Queen wasn't as easy as it might appear from the outside. She was fighting someone who was both a tank and a healer.

If the Dwarf Queen had a weakness, it was that she wasn't personally very good at dishing out damage.

Ken's entrance had helped finally sway the fight more towards her side. And his appearance also gave her a new boost of energy. She couldn't let Crimson's protégé show her up. Not to mention he was half her level!

For him to take on five dwarves that were twenty or so levels above him, nearly twice his level, was beyond impressive.

She couldn't have done it. Neither could any of the other high-level adventurers, save for perhaps Crimson had they been in his place. If his potential really was the second coming of someone at Crimson's level, then she would have to try harder.

She did not want to be eclipsed by the next generation, and it was a chance to secure somebody who could help protect her daughter in the dungeon.

Ken threw her sword down; his hand and arm were bright red like it was burnt. She winced as her sword clashed with the Dwarf Queen. Holding higher level gear wasn't pretty, and it would take him some time to recover.

Heather focused on the Dwarf Queen, seeing her opportunity. [Armor Break] activated and a drill-like form of mana wrapped around the tip of Heather's sword as she shot forward, closing the small distance between them.

Her sword punched into her opponent's armor, punching slightly through the center and surrounding it in a spiderweb of cracks.

She smiled, seeing her next steps clearly. She pressed hard with a dozen attacks, but the queen dodged back, giving ground rather than letting her armor crumble further. All the while, the chitinous black armor continued to heal itself.

Slugging back two potions, Heather kept herself going.

This battle was drawing out longer than she'd like, the Dwarf Queen was an opponent that could certainly wear her out. Heather was starting to consider that her opponent wasn't focused on fighting as much as surviving and producing an army. It was only thanks to the concept of a challenge between queens that she was even humoring a duel.

Heather was a bruiser herself, yet fighting an abnormally tanky opponent was frustrating her to no end.

It wasn't like she could... her eyes tracked to Ken, who was moving abnormally fast and had even moved to the point that Heather couldn't track him when he finished the dwarf soldier.

He could possibly slip in and follow up on her armor break.

Right now, the queen was fast enough that she escaped just when Heather could push her advantage for some serious damage. Heather needed someone to coordinate with her just long enough to hold the Dwarf Queen still.

Otherwise, Heather wasn't going to last much longer. Not to mention technically, the queen could send her elite soldiers to surround her and finish this in a minute.

Hopefully, the Dwarf Queen's hubris would hold out, and if this worked, before she could realize her mistake. She certainly looked smug as she danced away from Heather once again.

"Ken, can you pick the weapon back up?" Heather gritted her teeth and asked for help from the lower level adventurer. But she was starting to see him for what he truly would become. Ken was going to eclipse them all and give Crimson a challenge one of these days.

***

"Can you pick the weapon back up?"

The Harem Queen's voice broke through my thoughts as I carefully dodged and got scant swipes in with my blades. I wasn't trying to deal damage at that point. My main focus was keeping my stacks up and staying alive against the four dwarven soldiers.

I glanced over at the gladius and shuddered at the thought of putting my hand through more pain. Right now, the appendage had gone numb, which was certainly a poor sign for what was going to come after the fight.

The weapon was too magical for my body to handle. I had mana burns on my hand where too much flowed from the weapon into me.

Healing didn't fix the issue. It only solved some of the surface symptoms while making the actual burn worse by injecting more mana into it. The only thing that could really fix using a weapon of higher level was time.

But the Harem Queen would have known all of that, and she still asked me the question. Based on the looks of the fight, she was being held off to the point that she needed help to break through.

I gritted my teeth. I knew I was going to do as she asked, because it gave us the best shot of winning.

If we could end the fight, then I would take the mana burn and deal with the consequences later. Every second we wasted was likely costing more lives with the dwarves rampaging through the safe zone and into the floor above.

My eyes flickered back to the Harem Queen, watching for an opportunity, trying to understand their fight. I used all my grandparents' training to find the opportunity, watching while still fighting the soldiers around me. I let myself be patient, waiting for the right moment.

After a few attacks, I understood her strategy. The Harem Queen was cracking the armor, but it was healing too quickly for her to follow up the hit.

I struck the dwarf in front of me twice, timing my attacks with the cadence of the Harem Queen's blows.

Then, I took my shot.

The Dwarf Queen was backing up, avoiding the Harem Queen once again. I shot across the distance, scooping up the high-level gladius and moving into range of their fight. Thankfully, the pressure of their attacks were considerably less while the Dwarf Queen was too busy dodging and healing.

And both of them were in range of my [Liminal Space].

I activated the ability for the second time this fight as my stacks dropped sharply. I knew that this was going to be the final moment. We would either win or lose based on how the next series of attacks played out.

The world exploded around me and both combatants froze.

I moved quickly, jumping up and stabbing the gladius into the huge crack in the Dwarf Queen's armor. The blade glowed with dark mana as I used [Dark Strike] to push it in as far as I could.

The ability made my entire arm seize up as the blade bit two inches into the powerful opponent. To make matters worse, my fist clenched, and I couldn't let the sword go.

Throwing my other weapon to the ground, I peeled back my fingers with my other hand and dropped to the ground panting from the pain. It felt like I'd just stuck my arm in lava. Every part of it burned, all the way up to my bicep.

My fingers weren't responding, and I scooped up my blade before getting behind the Harem Queen and repositioning her so that she was mid swing.

I put her almost right on top of the Dwarf Queen before moving myself behind the Dwarf Queen and stabbing my sword into the ground behind her back foot.

It would have to be enough.

I rushed out of the area of the ability to deactivate it and get clear of what I was sure was about to be an explosive exchange.

As soon as I exited the space, the Harem Queen had a flash of confusion, followed by the Dwarf Queen stumbling and losing her momentum. As she stumbled, the Dwarf Queen quickly shattered my sword with a kick.

But it gave the Harem Queen the opportunity she needed. She shifted her strike and hammered in the gladius with the full strength of a Level 53 adventurer. Blue flames erupted everywhere as the gladius tore through the Dwarf Queen, spraying yellow goo.

If she had been stumbling before, then this attack had stopped the large dwarf in her tracks.

The Harem Queen exploded with even more blue fire, enveloping them both as her sword came crashing back down on the dwarf, severing her arm and then stabbing her through.

The Dwarf Queen had blue fire erupting out of her severed arm and between several cracks in her armor. The Harem Queen was cooking the Dwarf Queen with blue flames from the inside out.

The Harem Queen pulled the sword back with a smirk on her face as the Dwarf Queen collapsed to her knees, and the Harem Queen made sure she was dead by severing her head for good measure.

I was on the ground, panting while clutching my arm and grunting in pain.

The noise made Helen's mother glance my way and smile.

"AAAAH!" the dwarven soldiers shouted at the top of their lungs, the sound echoing through the whole safe zone as they went berserk.

The Harem Queen grabbed me and jumped clear of their on-coming rush. "Great job, by the way. Couldn't have done it without you. So let's get you clear of this before I finish them."

I got a good look at the Harem Queen. Despite her hair being frayed with blades of grass blown into it and her dress having seen better days, she had a brilliant smile on her face after the victory. It was a lot prettier than the smiles she'd shown so far.

Then again, fighting always put me in a good mood too.

She flew through the air in several leaps and landed back among the Haylon students who had pulled back to the building as the dwarves went crazy.

Despite the added frenzy, the other students seemed to have everything under control. The fortified building and the organized line at the front was able to handle the onslaught of remaining dwarves.

"He's damaged his mana channels. Heal him once and then don't do it again for at least several hours." The Harem Queen dropped me among the healers. "He saved my life and everyone in this safe zone."

The upperclassmen blinked in shock at her statement. Many of them probably idolized the Harem Queen, and while they'd seen me fight, the difference between me and someone like her was the same as a candle and the sun to them.

As for my class, they held no such reservations.

"Great job, Ken!" Selene rushed up to heal me.

Charlotte held a hand out. "He's mine." She cradled my arm and winced in sympathy as she cast a heal, slowly moving her hand up my arm.

The burning receded into my arm only to flare up worse like my bones were on fire, even if my skin was no longer bright red.

I hissed.

"No more healing," the Harem Queen warned and shot off to deal with the remaining high-level soldier dwarfs.

"So what happened?" Candice asked as she manned three runes in front of us.

"What happened here?" I countered.

Charlotte seemed to find the words to describe it first. "Helen pulled us back to the entry way. We weren't really making enough progress to matter, and a few of our healers passed out from mana exhaustion."

"It was the right move," Candice agreed with Charlotte. "We were only able to stretch ourselves out as much as we had because of you. And even if Helen would be loath to admit it, she saw the same thing before giving the order to pull back. Why her?"

I shrugged. "She's bossy enough to bully everyone into listening to her. Given we weren't all taught to fight together like this, it wasn't about who has the greater tactical mind, but simply, who can get everyone to follow directions. Being the daughter of the Harem Queen gave her voice a lot of gravity with the upperclassmen and Class B as well." Hopefully enough to get momentum so that everyone followed her.

"Ah." Candice smiled. "That makes me feel better."

"If we were needing tactical abilities the most, you would be an obvious choice." I decided Candice needed to hear that answer. "Hopefully when we get into the raid, we'll have a better chance to let you shine."

The Arcane Weaver was probably the smartest student in our class; I felt confident in her abilities.

"Well, you'll be sitting the rest of this out. It would be a good time to observe and think through strategies in the future." Charlotte huffed and put herself protectively between me and the dwarves.

"She's mad," Selene stage-whispered. "You ran off on your own and came back injured. Again. Or so I'm told."

I wanted to help, yet I had one arm that would be healing, and I had lost both my new sword and my dagger.

Sighing, I nodded, accepting the background role. "The Harem Queen needed my help, but I think you are right. I'm done with the rest of this fight."

CHAPTER 37

T wo days later, I found myself dressed and ready to see the UG leadership.

"Is it too tight?" Crimson fussed with the sling that currently held my arm. She both wanted to help, yet couldn't touch it without causing me pain. Our class had been given a week off after the attack, both for people to recover and for them to make arrangements.

I had several meetings with the UG coming up, and I needed to search around for new weapons. Both of mine had been lost during the fight.

"It's fine," I promised Crimson, who pouted and pulled at the sling like she wanted to do something. "Maybe a hair tighter would take the weight off better."

Even if I was the one who was injured, Crimson was distraught that she hadn't been with me to 'crush the stupid queen'. Although, there were times when she was talking that I wasn't sure which of the queens she was grumbling about.

I got the feeling she blamed the Harem Queen for not protecting me properly.

"He's fine." Des cut off a square of my omelet on a fork and held it over to me. "Say ah."

I dutifully ate the eggs. I'd long since given up trying to push back; besides, I wasn't great at some things with the single arm. Everyone in my life seemed intent on taking care of me at the moment.

Besides, this was temporary.

"Yes, you are one to talk," Fayeth said, coming around and giving me a brief hug with a lingering kiss. "Besides, I made the food."

"And I'm feeding him. As we discussed." Des' eyes pinched sharply in warning as she smiled.

This had been a problem yesterday as well as today. There was some slight fighting over who got to take care of me.

Charlotte came out of her room with a yawn. "Ken, time for your check up."

I shrugged, taking another bite from Des as she spoon fed me.

"This is an interesting behavior of the human pride." Felin sat on the couch watching. "When the leader is injured, it is the role of the rest of the pride to nurture him back to health?"

"Exactly." Charlotte patted Felin's head as she walked past. "Though if one of us would be injured, we would do similarly, only Ken would likely be out seeking revenge."

"Ah." Felin nodded in understanding. "I can see that logic. Ken isn't the nurturing type, so he would shed blood on your behalf."

I squinted, wondering if it was okay for Felin to be getting such misunderstandings.

"Arm." Charlotte came over and held her hand out, staring at me with the same look that a disappointed physician gave a patient.

"It's doing better," I promised as I held it out.

She squinted at my limb, running her hands over it and just a slight trickle of a heal touching my skin, but not going deeper. "It is." She almost sounded shocked.

I raised an eyebrow in question.

"You and Fayeth were loud last night." Charlotte pursed her lips.

"He didn't use his arm," Fayeth chirped. "I made sure of that."

"Uh huh." Charlotte wasn't paying attention to her as she poked and prodded at my arm. Since learning about the condition, she had become somewhat of an expert.

I hissed as she poked a particularly sensitive spot. "It's better when you aren't poking it."

"I'm examining it. Besides, the pain is just temporary. So far, it looks like it'll heal in the next week." Charlotte kept her face professionally impassive.

I let out a breath. "Good. It was worth it to help the Harem Queen."

"If I were there, you wouldn't have *had* to," Crimson grumbled something about Director Amato under her breath.

She had been very unhappy when she had returned to me with my arm in a sling. More than a few structures had to be rebuilt after she'd worked off her feelings.

"Alright, enough of this. We have to make the meeting," I reminded Crimson.

"Don't worry." She waved her hand and made a portal. "We'll be there on time. Really, I have no excuse not to be anywhere on time now."

"But you are still going to cut it down to the last second," I added.

"Millisecond," Crimson corrected me. "No need to waste time." She checked her CID. "Though, we must be going. We have the President of the UG again along with a number of other people. Lots of fact finding today. A ton of people died, and people with deep pockets are asking a lot of questions of the UG."

Des kissed my cheek, followed swiftly by Fayeth and Charlotte.

"Be good. Answer their questions, and Crimson will bring you back. Won't she?" Des glared at Crimson.

"Scout's honor," Crimson saluted. "He won't have to lift a finger. His arm is on full bedrest," she confirmed with Charlotte.

The druid nodded sharply, her eyes narrowing on me before shifting back to Crimson. "I should hope you can manage that." Dr. Charlotte was terrifying indeed.

"Let's go." Crimson pulled me through the portal into a bland hallway that had a simple wooden door. The door was already open with the Harem Queen and Helen walking through at that moment.

"Ken." The Harem Queen beamed at me with a smile that was tugging up at the corner of her lips infectiously.

"Heather." I nodded to her; I'd finally learned her real name.

"This is all just a formality." The Harem Queen walked in with us. "They won't have the balls to touch any of us, you included."

The room was bland, with a large horseshoe-shaped table filled with people I didn't recognize. On second glance, I did recognize two of those already present. Director Amato and the UG President were at the far end of the table.

"Welcome, Ken." The Director stood and recognized me out of the group walking in.

It felt... off considering I was walking with Crimson and the Harem Queen. Then again, it was also a statement.

"I hope things are going well." I forced a smile on my face. "Doubt I'm going to be much help for the time being." I shrugged the shoulder that held the sling.

"Nonsense." She smiled. "As we understand it, removing the queen won the war, even if we have some clean up to do."

"I hope so. I only have one good arm left," I teased, causing a few of them to chuckle as I took a seat between Crimson and Heather with Helen on her mother's other side.

"We just want a personal account from you," the UG President said. "Thank you for taking the time to come and see us. We did our best to make it simple by bringing the Harem Queen in at the same time."

I shifted a little uncomfortably. They were almost uncomfortably accommodating to me.

"Well, then let's get on with this. We have important guests that I'm sure have other things to attend to," one of the other participants encouraged, her eyes tracking me curiously.

It wasn't just me feeling odd. The others had also picked up on the deference that both of them were showing me. They had to be wondering if it was caused by Crimson and the Harem Queen or if it was all me.

"I'll start. If that's okay, Ken?" The redhead next to me cleared her throat when I nodded. Even she was making it clear to everyone in the room. "The Haylon building was attacked like many of the others. Spears with small explosive devices discharged that noxious smoke into our classroom. Ken led his class to assist the others in the building; he used an ability of his to see through the smoke and rescue my students. At which point, we cleared our building and its surroundings." The Harem Queen glanced at me.

"Yeah, that was the broad strokes. No permanent casualties," I added. "My ability identified that the Dwarf Queen was indeed in the safe zone, and I informed the Harem Queen before she made her way over to fight it."

"This ability?" one of the UG members asked.

"Eyes of Wisdom," I answered, not too worried. This level of people likely had access to much of my data.

"Ah, a rare one," another muttered, glancing at Crimson. "I believe Crimson has it as well?"

"Correct," Crimson spoke for the first time. "It is highly useful, but Ken acquired it on his own."

I paused. What she said was technically correct, though she had certainly been there while I acquired it.

The rest of them nodded along with her statement. It seemed the ability name settled something else that was about to be asked.

"Then Ken came and joined, fighting the elite soldier dwarves. They were comparable to upper forties in their strength. I was engaged with the Dwarf Queen who probably had the strength in the upper fifties or low sixties. It was lucky that I goaded her into a one on one. Her strength was in summoning an army and staying alive." She glanced at me to tell my part.

"My weapon was damaged from fighting the dwarves already and near breaking. I had hoped for something that could help me penetrate the higher-level dwarves. So I asked Heather for a weapon." Using her name was on purpose if they were going to set me up, I might as well play along.

There were a few brows raised at me not using her title, but when she sat back with a smile, no one said anything.

"I wasn't thinking and threw him my spare one-hander for tanking." She glanced at my arm in the sling. "He received those injuries protecting the safe zone by holding the weapon long enough to kill the dwarven healer."

"Then the queen?" the Director asked.

"I asked Ken for help, and he came through. He used his ability that makes him unbelievably fast, and he stuck that same weapon in a crack I'd made in the queen's armor. Then, I think he tripped her?" She hesitated.

I nodded.

"Can you give us details of the ability and how you used it?"

Heather spoke up, "Don't answer that and don't ask him that question again. I respect his right to privacy. Even if I had my suspicions, I wouldn't voice them here."

The UG member's mouth closed so fast that his teeth clacked.

Director Amato cleared her throat. "The records of the ability are sealed as well, please do not attempt to access them. Ken's CID is redacted on all of our records."

I froze. I was fairly certain that was the same level of treatment that Crimson received.

"As it should be." The Harem Queen nodded.

I could speak for myself and obscure things a little. Being insanely fast was one thing, stopping time was another. "Your assessment is roughly correct. I threw my sword into the dirt behind the Dwarf Queen. That's what tripped her and broke that sword as well."

The Harem Queen grunted in her agreement. "With Ken's help, I broke through her armor and pinned her down. Candidly, I didn't deserve to win that fight. If she had used those soldier dwarves while also attacking me, I would not have won. Ken's speed was instrumental in solving the fight swiftly so that she didn't get a chance to change tactics once her life was threatened."

"You two did a service to humanity," the President said while leaning back in his chair. "Am I to assume that you wouldn't feel comfortable fighting another queen?" he asked both of us.

I quickly shook my head. "My ability to penetrate such high-level armor is my biggest limitation." Having seen that the Harem Queen had an ability that seemed built for something like that, I had a goal to look through some ability glossaries later and find one of my own.

"It would be straining for me. My harem will be joining me in the dungeon shortly. With their assistance, I would estimate that it is possible, but I am unsure where this one ranked on their overall hierarchy. I can only assume their strongest wasn't the one being displaced and moving out." The Harem Queen worked through her thoughts as she spoke.

"A proper assessment," Director Amato said in agreement. "Well then. Thank you again. If you two wouldn't mind, I would like a moment alone."

"Crimson, please stay a minute longer for us to get your report," the President said. "We'll have Ken back before you're done."

Crimson looked at me like she was tempted to tell them to buzz off so that she could stick with me.

"It's fine. There's no threat to me right now. Besides, I won't be far," I sighed.

Crimson huffed. "I know that. Come back as soon as you are done."

The Director led the Harem Queen and me out of the conference room. Helen was trailing behind us, but the Director held out a hand for her to stop.

"This is for the two of them. Please wait patiently outside." The Director tapped a few things on her tablet before the door unlocked and she walked inside.

The space was a small, fortified room with a wire cage in the center separating the first half from the second half.

"What's this?" I asked, confused.

"A reward." The Harem Queen smirked. "You don't think doing all of that was for free do you?"

I shrugged.

"Rewards are what make everything work," the Director said and handed her tablet to the Harem Queen. "You'll receive a reward in currency as well. Also, Ken, the full analysis of your ability has been finished and I'll hand that to you now as well."

"Thanks." I glanced at what the Harem Queen was searching through.

There were a ton of high-level weapons and armors on the tablet with details on each, as well as a few ultra rare spellbooks. There were even two [Dodge] spellbooks on the list. Though not as flashy as many of the others, they were highly valuable.

The Harem Queen found something she liked based on the way her eyes lit up and she swiped at one of the entries a few times to get more details.

"This one." She pointed to her choice.

"I can do that." The Director looked at it and unlocked the cage before handing me the tablet and stepping in to grab a pair of bright red heels.

"Shoes?" I asked.

"You made me feel slow," Heather chuckled. "Those are about the fastest enchantments I've seen. Thirty percent base speed increase along with all the normal stats."

"They go for 2.4 billion. At least, that's the estimate," the Director said, carrying them out.

My eyes almost fell out of my head. "Uh. I don't think I can use most of these items. There really isn't anything for my level here."

The Director nodded and operated the tablet upside down. "If you don't mind, could I give you a few recommendations?"

"I'd love something better able to penetrate armor," I admitted.

She nodded and swiped quickly along the screen before coming up with a short list of expensive abilities. They weren't a billion-dollar number, but they were several hundred million in total costs. "These all fit your growing build as well as one to provide armor break."

I nodded, feeling slightly numb as I looked through the list and picked out an ability that cost over six hundred million. It had three strikes with a high chance to break armor.

"Perfect." She tapped on the tablet to record the transaction and then stepped back into the cage before giving me the spellbook and the report of my ability.

"Thank you." I couldn't keep the giant grin from my face.

The Harem Queen put her arm around my waist and led me out. "Well, that's what you get for saving a safe zone. Come on, let's get you back to Crimson."

We walked out of the room, and I couldn't control that giant smile on my face. But the smile vanished when I spotted Helen, who took one glance at my giant smile and her mother's posture and frowned.

"Pervert," Helen scoffed.

A breeze hit me as the Harem Queen moved around me and grabbed Helen's shoulder.

"I don't believe I heard you right, daughter." Her tone wasn't that of the celebrity or the flirty woman.

She was using the tone of a mother about to lay the smack down on her daughter.

I wanted to escape.

"Stay there, Ken. You need to hear this," the Harem Queen said, her voice softening a touch when she addressed me. "Because it seems I've raised a daughter who's ungrateful, spoiled and so damaged that she can't even acknowledge another person's accomplishments because she doesn't agree with his lifestyle. Or am I wrong?" She shifted her baleful glare to Helen.

The tank scowled right back like a mirror image of her mother. "You would defend him."

"Yes, I would defend your classmate who saved my life and saved your life too. Even when you've acted such that I don't think I'd blame him if he let you die out of spite." The Harem Queen snapped back her finger pushing into the center of Helen's chest as she tried to make a point.

Helen swallowed but was only on the back foot for an instant. "Mother, I'm a grown woman."

"Your fathers will be coming down here into the dungeon, and I will have this conversation with them. No doubt, regardless of how that conversation goes, you will end up talking to them about this. Your next few moves will determine how that goes."

I'd never seen Helen go so pale than at the mention of her fathers coming down into the dungeon.

"You wouldn't. They are retired," Helen shot back.

"I will," the Harem Queen said with conviction. "They are all coming out of retirement." She glanced at me. "Watching your classmate rush into danger far above his level and come out victoriously has made me reconsider retirement. I need to push the dungeon again and do away with the safe complacency of slowly grinding that we've all fallen into. I need to learn some of Ken's... insanity. For the first time in years, I crave to become stronger. We'll push for the fifty-fifth floor boss in a few weeks once I'm sure we've all knocked the rust off."

Helen stared at her mother and blinked slowly before shifting her gaze to me and tensing her jaw. "I am sorry. My mother doesn't speak lightly. You must have been a great asset."

I was pretty sure a part of her died saying those words. I could only hope it was the part that hated me so much.

"Better, but far from sufficient." The Harem Queen faced me and bowed low while she grabbed Helen's head and forced her into the same gesture. "Since my daughter fails to understand, let me express my thanks. The Dwarf Queen would have outlasted me if not for your aid. You have my respect, and I will demand that my family respect you as well." She shot Helen a sharp glare. "And you lost both of your weapons in the process."

The gladius that had destroyed my arm fell out of her CID.

I stepped back from it, my arm in the sling suddenly radiating pain just thinking about it.

The Harem Queen laughed. "Just tap your CID to it; don't touch it. Keep it as a souvenir if nothing else. It's worth quite a bit, but I think you'll find these a little more helpful."

She handed me a heavy wooden box, with a panel on the top that slid backwards to reveal its contents. Inside were a dozen blades, each of them radiated bright purple mana.

"I didn't have time to be picky. One of my husbands has a similar fighting style to you. I had him pick out a dozen weapons for someone in your level range. Hopefully, you can find a pair that are suitable for you, and I think he snuck a few upgrades in there as a thank you as well." The Harem Queen smiled at me.

The gesture from her mother made the dark cloud over Helen's expression darken. Yet she couldn't walk away. Her mother held her shoulder, rooting her to her current spot.

I checked one of the weapons with my CID. It was a stone blade with weathered wrappings around the hilt. Despite its looks, it was clearly epic-quality gear.

Blade of the Forgotten King : +28 Agility, +16 Stamina, +5 Mana, + 5 Magic. Requires Level 27.

"Thank you," I managed to push out. "These are incredible." And they had to have cost a fortune. "You really shouldn't help a low-level adventurer this much, though."

The Harem Queen waved my comment away. "Nonsense, you broke your weapons helping me. The least I could do was replace them."

I chuckled. What she was giving me was far more than 'replacing them', but I understood her intentions and let it slide. "As for Helen, even if she's a problem member, she's still a member of my guild. As the guild master, it's my responsibility to watch out for her."

"I don't—" She was halted by a look from her mother. "I mean. Thank you." She said the words like they were the most painful things she's said in her life.

"Better, but not good enough." The Harem Queen grabbed Helen's head like an unruly child and forced her into a bow. "Next time, try something more like 'I've been an ass and you've been too kind. I'll do better in the future.' Because you will, daughter. You will do better, or I will remove you from Haylon because I know it's a waste for you to learn to work with people."

Helen clearly wanted to argue, but she was stopped after glancing at her mother. Finally, she just stared at the ground.

"Well, let me do it right." The Harem Queen stepped into my space and wrapped her arms around me and pressed her chest to me. "Thank you for taking such good care of me and my daughter. If there's *anything* she can do, please let her know. Oh, and here's the contact information for my husbands. If you need anything, let them know. They are dying to pay you back for saving me."

CHAPTER 38

"**G**randson!" Grandpa blurred up next to me and glanced at how familiar the Harem Queen was with me. "Your luck is too good." He was practically crying.

The Harem Queen glanced at her daughter. "Now that is a pervert. You should be able to tell the difference."

"Agreed." Helen nodded sharply.

Grandpa clutched his chest. "You wound me."

"Says the man who gave me magazines as gifts quite frequently," I sighed and hugged him. "Good to see you. What are you doing here?" I'd expected them to be back on the surface managing and protecting the clan.

"Oh, just a quest from the guild. Time to kill dwarves and such. Given it was near your location in the dungeon, we couldn't pass up the opportunity." Grandpa grinned.

"It also paid quite well." Grandma Sakura came at a much more sedate pace. "We have a meeting with the UG to report here in a few minutes."

"That makes sense. Crimson is finishing up." I noticed my grandmother staring at my arm in a sling with a burning question.

"You two have a fantastic grandson." The Harem Queen held her hand out to my grandmother. "He saved me and many others. If you or Silver Fang need a hand, please let me know."

Grandma Sakura shook the Harem Queen's hand thoughtfully. "We will. It seems my grandson has yet again gotten himself mixed up in trouble."

"Adventuring is full of conflict. Even if the school tries to mitigate most of it, it is almost like the dungeon just keeps shoving volatile elements together." The Harem Queen was all smiles. "If you'll excuse me, I need to have some further words with my daughter." She pulled Helen after her.

The door to the nearby room opened up and Crimson flashed out into the hallway, spotted my grandparents, and bowed her head to Sakura. "I failed to prevent harm to your grandson."

"All is forgiven," Grandpa was quick to jump in. "He's whole and healthy. Looks like mana burn? He should be at fault for picking up a high-level weapon."

I shrugged. "It's fine. It will heal by the end of the week, and I'll be back at it. Crimson is going to teleport us to an event to grind out the whole class to the thirties so we can join the raid before holiday break."

"She has teleport?" Grandpa's eyes unfocused as he did the mental gymnastics before he blurred to my side, tears pooling in his eyes. "My grandson. I'm so proud of you. Your abilities awe this one. Please, teach me."

Grandma Sakura pulled at his collar until he was forced to let go of my hand. "Please don't do that. If we let my husband have his way, he'd repopulate humanity," she sighed. "Congratulations, you two."

"Thank you." Crimson smiled and bowed before more confidently putting an arm around me.

I suddenly realized how lucky I was that Crimson hadn't come out of the room when the Harem Queen was in a similar position. Sweat beaded on the back of my neck in horror at the thought. The whole building would be destroyed, if not the whole safe zone.

"Well, we'll be off," I told them both. "Come visit us when you are done. We'll be in the Haylon building. The students that stuck around are largely taking jobs to help rebuild and expand into the dwarven area."

"We saw the fort being built over the boss stairs that lead to the rest of the dwarven section of the dungeon." Grandpa nodded. "We probably won't stick around if you are heading out. No sense in it, but we'll visit tonight."

There was a massive undertaking to seal off the dwarven section of the dungeon. The hope was to be able to stall any dwarven army long enough for higher-level adventurers to come solve the problem.

In the end, we'd lost over two hundred adventurers with the invasion.

"Wonderful," Crimson's voice returned me to the conversation. "We'll get something nice whipped up for you. Now, if you'll excuse us, I have to get him back to Charlotte, or she'll start accusing him of training while he's supposed to be on light duty."

I rolled my eyes. She would probably strap me down if that's what it took to get me not to re-injure myself. As an adventurer and an assassin, sometimes I got hurt. They didn't need to fawn on me quite so much.

"See you later, Grandson. Don't hold back on our account. If you need more time with your ladies, just let us know," Grandpa chortled to himself.

I shook my head. "Let's go, Crimson." Nothing got me moving faster than Grandpa wanting to talk about what happened in the bedroom.

Crimson waved a hand in the air and a portal ripped itself open back to our suite.

"A very useful skill. Maybe they could visit more," Sakura murmured as we stepped through.

Crimson closed the portal behind me just in time for Charlotte to bound up to my side and pull me gently down to the couch to inspect my arm.

"I haven't even been gone an hour." Sighing, I put up with her prodding again. "Oh, but I got a few new things." I grinned and pulled out the box of weapons and slid the lid open.

"Confiscate those," Charlotte demanded.

Crimson had them pulled away in an instant. "These are nice. From the UG or Harem Queen?" She picked two of them out of the box.

"Hey, they are level appropriate." I didn't even try to get them back from Crimson. I knew that was a losing battle.

"No weapons until your arm is healed," Charlotte spoke with a finality.

"Ken." Des clicked her tongue as she walked out of her room, hair still wet from the shower. "It could delay your healing." She walked over to Crimson and poked at the weapons. "Oh wow, the Harem Queen really went all out."

I glared at her.

"What? You love me playing with your weapons," Des flirted. "I'll make it up to you." She pouted and kissed a dagger sensually. I tried not to show what the image did to me.

"I'll keep them in my CID, along with the other weapon the Harem Queen gave me. She gave me the weapon I burnt my mana channels with, as a souvenir," I clarified.

"They go into your CID and stay there," Charlotte released my arm.

"Yes, Dr. Charlotte," I teased.

Crimson handed me back the box only for it to disappear into my CID as she sat down next to me, sandwiching me between the two beautiful ladies.

Des came up behind me and kissed the back of my neck. "Don't worry. We have a week where you can't train. I'm determined to keep you busy, and I think we all know exactly how that'll turn out for you."

Charlotte leaned in. "You'll put up with us until your arm heals?" The cute druid was trying to be flirty.

"Yeah. I think I can manage. Oh, and I got a new spellbook too."

The look from all of them told me to just put it away for the moment.

"That was the reward from the UG?" Crimson asked.

I nodded, feeling a bit of pride at having even earned it.

"They really are treating you like a high-level adventurer." Crimson nodded. "The analysis from Director Amato was one thing, but the way they treated you in that meeting..." She trailed off with a smirk.

"How did they treat him?" Charlotte got defensive.

"Way too nicely." I patted Charlotte to reassure her. "Like I was Crimson or the Harem Queen." Or even higher.

"That's not so bad." She settled down. "Maybe they'll respect that you need some rest."

"Yes and plenty of food to recover." Fayeth had a bright smile on her face as she came around with muffins.

"He'll need plenty of stamina and hydration these next couple days." Des draped herself over my back. "And since you can't use your arms, just let me help you." She grabbed a muffin and pretended to be my arms as she fed me.

Felin simply sat nearby in her nest of pillows, watching with wide eyes.

I leaned back and let them pamper me. Soon I'd be diving the dungeon again, and we likely wouldn't have the same quiet moments.

***

Des glared at me across the table.

Ami had come with my grandparents, and my butler was currently attending to me. She lifted a cup of tea for me to take a sip from and put it back down. The butler's eyes were like two sparkling gems as I recounted my first use of [Liminal Speed].

"That's nothing. Wait until I tell you about training with Crimson at full speed even while she's using Limit Break," I said.

I was fairly sure I had just gained an admirer based on the way that Ami was staring at me.

"So, you can control that ability better?" Sakura asked Crimson pointedly.

"With Ken, it is much better. Even in that state, I can stay focused on him." Crimson sipped at a cup of tea with a calm expression.

"Good to hear." Sakura narrowed her eyes. "I'm glad that Ken was able to gain so much in the short amount of time. I heard that he defeated the remnants of Kaiming?"

"Yes." I bowed to my grandmother. "My parents have been avenged. The organization that killed them has been put down."

"Don't wallow in revenge," my grandmother chided me. "Focus on the future." She glanced at all the ladies around the table. "You have much to live for."

"Lucky bastard," my grandpa grumbled.

He had a lump on his head. I had no idea what had led to the bump, but the fact that it hadn't been healed by Grandma Yui spoke volumes.

Bun-bun sat next to Grandpa with a lump on his head too.

They both probably deserved the lumps.

"You will be heading to the thirtieth floor safe zone after this?" Grandma Akari asked.

I nodded my head rapidly. "That's the plan. We'll portal to the vampire event from there. We all leveled quite a bit during the dwarven attack."

I glanced at my CID.

Ken Nagato
Class: Emperor
Secondary Class: Demon Lord
Level: 29
Experience: 71%
Strength: 81
Agility: 150
Stamina: 114
Magic: 98
Mana: 112
Skills:

Dark Strike, Earth Stomp, Charm, Metamorphosis, Sprint, Absorb, Discharge, Dark Blades, Shadow Arm, Camouflage, Shadow Ambush, Elemental Shield, Portal [Special] [Restricted], Mana Burn, Hydra [Elysara], Cleave [Fayeth], Spell Mirror, Dungeon's Blessing, Blades of Shadow, Mana Implosion, Shadow Wave [Desmonda], Revive [Charlotte], Shadow Phase, Dodge, Liminal Speed, Eyes of Wisdom [Crimson], Delirious Pleasures

My ability list was giving me a headache; I'd have to fix that. I wasn't wearing any gear. That had been Dr. Charlotte's orders.

We had leveled almost too quickly from the dwarves. Now we needed to focus on our stats. The gear from the raid would be a big part of helping us progress our stats. At Level 30, we should be at about 600 stats.

With my new weapons and old gear, I was fairly certain I could push myself just over that limit.

"When you are a high enough level, you'll move onto the raid?" Grandpa asked. "Raids are difficult."

"They will be fine," Crimson insisted. "We'll have someone on staff to revive and run them through several scenarios so that they learn to keep someone who can revive them alive. We are still a top dungeon college and precautions will be kept while they are here."

"I would expect nothing less," Sakura replied calmly. "Take care of our grandson."

Crimson bobbed her head repeatedly. "Of course."

"Not too much, though," I reminded her. "It is important that I have room to grow."

Crimson squinted in thought for a moment and then smiled at me.

"Can we talk about the elephant in the room?" Grandma Hemi glanced at Felin.

The Nekorian blinked. She had moved across the room and was halfway to swiping the whole grilled fish from the serving place. She carefully put half of it back. "Hi. I'm Felin, I've been called many things, but what is an elephant?"

"A very large animal, one that is hard to ignore," Fayeth answered like she was reciting from a book.

Felin glanced down at her stomach and poked it. "I don't think I've put on *that* much weight."

"You haven't put any on at all," I sighed. "They are saying that the topic of you is too big to ignore. Grandparents, this is Felin, she's a Nekorian shaman."

"I marked your grandson," Felin added with a big smile.

I smacked my face while Grandpa fell over sideways. "She tattooed me. It's a thing, let's step back and tell that story while we have a chance."

Felin nodded eagerly and dug into the fish with gusto.

Fayeth watched her. "Are fish a delicacy to Nekorians too?"

Felin spoke with her mouth full, "No. It's just delicious. Almost as good as milk."

"And your position in all of this?" Grandma Hemi asked.

"Oh. Ken's class needs two spots for the raid. I am going to take one of them." She finished all of the fish on her plate and looked meekly at the remaining portions.

Grandma Hemi used her chopsticks to serve her more. "Is that so?"

"Yes." She nodded eagerly, though I thought the excitement was more about the fish than the question.

"Well, then take good care of our grandson." Sakura gave me some serious side eye.

I ducked my head into my own meal.

***

I rolled my shoulder, finally free of the sling. It felt good to be back in action. Bedrest had certainly been exciting, but there was nothing like diving the dungeon.

"Ready?" Des was geared up, her eyes focused for the first time in almost a week. We had tested Demon Lord Snu Snu's new present, and she'd been quite smitten until she'd gotten her second dose this morning.

Charlotte was ready to go. Her staff was out and she was warming up as Fayeth came out from packing up the kitchen.

"This place felt like a home briefly," the elf said, looking around.

"Home is where the pride is," Felin chimed in.

"Couldn't have said it better myself." Crimson put her arm around Felin. "Let's go get the rest of the class and get moving. Slacking time is over. The best adventurers don't stop pushing, and you all are going to be the best."

Crimson ripped open a portal to the Haylon building, our next stop on our way to dive deeper into the dungeon.

AFTERWORD

Hey Everyone,

I hope you enjoyed Dungeon Diving 201. Crimson X Ken finally happened and Ken stepped up in the world, in a big way. Excited for the next installment of Dungeon Diving coming this summer and for the coming webcomic of the series at the end of the spring.

Me and the family are doing well. The new little one has settled in, his time in the NICU was stressful, but we are past that and moving forward.

As for the writing, Ard's Oath 3 just needs the finishing touches and will be out for you all on April 9th. Not sure what's coming after that. I could loop back to Dungeon or start a new series. TBD.

Please, if you enjoyed the book, leave a review.

Review Dungeon Diving 201

I have a few places you can stay up to date on my latest.

Monthly Newsletter

Facebook Page

Patreon

ALSO BY

Legendary Rule:
Ajax Demos finds himself lost in society. Graduating shortly after artificial intelligence is allowed to enter the workforce; he can't get his career off the ground. But when one opportunity closes, another opens. Ajax gets a chance to play a brand new Immersive Reality game. Things aren't as they seem. Mega Corps hover over what appears to be a simple game. However, what he does in the game seems to effect his body outside.
But that isn't going to make Ajax pause when he finally might just get that shot at becoming a professional gamer. Join Ajax and Company as they enter the world of Legendary Rule.

Series Page

A Mage's Cultivation – Complete Series
In a world where mages and monster grow from cultivating mana. Isaac joins the class of humans known as mages who absorb mana to grow more powerful. To become a mage he must bind a mana beast to himself to access and control mana. But when his mana beast is far more human than he expected; Isaac struggles with the budding relationship between the two of them as he prepares to enter his first dungeon.
Unfortunately for Isaac, he doesn't have time to ponder the questions of his relationship with Aurora. Because his sleepy town of Locksprings is in for a rude awakening, and he has to decide which side of the war he is going to stand on.

Series Page

The First Immortal – Complete Series
Darius Yigg was a wanderer, someone who's never quite found his place in the world, but maybe he's not supposed to be here...Ripped from our world, Dar finds himself in his past life's

world, where his destiny was cut short. Reignited, the wick of Dar's destiny burns again with the hope of him saving Grandterra.

To do that, he'll have to do something no other human of Grandterra has done before, walk the dao path. That path requires mastering and controlling attributes of the world and merging them to greater and greater entities. In theory, if he progressed far enough, he could control all of reality and rival a god.

He won't be in this alone. As a beacon of hope for the world, those from the ancient races will rally around Dar to stave off the growing Devil horde.

Series Page

Saving Supervillains – Complete Series
A former villain is living a quiet life, hidden among the masses. Miles has one big secret: he might just be the most powerful super in existence.

Those days are behind him. But when a wounded young lady unable to control her superpower needs his help, she shatters his boring life, pulling him into the one place he least expected to be—the Bureau of Superheroes.

Now Miles has an opportunity to change the place he has always criticized as women flock to him, creating both opportunity and disaster.

He is about to do the strangest thing a Deputy Director of the Bureau has ever done: start saving Supervillains.

Series Page

Dragon's Justice
Have you ever felt like there was something inside of you pushing your actions? A dormant beast, so to speak. I know it sounds crazy. But, that's the best way I could describe how I've felt for a long time. I thought it was normal, some animal part of the human brain that lingered from evolution. But this is the story of how I learned I wasn't exactly human, and there was a world underneath our own where all the things that go bump in the night live. And that my beast was very real indeed.

Of course, my first steps into this new unknown world are full of problems. I didn't know the rules, landing me on the wrong side of a werewolf pack and in a duel to the death with a smug elf. But, at least, I have a few new friends in the form of a dark elf vampiress and a kitsune assassin as I try to figure out just what I am and, more importantly, learn to control it.

Series Page

Dungeon Diving
The Dungeon is a place of magic and mystery, a vast branching, underground labyrinth that has changed the world and the people who dare to enter its depths. Those who brave its challenges are rewarded with wealth, fame, and powerful classes that set them apart from the rest.
Ken was determined to follow the footsteps of his family and become one of the greatest adventurers the world has ever known. He knows that the only way to do that is to get into one of the esteemed Dungeon colleges, where the most promising young adventurers gather.
Despite doing fantastic on the entrance exam, when his class is revealed, everyone turns their backs on him, all except for one. The most powerful adventurer, Crimson, invites him to the one college he never thought he'd enter. Haylon, an all girls college. Ken sets out to put together a party and master the skills he'll need to brave the Dungeon's endless dangers. But he soon discovers that the path ahead is far more perilous than he could have ever imagined.

Series Page

There are of course a number of communities where you can find similar books.
https://www.facebook.com/groups/haremlit
https://www.facebook.com/groups/HaremGamelit
And other non-harem specific communities for Cultivation and LitRPG.
https://www.facebook.com/groups/WesternWuxia
https://www.facebook.com/groups/LitRPGsociety
https://www.facebook.com/groups/cultivationnovels

Made in United States
Troutdale, OR
09/29/2024

23237052R00195